Pride

Book **1** in the **S**torm**E**dge Series

By
Vanda **T**awhai

Trigger warning: The book contains sexual contents, violence and reference to past trauma. Reader discretion is advised. This book is recommended from 18+

The magnificent Jaguar on the cover is Neron from The Big Cat Sanctuary.

Cover design by Bjørn O. Holter- Symbolic Ink Årnes

Editor Satine von Gersdorff – Sleipnir Translation & Editing

ISBN - Paperback: 978-87-975010-0-9
ISBN- Epub: 978-87-975010-1-6

First Edition: December 2023

Chapter 1

This was a once-in-a-lifetime opportunity, Grace reminded herself sternly.

Sophie huffed for the umpteenth time this hour alone.

"Grace, are you sure? You could stay, you know. It's safer here, and I know daddy won't mind if we just move you in here permanently," she said, her London accent thickening as she spoke.

Grace sighed and rubbed her hands on her thighs, blowing a lock of her long hair out of her face.

"I know I could, Sophie-bear, but I'm done running. I need to do this. I can't live in your pretty mansion forever and I won't keep hiding. It's been a fucking year!"

Grace really was done running and hiding. She'd done more than enough of that since she was a kid. If she wasn't running away from yet another shitty foster situation, she was hiding in the streets. Just when she finally had her legs firmly under her, had finished her veterinary nursing degree, and gotten a great job at the Auckland Zoo, a damn stalker weaseled into the picture. Sophie, whose dad owned and operated New Zealand's largest private security firm, had damn near bundled Grace up and carted her from her tiny one-bedroom apartment to Sophie's huge - and scarily secure-home.

"We will catch whoever this is. I know we will. And the coppers are-"

"The cops aren't doing shit, Soph." Grace interrupted. "And they're not gonna do shit. If *you* were stalked, sure, but for a former street kid, not so much," Grace teased. "Look, I want this. I want this adventure, and it's not like they'll follow me to fucking Canada!"

The stalker thing had started not long before her almost mom's car accident. At first, it was just a feeling of being watched at work. Then, her car malfunctioned three times in one week. Her apartment was broken into, though nothing was taken. Then, it became a constant feeling of someone following her, culminating in her neighbor's death. The police found Grace and Leanne's door numbers had been switched. That's when Sophie's dad, Martin, gave Grace a very illegal taser, and Sophie started packing Grace's shit.

Sophie threw a soft pillow at Grace, frowning.

"You're my best friend. I'm supposed to not love you leaving."

Grace knew Sophie was nervous about this whole thing. They hadn't been apart much since the beginning of their oddball friendship some ten years ago. Grace was a foster care kid with a case file the size of 'The Hobbit,' who spent her teenage years playing with compound bows. She never fit in anywhere. Too aggressive for the good kids and too sensitive for the bad kids. Sophie was the polished daughter of a London security entrepreneur. She moved to New Zealand with her dad when she was five after her parents divorced.

"Daddy almost made me put a tracker on your phone," Sophie chortled.

Grace snorted. Sophie's dad was a smidge overprotective of them both, constantly worrying the big bad wolf would come to eat Sophie. He also had what Grace deemed a questionable moral compass. Since the accident, Grace had been living with Sophie most of the week. *Time to move on. Way on,* Grace concluded.

"I'm going, and you're going to support me because you're my best friend! This is my chance at an epic adventure. Thank you!" Grace huffed and got up.

Sophie stood with her, her hands on her hips.

"But I just really thi-"

"I *said*, thank you!" Grace pointed a finger at her best friend, mock frowning at her.

After a long pause, Sophie seemed to dig out a sliver of enthusiasm.

"Ring me the second you're settled, and I want pictures of all the Canadian hot blokes at the sanctuary! Not just big cat this and big cat that!"

Grace snickered.

"Yeah-nah. There will be no hotties for me." The last thing Grace needed or wanted was another pompous douche telling her to wear more feminine clothes or complaining when she served lasagna for the fifth time in a row.

Grace considered herself the perfectly toned version of average. Average height (so kinda short), average weight, and average features. She did have a nice year-long tan, compliments of her Māori blood. Sophie was sure her long, thick, reddish hair had come from a European parent. Grace knew little about her parents. Two names on her birth certificate by the nurse who found her. That same nurse knew her mom's first name because she'd treated her more than once for the various STDs the prostitute collected, like Pokémon cards. Aroha. Father unknown. Grace had been named by that same nurse and kept her super fantastic and not at all telling surname. Doe. As in Jane Doe. Grace fucking Doe.

Grace looked at the time.

"Ok, Soph, time's up. Don't wanna miss my broomstick." She winked.

Sophie rolled her eyes.

"I see our Peter Pan complex is alive and well." Sophie looked out the window. "Taxi is here."

Grace hugged her and grabbed her single duffel bag and her small backpack.

After a two-hour layover in Auckland, another four in San Francisco, and one very frustrated customs officer later, Grace settled into the last leg of her (epic!) journey. She was set to land in Ontario, Canada, on October sixteenth.

Chapter 2

48 Hours later

Pogue shut down the computer and backed away from the bulky screen. Sighing, he ran his hands over his face, trying to will life back to it. Gods, he needed a shave. His auburn whiskers were getting to the point of braiding. He'd grab a bath as soon as this day finally ended.

He looked at his hands to find pencil and charcoal smears all over his fingertips- and on the keyboard by the screen. Again. Sighing, he took out a small cloth from his pocket to wipe it. Doodling was his favorite pastime, but it had the unfortunate side effect of leaving him with smudged fingertips more often than not.

"We have got to get someone to do this shit for us," he grumbled as his twin brother strode in the door and plopped down in one of four oversized bean bag chairs, he insisted were better than using an office chair like a civilized Shifter. Caden ran his hands over his buzz-cut hair and stretched his long arms over his head, cracking his neck as he did so. He then reached over to grab his old acoustic guitar and started plucking the strings softly as Pogue got up and stretched.

"I know... Sometimes, it seems like we spend more time doing paperwork than actually managing the Pride." Point in fact, Pogue nodded to a piece of paper on the desk. Another Challenge notice. StormEdge, their Pride, had been challenged more often than any Community he knew of in the sixteen years since they'd been approved by the local Council to form it. This one was yet another Challenge from a Pack of wolves, IceFjord. What was the fucking point of having laws that required you to file a request to Challenge if the response was always yes? At least they'd managed to get their Pride member Nadya back three days ago. IceFjord, a pack of Purebloods with just one animal in their lineage, was always picking

4

on them. IceFjord believed in Primus DeCoill's archaic notion that mixed breeds were equivalent to wasting blood. And StormEdge was a mixed pride.

Pogue and Caden had decided not to exclude anyone when they founded the Pride, and they'd gained a solid Pride with bone-deep loyalty for it. Pogue knew DeCoill was an asshole and a dangerous one at that. Their Pride lawyer, Tari, had spent more time defending the same-sex mated couples they had accepted into the Pride than actually performing his job as a liaison between the Council, the Academy, and StormEdge. Not to mention, DeCoill had made sure of a hellish long wait for approval of mixed-breed transfers.

Pogue detested how old-fashioned their laws were, although he liked the simplicity of their world as a general concept.

"How's Nadya holding up?" Pogue asked. Getting her back was the third step out of four in the upcoming Challenge.

Caden tensed.

"Left her with Claus and Liam," he said, referring to Nadya's foster parents. "She's shaken, but she'll be fine."

When one Community wanted to issue a Challenge, there were four archaic steps they had to abide by. First, the offending Community would steal a member from the defenders. If successful, they would then petition the Council to initiate a Challenge. The next step would be for the defending Community to reclaim its member, much like a ridiculous game of capturing the flag. The final phase would be an Alpha fight or on rare occasions, a Turf War.

If you won a conventional Alpha challenge, you were legally entitled to their land if you wanted it. A Turf War usually meant the eradication of an entire Community. With Shifters becoming extinct, Challenges like that made no sense, but DeCoill seemed to enjoy approving them the same way he seemed to enjoy dragging the local Council around by their balls. Pogue had been getting increasingly more frustrated, not just with DeCoill but the Council as a whole over the past few years.

The Council, in short, were the judge, jury, and executioner of their world. The Global Council was their highest authority, and the local ones scattered across the globe were, in essence, local courts. There were five council members in each local Council. Four Shifters and a Wielder. Two of the Shifters serving in their Council were polar opposites from what Pogue knew. DeCoill was the bane of his existence. On the opposite side of the spectrum sat Archer. Pogue knew him to be open-minded and progressive. Unfortunately, StormEdge had to deal with DeCoill as he was Primus for the Alaska-Canada region. Tari and either Pogue or Caden would travel via Portal to the Local Council headquarters in Ontario every time they had to meet.

Pogue leaned back, absentmindedly straightening his blue business shirt. Though most Shifters were fans of hand-me-downs, Pogue liked new and modern clothes. He studied Caden's expression as he read DeCoill's notice, but his brother played his cards close as usual.

"Did the fucktard at least send the latest tally?" Pogue asked, lighting up his smoke. The fucktard in question was, of course, DeCoill.

Caden frowned at him.

"Let me look at the damn challenge notice first, man."

Pogue held up his hands in surrender and tried to instill some patience as Caden went over the notice, his frown deepening as he read.

Caden sighed.

"Let me have Tari go over the notice. I wanna make sure I understand the specifics. Ok, so the tally," he said and went through it. In the Alaska-Canada region StormEdge called home, there were eight cemented Communities. Two of those were non-predatory. It was very few Communities for such a large area. There were, however, multiple clusters of Nomads spread out. The Council had little to no control over them, and keeping track of their numbers was a guessing game. Nomads were Shifters without any absolute allegiance.

The closest Community to StormEdge was FireQuill, an avian Community. For no particular reason, the different communities didn't have much to do with each other apart from trade.

"IceFjord. Pack. Northeastern Territories. Thirty-nine Shifters. Stellan has recently taken another Mate. Five cubs. RazorSea. Sleuth. Northern Alaska. Currently at twenty-six. Bears, aside from their one avian and three wolf Shifters. No cubs in the last ten years, but rumor has it, Benoit has taken a third Mate."

Pogue snorted. The Alpha, Benoit, could take a thousand Mates, and he still wouldn't produce offspring. They needed cubs. No one knew why so many Shifters died birthing cubs or lost them before term. On top of that, an alarming number of Shifters had gone missing, never to be heard from again. Caden had wanted to dig into it, but Pogue wasn't sure. He tried to avoid sticking his nose in Council business that didn't directly involve them. Especially as young as the Pride was. They didn't need the complication. But it *was* a problem, and Pogue had a nasty feeling StormEdge couldn't stay out of it forever. No matter how much he wanted to.

Caden pulled him from his thoughts.

"Mom and Pop say hi." Their parents' Pride was mixed, though less than StormEdge. "ShadowCast is still at sixteen. Luna and Kellan are the only juveniles left. Still haven't taken in new Pride members, but they seem fine."

Caden was about to recite the numbers of the remaining six Communities when Pogue's phone rang. Pogue grabbed the phone and flipped it open, pulled up the antenna, and pressed the speaker button. Henley, their tracker, was on the other end.

"I completed the perimeter check. Nothing to report, but Beau caught me on the way home. Told me the newest shipments of gems is ready. You want Micah to go cross over?"

Caden nodded as Pogue answered.

"Yeah, have him cross today if he can." Micah, their Beta, had a keen interest in the human world and was happy to cross the Barrier to trade the gems the earth provided for human world currency. They didn't need much, but some basic modern conveniences just made their lives easier. Technically, only the Alpha of a Community was allowed to be the breadwinner. Another archaic law designed to make sure no Community grew too large for the Alpha to keep them safe. StormEdge kept the leniency they practiced on this matter, discrete.

Chapter 3

Council

Archer

Archer smiled widely when he ended the call. His informant had just given him an early Yule present. The plan had worked, sort of. If she was still alive, of course. Now, Archer had an important call to make. A call that could, in the end, allow him to keep his word to a man who was most likely dead now.

Archer had been waiting for a very long time. Watching over the poor human as best he could as she grew up.

The fates had not been kind to her. Archer had only been able to check in with her periodically, and to do so, he posed as her caseworker. He'd move her around the large city of Wellington, New Zealand, and several times to different cities and backwater towns. When Archer couldn't go, he sent one of his trusted people to look out for her from a distance. But DeCoill's latest attempt to get to her had almost killed her as it did her foster mom. The first good foster family he'd managed to secure for her. Now, he couldn't risk waiting any longer.

DeCoill had taken the Wielder, and Archer had let him. If he hadn't, the life of his True Mate was forfeit. Archer, unlike many others, knew not to underestimate DeCoill. He only knew of her existence because he had happened upon DeCoill as the man was pulling the most important Wielder Archer knew through a Portal. The half-Wielder was kicking and screaming as he screamed out her name to Archer. For years, played a game of hide and seek with the girl as the prize. The time for hiding her was over. Now, Archer could only move the chess pieces and hope for the best. Hope StormEdge really was as progressive as he expected. Pray she would find the truth and a safe haven with it.

Archer knew DeCoill would chase her. He knew the lion Shifter was hellbent on destroying her particular bloodline and any other mixed bloods.

So, Archer had played defense while watching StormEdge cement themselves, growing strong.

Then, he had exchanged favors —a lot of them. A Displacer Wielder was already on the flight with her, and a powerful Portal Wielder was on standby to create a massive Portal for the Displacer to drag her through. It was a gamble. The Displacer could lose focus, making them appear in the sky and fall to their deaths. The Portal Wielder could mistime her Portal or worse. Nobody really knew how Wielders worked, including Archer. Shifters bought their services from them because they wielded magic. Magic that, amongst other things, enabled Shifters to travel long distances, create homes in under an hour, and much more. He didn't mind not knowing the ins and outs as long as he could hire them and be confident, they could do the job. Archer had weighed the cost-benefit ratio of this gamble several times, but this might be his last chance. He dialed his Mate, who answered on the third ring.

"Hello, darling."

Archer's distress was relieved by his Mate's gentle voice.

"I don't have much time, love. I need you to do something for me." His Mate said nothing, clearly waiting for Archer to continue.

"Have you found your Pridemember?"

"Days ago. Why?"

Archer let out a breath.

"A plane crashed near you. Make sure your Beta is there, and please, I beg you, do not let them kill her!" he urged. It was law. A human inside the Barrier would be killed on sight unless a Community had applied for permission to keep them as a pet beforehand.

"I'm going to assume you can't tell me who it is or why we're not killing her?"

"I'm sorry. I wish I could. She is of no danger to StormEdge. At least not by her own choice."

"Then that'll be enough. I have to go. I love you."

The line went dead before Archer could say anything else.

Chapter 4

An hour later, Caden's phone rang. Pogue watched as Caden's jaw tensed. He pressed the phone so hard against his ear Pogue couldn't hear clearly what was being said on the other line.

"Where?" Caden's words were clipped. Pogue recognized Grayson on the other end. "Pogue's on it." Caden hung up and looked at Pogue, who was already by the door, pulling on his leather boots and lacing them up with a practiced routine. He was donning his brown winter jacket when Caden shook his head, signaling to Pogue that his cat would run tonight. That meant accuracy, a small team, and possibly—probably—rapid execution.

"What?" Pogue asked.

"Seems an airplane crashed about sixteen kilometers from here, due east, toward Fawlks."

"How the fuck did the Council not find this before us?" Pogue frowned as he stripped down to his boxer briefs. It just made shifting easier and cut down on the amount of clothes he'd need to replace cause he'd shredded them in a shift. Most Pride members had no problem with mended clothes, but Pogue and his cat preferred the feel of new, soft fabric against their skin. His cat, like the man, was a creature of comfort. He'd trade paintings or drawings to Micah, their Beta, in exchange for clothes from the human world. Their deal worked out great as long as Micah stuck to the very precise list of clothing to buy. As solid a Beta as Micah was, his fashion sense had died somewhere in the late nineties, and to him, polyester/cotton blend was an acceptable fabric.

Pogue winced internally as Caden interrupted his thoughts.

"I don't know, man, but Henley said nobody has been out there. We'll figure it out later." Caden's words were clipped. Pogue huffed a breath and plucked his phone from his discarded jeans to assemble a small team. He nodded at Caden, who was already dialing up people. They both knew what to do and worked perfectly in sync, as usual.

"Taking Micah," Pogue said as he swung open the office door. The only answer was a thumbs up as Caden turned around, already in conversation.

Pogue dialed as he descended the stairs.

The lion picked up on the first ring.

"I'm at Doc's. Meet you at the front door?" Micah asked in a no-nonsense tone.

"Grab Dina on your way. Henley's en route," Pogue said as he passed the second level. "I'm getting Hannah and Taruk."

"Taruk?" Micah asked, his voice rushed. Pogue could hear the rustling of a backpack.

"Runner," Pogue replied courtly before hanging up.

Pogue jogged towards Hannah's apartment, situated in a narrow hallway adjacent to the dining hall.

He was about to turn into the hallway when Taruk came sprinting through the saloon doors of the dining hall, a bagel in his hand. Pogue nodded to him.

"Toss the bagel. Your wolf runs with Micah."

Taruk puffed out his chest, a sharp, toothy smile on his lips. Taruk thumped his chest with his fist just above his heart once. A human would compare it to a salute. It was not. It was more.

"Alpha!" Taruk said, loud and clear. He turned around to run but stopped in his tracks before he had gotten more than two steps away, turning back with a sheepish look on his young face.

"Uhm, where is Micah?"

Pogue rolled his eyes.

"Doc's." Pogue was already jogging again as he yelled after Taruk, "And Toss the damn bagel!" He made his way down the hallway to Hannah's apartment.

Pogue stopped at the red-painted steel door with some kind of odd symbol on it. It changed from time to time. If he didn't know better, he would say it depended on her general mood of the day. Pogue was just about to knock when the door swung open, revealing Hannah. The young Wielder was dressed for... Well, he didn't know what the hell she was dressed for. She wore green and black striped leggings, a black bustier over top of a dark green t-shirt, and a short cape with slits instead of sleeves. And a hat. Pogue pinched the bridge of his nose and shook his head. Today's choice was a black pointed hat with green and black stripes and snakes- no doubt a tribute to her favorite film. Pogue knew she could dress normal-ish. When she wanted to, that was. Her caramel-colored eyes were slightly slanted, her lips rosy, and her short pixie bob suited her, giving her a wicked look.

She huffed at him as a greeting and unceremoniously pushed him out of the way, yelling back at him as she ran.

"Well, are you coming, Alpha? Caden called already!" She sprinted down the hallway, her cape/coat, whatever the fuck it was, flowing behind her as she made her way toward the front door. *Cranky Hannah it is,* Pogue thought, shaking his head as he jogged after her. *Let's go kill shit, then.*

The snow was almost tiny flecks of sleet as the team assembled by the front door. All but Pogue were fully clothed, none batting so much as an eyelash about the fact that their Alpha wore only boots and boxer briefs. Pogue noticed Micah had taken it upon himself to invite the good Doctor, probably in case they found someone alive. Pogue decided not to say that whatever was out there probably wouldn't need a doctor as much as a quick death. Humans didn't belong in their world as anything but pets, and StormEdge did not keep pets.

Pogue stood in front of the now-assembled team. He looked to Micah, arms crossed, hands in his armpits.

"You, Hannah, Taruk... *And* the Doctor," he added after a slight pause, "*behind* us. Taruk, eyes open!" Taruk and Micah nodded before a small frown creased his forehead.

"Shit. Only way of getting the spare clothes and the first aid kits there is-...."

"Hannah," Pogue smirked, finishing Micah's sentence. He knew Micah hated to fly. Flying- well, getting levitated by Hannah was probably like flying. But without any control. He pointed at the rest of the team and then back to himself.

Micah nodded again, then organized who carried what as he drew his knit cap lower to cover his ears, his lion part not liking the cold. Pogue's eyes settled on his group.

"Henley, wide perimeter and stay downwind. Dina, up. I wanna know what we're dealing with."

Micah rocked back on his heels, hefting up his backpack, and added

"We don't know what we'll find. Could be humans alive, or... Well, not."

Micah held out his hand for Pogue's phone, knowing his Alpha would shift.

Dina and Henley nodded as Dina broke out a big, toothy smile. She started stripping off her clothes right where she stood. In the fucking snow.... Nudity wasn't a big deal among Shifters, but most preferred to shift alone, or at least not in public. Not Dina, though. That woman had no inhibitions, no matter how much Caden had tried to teach her. Pogue's lips twitched as he shook his head at her. Pogue didn't mind much as long as it was within the Pride's borders. The one time she shifted outside the bar in Fawlks, she'd started a fight between three black bear Shifters, and Pogue had to separate them. Twice... Fun times.

Dina smiled before body transformed into a fully shifted hawk in a blinding flash of light. She hovered briefly in front of Pogue before shooting straight up.

Henley emerged silently from behind a large oak, already shifted into his fox. He trotted over to one of the many 'dump boxes' they had installed all over their land, inside and out, and placed his clothes inside. It made it so much easier not carrying your clothes when in your other form. Knowing that most of their animals, like their wild counterparts, were close to color blind, the boxes were blue and yellow. Yellow for dirty, blue for clean.

Pogue moved aside and finished his own transformation into his melanistic black jaguar—a sharp contrast to his tawny-colored twin—using the same oak to hide him as he did so. Pogue and Caden's cats were roughly double the size of a wild jaguar.

Pogue didn't need to say anything as his cat roared its joy, knowing it was in for a good hunt. He knew they would follow. They always followed.

The sharp cry of a hawk pierced the icy wind from above Pogue and Henley as they ran through harsh weather. Dina flew down and hovered next to Pogue, signaling him to stop. In a flash, she shifted.

"The sleet and wind are too strong! Fuck a duck, it's cold," she shouted, rubbing her hands up and down her bare body to try and retain the warmth.

"Almost close enough," Pogue answered after he had shifted. "Shift back and latch on to the back of my neck. Flat as you can!" He said, his voice carrying over the wind as Henley paced beside them.

Pogue didn't waste time waiting for an answer; he wasn't asking a question. He shifted back into his jaguar. Dina nodded and shifted, too. Carefully, she settled between his shoulder blades, barely holding on. She was very clearly not comfortable with this. *Oh, for fucks sake, just dig in what needs to be dug in already!* Pogue bared his teeth and snarled at her, signaling her to hurry the fuck up.

Henley was still pacing back and forth, high on adrenaline but well-mannered enough to wait for the Alpha to move again. And so, he did.

A couple of minutes later, they reached the scene of the crash. They stayed in animal form to wait for Micah's group. It was brutal. The front of the plane was gone; he would have to send another hunting party out to look for it. The back half of the aircraft was in pieces. There were small scattered fires, but the sleet was keeping them contained. Pogue's nose was offended by the mix of disgusting smells that hit his senses like a battering ram. Henley also smelt it, his fox sneezing to clear his nostrils.

Pogue signaled with his large head for Henley to start tracking to find out if anyone was still alive. So far, all they'd found were dead bodies or parts of dead bodies. Pogue signaled Henley to circle around the plane. Years of charades and game nights had honed the Pride's skills in cross-species nonverbal communication. Henley took off immediately.

Pogue padded around the wreckage, using his senses to look for anything relevant. His large paws trod softly on the ground, mindful of the many sharp objects in his path. Between the unpleasant odors, the only scent he couldn't place was a hint of wildflowers. That doesn't belong there, he thought, confused. He circled back, shaking his head, his long tail twitching in agitation.

About fifteen minutes later, the other group came into view. They were jogging, and it appeared Hannah had cast a shield around them, protecting them from the weather. As they reached them, Hannah dropped the shield and dropped to her knees. They were all drenched in sweat.

"Sorry, folks," she panted. "Almost out of juice here," she said as she turned to Pogue, who shifted and caught the sweatpants and hoodie Micah tossed to him, swiftly followed by boots. It would have been too cold for most other Shifters, but as an Alpha, Pogue ran hot. Dina left his shoulder, as he dressed, to settle down on Micah's. Micah stroked her feathers lightly in greeting.

"What happened?" Pogue asked, his voice easily overcoming the harsh wind as the group huddled close. Taruk's gaze remained fixed on the wreckage, his eyes wide with shock. His complexion had paled, absorbing the gruesome sight of mangled forms amidst the blood-stained snow.

"The wind is too strong! Took too much energy. I put us down about five kilometers back," Hannah yelled as she slowly got back to her feet and wrapped her arms around herself.

"Do you have enough in you to check for magic?" Pogue asked her.

Micah looked over at their Wielder. He shook his head slightly at Pogue and said,

"She can take a little from me."

For Wielders, magical power wasn't boundless. If they depleted their reserves, they'd either need to bide their time or siphon from another, exacting twice the toll. Typically, it was the strongest Shifters who volunteered. Pogue hesitated, reluctant to diminish his Beta's strength when he didn't know what the hell they were dealing with here- regardless of Micah's substantial inner strength.

Henley poked Pogue's leg with his soft nose, looking up at him.

"You sure?" Henley let out two short, high-pitched barks. "Thank you," Pogue said and turned to Hannah.

"Take as little as you can. We'll put you on Doc's back for the run home."

Doc lifted a white bushy eyebrow at his Alpha.

"We are going to place whom where?" Pogue leveled him a flat stare, his cat not liking defending or explaining an order.

"*We-*" he pointed to himself. "Place the *Wielder-*" he pointed to Hannah, "who *doesn't* have an animal to shield her from the weather on the largest fucking *Pridemember* here." He pointed to Doc, trying and failing to keep the growl from his voice. Pogue didn't care.

Doc seemed to think about it for a few seconds and then nodded.

"Right you are; of course, we will. It is the logical choice. I agree."

I don't need you to fucking agree. I need you to follow orders! Pogue mentally rolled his eyes.

Henley trotted over to Hannah, who smiled at him before mumbling an apology and thanking him for his sacrifice—a custom all Wielders abided by whenever they were given energy from another being. She then placed a hand on each side of his furry face, putting her mouth close to his muzzle, her thumbs gently caressing the sides. After a short while, she inhaled. Pogue watched as a shimmering fog seemed to pass from Henley to Hannah. It always made him yearn for a cigarette... Hannah's energy increased with each inhale, while Henley's weakened. After the third inhale, Hannah stopped, letting go of Henley, who sat down huffing. Doc went to him and bent down to administer a small pill—probably one of his energy cubes.

Pogue shifted his gaze from the group, seeking out Taruk. The young Shifter was crouched nearby. Taruk, Pogue noticed, had recently parted ways with his bagel. And whatever else he'd eaten today. Pogue couldn't blame him.

Hannah nodded sharply to Pogue and turned towards the wreckage. She mumbled a few phrases under her breath, and Pogue felt energy shifting, like pins and needles up and down his back. Hannah and everyone else didn't move for thirty seconds until the pins and needles subsided.

"There's something here, but it's faint. Feels like Portal residue and some kind of transport spell, but not a well-made one. That's probably why the plane crashed. If I didn't know better, I'd say both Displacement and Portal Wielders were involved, and it feels hurried," she said, frowning.

A Portal Wielder had a simple task: create a Portal to let people pass through the Barrier. A Displacer worked a bit differently. They could transport themselves, literally popping in and out as they pleased and sometimes taking one or two people with them, but as far as Hannah knew, they couldn't cross the Barrier that kept Shifters and Wielders hidden from humans. Pogue hated being Displaced. It felt like your entire body had all the air sucked out of it and then dumped in ice-cold water. Portals were fine; unlike many others, he never really experienced the nausea and dizziness that usually came with it.

"So, either hurried or inexperienced, maybe?" Pogue asked Hannah.

Hannah leveled a stare at him.

"No Pogue. Either Voldemort powerful, or there were two, and they were in a rush. But even then, it takes extreme power to pull through a plane, and I don't buy into it being just one Wielder. " *What the fuck is a Voldemort?!* Pogue thought. No time to dive into it either way. They needed to go.

"Shh!" Pogue hissed after they decided to wrap things up a few minutes later. Everyone fell silent. His cat had picked up on something. There was an odd feeling in his chest like he was searching for something he'd lost... He pushed the thought away and refocused on the task ahead.

Pogue's head whipped around as he scented something not there five minutes ago. Fresh blood in the air overrode the putrid smell of burnt flesh, plastic, and smoke.

He signaled Henley to do another sweep, as Micah did the same, Taruk in tow, and Dina flew up and circled. It didn't take him long to follow his nose to the crumpled-up form of... *What is that?* That wasn't there before, Pogue knew. It must have been buried under debris. He examined the small form. She was dressed in blood and piss-covered torn leggings and a semi-burnt and bloodied T-shirt proclaiming, 'What doesn't kill you, gives you XP,' whatever the fuck that was. He brushed her lengthy hair, or what was left of it, from her face.

Alive but weak. Female. He detected something he knew was important without knowing why. Another scent lay beneath the piss, blood, soot, and grime layers. *Wildflowers.* His cat wanted to lick away the disgusting layers to get to the one that mattered. Pogue mentally yanked it back, signaling the others to come to him.

Her hair was the color of wet autumn leaves. Again, he had to wrench his focus on the task as something dawned on him.

"Tell me that's not what I think it is!" Pogue growled.

"I..." Micah hesitated, standing next to him with a sheepish expression. "It's a human, Pogue." Pogue stood up and hissed at Micah, his voice hurried,

"Thank you, Captain Fucking Obvious! You're the human expert. How is it a live one, considering everyone else isn't? That shouldn't happen, Micah, and you fucking know that."

Micah kneeled and placed his head close to hers, undoubtedly smelling her.

"Adult. Female," he said. Pogue noticed how gentle Micah was as he lifted her upper body slightly and put his ear close enough to hear if there was a heartbeat. Pogue could hear it from where he stood. Faint, but it was there. Taruk, who had never seen a human before, was curiously edging closer, his wolf peering through his eyes. Pogue pointed a finger in his direction while maintaining focus on the body on the ground.

"Leash your wolf!" He commanded sharply. He knew Taruk had heard him as he moved backward.

As Micah gently lowered the body, a faint, almost imperceptible moan slipped from her cracked lips. Micah made sure she wasn't in direct contact with the ground, placing his jacket beneath her to shield her upper body from the wet, cold earth. He then straightened his shoulders and looked Pogue dead in the eye.

"We need to take her home, Pogue. I'll vouch for her," Micah said, a determined look on his face. Pogue knew Micah had a soft spot for humans, but his reaction was more potent than Pogue expected. Vouching for someone wasn't something you just did. He was basically saying, 'She fucks up; I accept being excommunicated.' Exile was a big deal. The prospects of finding acceptance elsewhere were slim, and Shifters were inherently social beings. They didn't thrive in solitude. Pogue studied his Beta. Micah stood about a head shorter than him and lacked the same broadness in the shoulders. The freckles across his nose, combined with his shaggy, wheat-colored hair and easy smile, always reminded Pogue of someone far younger than the lion really was. He was, after all, only twenty years younger than Pogue. Nothing in Shifter terms. They both looked to be about thirty years old.

"Careful, Micah," Pogue growled as he smiled flatly, his canines peeking out from under his upper lip. "We can't bring home every stray we find." His cat was getting increasingly agitated.

"Can you *guarantee* she's safe?" Pogue stepped closer and placed his hand at the back of the Beta's head, looking him in the eye. His hold was part grounding Micah's lion, who was too close to the surface, and part dominance display, reminding Micah *he* was not Alpha.

"There's something familiar... My cat is pacing like crazy," Micah murmured as he rubbed his right pec before averting his eyes.

Pogue sighed. Micah had never made a serious mistake. He always told Pogue, when in doubt, to trust the cat. His cat, Pogue thought, annoyed, just wasn't being fucking helpful right now! But having a Beta was pointless if you didn't show them trust. So, Pogue would trust him now and deal with the consequences later. They needed to get home.

"Let Doc and Hannah look. If they deem her safe, I'll take the hit from Caden, but you *will* owe me."

Micah's face now bore a shit-eating grin. He turned and motioned for Doc to hurry up. The rest of the group quickly gathered around the small form on the ground. Dina's hawk was perched on Hannah's shoulder. Poor Henley trotted slowly to them, his head downcast.

"Shift, Henley. Get some strength back," Pogue turned around and knelt before his Pridemember, gently scuffing him. Shifting didn't heal all, but it would speed up the process.

Henley shook his head and looked at the body on the ground.

"It's human and weak." Henley nodded and left to go shift. Pogue snapped his fingers after him to get his attention. When Henley looked, Pogue held up three fingers to convey he expected a minimum of three shifts. A soft bark was his only answer as the fox slid behind a large fir close to the group.

"May I assess the patient now, Alpha?" Doc asked, his tone neutral, as he ran a hand across his face, trying to clear some of the sleet from his eyes.

Pogue snorted and nodded. She won't make it, he thought to himself, even as that same thought added to the odd feeling in his chest.

Doc kneeled, his large, slender frame bending over the small body.

"Micah is correct; she does appear to be an adult. However, young. She's quite damaged," Doc observed, peering over his narrow shoulder at Pogue. "The wound on her back, though slim, looks quite bad, and her body is clearly in shock. I dare to say she got off lightly, but she is still in awful shape," he said, standing up to face his Alpha. "She will die if we do nothing. She should have been already. I have no plausible explanation as to how she survived this." He straightened and placed his long arms behind his back. However, Pogue knew he already considered the human a patient to be cared for. Doc didn't look like much—tall and lanky with white poofy hair and a long, sharp nose. But he was a damn good Healer, not to mention a polar bear.

Healers in their world were either very good but could only heal one type of Shifter, or, like Doc, they were less effective on a specific Shifter but could, in turn, heal many types. Doc was one of the only Healers he knew who could heal

Wielders and most Shifters. Pogue wasn't sure if he could heal humans. They'd never had one to try it on.

Caden is gonna string me up by my balls, Pogue concluded as he made the decision.

"Why the fuck am I carrying her?" Micah grumbled.

Pogue raised an eyebrow at the lion Shifter hopping around, trying to ward off the chill. It struck Pogue as a quirky behavior. As an Alpha, he naturally ran hotter than most Shifters and humans. However, Shifters were generally more resilient to the cold than humans. He couldn't help but notice Taruk mimicking him. *Great... Just great...* Pogue thought, rolling his eyes before returning his focus to Micah.

"One"—he held up a finger—"she's human," he stated, thinking it should be obvious that the human expert carried the human.

Micah stared at him flatly.

"Oh, mighty Alpha, please elaborate on your ever-so-eloquent and lengthy explanation."

Pogue growled softly at the dumb lion.

"Two"—he held up his middle finger—"you're the one insisting we bring her home."

Micah's jaw fell open for a moment, then he squared his shoulders and gave a brisk nod.

"Fine, but the piss pants are coming off!"

"Whatever you say." Pogue shook his head and gave Micah a rough pat on the shoulder.

"You carry her. All the way home", he said, smirking at the blonde, who froze in place, halfway bent to pick up the tiny human.

"All the way? Really?!" Micah exclaimed. "That's like twelve k's!" Pogue rocked back on his heels, jamming his hands in his pockets.

"Sixteen. Move out!" He barked, then turned to Taruk. "Run fast. Let Caden know we're inbound. Do *not*," he stressed the word, "tell Caden we're bringing a human."

Taruk nodded sharply and shifted without taking off his clothes. Pogue sighed, collecting Taruk's torn clothing, and gave the wolf a disapproving glare—no litterbugs in StormEdge. Taruk lowered his head in apology. Then he bolted, his wolf vanishing amidst the brutal weather and towering fir trees.

Pogue turned to Doc.

"Doc, shift so we can get Hannah home before she turns into a popsicle."

Doc nodded and stepped away from the group. The sleet and wind obscured their view, making hiding unnecessary, especially with the low afternoon sun. Not long after, a massive polar bear trudged through the snow with a pile of clothes neatly folded in his large maw. He walked over to Hannah, who smirked and took it from him to put into the backpack Micah had brought. Pogue then unceremoniously grabbed the small woman around the waist and threw her onto the large bear's back.

Doc stood nearly two and a half meters tall. Pogue would hate to ever have to fight him. Not that it would ever come to that. Doc was a healer, not a fighter. Hannah grabbed his thick fur and lowered her upper body, mumbling a few words. Pogue felt the pins and needles again. Before the group's eyes, a saddle materialized on Doc's back. Unaware of Hannah's plan, Doc freaked out and rose to his hind legs, roaring his outrage and sending Hannah flying, landing on her ass on the wet ground. Dina, who was perched on Hannah's shoulder, let out a loud and somewhat undignified squawk as she was launched off Hannah's shoulder. Doc stomped around, trying to dislodge the offending item strapped around his chest and belly.

"Stop!" Pogue commanded, his lips twitching with the effort not to laugh, though his dominance rolled off him in heavy waves. Doc froze but started whining. It was pathetic but comical. Pogue had to keep chanting internally to keep from showing the irked Shifter just how fucking funny it looked. *Don't* *laugh at the polar bear, don't laugh at the polar bear, h*e chanted as he walked up and grabbed the bear by the jaw.

"I know. Trust me, I *know*. But Hannah will never be able to stay on you otherwise, and she *will"* -he looked at Hannah, who was dusting sleet from her cape, an annoyed expression on her face- "take it off the second you reach the Den." Pogue then walked over, grabbed Hannah, and threw her back onto Doc. They took off, Dina perched back on Hannah's shoulder. "Dina, check along the way." Dina's hawk gave a sharp cry, indicating she'd heard him.

He then looked to Henley, who still looked tired, his head down as Pogue snapped his fingers to get his attention.

"You good to run?"

Henley nodded and started after Doc.

Pogue was left with Micah.

"Alright, lover boy. I'm not leaving that-" Pogue pointed to the small woman "-out of my sight, so I guess we're going on a date."

Micah grinned sharply.

"And you didn't even buy me flowers."

Pogue snorted as Micah bent to pick up the body.

"No, but I apparently got you something else... But *you* have to feed it, clean up its mess, and"—Pogue smelled the small human— "for the love of the gods, *bathe* it," he said, scrunching up his nose. Micah nodded as he lifted her and protectively tucked her now half-naked body against his chest, trying to keep his jacket on but throwing it over her as well. He stared at Pogue, an urgent expression on his face.

"I've never had to carry a human in this condition before. What if I break her? Or if her legs and ass freeze off. I mean, literally?!"

"Then she dies." This was clearly a bigger deal to Micah than Pogue had seen coming. It usually took quite a bit more to faze his Beta.

"I know I owe you; I do... Can I owe you one more thing, tho?" Micah asked as he jostled her around.

Pogue sighed, pinching the bridge of his nose, willing Micah silently not to ask.

"What?"

"Can I owe you a new hoodie?"

Caden is gonna kill me. I'll come home with my chest hair frozen off and Micah adopting the damned thing like a lost puppy! Pogue shook his head at his mental visions, a wry grimace tugging at his lips. This was becoming absurd.

Micah gently raised her small limp hand and waved it in Pogue's face.

"Seriously, man, feel her hands! They're frozen." He juggled her around, trying to show him the gash on her back, too, while trying to keep a hold of both her arms.

Pogue put a single finger on her forehead. She really was freezing. The faintest scent of wildflowers distracted his cat from the smell of piss, blood, and everything else.

"You just took my kitchen duty for a week, my friend." Micah just nodded. The whole Pride took turns in the kitchen. Pogue hated it. He was not in any way, shape, or form adept at cooking, which meant he ended up cleaning. A lot...

Pogue removed his warm hoodie and helped Micah put in on the small body. It reached all the way to her knees.

"Let's go home," he said, setting a brutal pace back to the Den.

24

Chapter 5

They made it back to the Den a little before dawn. Pogue ordered Micah to the infirmary and told him to stay there until he returned. His cat wanted to follow. He ignored it.

He walked up to the front door, already open and inviting. He found it odd that their Wielders, Hannah and Nigel, accidentally gave the door a personality, years back, but he appreciated how it seemed to favor the Alphas, opening and closing as needed. Well, most of the time. Pogue knew his brother wouldn't have gone to bed. He would have waited for the team to come home and then waited for Pogue to find him. Pogue found Caden sprawled out in a beanbag, shirtless and sockless. A spilled bag of nuts lay beside him, and he had one hand tucked into the front of his jeans. Unable to resist, Pogue quietly made his way to the desk drawer and retrieved the Polaroid camera. He moved soundlessly, shoes left outside the office, and quietly approached his brother.

"Morning, sunshine!" he sang right by Caden's ear as he snapped a picture.

Caden bolted up and fell face-first out of the beanbag chair and onto the floor, his hand still in his pants.

"Oh fierce, graceful Alpha, thy brother has returned," he smirked. "And thy hand is still in thy pants," he added in a dry voice.

"Ow..." Caden mumbled, his face squashed into the soft carpet.

Pogue walked over to a small fridge in the corner of the room, grabbed a bottle, and drank two large gulps of water before turning around.

Caden was facing him with a scowl on his sleep-rumpled face.

"Asshole!" Caden wasn't really a morning person. Before coffee, anyway. "Taruk got back OK," Caden said before yawning as he stood up. He grabbed Pogue's cigarettes from the desk and handed them to him.

Pogue shot him a quizzical look.

"Cades... Why are you handing me smokes?"

Caden sighed and wiped his brow with his hand. Pogue groaned softly on an exhale. He was exhausted, hungry, and smelled like he had just completed a fifty-kilometer run. It wasn't far off. Now Caden was handing him cigarettes even though he detested Pogue's bad habit.

"What the fuck now?!"

Caden grabbed his guitar pick and started biting the edge.

"DeCoill rang while you were out... The terms for the Challenge."

Pogue lit a cigarette.

"This warrants you feeding me smokes how?" he asked as he opened a window.

The IceFjord wolves, notorious Purebloods, were led by Stellan, who ruled with strict adherence to old traditions, punishing even minor infractions severely. They had challenged before. Pogue had defeated Stellan three times.

Caden sighed. Clearly, he was about as done with IceFjord as Pogue was.

"IceFjord is initiating a Turf War," he said as he sat down on a bean bag. "They're coming for everyone."

Pogue felt as if the air had been punched out of him. A Turf War was rare. Council-approved war, stamped and sealed.

"When? Why?" Pogue asked, feeling his cat snarl inside him.

"Yule. They're cleared to enter Pridelands at midnight on December twenty-fifth." Caden dug his feet into the thick carpet, a frown forming. "Gives us about two and a half months. The why part? I'm honestly wondering that myself. They *know* we're the stronger Alphas. They must know they will lose their wolves?"

Pogue started pacing as Caden tossed the guitar pick on the desk.

"This couldn't have come at a worse time," Pogue groaned. They held each other's gaze for a moment, a silent understanding passing between them. They would beat this. Now Pogue just had to get rid of the human.

Caden called Micah to inform the Beta about the notice before grabbing a beer and trying to unwind. Fortunately, that was something they both excelled at. As Alphas, you had to be able to roll with the punches. Caden was better than Pogue at decompressing quickly. Pogue had a tendency to think about things. Many Pridemember, to his face, called it brooding. Obviously, they were wrong. At least that's what he told them all. Repeatably.

A while later, Caden smirked and pointed his beer at Pogue.

"You think Micah went home yet?"

"Infirmary," Pogue answered as he took another swig of his beer.

Caden's lip twitched, the pick dangling from his fingers.

"Oh really? Why would our Beta go to the infirmary? Is he injured?"

Pogue suddenly felt like he'd just lost a bet and was about to pay up. Caden's voice was a little too kind.

"Micah is fine. But he sort of brought home a stray," Pogue mumbled as he sipped his water.

"A stray what, Pogue?" Caden pressed as if he didn't already know.

Pogue could almost taste his brother's smugness, his cat's eyes glinting with mischief.

"Human," Pogue muttered under his breath.

"Sorry, Pogue, I didn't quite catch that. Repeat, please?"

Pogue groaned and looked Caden in the eye as he reached to close the window.

"He brought in a stray human, a survivor from the crash. Gotta send a team out tomorrow to find the rest of the plane. We only found the back half."

"Mhm... I'll send out a team. You need your sleep so you can be awake and coherent at noon tomorrow," Caden smirked.

Pogue knew what was coming, but like a dumbass, he asked anyway.

"Why do I have to be awake and coherent at noon? Which, by the way, is in five hours."

Caden grinned. He strolled over to a metal filing cabinet near the door and yanked out The File swiftly turning to page seven, pointing out a paragraph and tapping it with a finger. Pogue didn't bother to look. He didn't have to. Instead, he walked over, pushed Caden aside with his hip to open the window again, and lit another cigarette.

"Page 7, section 4, paragraph 3.4. You, dearest brother," he grinned, "are on punishment for your offense against the Pride and me, your fellow Alpha! And I even planned your awesome punishment, so you don't have to worry about it. Isn't that nice of me?" Pogue noted Caden's evil grin as he puffed, his annoyance growing with the promise of sunrise behind the trees surrounding the Den.

They had rules in place, mainly to avoid conflicts and plan for contingencies in case of mental instability, severe injury, or disappearance. Some of their childhood rules they had kept were ridiculous, like how they could never play chess together (because Caden was a piss poor loser). This rule allows the other Alpha to decide and enforce any punishment until the offense is resolved.

Basically, Pogue would be his brother's bitch until this clusterfuck was resolved. *Fun times.*

"Cades, I'm fucking tired. What is my punishment so I can go sleep?"

Caden flashed a toothy grin.

"You're going to work on your people skills by gluing the human to you. She's your responsibility. We'll see if we can use her for anything. I'll take any advantage we can get right now. If not, we'll turn her over to the Council, OK?"

Pogue felt his jaw drop as he stared openmouthed at his brother, who just stood there looking way too pleased with himself.

"But it's Micah's human!!" he whined as dignifiedly as he could muster, which really wasn't a lot. *Great, now you sound like a five-year-old,* he mentally facepalmed.

"You brought it home." *Aaand there's Caden, five years old...*

Chapter 6

48 hours later

Grace opened her mouth a little to lick her lips. They felt like sandpaper. Her brain slowly started to receive signals from every part of her body, none of which seemed happy. Her brain was frantically trying to remember where she was and what had happened. Grace opened her eyes, and the whole world was blurry.

"Ah, you are awake. Good." A baritone voice came from her right side. Soft-spoken, with a little accent she couldn't place. Maybe British?

When she tried to sit up and speak, as she rubbed at her eyes, a gentle hand on her arm stopped her.

"Please do not try to move. You may inadvertently rip out your IV. Hold on". She heard footsteps moving away from her. A moment later, the sound of a cup being filled. The footsteps returned, and a hand supported the back of her head.

"Sip it slowly, please. It's a soft drink infused with vitamins. It'll aid your recovery. The smoke might have irked your eyes; give them a moment to adjust. You've been through quite an ordeal. I wasn't certain you'd pull through the night."

Grace ignored the slow part and swallowed the whole drink until she could hear the slurping of the straw, reaching for the last precious drops of liquid. The doctor, she assumed, chuckled and said

"Sleep a little bit more if you can. You are safe for now. I will see to your health. My name is James St. Nick." She tried to smile at the name. Santa was her doctor, she thought, just before darkness swallowed her once again.

"How's our girl doin', Doc?" Through the haze, she registered a clear voice. Grace blinked her eyes open. Her vision was still fuzzy, but she could see a mop of wheat blond hair and a huge smile that lit up the entire room. She didn't have enough coffee in her system to handle that level of happiness right now. Her eyes gradually adjusted, and she was able to look around.

She found herself in what looked like a fancy mountain cabin - all wood and a vintage stove in the corner. Four hospital beds were neatly arranged along one wall, with her on the left of the middle. It had a bit of a '60s movie vibe, she thought. Everything seemed well-kept, though. *Shit. What happened? Did the plane crash?*

"Good evening, Micah," the doctor said. She looked toward the voice to see a tall, lanky man with white poofy hair. He smiled at her as she looked at him. *Huh, kinda looks like Santa, too,* Grace mused.

"Update, please," mop head prodded.

"She woke up about four hours ago and managed to take fluids orally but then slipped back into sleep. I have healed what I can, but I have had to apply human techniques for many of her injuries. Her back has thirty-four stitches."

"Stitches?" The mop head, Micah asked. That would explain the searing pain in her back, she reasoned as she tried to resurrect her limbs. Unsuccessfully...

"Required. Her skin will absorb them as she heals. I will work on her every few hours to help it along," Doc replied.

Grace tried to sit up, wincing as she lifted her head. *Yeah-nah, ow....* She moaned.

Mop head quickly eased her back down and gently patted her head, kinda like a child petting a cat. It was odd but felt nice. Her *everything* hurt.

"Hey there, little one, wanna tell-" he spoke softly to her, as poofy man interrupted, "Micah, you are aware she is a young *adult,* right?"

Micah, apparently, cleared his throat.

"Well, yeah, but to be fair, I'm not really sure if their adult is the same as ours."

"Miss, can you hear me well enough?" poofy hair man asked.

"No," she answered. The doctor didn't seem to be fazed by her sarcasm. Maybe he was used to it from whoever else was around.

"Ah, good. I am going to reduce the muscle relaxants slowly now. This will allow you more motor function, and you should feel more awake in a few minutes. Please take it slow; you have been asleep for forty-eight hours. Do you understand?"

Grace tried for a thumbs up. Micah kept petting her, and moments later, she felt a cold sensation in her arm and a slight pressure. She winced and opened one eye, glaring at the doctor.

"Apologies. Just flushing your IV."

"How long?" Micah asked.

"A few minutes. She isn't ready for an interrogation just yet, please. You know the rules as well as I. My clinic, my patient," Doc said, a touch of steel in his otherwise pleasant voice.

"I know. But I must let them know she's awake," Micah sighed. They? Who the fuck is they?

"Yes, of course."

Time ticked on. Micah remained still, now giving her hair comforting strokes. It distracted her from the pain but also had her mentally weighing the pros and cons of giving Mister Touchy-Feely a throat punch. The logistics of that feat, however, seemed daunting, especially when even a paper cup felt like a weightlifting challenge. Grace felt tingling in her toes as sensation started to return. She tried using her abs to sit up, causing her to tilt slightly to the side as they protested much. They were not in any way inclined to help her right now. They wanted heat and peace, thank you very much!

"Careful, darlin'." Micah's hand smoothed down her arm and gently patted her hand as he placed it on her stomach.

"I wanna sit up!" Grace whined.

"Shhh. It's OK, darlin', it's gonna be OK." Micah's words were soothing but not enough to stop the cold sweat starting at the base of her spine. Not good. Grace didn't get panic attacks but had these spaced-out moments called dissociative fugues. They'd make her zone out and forget things for a bit, lasting from seconds to hours. Sometimes, she'd wake up in odd places, lost or miss half a chat while talking to someone. It usually hit when she felt super stressed. Therapists said it was a result of childhood traumas.

Grace turned her head toward the doctor. She clenched the sheets, frantically trying to get a grip on reality.

"I need facts. Please. Facts calm panic. Please, any facts," she pleaded as Micah continued to stroke her hair with one hand and gently took hold of her much smaller hand with his other.

The doctor cleared his throat.

"Certainly. Firstly, please know you are safe here. You were in a plane crash, but you will be just fine." He hesitated. *Safe. Plane crash. Gonna be fine.* Grace nodded for him to go on. "You were severely hurt but are in a safe place." *I'm safe. The doctor fixed me. The creepy dude has soft hands.* Grace nodded again. "You still have several injuries, but most of them will heal on their own, and the others I have been working on."

The doctor smiled down at her. She glared.

Sighing, he continued.

"I suspect you will heal up quite quickly. Now, you have a long, narrow wound reaching from your right shoulder blade and down across your buttocks, stopping at your thigh. It was quite bad and will need to be cleaned daily. Are you still with me?"

"Give me a second. This is a lot." She found herself clinging to Micah's hand, attempting to ground herself. He squeezed her hand lightly.

"Where am I?" She looked at the creeper/golden retriever dude, Micah, next to her. "And who are you to me? I don't remember you."

"I cannot tell you out location, miss, " the doctor said calmly.

"Tell me!" Grace screeched before going into a coughing fit. Was this it? Like in the movies where the stalker kidnaps the blond and kills her? Her mind quickly came up with all sorts of possible deaths she might endure soon. Micah helped her sit up more and ran his warm hands in circles on her back, mindful of the long gash. A moment later, a cup was placed in her hand. She tried to lift it to her mouth, but her fingers wouldn't grip properly. It spilled out all over her hospital gown.

The cup was taken, and moments later, another one returned. This time, Micah held his hands over the top of hers and helped her bring the cup up.

"This is so mucked up... All I wanted to do was go to the wildlife sanctuary... It was just four months. Leave creepy stalker in NZ. Work with the big cats. Pet the cats, then go home. Be fucking happy! That's it! This was supposed to be my big magical adventure, not my fucking nightmare on Elm Street!" Grace exclaimed, her voice high-pitched and wheezy.

"Think of me as your emotional support lio-uhm, man, okay? Just here to help. What's this about a wildlife sanctuary?" Micah asked at the same time as the Doc asked,

"What's Elm Street?"

"Freddy Kruger, you know... And yeah,"- she waved her still half-numb hands about. "It's this fantastic place outside Ontario that takes in big cats from all over the world. I was supposed to have this great fucking adventure, and instead, I *Wingardium levio no no'ed* into ...Where *am* I?"

"We'll get to that, darlin'. Just rest for a little, and know you're safe, okay? I'd like to know about this stalker business, too, but for now, just rest." Grace knew Micah was trying to be soothing, but this was just too fucking much.

Grace proceeded to go into a total meltdown. She bawled her eyes out, her body shaking so bad the doctor pleaded with her repeatedly to stop so she didn't tear any stitches. But she kept going, and going, and going...

That is until Micah stopped her as he blurted out,

"You can stay here! We can help each other!"

A metal tray fell to the floor, and the doctor hurriedly started picking up the utensils now spread out on the floor. Grace was shocked out of her panic and turned her head towards Micah.

"Stay here?"- she said, sniffling-" What do you mean stay here? How the fuck can we help each other? Where *is* here?!"

"Well, darlin', you wanted to work with big cats. And leave the stalker thing. You're not the one stalking anyone, right?" he asked, a hint of humor in his voice.

Grace shrugged.

"I'm a veterinary nurse. We all wanna play with big kitties. I actually specialize in them. And no, I'm not the stalker; I'm the stalkee, I guess. What's it to you?"

She stared daggers at him. Why wouldn't they tell her where she was?! Micah seemed to think for a minute, then looked at her.

"Grace, do you believe in magic?"

Grace stared blankly at him. *I've landed in some backwoods pot-smoking commune... Super...*

Micah frowned slightly.

"What if I told you that magic is real? Not just that, but that some people turn into animals?" Grace kept staring at him. He smiled as his blue eyes slowly changed color, yellow bleeding into the bright blue.

"What if I told you I'm a Shifter? That I can turn into a cat. Big one at that."

I'm going crazy... This must be shock. You're high. That's what she thought. But somewhere inside her, her Peter Pan complex poked its head up. Grace had always had an open mind about the supernatural. She'd never seen any proof but wanted to think it could be real when she read her changeling romance novels, Harry Potter or Percy Jackson books. She'd enter that realm whenever another foster parent hurt her or she was put in a cupboard for not eating her veggies.

"I'd tell you; you should have shown up between foster parent two and six. Cool eye trick, though," she mumbled before yawning. "Also, you're high, and if you're gonna kill me, at least give me some of whatever you're smoking first."

Micah started stroking her hair again.

"How about this," he tried as he pulled out what looked like a thick, worn notebook from a satchel on the floor. "You read this and consider my offer. I'll come by when you've read it and slept, and then we'll go over it together."

"Offer?" Grace asked, her curiosity spiking despite everything.

"We might need a veterinary nurse very soon. You help us with that, and you get to pet as many big cats as you want; we'll keep you safe from your stalker, plus we won't have to hand you over to our Council, who *will* probably kill you." *Pot smoking commune meets cannibal-murder mother-brother same-same commune. Gotcha...*

Grace said nothing as his words sunk in. His many confusing words. What was the Council? Some kind of backwoods police, maybe? *But he said kill. Holy shit, I'm kidnapped?! Is this like a mob thing? Is Santa really The Godfather and Micah is his Godson brother-husband?* Grace wasn't necessarily a brave person. But she was a survivor, and when words like 'kill' were used, she listened, and he sounded dead serious. Rule number one when you're kidnapped. Don't be a dick. Make them like you. She didn't want to die, and if she was honest about it, she instantly liked Micah. Not that she knew why, but it had to be that complex where the victim starts liking the bad guy, and she must just be like, really, really fast to fall for it. And he probably wasn't related to the doctor...Right? Either way, she knew one thing: She knew how to adapt. At least until she knew more, it seemed smart to play along.

Grace held out her hand for the manual.

"Let me read, and then we talk. Do the eye thing again," she ordered.

Micah leaned a little closer, and she watched as they changed color from blue to golden and back to blue again.

"Woah," she whispered right before yawning. "Okay, maybe a little sleep and then reading." *Either you're high, or I am, and if I'm not, I fucking should be...*

"No problem, darlin'."

Grace closed her eyes, and soon sleep embraced her.

Chapter 7

"You said what?!" Pogue and Caden simultaneously roared at Micah . Pogue crossed the office in five quick steps and grabbed their Beta by the throat, easily lifting the large Shifter up and pushing him against the wall opposite the windows. He did not need this shit right now.

Micah lifted both his arms as he shrugged, an innocent look on his face. Doc stood silently by the door, hands in his pockets.

"Explain to me how the fuck you think this is gonna play out, Micah," Pogue growled in his face, his cat itching to swipe at the dumb lion.

Caden stood, leaning on the desk, his hands grabbing the edges tightly. Doc discreetly cleared his throat, and Pogue whipped his head towards him so fast he felt his neck crack.

"What?!"

Micah was grasping Pogue's black knitted sweater at this point. Pogue knew Micah's lion could remove his arm, but he didn't fight, probably because he knew things could quickly escalate.

Doc moved slowly forward. He kept his eyes downcast, his head tilted to the side, throat slightly exposed. He trying to balance his impulse to safeguard Micah and his need to be subservient to his Alpha.

"I do believe young Micah might better be able to answer your questions if he could breathe."

Pogue looked at Micah, whose face was an ugly shade of red. Micah wisely averted his eyes from Pogue, despite undoubtedly being pissed. No Shifter appreciated anyone lifting them by the throat. The Beta of StormEdge was no exception. Pogue shifted his attention to Caden as he allowed his cat to surge to the surface. Caden's claw-tipped fingers delicately tapped the wooden surface of the desk. A quiet understanding was reached, and Caden nodded. Pogue let go of Micah, who slid down the wall palming his throat, wheezing hard.

Doc looked torn between wanting to go to what was now a patient and not angering two angry Alphas. He settled on looking to Pogue and then to Micah.

"Pogue..." Caden's voice behind him penetrated his cat's anger at a Pride-members stupidity.

Pogue took two large steps back and threw up his hands, his claws shooting out for a second before resettling in his human skin. He noticed Caden signaled to Doc, who swiftly approached Micah. Doc's fingers gently touched Micah's throat, emanating a soft, warm glow as his healing gift worked Micah's throat. After a minute, Micah took in deep breaths, coughing to clear his throat.

Caden extended a hand to Micah, who grabbed. Caden then yanked him so forcefully that the Beta went airborne, swinging onto the desk. With a resounding crash, Micah landed and toppled over the edge, bringing the high-backed leather desk chair down with him in a tumble to the ground.

"Talk, Micah," Caden said, keeping his tone even though his fingers were still claw-tipped. Micah flowed up from the floor to stand in front of his Alphas as Caden continued. "What possessed you to tell the human about us? That she could stay? That we wouldn't turn her over?! We've never had a pet Here! We would never do something like that. Micah, we don't keep slaves! And yet, you just handed it to her as if it were a lifeline!? You are not the Alpha! You can't make that choice for her or for us."

In their society, a pet was a person tied to a Community, belonging to a high-ranking member. Essentially, they were slaves. This practice wasn't embraced by StormEdge. They firmly believed that ownership didn't guarantee loyalty, and they wouldn't accept anyone in the Pride who wasn't completely dedicated to them.

Micah looked up; his gaze fixed on Caden's chin. Pogue stood silently, his right-hand fidgeting with a loose thread on his sweater while he stared down the young lion. He snapped it off, only to look at his fingers. Black smudges coated his index finger from the doodle he was working on last night just before bed.

"I'm sorry-" Micah started.

"Not fucking good enough, Micah," Pogue hissed at him. Micah didn't flinch.

Doc had slowly retreated to the door, clearly waiting for a good time to exit. Caden nodded to him and he slid quietly out the door, closing it softly behind him.

"Try again," Caden prodded. Micah took a deep breath.

"I recognize I should have talked to you both first, and I acted above my rank. But I didn't tell her about the Turf War, just so you know, " Micah started quietly.

Caden shifted his stance, shaking out his hands as his claws retracted.

"Then why? And how the fuck did you explain? Does she even believe you?! This could cost you your rank."

Micah looked directly at Caden; his eyes wide. Micah loved StormEdge and had worked hard to earn his position. Pogue recognized his irreplaceable worth, and not just as a Beta. Micah was like a brother to him and one of his closest friends. Still, it didn't change the fact that Micah had fucked up.

"Alphas, I..." Micah's voice faltered as the seriousness of the situation dawned on him. He cleared his throat. "I showed her my lion's eyes and gave her the manual I've been working on for a few years. It's sort of an intro to our world. In case we ever had a human here. I told her to read it and that her skills could be bartered for protection from her stalker and the Council. Most importantly, I do *not* believe she is a threat to the Pride. And I do admit to having a soft spot for her. But she is *not* a danger," he stressed, rubbing his pec with his knuckles. "My cat just feels like we're supposed to keep her."

"It's not a damn puppy, Micah!" Pogue said, exasperated.

"I know, trust me, I do. *She* is a human," Micah retorted softly. He stuck his hands into his pockets, rocking back and forth on his heels.

Pogue and Caden both pointed a finger at Micah as they, in concert, barked, "Don't sass me!"

"Sorry," Micah said crestfallen.

Caden's thawing was inevitable. Like Pogue, he genuinely loved Micah. But Pogue, unlike his brother, had no reservations about punishing him. Cades had always been gentler than him, Pogue thought as he watched Caden's shoulders relax.

"Under normal circumstances, you're a solid Beta. Help me understand what happened. Step by step," Caden said, his voice slowly softening. He leaned his body toward Micah and inclined his head.

Oh, for fuck's sake, Pogue groaned as he envisioned himself banging his head against a wall. *Help me understand?* Pogue thought. *Who are you, a Maternal? Wanna offer him a cookie too?!* Pogue mentally rolled his eyes.

"I saw that," Caden said, his lips twitching.

Pogue flipped him off.

"Explain, Micah," Pogue said sternly.

Micah took a deep breath and shook his hands out.

"Well, she woke up," he started.

"No shit," Pogue interrupted and glared at him.

Micah's jaw tensed. He waited until Pogue finally held up his hands, palms out, before continuing.

"And then she panicked a little. Then Doc started talking about all her injurie s..." Micah hesitated. Caden rolled his hand slowly, encouraging him to continue. "Well, then she was kinda crying a lot, and it just got worse and worse; my cat got so sad, and she squeezed my hands so hard and was te..."

Pogue held up a hand to stop his thousand-kilometer-an-hour blabbering.

"Slow! Breathe, man!"

Micah nodded and continued after taking a couple of deep breaths.

"She was telling us about why she was on that plane to begin with. She is a vet nurse. She specializes in big cats. With this Turf War and all.." he trailed off.

Pogue raised a brow at him.

"Still not explaining the why, Micah."

"If we petition the Council for her to stay on a probationary basis as a pet, she can help Doc with any injuries. She could help save some of our people! You know one healer for all of us won't cut it!" he ground out, frustrated, before composing himself. "She just... She just looked so small. My cat wanted to protect her, and I can't explain why," he shrugged.

"Micah, one of these days, this hero complex will end you." Caden sighed. "What scents did she give out?" Micah scrunched up his nose.

"Now you mention it. None," he responded, perplexed.

Caden frowned.

"No fear, anger, anything?"

"Nothing, but I'm not *actually* sure humans give off a scent. I've been so focused on learning about their society and their psychology," he mused, running a hand through his shaggy hair. "I don't know why I never took notice of that. I mean, other than piss and blood and stuff. That's reall-"

"Wildflowers," Pogue interrupted as it dawned on him why the scent didn't belong at the crash. It was her scent. He couldn't figure out why he knew that or why it seemed so important to his cat. He knew that as an Alpha, his senses were more acute than those of a typical Dominant Shifter, but that didn't explain why his cat had picked up that particular scent. He dragged himself out of his internal monologue to see his brother's green eyes sparkle with the cat's curiosity. Pogue could almost see a small smile form on his brother's lips as he grabbed one of his guitar picks and began biting the corner before asking.

"Come again?"

Pogue shook his head and lit a cigarette. He instantly regretted blurting it out. He shouldn't give a fuck what the human smelled like, let alone remember it as vividly. Caden snatched the pack and tucked it into his jeans. Pogue let out a sigh. it wasn't like they'd kill him. Shifters, as a rule, weren't prone to human diseases. Doc had explained that viruses were no match due to their robust immune system. Bacterial infections were possible, but usually cleared up after a couple of shifts. Micah once shared that mental health didn't seem to be something they were less susceptible to, but he figured that their connection with their animal side kept the more severe issues from fully emerging.

As a result, Shifters had a low rate of severe mental illness. Micah had told him that if they actually had a working relationship with other Communities around the world, he'd be able to get better numbers. Pogue had told him no. That was a matter for the Council. Now he was starting to think Micah and Caden were right when they'd discussed creating some kind of information network...

40

Pogue realized he'd been sucked into his mind once again as Micah and Caden looked at him, their heads cocked waiting for his response.

"The only scent she has is wildflowers."

Caden's lips twitched.

Pogue pointed a finger at him, "Shut it!"

"So, where do we go from here?" Micah asked, his stance relaxed a fraction, mirroring Caden's.

"You tell us," Pogue said as he blew a smoke ring.

Micah was quiet as he thought it over. After a while, his head snapped up, and he smiled widely, showing his teeth.

"Get Tari to do the necessary paperwork. It's easy. We keep her as part of the Pride," he said, a hopeful look on his face.

Both Alphas looked at Micah wide-eyed. Pogue started toward him.

"Right! You don't wanna breathe after all!"

"No, no, no, wait," Micha said as he swiftly moved behind Caden, who huffed indignantly and tried to move aside. Micah shadowed behind him with catlike grace as Pogue tried to reach around his brother to get to him, gripping the cigarette between his teeth.

"She quoted Harry Potter! Her t-shirt talks about experience points! She probably wants to believe in magic! She's susceptible to our world! This isn't impossible! She could be integrated. Be an asset! She'd be the perfect case study; we know there have been human/Shifter matings in the earlier days! They can teach us so much, and she's a fucking vet nurse!" The words came out with lightning speed as he left Caden's back to pick up a large potted plant to shield himself.

"We didn't *ask* for a human veterinary nurse, Micah," Caden stated. He began flanking right while Pogue went left, gradually encircling Micah in the middle, his back against the water cooler next to the mini-fridge. Micah was on his best behavior, and Pogue knew it.

"Well, you got one," Micah remarked.

Pogue's low rumble deepened in his throat as he moved forward.

Micah held out his hand.

"Plus, because we're such a young Pride, it's a great educational opportunity for us- many in the Pride haven't ever interacted with humans, and all she wants to do is play with big cats, so we let her! *Educational opportunity* Alphas! Use your words, not your claws!"

Both Caden and Pogue were now standing in front of their Beta, who had slid partially down the wall, holding up the plant almost like an offering. *This is what we're reduced to?!*

Pogue felt his lips twitch as he took in the scene. Caden glared at him but then looked down at Micah, whose head turned sideways, his eyes squinting shut, and the stupid plant held up towards them. Then Caden started snickering, and soon both Alphas were laughing so hard, Caden had tears streaming down his face, and Pogue had both hands on his knees. That was until Micah tentatively let out a small laugh. They both abruptly stopped and glared at him.

"So, your brilliant solution to this whole clusterfuck is to offer her protection, let the Council know we've got a human from a plane crash we can't explain, and then somehow get the Pride to just accept a human on top of the possibility of having to face death too?! Caden asked, exasperated. It wasn't unfair for Caden to be a bit taken aback. In their world, humans were pets, and pets only. Pogue had never come across any other role for them, and the few pets he knew of were unfortunate folks who had somehow stumbled through the Barrier, only to end up enslaved. It wasn't a pleasant life, even if it was better than death. Certainly, wasn't a dignified one.

Micah shrugged, holding the plant close to his chest as he responded.

"Educational opportunity. And maybe not say anything to the Council until we know we can trust her?"

Pogue and Caden tilted their heads and rolled their eyes simultaneously. They tended to freak people out when they did things like that.

"We'll talk to her tomorrow, and then we'll see. Fuck off now." Pogue sighed.

Micah grinned as he thumped his chest once with his fist and started out the door.

"Leave the plant, Micah!" Caden yelled. Micah barely stopped as he dumped it by the door, not bothering to tidy up the dirt that fell from the pot. "Our lives are about to get a lot more complicated," he added with a smirk as he grabbed the acoustic guitar and started playing 'Here Comes the Sun'...

Chapter 8

Council

A^{rcher}

Archer lovingly rubbed the pendant on his necklace as he picked up the toothbrush from its holder. He'd gotten word that the Alphas had her. She was in StormEdge now. His Mate had seen her. *My Mate...* Stars Archer missed him. How long had it been since he last saw him? Held him? Too long. Far too long. Archer chuckled as he looked at himself in the mirror. His Mate would slap him silly if he saw this scruffy beard, Archer mused as he ran his hand through his blond mess of a beard.

Now for the next step. StormEdge must win the Turf War, and Grace must be protected from DeCoill. He had been pleased to hear that the young lion took so quickly to her. It would make things easier with the Alphas. They trusted their Beta.

DeCoill's volatile nature worried him. The Shifter was getting increasingly erratic. Archer noted that it aligned with the times he crossed the Barrier into the human world. Archer couldn't find out why, and he'd been too busy scrambling to keep the human safe to dig into it.

Archer hated that he couldn't give Grace a choice or let the human enforcers take care of her, but they'd proven useless. Only his own people had been able to stop DeCoill's attacks. Hopefully, she would forgive him when all was said and done. Archer had been careful in reaching out to Masters, a member of the Global Council, the top authority for Shifters. He inquired about the legal options if there were concerns about a Shifter hunting a human, only to be reminded of the Slander laws. The law was straightforward: no evidence, no crime. Accusing another Shifter of a crime without proof, especially by name, was a punishable offense. So, it was another dead end. Archer wasn't even sure if these laws applied to pets. In hopes of leading Masters to DeCoill, Archer sent him the latest list of missing Shifters. It was unrelated to Grace but could put Masters onto DeCoill's trail. And it *was* an important issue that needed addressing. So far, no response to that one. He'd known for years that Shifters, particularly mix-breed and same-sex mates, had vanished, and he had a feeling he knew who was to blame. However, the path from knowing to proving was long, tedious, and lonely.

The Council was utterly redundant. Even if Archer served on it. There simply weren't enough Shifters left to warrant this level of supervision. *End game,* Archer reminded himself. Take one step back and rebuild. Keep her safe, earn credit with StormEdge, and *then* change the world. Simple, right?

Inside Archer, his wolf lay down, head on its paws. It missed its Mate so much it was a constant physical pain in his chest. The wolf didn't understand why they couldn't go to him. Trying to explain politics, blackmail, and genocide to his wolf was, to say the least, an uphill battle. It insisted they could keep him safe. Archer couldn't take the chance. He couldn't lose him. And so, they would continue to sneak around as they had been. His Mate would continue to become less and less understanding of the why of it all. And Archer would continue to beg for his patience, with the promise of a thousand nights in the home he would build them. But Archer wasn't dumb. He was well aware time was running out. For him, for StormEdge and hopefully.... For the Council and DeCoill.

Chapter 9

24 hours later

Grace was jolted awake by the sound of approaching footsteps. She struggled to open her eyes, craving a coffee or five. Confusion and irritation quickly followed. Mornings were the worst, especially in a place where she felt uneasy and out of place. When she woke up during the night, she'd read, and re-read, what turned out to be an 'Introduction to Our World' manual. It seemed to have been written by Micah. Grace thought of herself as someone who could roll with the punches, fake it till you made it, and all that. But as she read the manual and thought back to how Micah's eyes had changed, it all became very, very real. Or surreal as it may be. Grace then spent from four to seven in the morning coming to relative terms with the fact that this could actually be real. Very fucking real.

The manual outlined that Shifters had coexisted with humans, hidden in territories shielded by an invisible Barrier crafted by people called Wielders. Essentially, they were a blend of mages and witches. Shifters appeared to have limited knowledge about them. Grace made a mental note to inquire further. To travel between the two sides, a Wielder known as a Portal Wielder was required. The manual mentioned that there could be holes in the Barrier, which Micah suspected was how the odd human stumbled through on occasion.

But the Barrier generally kept humans out of Shifter territories and away from the safe houses Shifters had in the human world. Thanks to magic, and a lot of it from what Grace read, people would be compelled to move away from the Barrier if they came close.

The manual stated that for centuries, folklore and strategically placed scientific evidence have worked to keep humans out. Certain volcanoes or mountains were known to be too volatile for research, and some locations on Earth were too dangerous to visit. Many of those places, it seemed, were Shifter territories. Researchers who get too close would find their equipment malfunctioning or give readings that make sure they will never attempt to get closer. The Barrier would magically turn them in the other direction if they persist. If all *that* failed... All Shifter Communities, predatory and non-predatory, did patrols. Made sense when she thought about it. Shifters and Wielders being exposed today would end up somewhere between a lab and a war.

Accidents happened, though. Micah suspected the Barrier had weak spots or maybe even holes here and there. Paragliders went off course, and planes malfunctioned. The Council would send something called a Regulator to ensure that the plane and its passengers vanished. Any GPS device would send a signal to a location far away from where they actually landed. *Well, that's a notch in the kidnapping theory...Or maybe they're just being nice and helping me not die,* she thought as she read that airplanes' black boxes have the same result. But they brought me here, Grace thought as an uneasy feeling settled in her stomach. What's so special about me?

From what she gathered, Shifters didn't mingle much with humans or their world. However, they did incorporate some practical elements, and a few Pride-members had ties to the human realm for various reasons. Micah had listed a few examples. They used basic cell phones without video calls. The ones with an antenna you had to pull out. They had washing machines, kitchens, and other conveniences, but all seemed stuck in a time capsule from the '50s to '80s. As for weapons, they stuck to bows and knives. Grace chuckled as she read a hastily written note in the margins of the page, mentioning how a gun would come in handy against claws. The note had then been crossed out, another one replacing it. This one said, 'can't afford to lose more'. Grace filed away yet another thing she'd like to ask about. *Like you're gonna remember all this in an hour. Dumbass,* she shook her head.

There were many different types of Shifters, but there didn't appear to be a large number of them. Micah had written that their numbers had been steadily declining. They had something akin to Hogwarts called the Academy for Wielders and a Council that oversaw local and global Shifter legal matters.

There were predatory or non-predatory Communities, and all had Submissives, Maternals, and Dominants. They were described as the heart, brain, and sword, respectively. It was underlined that one's nature did not denote one's personality. Submissives were not necessarily gentle or shy, and Dominants weren't necessarily authoritative and extroverted. Micah didn't seem to have the full explanation of how or why someone was born into their specific designation. The notes in the margin, marked by a star, hinted that genes could play a role. Alphas tended to have Alpha offspring; if a Maternal Mated with a Dominant, the child was more likely to lean toward the Dominant side. Similarly, if the parents were mixed, the offspring would automatically shift into the same animal as the stronger parent. Hmm, interesting, Grace thought. What does he mean by mixed, she wondered. As a veterinary nurse, she'd often considered diving deeper into genetics, but that required her to advance to vet and from there... *Yeah, not really what we need to focus on right now, cuz*, she reminded herself.

She'd just gone back to sleep when the hospital bed dipped. For a second, panic returned. She remembered footsteps before. How long was I out, she mused. Turned out it was Micah, who had hopped up on her bed and patted her thigh before rubbing his cheek on her hair. She grumbled at him and shoved at his head. She wasn't sure what drugs they'd pumped her with, but she wasn't really hurting anymore. The drugs also made her whole body feel heavy and slow. A stranger touching her would usually result in a black eye. But her body was too tired to respond, and her mind was too muddled to react. Grace assessed her injuries as she gradually awoke. She was achy all over and felt the long gash on her back. She figured it wasn't so bad after all. Maybe Doc had given her some kind of super-healing medicine while she was out?

"Top of the mornin'," Micah said in an exaggerated Irish accent.

"Fuck off, Paddy," Grace grumbled.

"Touchy today, my little stink beetle huh?" Micah chuckled as a towering man entered the room.

Okay, he wasn't just a bit tall, she observed as she sized him up. He embodied the classic swimmer's physique—tall, lean, with broad shoulders and a sculpted chest that narrowed down to a trim waist. His dark green eyes stood out against his snug gray t-shirt. She caught sight of a small scar on his upper lip, which gave a rugged touch to his clean-shaven face. Her gaze followed as he ran a hand over his auburn buzz-cut hair. Micah, in her eyes, didn't strike her as particularly dangerous - at least not in the way he probably should, considering she didn't really know him. But this man... He was on a whole other level. The way he moved and the intensity in his eyes told her he was an apex predator.

"Hello Miss... Erh-" he looked to Micah.

"Shit... I don't know how I managed to not even ask," Micah winced.

"My name is-" The door swung open, revealing another tall man. Grace's gaze fixated on him, a subtle force drawing her attention. Twins, she concluded. This one had the build of a swimmer, too, but with more muscle, and his hair was longer on top and shorter on the sides, a rich auburn shade that matched his brows. Her mind seemed to blank out for a moment. Despite herself, a strange mix of attraction and irritation stirred within her. It wasn't clear if it was his insanely good looks or the fact that his mere presence irked her for reasons she couldn't quite fathom. He looked like the other guy, but Mr. Buzz-Cut didn't have the same effect on her at all. The newcomer leaned against the wall just inside the door, hands casually tucked into the front pockets of his well-fitted black jeans. His gaze was fixed squarely on her. While Micah and the other man were sporting what could be called hand-me-downs, this guy was clearly conscious of his appearance. His jeans were stylishly distressed, and the azure t-shirt seemed freshly bought. She observed him take a slow, deep breath through his nose, his eyes narrowing to slits. Another predator, she thought. But while the first one had made her cautious, this one instilled a mix of terror and anger. Grace had to wrestle with the urge to growl at him for his infuriatingly cryptic demeanor.

A cough from Micah pulled her focus back to the conversation.

"Grace. My name is Grace," she managed to grind out. Even as she spoke up, her eyes remained on the newcomer as he glared right back at her. "I need to call home right fucking now!" she snapped, a little more than she meant to.

"Sorry, Grace, no can do right now," Micah informed her, his voice soft as he spoke. "That's Caden, by the way," he indicated to the tall man. The non-scowly one.

"Super, but not cuz. Also, I have a shit ton of questions, and you'd better have an equal amount of answers," she snarled, looking at Caden before her eyes shifted back. Sexy McCreeper was still glaring at her...

"The fuck are you *staring* at?!" she motioned to him, feeling her temper snap. *Way to play nice, Grace. They're totally gonna let you go if you piss them off enough. Oh wait, that's how you get eaten,* her brain facepalmed.

Scowly-man pushed off the wall and stalked towards her, his eyes changing from a pale green to a darker and definitely scarier type of green as they grew slightly slitted. A predator's eyes. *Woah, that's a lot, she thought.* Caden gave a throat-clearing cough and shot a meaningful glance over his shoulder, bringing scowly-man to a halt. The man frowned, folding his arms across his chest and tucking his hands under his armpits, his gaze fixed firmly on Grace.

"My name is Caden. I need to ask you a couple of questions, and then we'll go from there, okay? I'm sure we can answer whatever questions you have, too." He smiled warmly at her.

"And then I get to call Sophie? Please..." She whispered, and Micah moved up beside her to hug her, carefully placing an arm around her shoulder. A part of Grace wanted to knock away Micah's arm. Even if she wanted to believe he meant no harm, the touchy-feely was a little creepy. Another smaller but growing part of her was comforted by his closeness. "I just want her to know I'm alive. Please," she almost begged, her gaze shifting from one tall man to another, then to Micah, as her steely resolve gave way to fear.

"Shhh, it's okay, darlin'. Once we're done here, I'll get a message through. Just tell me where to ring," Micah offered.

Grace rattled off Sophie's phone number and added.

"There's no one else. Please tell her I'm okay."

"He will," Caden said gently. "Where are you from?"

"Wellington, NZ," she answered quietly.

For a moment, the only sound in the room was the flicking of the lighter held by the man near the door. *Huh... He must've stepped back. How did I miss that?* Even amidst her swirling emotions and a growing headache, she could still sense his gaze on her. He exuded an air of danger, but at the same time... not. At least not to her, perhaps?

Scowly McSexy retrieved a pack of cigarettes from his jeans. Just as he was about to light one up, the doctor smacked his hand.

"Not in my clinic!"

Pogue growled, and in a flash of blindingly bright light, there was a large feline in the room.

Micah jumped off the bed, positioning himself before Grace and shielding her from the massive beast. It emitted huffs and growls of protest. It was the largest feline she'd ever laid eyes on. Easily twice the size of any she'd seen. Unnaturally large even. Shredded clothes lay strewn around it, a torn pant leg still clinging to its hind paw. The cat hissed at the doctor, who quickly retreated two large steps, hands raised and head lowered.

Grace felt her eyes widen as her brain registered what had just happened right in front of her. That's... Scowly man turns into a giant cat.

"Holy shit, this is real!" she burst out as excitement (or serious lack of understanding of Darwin's law) overtook her. Micah shot her an incredulous look before he started walking toward the giant cat. The tip of his tail swished widely back and forth, a clear sign of agitation.

"Come on, Pogue, can we not eat the human, please?" Micah held up his hands in a placating gesture as he maneuvered himself between Pogue and the hospital bed, blocking her view.

Grace lost all composure, and while curiosity might get her killed by the cat, the questions poured out of her.

"That's a Jaguar, isn't it? Or is it a leopard? Holy shit, how much does he weigh? He's huge! Can he hear me? Like, does he understand me?" Grace scowled at the jaguar. "You're a dick" she told it for good measure before averting her attention back to Micah. "Can I pet him?" she rattled off the questions like a kid making a wish list for Santa. Cats she could deal with. To her, animals had always been easier to deal with than humans, and they didn't scare her. Animals, cats, in particular, were logical. They don't lie. They like you; they purr. They don't; you get clawed. Simple. The cat paused its pacing and began slinking toward her. He sniffed her bed, then gave her the most human flat look a cat had ever produced before turning around to pad out of the room, Caden close behind.

Micah's lips quirked a small smile at her.

"Sorry about that, darlin'. He's a bit temperamental, but maybe you can pet him later."

Soon after, Caden walked back in, chuckling as he gently rubbed the knuckles on his left hand.

"Let's try this again, shall we?" Caden said as he dragged a chair over to sit in front of her bed, his forearms leaning on the edge of the bed. "Have you read the manual Micah gave you?" Grace nodded, her brain still computing what she'd seen a minute ago. "And you feel you understand and believe it?" Again, she nodded. Micah looked at her, his eyes searching, probably for signs of shock. Satisfied with his findings, he nodded to Caden, who continued. "And you are aware of our situation?" Caden asked, a serious expression on his otherwise charming face. Grace shook her head.

"No. I remember Micah saying you might need a vet nurse soon for something. Uhm... Yeah-nah, that's it. I have questions. Lots of them," she grumbled.

Caden gave a sharp nod back. Micah squeezed her hand gently.

"Let me be very clear, Grace. You have two options. One, we turn you over to the Council—they're like the police—and they deal with you. Chances are they will kill you, as you're unclaimed, and we can't explain how you wound up here," he said. "Two, you will be in our clinic helping patch up our people, and in exchange, we will petition the Council for you to stay here, and we'll deal with everything after. I can't afford you to think about this for long. I'm sorry. But the safety of our people is everything, and we don't have long to prepare." His words set off a whole cascade of new questions, adding to the already lengthy list.

"If I said I wanted to go home?" Grace asked, steeling herself. She needed to know if she was a prisoner or a guest. Caden crossed the short distance between them and bent to sniff her. "Rude, cuz!" Grace finally snapped, pushing at his face. Caden didn't move, his facial expression looking a little confused as he drew in another breath, his lips almost touching the side of her neck. Grace tensed up, afraid to move and wanting to smack the fuck out of him simultaneously.

Micah seemed to sense her trepidation and cleared his throat.

"Uhm, Cades, humans get worried when random people sniff them," Micah explained.

Caden shook his shoulders as he lifted his head just a little to smile at her, his nose—and therefore teeth—too close for comfort. Yup, he might look all nice and friendly, but she was in no doubt—he had the same teeth and claws as his dark counterpart.

"My cat is confused that you don't give out any scent markers," Caden said, straightening up. "Micah mentioned something about a stalker? Maybe it's best for all of us if you don't go home just yet. Ask your questions now." Caden turned from her and sat down again, motioning for her to proceed.

"Just to be clear, nothing you just said made sense, and your behavior is fucking weird, cuz." Caden didn't speak. He just angled his head and blinked. When his eyes opened, a cats eyes were looking out at her. Micah squeezed her hand again. She drew in a deep breath. "All right then. Ignoring the awkwardness. Right, so if the only way to get to and from my world is a Portal, does that mean there's always one open?"

She noticed Micah getting out a pad of paper and a pen as he gently pushed her to sit beside her on the bed, his legs bent at the knees as he took notes.

"No. You need a Wielder specialized in Portals," Caden answered.

"Kinda like a doorman," Micah supplied.

Grace took a drink of water from the cup on a small table next to her.

"How is it that cell phones work?"

Caden and Micah looked at each other for a long minute before Micah answered.

"Very astute question, Padawan," he grinned. "The Barrier doesn't block signals, and Wielders do something I can't explain to make sure there's a signal almost everywhere here. We're still on Earth, Grace. We're just hidden."

"What *exactly* are you?" she asked.

Micah placed the manual in her lap as he casually sat beside her, slinging his arm around her shoulders. Grace noted Caden's raised brow, though he didn't say anything.

"Shifters are individuals with both human and beast coexisting in one body. It's not a matter of one being more dominant than the other; you'll see traits from both sides when you interact with us. Some of us may lean more towards our beastly nature, keeping it closer to the surface than our human side. Remind me to introduce you to Gray," Micah smiled and went on. "There are many types of Shifters, though it seems ninety percent of what remains of us are large mammals or birds. And before you ask, no, you're not gonna find a Shifter dragon, but you might find a whale."

Grace nodded slowly, moving on to her next question.

"Can you explain the lifespan thing? I'm not sure I get that, and your handwriting sucks, by the way."

Micah nodded and took a breath.

"We age about one-third slower than humans. Wielders, a little faster. We age normally, like humans, until we transition from Juvenile to Adult. Usually, when we're around twenty-one. We're not big on keeping track of age," he shrugged and pulled the blanket up around Grace's shoulders. She hadn't even felt the cold before he did it. "After the transition, it slows a bit. When we're around thirty, we're considered in our optimal genetic state, and here our aging slows to a crawl." From what Doc has told me, the Barrier then acts as a filter of sorts. Our DNA basically renews itself magically somehow, as long as we stay within it." Grace tapped her nose absentmindedly as she tried to sort out all the information Micah was throwing at her. It was a lot to take in, even if she had read most of it in the book.

"You with us so far?" Caden asked, his voice neutral.

She could feel him assessing her, though, so she took a deep breath and nodded.

"I think so. What are Regulators, and why am I still alive when the manual stated Shifters kill on sight?" Brain, filter mouth, she facepalmed internally.

To her surprise, Caden chuckled as he answered.

"You're alive because Micah is putting his head on the chopping block for you. Now, a Regulator is the equivalent of..." he frowned, trying to find the right word.

Micah held up a finger and answered before Caden could.

"Like a mix between an assassin, an entire SWAT team, and Superman rolled into one."

Grace frowned.

"How about we don't call them? You call yourself a Pride in the manual. Are you only cats, then? Are you all panthers?"

Micah smiled and nodded to the doctor, who'd silently entered the room and now stood leaning against the wall.

"We won't call the Regulators. As you read in the manual, a Community, that's what all organized Shifter groups are called as an umbrella term, is defined by its Alpha. Our Community, StormEdge, is led by dual Alphas. Caden and Pogue, who you just saw, shift. They're both felines and so this Community is called a Pride. If they had been wolves, we would have been a Pack. StormEdge is about sixty percent feline, but we have avians, bears, and wolves, too. Makes sense?"

Grace thought for a bit, thankful the men let her have the time to do so, before asking.

"Yeah. Uhm, your brother, I assume..." she started. Immediately, she felt, more than she saw, Micah tense up as he gently squeezed her thigh once before removing his hand.

"He won't hurt you." Caden's voice was careful.

To her surprise—and very obviously theirs—she blurted out.

"I know that. I meant, like, is he a jaguar? Or leopard? I always get those confused. Jaguar, right? No?" Caden, the doctor, and Micah just stared at her. She blushed. "Sorry, I don't get to see many of either type, and it really was a fantastic feline specimen. A little fluffy, but still."

Caden regained his composure; his smile deepened as he answered her.

"I'm sorry, Grace. That's just not a statement I'm used to hearing about Pogue. Normally, people find him intimidating at best. Not, you know, a fantastic specimen of anything. And you're... well, human," he mused, his head angled in a very feline gesture, his eyes flitting between a dark green and a much paler version of his animal side. "Also, the spots inside our rosettes set us apart from leopards," he added, almost like an afterthought.

"Ok... So, if I stay and help with this thing, it means I get to basically stay in Narnia for a bit in exchange for my services, and you'll patch me up. And I get to work with big cats. And also, you won't kill me." she started. "And if I don't, I'm in a world of trouble, but you'll try to get rid of me in the nicest way you can?"

Caden made a 'so so' gesture with his hand, most likely referring to the latter part of her question.

Home wasn't exactly a safe haven these days for Grace. She was used to having to fight, and purely surviving was becoming a routine. She knew these people were a threat, but the alternative seemed like a surefire death sentence—only marginally better than the perpetual fear she'd face back home, not to mention the ordeal of the plane journey it would take to get her there.

"Am I safe here? During the thing, too?"

"The Healer's residence is off-limits, so yes. "It's the law," Micah said, shrugging.

"What do I need to know that I don't already know?" Grace asked.

Caden's lips quirked. He motioned for the doctor to leave. He nodded and took a step outside.

"No one knows this except Pogue, Micah, and I. What's coming is the equivalent of a controlled war. It's called a Challenge. Not an Alpha one. It's a Turf War. It means the Shifters that are coming will try to kill everyone here."

"But I'll be safe?"

"Yup," Micah said.

"Uhm, ok..." *Fake it till you make it. Out of here...*

Caden tapped his fingers in quick succession on the edge of her bed.

"Ok. So, it's a deal. We keep you safe while your human police capture your stalker. You help us here and get to pet cats. Many here will be asking you questions, so you'll have to adjust to that. And you have to do as you're told. Let me just go fetch Pogue. Hang on." He turned faster than a human could and disappeared out the door while Grace nodded. He didn't need to see her fingers crossed under the manual in her lap. A short while later, he walked back in with a now-redressed McGrump. He stayed by the door and just glared at her as Caden spoke again.

"You're not allowed to wander, at least not yet, so you'll be escorted. Now, I'd like to formally introduce you to Pogue, my twin brother and your uhm... Handler," Caden said as he turned to him. "Are you gonna go shake her hand?" Caden asked pointedly.

"Nope," Pogue said, making a popping sound as he jammed his large hands in his jean pockets.

"Seriously, bro, don't be an ass!"

"The fuck did I do to you, sourpuss? Someone piss on your catnip?" Grace quipped. She watched as he curled his upper lip, revealing the tip of his canines. Half her brain told her to cower and apologize. The other wanted to sock him in the mouth if she could just reach him.

"You *breathe*. It pisses my cat off." The way he said it partly irked her and partly made her want to insult him some more just to hear him speak. Like fire and ice, whisky and honey, his voice shot directly into her core. Must be shock, she concluded.

"Well, tell your kitty to go eat a fucking ball of yarn!" *Ok, maybe a little less effort in the Darwin Award race, Grace,* she thought as she watched him move.

Pogue moved with a fluid, predatory Grace, drawing closer until he stood beside the bed. He leaned in, exuding confidence, a self-assured, masculine smile playing on his lips, teasingly hinting at what she was almost convinced were the world's sexiest dimples.

"How about I eat *you* instead?" he purred.

Grace blinked. She usually gave as good as she got, but something in how he said it completely stumped her. She ended up just flipping him off, breaking eye contact.

"Maybe not. You fucking reek!" Pogue snapped, swiftly turned, and walked back out the door. He did that just to mess with me! Grace felt her newfound confidence shatter in an instant. Caden sighed, and Micah gave her arm a comforting rub, then exchanged a glance with Caden.

"How about we let her get clean and settle into a room? It'll give Pogue time to take his meds, and I can do that meeting, you know, while she's bathing."

"Medication?" Doc asked from where he was sitting on a saddle stool. The headache was still building, and she was getting tired again. "Ah, yes, of course, his medication. The erh... What is it again, Micah?"

"The Prozac. You know, for his mood swings." Micah said.

Caden chuckled as Grace answered.

"Actually, I'd really appreciate it if that's an option. I feel disgusting... I also don't have anything to wear, so maybe if you have an extra pair of scrubs, I can borrow? And some pain meds, maybe?"

"Oh, I'm sure we'll be able to find something," Caden said. "Doc, anything we need to be aware of?"

"Yes, sir. She will need this balm applied to her back; she won't be able to reach it," he said, holding up a small glass jar.

"Pogue will do it. Get her into a shower, and I'll send him over," Caden smiled wide.

Grace held up a finger.

"Yeah-nah! Sorry, but I'm not okay with that, and not just 'cause he pisses me off."

Micah bent down to her ear and whispered.

"It's fine, darlin'. He's flaming. And he has a lot of medical training. He's also the Alpha, so he'll be able to protect you once his meds kick in."

Grace looked at him, her mouth forming an O.

"I don't give a shit which way he swings cuz. Doesn't really make me comfortable with that. Like at all," Grace mumbled. Micah glared at her; his easy smile replaced a tense jaw. Grace huffed out a long breath. "I don't really have much of a choice here, do I?"

Micah shook his head.

"I know it's a lot, Grace, but I won't hurt you, nor will Pogue. But the fact is that he can protect you better than anyone here."

"So can Caden and you, right?"

"Yes. But Caden has stuff to do. And so do I, for that matter. Just please try and go along with this, okay? I promise it'll all look much brighter once you've had a bath and decent sleep. Maybe some food, too, right?"

Grace thought about it for a bit as Doc came over and handed her two pills and a fresh glass of water. In the end, no, she didn't have a choice.

Chapter 10

S hortly after, Micah cocooned her in a blanket and gently transported her outdoors. The scent of crisp winter air felt like a slice of heaven, even though her toes quickly objected to the cold. As they moved (or rather, as he moved while she was carried), Micah provided a rundown of the compound's layout.

In front of the clinic, Grace had a clear view across a spacious, open area that Micah pointed out led to the Den. This structure was nestled into a small mountain's rocky facade. From outside, all you could see were towering, curved windows conformed to the mountain's shape. Micah mentioned that a massive oak tree cleverly concealed the main entrance. When they stood before the main gate, he turned around to give her a better view. Grace was speechless- not something that happened a lot. Looking upward, she spotted a wooden and steel walkway extending from the Den to...

"Oh, my fucking God, are those tree houses?"

Micah laughed at her enthusiasm.

"Aeries, yeah. Our Wielders, Hannah and Nigel," he clarified, "made sure they're all linked up with those wood walkways reinforced with steel. Once you've got the run of the place, those paths will also lead you to the forest homes, but steer clear for now. It's a maze if you're not familiar. Pogue will probably tell you this a thousand times, too. Stick to the inner routes of the Den grounds, alright? You definitely don't wanna stumble upon old man Hans' spot. He's a grouchy old guy." Micah chuckled. Grace simply nodded, still processing it all.

Finally, he carried her through the front door. Grace had her eyes closed and her head leaning on his shoulder. She was drained.

"Feels like a library in here," Grace murmured. She was accustomed to the constant hum of human activity around her. Her apartment was sandwiched between neighbors above, below, and on both sides. It felt weird a place this big was this quiet.

"Evening meeting. I gotta go too as soon as I get you settled in the tub."

"Are you gay too, Micah?" Micah shook his head, a confused look on his face.

"So, you're not gonna be settling me in anywhere!"

Micah carried her to a small guest room, sat her on the comfortable bed, and went to get the shower and tub ready for her. He handed her two towels and a pill from the doctor for the pain. She accepted it gratefully and swallowed it dry, nodding her thanks. Micah leaned down to gently kiss her forehead, which didn't prompt the usual knee-jerk slap-his-face reaction. Though her body protested every step, Grace managed to navigate into the shower stall without adding more injury to herself. It wasn't that she didn't long for a soothing bath—now that would be a luxury—but first, she needed to rid herself of the crusty blood and grime, so the tub would have to wait another day. Someone had clearly taken care of the worst gore while she was out cold, thankfully- depending on how you look at it- avoiding the more sensitive areas.

And so, Grace began scrubbing off the aftermath of a plane crash.

Chapter 11

Pogue accepted the travel mug from Caden's hand as they entered the spacious dining hall. Most of the Pride had already gathered, forming smaller clusters on the many benches and chairs. Thanks to Micah, the dining hall was fashioned to resemble what he claimed American high school cafeterias looked like in movies. Pogue had to concede it was a pragmatic choice.

The kitchen was adjacent to the dining area, separated as its own space. It had an expansive serving counter equipped with a tray rack.

The arrangement of tables, chairs, and benches had no rhyme or reason. Some were made of steel, while others were long tables with well-worn wooden benches. Pogue disliked the fact that no two were alike. Caden thought it was charming, but Pogue preferred a more streamlined appearance. He didn't like chaos, even if he was good at navigating it. Pogue preferred that his clothes match. He appreciated keeping his apartment clean and always rinsed out his coffee mugs. It was just his thing. He liked control.

The hall began to quiet down as they approached. Micah was already there, perched on a tiny dais beside a round wooden table, talking to Lucy, another lion Shifter. She was close to transitioning into adulthood and edgy because of it. Transition hit different Shifters in different ways, but there was one thing they all had in common: raging hormones. This meant that Juveniles going through it were more likely to have mood swings and, well, let's just say, a super active sex drive by human standards. This was especially true for the Dominants, though Pogue had seen his fair share of Submissives and Maternals going through intense emotional roller coasters, too. Pogue watched as Micah softly brushed his lips against hers and sent her on her way. To them, this was a greeting, reassurance, or scent swapping. Micah could have just as easily hugged her, which he might have with a male, especially a Dominant.

They made their way over to him.

Caden bumped his shoulder, jarring him from his thoughts.

"What was with you today?" Pogue just stared blankly at his brother. "I know you're an ass, but that was a little much even for you. I wasn't sure if you wanted to eat her or *eat* her," he smirked, earning him a soft punch on principle.

Pogue shrugged.

"She pisses me off, is all," Pogue shrugged. But what if that wasn't all? His cat's reaction to her was unlike anything he'd felt before. Not even Rosita managed to provoke that kind of response from his other half, and she'd sure as hell tried. Pogue knew well enough that all Rosie wanted was an Alpha bite. a Mating agreement. He was pretty sure she didn't even like him much as a person.

They arrived at the dais, and Pogue took a deep breath, steadying himself. Speaking to large crowds wasn't exactly his favorite pastime unless it was a crisis situation. It didn't make the experience any more enjoyable, but having something urgent to focus on helped him push past the unease. Raising a hand to hush the assembly, he began.

"We had to check on a plane crash near Fawlks. Someone survived,". Pogue snapped his fingers, silencing the Pride as some started talking.

"We don't bring humans here, you know this. That, apparently"-he glared back over his shoulder at Micah and Caden- "changes today."

Questions were shot at him so quickly that he didn't have time to respond.

Pogue looked to his Beta.

"Micah, you're up." He turned his back and motioned to Micah to get to it before he sat down.

Micah got up and faced the firing squad, but not before shooting Pogue a dirty look. Micah had probably expected Pogue to deal with this shit. Yeah, well... Sucks to be Beta Pogue smirked to himself as he cradled the travel mug between his hands.

"Why will that change? Are you saying a Pet is to be brought in?" A Maternal asked, her head quizzically tilted to the side, more curious than anything else, it seemed.

Pogue gnashed his teeth as the thought of having a human Pet grated on his nerves. He barely held back a hiss as he answered before Micah could.

"She is not a Pet!"

Micah shot him a look over his shoulder. He quickly turned back to the Maternal Shifter, answering her question.

"As the Alpha said, she is not a Pet. You know we have not and will never keep Pets in StormEdge." The Shifter nodded and returned her attention to her coffee.

"What kind is it?" someone in the back shouted. What kind? What the fuck kind of question is that even, Pogue thought. The Pride, it seemed, needed to be educated better. He added it to his mental 'to-do list'

"Does this mean we can't shift?" An eagle Shifter, Mac, asked, annoyance clear despite his calm tone of voice.

"How are we going to keep the kids safe?" Louisa, a very nervous, low, hierarchy Maternal, asked in a severe tone.

"Enough!" Caden exclaimed, exasperated. He rose and smacked his palms on the table, knocking Pogue's' coffee off the table a second after Pogue had put it down. *Wasn't gonna drink that anyway, asshole,* Pogue thought as he bent to pick up his now empty travel mug off the floor.

Micah took a deep breath, nodding back at Caden, who sat back in his chair and nodded for Micah to continue.

"All right, folks, from the top. Firstly, *she* is not in any way dangerous. This is a quid pro quo situation. We help her recover from her injuries, and she helps us in the upcoming Challenge if needed." Micah hopped down from the dais and began pacing back and forth as he spoke clearly before the crowd could pick up again.

Pogue knew Micah wouldn't spill the beans to the Pride about how this seemingly ordinary Challenge could escalate into a full-blown war. They had to dig deeper into Grace's situation, understand how and why she ended up here, and ensure all the paperwork was in order. Pogue knew Micah was doing his best to convey as much as he could without dropping that bombshell.

Micah was still trying to explain.

"*She*, Grace, will also be an opportunity for all of you to study her. Many of you have never interacted with humans before. While our worlds coexist, humans are far more advanced in terms of material things. Their social structure, as well as how they learn, hunt, and live, is different too. This is a once-in-a-lifetime opportunity for you."

A hand raised somewhere in the middle.

Micah pointed to it.

"Yes, whoever you are, 'cause y'all are so many, and I can't see shit from here." Pogue could see why. Putting forty-eight Shifters in one room took much more space than one would think.

A short, sturdy Shifter stood up and scratched his black beard before running his hand down his checkered shirt. Michél looked every bit the lumberjack, Pogue noted as Michél spoke.

"You're gonna set it loose among us?"

"For the love of all women," Micah rolled his eyes. The crowd chuckled, "*Her* name is Grace. And yes, Michel, I want to let her loose once she is ready and able. Right now, she is not due to her injuries. And before you start, she will never be without an escort. Pogue and I will be her primary handlers." But when she is allowed to roam, keep in mind she can't hurt you. She's physiologically much weaker than anyone here, the cubs excluded." Michel nodded once and sat back down. A couple of hands disappeared.

Zia, a Maternal jaguar, stood up, her fluid movement quintessentially cat. Zia was, Pogue knew, very perceptive. Today, that was not a good thing.

"Why would there be a need for help? We've got Doc," she shrugged. "And what does she have to offer us?" Zia wasn't being aggressive. Her calm demeanor showed her intellect and self-control. "Does she even know what we are?"

Micah bent his head and scratched the back of his neck, a sheepish expression on his face.

"Yeah, she's in the loop. She's a veterinary nurse, and she'd like to help where she can as a thank you for saving her. And she may have been promised to pet a large cat or two after she saw Pogue sort of lose his shit and shift in front of her at the clinic earlier." Micah looked up with a smirk on his face.

He pointed to Louisa, who had raised her hand.

"Where is she going to stay? And, uhm, well, I don't mean to sound trivial, but if she was in a plane crash, will she need anything? That you can't provide, that is? Will she need help getting dressed and such?"

Micah smiled softly at her.

"We've got that covered, darlin'. But if you have any clothes to spare, that'd be great; she's about your size of tiny, I think," he said, turning to face Maude, who was propped up against a long steel table, holding a coffee cup. Her blond curls bobbed as she tried to suppress the laughter that was undoubtedly trying to escape.

"Can ya' all repeat the part about Pogue?" she asked, a smile tugging at her lips. The room was so quiet that you could hear crickets. Maude, his childhood babysitter, looked him in the eyes, her cougar smirking as she discreetly scented the air. Normally, this wouldn't bother him, but he didn't want her to sense his confusion. Pogue had left the clinic earlier, rock-hard and angry as hell. Not a good combination, especially when it resulted from a five-minute verbal sparring match with a fucking human, he thought as he mentally prepared himself to growl everyone into submission.

"Which part, darlin'?" Micah asked, his lips twitching.

Thanks, fuckstick, Pogue groaned internally. The Pride was nosey as hell. They'd love nothing more than to rip into this little tidbit like a juicy steak, and he'd never hear the fucking end of it.

"Pogue, did you have an *accidental* shift?" Maude's lips were curving. Yeah, his childhood babysitter was loving this, he had no doubt. Involuntary shifts were sort of a gray area of embarrassment. If your animal shifted to protect you, everyone thought it was smart and shit. If you did it because the woman you'd been staring at for ten minutes pushed your buttons, it was a different level of embarrassment.

Pogue felt like banging his forehead against the table. He settled for sighing deeply instead. Maude smiled wide, not even bothering to hide it, as she took a sip of coffee, taking that as a yes.

"So, do we get to keep her?" Brody, a tiger Shifter, inquired. Inside him, Pogue's cat extended its claws, not liking the meaning behind Brody's question. Usually, Brody was a polite young Shifter with a nurturing instinct rivaling a Maternal. But Brody was going through transition, heavily influenced by hormones. He likely had a couple more months to go before his cat would mellow out.

Micah replied sternly, echoing Pogue's earlier words.

"Brody, she's not a puppy!"

"I was more thinking she could be my pussy... cat," Brody smirked, running a hand through his messy brown hair.

Pogue could feel a distinctly feline growl rising in his throat, reacting more intensely than usual. He shot up, accidentally toppling his chair, and swiftly navigated through the crowd, which promptly made way for him. Upon reaching Brody, the young man offered a wry smile and tilted his head to the side, baring his throat.

"Hormones talking out my ass again?"

Pogue glared at him and grabbed him by the collar to walk him out of the room. Brody went quietly. *Yeah, you know you fucked up!* Pogue didn't say a word as he reached the saloon door opening up into the hall. Just kicked one open, threw Brody out, turned, quietly walked back to the dais, and stood beside Micah.

"Let me make this crystal fucking clear. Tari has petitioned the Council for temporary Pet status, so we can figure out what the fuck to do with her! We do not keep her! But we will keep our paws and claws to ourselves so the Alpha doesn't have to wipe the floor with our asses! Is that clear?!" he roared.

Anyone hear a cricket? Pogue wanted to bang his head against a wall until his cat settled the fuck down instead of acting like a fucking Juvenile. One thing was the roaring; the Pride was used to that. But he was well aware his Pride worried when he started using full sentences. He had to get rid of the adrenaline and regain control before the gossip mill started.

Caden coughed into his fist, trying not too hard, Pogue noticed, to hide a smile as he stood.

"As long as she's bedridden," Caden said, "we'll have about half of you visit in small groups. It'll settle your animals; you get to ask her some questions."

Micah held up a finger. Caden nodded, giving him the floor.

"Rule of thumb: come to Pogue or me when in doubt. Caden will deal with the Council. Officially, she's not here, so mouths shut. Also, remember, humans do not have senses like ours. Theirs are much duller. They are fragile creatures, so no roughhousing. Any questions?" As hands shot up, Micah signaled Pogue with a glance at his watch, indicating it was time to assist the human - his first punishment task. Pogue sighed, rolled his eyes, and quietly left the room. *Smartass lion. Exceptional opportunity, my ass,* he thought as he started towards his quarters, grumbling all the way along the hallway leading there, knowing she'd be in the small guest room next to his apartment.

Grace was fast asleep when he entered the room quietly. She'd taken a shower, judging by the wet carpet and towels on the floor. A lot.

She's also a fucking slob. As he bent to pick up the towels and wake her up, he rolled his eyes at the ceiling. The scent of wildflowers piqued his interest. He chose to ignore it. His cat, on the other hand, did not. It sat up, curious about this human who smelled like... Mate! Pogue mentally smacked his cat for the misinterpretation. She couldn't be his Mate. She would have the scent markers, human or not. He would have also changed his scent, but he still smelled the same! Also, she pissed him off! Pogue paused for a second. Just to get his head straight.

Pogue crept out of the room before she noticed him as morning rolled around. He wondered how she had managed to keep him standing next to her bed all night. She wasn't anything special. She had a button nose, nothing special. Her high cheekbones and chestnut hair were ordinary, and her lush lips did nothing for him. Nothing at all. And yet, the sun was rising by the time he moved...

Chapter 12

1 week later

Grace was over being confined to her room. Not that she had been lonely, but she missed her yoga and the feeling of fresh air on her face. She'd spent most of her time sleeping or being pummeled with questions.

She was also introduced to the Vigilia. They were sort of squad leaders. Essentially, soldiers in charge of keeping the perimeters safe. Caden had decided to invite them to be her first visitors. They all seemed nice but a bit distanced. Beau, a mountain of a man, was the most outgoing. His hair was a deep purple with black tips. She liked him immediately for that reason alone. The Vigilia were always present—at least two when Pogue or Micah weren't around. She knew she was being watched, but having them there gave her an odd sense of security. Despite everything, this place somehow made her feel safe.

Doc would check on her once a day, in the morning. Although she had been told he was responsible for her, Pogue was nowhere to be found. For some ungodly reason, this irritated the hell out of her.

Every day, she was bombarded with questions from all sides as they sniffed her. She had tried to explain how incredibly rude that was to a human. They didn't care. They were all confused because she gave out no scent markers. Scent markers were the equivalent of a shifter's fingerprint. Shifters nearby could smell you if you were Mated, just as it would tell them if a woman was pregnant or an elderly Shifter was nearing the end of their life. Scent markers imprinted the Shifter with a scent that was unique to that Shifter.

Nadya, this sweet young woman who happened to transform into a wolf, filled Grace in on the Pride's background. Many of them hadn't interacted much with humans, so Grace was a bit of a novelty to them.

Grace learned that Nadya was the only Pride member aside from the doctor, and Micah with a direct link to the human world, though Claus used to teach disabled human kids for a short time. Nadya attended a fancy dance school, often with Brody, her best friend and practice dance partner. They went out together about once a week. Evidently, most Pridemembers liked to dance and play games. The last part wasn't overly surprising to Grace, considering over half the Pride were cats.

Generally, the Shifters were forthcoming. Many had been really cool about shifting for Grace, and as the days passed, some even came in in their animal form just to hang out.

Grace knew she should feel scared, but surprisingly, she found herself relaxing and actually anticipating seeing them. The primal fear she should have felt for these powerful apex predators waned as they gently stroked her hair and planted kisses on her cheeks. Yeah, Shifters seemed to be a touchy-feely bunch, at least most of them. Grace was starting to find it intriguing, observing how they interacted. There seemed to be a strict social hierarchy within the factions. Something she hadn't quite figured out yet. But she had noted that the Submissives were more touchy-feely than the Dominants and would seek out their touch more than the other way around. Not for the first time, she wondered who Pogue allowed close. Who did he turn to when he needed touch? Not that she cared. It was just a professional curiosity.

She had asked them about the Challenge. Most seemed excited about it. Grace found it odd. *Who gets excited about war?* But then she remembered they didn't know. A tall blond man had said they got Challenged a lot, and by now, it was mostly a chance to see Pogue wipe the floor with someone's ass...

Hannah, whom she idolized from the moment she saw her Slytherin blazer and green, spikey pixie bob, stopped by often to discuss Harry Potter and romance Shifter novels. She was a bit of a nerd and a fan of Big Bang Theory and snarking at the Alphas. They got along famously. Grace had tried asking Hannah about magic, but it seemed there was a lot she wasn't allowed to share. Grace often asked questions, and Hannah looked away or choked on whatever she ate or some other deflecting action.

Pogue finally appeared on day four. He didn't knock as he walked into the room. He didn't even greet her as he shut the door and turned to face her, a scowl on his face.

Grace swiftly pulled the duvet up to cover herself, studying him. Pogue was casually dressed in worn jeans and a plain black shirt, its sleeves rolled up, show-casing his sun-kissed forearms as he crossed them over his chest and shot her a glare. The fabric clung to his biceps and chest as he flexed. Grace tried to hide the small jolt that zapped through her. The look on his face told her she hadn't succeeded.

"Done?" he asked, a hint of smugness in his voice. That voice... How could one word be that sexy and piss her off that much at once? Grace raised her eyes to meet his. He arched his brow and popped his jaw. *So, he noticed you staring at him. Whatever,* Grace reasoned, telling herself it didn't matter. He was too much of a jerk to be attractive anyway. She gathered her stupid fluttering stomach and mentally punched it.

"Aren't you supposed to be watching me all the time?" she asked, her tone harsher than intended. Pissing off an Alpha was not on the list of wise life deci-sions. Grace had found herself relaxing around the Pride for the past few days. But not Pogue. That man changed everything in her from zero to fuck you in a second and had done so the few times he'd been by to deliver messages to her visitors.

"What makes you think I haven't?" Pogue retorted, the slightest hint of a smile playing on his lips. Then, with a quick shift, his expression turned into an impressive scowl. He held his ground by the door.

Why is he being all weird? It wasn't like Pogue had been the epitome of a social butterfly around her, but still. He was an Alpha. Shouldn't he be more... People friendly? Grace silently urged him to say something as he stood there frowning at her. After a tense minute, Grace realized she was just as silent as him. *Snappy comeback, Grace,* she urged herself. Another thirty seconds later, she still hadn't found the right words.

"Whatever, Sour McBroody." *Well, hello, teen me,* she thought as she mentally facepalmed. *Use normal fucking words, Grace!* It wasn't that hard. Right?

Pogue moved closer, letting out a quiet breath. His posture seemed a bit uncertain, which in turn made Grace feel awkward, which then annoyed her. She huffed and spoke up.

"Are you planning on staying, or is this just a glare and run?"

He nodded sharply but said nothing. He was tense, and Grace couldn't tell if he was angry or nervous. She leaned toward anger. That seemed to be his default mode. *Play nice. He's a feline. Treat him like one.* A small part of her wanted him to like her. He was one of the leaders here, after all. Grace dug into her knowledge of feline behavior. First thing a cat did to the allergic human at the table? Jump up on their lap. Cats, being dicks, generally speaking, had an innate sense of knowing who didn't like them. That, of course, made that particular human their prime target. So...

Grace ignored Pogue and reached for the romance novel Micah had purchased for her on a small bedside table. Cats were naturally inquisitive. She was banking on Pogue being enough cat that he would be too. After nearly fifteen minutes, she mustered the courage to look up. There he was, standing by her bedside table. It startled her; he had gotten so close without her even realizing. Pogue tensed, shooting her a glare, but she could see a glint of curiosity in his eyes as they fell on the book. *Gotcha*, she thought smugly as she tried to calm herself again.

"I won't harm you." He informed her as soothingly as a wet blanket, switching his weight from one foot to another. Grace put down her book and looked up at him. She blinked slowly, the cat equivalent of a smile. No dice. He continued to stare at her. She did it again, feeling a little dumb now. They weren't animals. She knew that. But, from what she had learned, they were two halves of a whole, and one half *was* animal. Or at least they had their traits. As she turned her head, she caught what she thought was a blink, as Pogue's' pale green eyes darkened and the pupils elongated slightly. At least his cat seemed to sort of, almost kinda like her. The realization hit her like a punch between the eyes. *His cat likes me... His cat is a part of him. It doesn't matter Grace, he's gay and currently keeping you quasi captive...* Still, Grace rubbed her suddenly sweaty palms on the duvet. Pogue's gaze immediately went to her hands. Cursing inwardly, she clenched her fists in the duvet.

"You're giving me a kink in my neck." It came out more like a question than a statement, she realized. What she really wanted was for him to actually sit down and make this weird tension evaporate. His looming over her wasn't helping anything.

Pogue

Why am I acting like a dumbass? Pogue cursed himself as he finally made his body obey and sat down in an old brown recliner Micah must have dragged in here. He was not usually this dense. He had game, dammit! Not that he needed game here. But a certain amount of basic social skills would come in pretty fucking handy right about now! *Words. Right the fuck now,* he commanded his brain.

"You're short." *Wow,* he thought dryly. Pogue mentally slapped himself. *I am an Alpha! I can talk to people! She* is *people!*

She shrugged.

"You're really tall."

Another minute of silence. Then,

"You in pain?" he found himself asking. He wasn't expecting the sinking feeling in his stomach when she held up her thumb and index finger, measuring out a little, while a weak smile ghosted her lips. "Tell me." He spoke more sternly than he intended.

Grace indicated her back.

"It itches like hell, and my skin feels like it's ripping apart."

Pogue placed a finger on her shoulder and gently pushed her forward to examine the long, narrow, healing wound on her back. He noticed the hitch in her breathing when he pulled out the white tank top she wore to get a decent look at it. It was healing nicely, but he could see how it would itch. It was wholly scabbed over.

"Ointment." Pogue got up and ducked into the bathroom to get the salve Doc had recommended to help heal and ease the discomfort. When he returned, Grace had discarded her tank and clutched the duvet tightly against her breasts. His gaze was drawn to the side of them, where the barest hint of skin was showing. He clenched his teeth and returned his focus to the task at hand. He began to rub the salve on the long, narrow gash with only the tips of his fingers. Her skin was cool to the touch but soft. He was surprised to see how well-defined she was.

"You work out?" he asked, trying to focus on the task.

Grace nodded.

"Yoga. I mostly do Yin 'cause I like the stretch. Uhm, as in, I'm limber. Not in a weird way, "she quickly clarified. "I try and get in some power yoga at least once a week. Why?"

"Muscle definition. You're cold."

Again, she nodded.

"I *am* cold. It's winter, and I'm pretty sure the duvet is a summer duvet." She sounded almost as tense as he felt.

From within, his cat clawed at him. For some inexplicable reason, his other half was irritated that Grace was sore and cold.

He sighed and ran his hand down his face. He then placed the small glass jar beside him on the bedside table.

"Don't move. Let it settle on your skin."

Of course, she moved. She twisted toward Pogue, wincing when the skin stretched with the motion. He hissed at her before he could catch himself. Control around this human was a losing battle. Her face went from conveying her pain to sheer annoyance as she pointed a finger at him.

"Don't you fucking hiss at me, Sourpuss! I'm munted all to hell and doing my best here!" she snapped at him. She tilted her chin up as she spoke. *Defiant little fiend*, he mused, oddly pleased by her sass, though he could almost feel the uncertainness in her voice.

"I'm not hissing!" he retorted. "What the fuck is a munt?"

Grace pulled the duvet higher, covering her shoulders and hiding the soft flesh from his gaze.

"Means broken. And it's munted. And you did fucking hiss!"

He had, and he knew it. *Put on your damn big cat pants*, he silently told himself. He sat on the edge of the bed and gazed at her. Her breathing was a little faster, but she didn't look scared, though her gaze was fixed on his hands. He raised his hands, palms out, and got up to put distance between them.

"I'm an Alpha. Protection is in my nature. Won't hurt you."

Grace snorted.

"And hissing comes with protecting? Cause it makes me feel oh, so safe?"

"You piss me off." He muttered.

Grace pulled the duvet tighter. He reached out to touch two fingers to her forehead. Not because he actually needed to feel her temperature, but because his damn hand acted before his brain could stop him. To her credit, she didn't flinch, though she did frown at him. "Put on your top. You're cold."

"The ointment sticks to anything for, like, half an hour," she said. The frown and pouting of her lips made her look younger than she probably was.

Pogue rolled his eyes and turned his whole upper body away. She was cold. She needed to get warm.

"Now!"

"I think the word you're looking for is please and thank you," she smiled, baring her teeth at him. Pogue ignored her and went to a cupboard to grab one of the heavy-knitted blankets he knew Juno had left in there. When he returned, Grace was dressed again, and the duvet was pooled around her waist, giving him a much too distracting view of her slim waist and slightly puckered nipples under the tank. He clutched the blanket in his fists.

"Lay down." He told her, his voice coming out more gravely than he expected. When she didn't move, he held up the blanket and shook it as he looked at her pointedly.

Grace

For a second, Grace almost thought he had been checking her out. But then the asshat returned to his shiny personality of 'go fuck yourself.' Now, he was back to ordering her around. His eyes returned to pale green- a sign his cat had retracted from the surface. Now he just looked pissed. Again. And her stupid mouth wouldn't form actual words.

"Uhm..." she managed to croak out. Pogue rolled his eyes and threw a large, thick blanket at her. She managed to catch it, but the motion made her wince. She froze when he stepped toward her, reaching his hands out slightly before seemingly stopping himself. Grace looked at his clenched fists and the tightness of his jaw. She held up a corner of the blanket, unsure if the tingles she felt down her back were because she wanted him to or didn't want him to tuck her in. To get closer. In the end practicality won out.

"Can you help me here? It's kinda big." Pogue grabbed the blanket again and waited for her to lie down. When she did, he lifted the blanket and gently floated it across the bed, covering almost the entire surface. Grace shifted around a bit to get comfortable, or as comfortable as one could, on her stomach as Pogue sat down on the very edge of the bed, his posture stiff as he looked down at her. He was close enough that she could feel the warmth of his body. He smelled like just before it rained, mixed with a slight citrusy undercurrent she couldn't quite put her finger on. A faint trace of cigarettes mixed in with his natural scent.

They stared blankly at each other for what felt like forever before it dawned on Grace that she was breathing him in. When she blinked, Pogue seemed to tense up, his upper body edging the slightest bit away from her. *Dammit! Say something. Anything*, she coaxed herself. She was filled with questions but knew she'd have to pick her battles with this man. She also had to actually form words, seeing as Pogue, it seemed, was not going to oblige her. *Simple questions*, she reminded herself as she asked.

"Can I ask about the Pride?"

"Mhm," he answered and abruptly stood again. He jammed his hands into his pockets and rocked back on his heels. "Ask."

"Micah has an accent, but it's different from yours. And Caden's. Are you all from different places?"

Pogue shifted his weight from one foot to another, but her question seemed to ease a little of the tension. He sat down on the edge of the recliner and clasped his hands loosely in front of him.

"Micah is from Louisiana; I was born here."

Does he ever use more words than absolutely necessary? she wondered.

"Is everyone else from Alaska or Canada too?"

"No."

Before she caught herself, she'd reached out to lightly tap his knee with the back of her hand.

"More words." Grace braced herself for the adverse reaction she was sure would come. It didn't. The only response was a slight twitch in his fingers and the darkening of his eyes as he glared at her. Kitty cat on the way back, she noted.

"Most are from this continent, a few from Northern Europe, and Gray is from Middle Eastern Europe."

"And now you have a Kiwi." *That came out so wrong,* she mentally facepalmed. "Uhm, a Kiwi is a person from New Zealand." She wanted to slam her head into a wall as a nervous giggle escaped her. She started studying her short nails. And like the idiot she was, her mouth opened again, spewing more dumb shit. "It's a NZ saying. Kinda like yeah-nah. And uhm..."

"Grace?"

Grateful for the reprieve, she sighed. For a second, it almost sounded like Pogue had chuckled, saying her name. But that would mean he had a sense of humor. *Nah, must have been something else.*

"Yeah?"

"How do I make you shut up?" His voice was so damn... *Good!* An idea popped into her head. *No, he wouldn't... Would he?*

"Well, in the spirit of you not killing me, I offer two choices. Twenty questions or read to me."

To his credit, he actually seemed to weigh the options before answering.

"Give me the damn book."

Excitement gave way to any nerves she had as she dug the book out from under her pillow and handed it to him. Pogue grabbed it and took his time settling into the recliner. Sitting there, He looked huge, and she knew the recliner wasn't exactly small. Pogue just seemed to be bigger than the average man. He opened the book, scoffing as he must have noticed she had donkey-eared the pages to keep track. His fingers seemed to itch to smooth them out. So, he did. All five of them. He opened the book to the page with the last donkey ear.

Based on the tensing of his jaw, Pogue had just realized what kind of book this was.

Paranormal romance. Changeling paranormal romance. With cats. He didn't say anything momentarily, and she thought he would balk. But. To her surprise, he didn't. Nor did he flinch or stutter when he read some extremely descriptive intimate passages. The only time he reacted was when a description of how a changeling cat scaled a building made him scoff and mumble how that just wasn't realistic.

Grace settled down to listen to Pogue read to her. He eventually kicked off his boots and put his feet on the edge of the bed. Grace eventually forgot how much he pissed her off and just let herself listen as his slightly raspy and wholly husky voice allowed her to emerge herself into the story. She must have dozed off because Pogue was gone when she awoke. The blanket and duvet, on the other hand, had been tucked closer around her, and her book now had an actual bookmark. Pogue, or whoever it belonged to, clearly enjoyed reading post-apocalyptic fiction.

Chapter 13

All Grace knew was to fight. She fought for her life as a newborn, left in a dumpster behind the hospital. Then, she fought her way through foster care and life on the streets. Now she fought to just keep the damn stalker off her back and to survive all of this. By contrast, she had never had anyone to fight for except Sophie. Sophie, whom Grace had entrusted Micah to keep in the loop for her. Micah, whom she barely knew, and yet felt so unexplainably safe around like most of the Shifters here. The longer Grace stayed here, the more she wanted it, even if they weren't her family. A part of her wanted to help them stay alive and make them want to keep her.

Micah, whom she had sort of adopted as a big brother, walked in the door late that evening, a wide smile on his tanned face.

"Guess who gets to take a bath on this fine morning?"

She glared at him. It wasn't a case of her not being allowed to have a bath, as much as Doc telling her showers would be best while she was healing and then telling Micah off because he dared to draw her a bath weeks ago. Go figure...

"Your lion? Again?" He grinned and pointed at her. She squealed, making him wince as he held a hand to his ear.

"But before you get all wet," he leered. She flipped him off. "I was wondering about something." She just nodded, a sinking feeling in her chest slowly settling like lead. Grace just nodded, a heavy feeling settling in her chest like a weight. This wasn't the first time someone had picked up on her. Usually, they just brushed it off as her being a bit weird or lost in thought. But Micah was different. Despite his easygoing demeanor, she suspected he saw much more than the average person.

"I'm not trying to come off all psychologist-like, but I need to ask you something, Grace." She nodded.

Micah took a breath and settled on the bed beside her. He gently cradled her hand in his, his thumb moving in soothing circles on her palm.

"Grace, do you suffer from Dissociative Amnesia Disorder?" Grace sat up straight. Did I have a fugue? Is that why he's asking? How would he even know what it's called? She wondered, a touch of unease creeping in. The drugs and stress made it difficult to piece together the events clearly.

"What have you seen? What did I do?" she asked.

Grace had dealt with the fugues for years since her early teens. She hated the loss of control over her own mind and body. The fugues had their scary moments, of course. Yet, more often than not, they were a mystery band-aid on a wound she couldn't recall getting or discovering lasagna on the kitchen counter with no memory of making it. And then, there were the times she'd wake up in unfamiliar surroundings. Fortunately, she had only experienced the unsettling feeling of waking up once in a stranger's bed once. She was just fifteen.

Micah held up his hand to stop her when she was about to ask him more.

"Nothing major. I promise. Pogue mentioned the recliner being moved, and Doc said he'd found you standing by the door looking into the wall, but he put it down to the drugs he gave you. You asked Beau if he would like his lasagna cold or warm. Small things, Grace, nothing major, and you haven't done anything you should be embarrassed about. Am I right, though? If I am, I'd like to know so I can read up on it and help you avoid dangerous situations." Micah looked down at his hands, a wry smile on his lips. "And, as promised, I've kept in touch with your friend. She mentioned you have, uhm, had," he amended, "some pills to calm you down after a fugue or if you felt one coming on. Is that true?"

Grace nodded. She then looked at Micah as a thought occurred to her.

"They were in my backpack. Must have lost it in the crash. How do you know what DAD is?"

"I dabble in psychology. It's ok, you know. I'll help you deal with it if you'll let me. And I can ask Doc to see about getting a new prescription if you'd like?" He sounded so damn sincere.

Grace sighed.

"No, Micah, you really can't help. It's been happening since I was a teenager, and the therapists say the treatment could make me worse. Like uncovering stuff, my brain forgot to protect me. It's a life with kind of thing," she shrugged. "Usually, it's small things. I'll kinda zone out, go somewhere else in my mind."

Micah nodded seriously.

"Because where you are isn't safe?" he asked, his voice quiet.

Grace shook her head.

"Not necessarily, but sometimes, yeah. But anything can trigger it. Sometimes, it's a smell, sometimes a sound, or someone moving in a specific way. My therapist told me the best anyone around me can do is time it if I'm not in any danger. Just, you know, wait it out. Then, when I come out of it, it calms me to know how long I was out for. I've read pressure point therapy can work. You know, like when a dog is scared of fireworks, and you put a 'Thundershirt' on it? It puts pressure on specific zones that release endorphins and help it calm down."

Micah scrounged up his nose as he replied.

"And if you are in danger? What if you're about to walk out in front of a car?"

Grace shook her head.

"Won't happen. It's like my brain still works, but I'm on autopilot. Like, I still look both ways before crossing a street and put on gloves before sticking my hands in the oven. Sophie tried restraining me once. Didn't turn out well. I get... reactive," Grace said, her cheeks heating with embarrassment.

"OK, so I'll talk to Doc and the Alphas. I'll read up on DAD, but I imagine the stress of all this isn't helping?" he asked as he hopped onto the bed and pulled her in for a snuggle. Micah was a quick study, it seemed. He knew exactly where to put pressure. Grace didn't snuggle, but Micah just relaxed her- the pressure points notwithstanding.

"Not really, no. On a side note, feel free to explain why you automatically lower my stress levels," she grinned wryly.

Micah shrugged.

"Good looks and charm."

I call bullshit, she thought, cuddling into the heat of him.

Micah passed along updates from Sophie almost daily, which Grace greatly appreciated. He also prepared the bath for her before he left today. She knew she'd need help with her back, as twisting still caused discomfort, even though she was on the mend. Doc seemed to be taking extra precautions, treating her like she was wrapped in bubble wrap just because she was human. He'd also dropped by a small bottle of pills. A panic pill, basically, for her to take after a fugue, if it was too bad.

Micah assured her that Pogue would be coming by, and there was no need to worry. He mentioned that Pogue had spent the last two nights at his boyfriend's place, so he'd be as gentle as a lamb. He added a playful remark about Prozac with a wink.

While Grace still had some reservations, she knew a bath would do her good, and she couldn't reach her back properly.

The warm water felt like heaven on her skin as Grace sank down in the bubbles that smelled like lavender. *Thank you, Micah!*

A knock on the door a minute later jolted her out of her relaxation.

"Come on in," she shouted, her voice a bit shrill.

Nothing... "Halloo, you can come iiinnn," she called out again.

"Stop shouting," Pogue muttered from right beside her. Grace screamed and slipped under the water. She was quickly pulled up by her neck.

"Arrgh ow, ow, ow!" she exclaimed.

"Shit, woman!"

Grace quickly concluded that the boyfriend didn't do a good job on the gentle as a lamb part.

Pogue picked up a washcloth she'd left on the floor and wiped the water and an insane amount of bubbles from her face as she spluttered.

"What the fuck did you expect?! Do you actually walk on the floor, or do you just kinda float like Voldemort?!"

"Don't know what a Voldemort is, but yes, I walk," Pogue replied stiffly as he reached for something in a small cupboard opposite the large bathtub. "Sit up."

"Why? Are you gonna try to drown me, and you'd like resistance?" she quipped. Pogue held up a sponge, giving her a flat stare. "Fine, but if you try to drown me, I will hurt you!"

Grace sat up straight. The water reached about halfway up her breasts, and she scooted down to make sure the bubbles covered her more.

Pogue sat on the bathtub's edge, dipping the sponge into the water beside her. He squeezed the water from the sponge as he placed it below her neckline. Grace moaned softly and leaned forward, enjoying the sensation, until the sponge caught on something, and she hissed. The sponge was dropped.

"Scab."

"You really don't talk much, do you?" Grace asked softly. *Talk to me more, Pogue, a small* voice deep inside her whispered.

"No."

"Thanks for not being a dick about this," she mumbled.

"Mhm," was his only response before he stood up and cursed as his hand slipped on the edge, splashing water.

"Sec."

Grace kept her eyes closed, enjoying the pampering despite the unwillingness she was sure Pogue felt. They'd come a long way in terms of being around each other. He certainly growled less, and the awkwardness had tampered down a bit.

She could hear the rustling of clothes as he moved away from her.

"Up," he ordered.

Grace wasn't particularly shy, but she felt the heat seeping into her cheeks. She gripped one side of the tub, but her right hand slipped. She would have hit her chin on the edge if it hadn't been for two solid, naked arms holding her up.

"Sorry. Slippery," she managed to say, feeling like an idiot.

"How the hell do you keep yourself alive?!" he burst out. Pogue's short-bristled jaw scratched slightly on her cheek as he propped her up while her knees slid around like a three-year-old drunk.

"Well, I always throw spilled salt over my left shoulder and keep rosemary by my garden gate. I plant lavender for luck, and go fuck yourself," she said sarcastically, quoting one of her all-time favorite films, Practical Magic. Grace tried to get her feet under her, splashing water and bubbles everywhere.

"What?!" was the confused response as he let her slide back into the tub. He sighed and then huffed at her. "Stay!"

"Not a dog, dumbass," she retorted, crossing her arms over her chest.

"Oh, for fucks sake, fine!" he snarled.

Pogue's arms entered the water, causing a small splash. Swiftly, he slid one arm under her back and the other under her legs, effortlessly lifting her from the tub and placing her onto the soft rug. *This is a whole new level of embarrassment*, she thought, squeezing her eyes shut and trying to shield herself like a five-year-old. *If I can't see you, you can't see me. Hang on. Is he...?* she wondered, her fingers inadvertently brushing against something firm. She cautiously opened one eye, confirming that his upper body was indeed naked. Whoever his boyfriend was, they hit the jackpot. Pogue had a light dusting of auburn hair on his well-defined chest and chiseled abs, leading down to a narrow trail disappearing into his jeans. And the gods dammed Adonis belt. The V-shaped muscular groove made for licking. *No! No licking!* Grace forcibly redirected her thoughts, dragging them out of the gutter. She must have shifted closer to him because he gently pushed her shoulders as if to steady her.

Pogue went to get something. A large towel hit her in the face seconds later. She snatched it and wrapped it around herself. Soon after, another towel was placed on her head, and a couple of large, strong hands attempted to jolt her brain out of her skull as he dried it. Grace reached up, clasping his right hand while using the other to secure the towel, wincing as her nearly healed wound pulled. It was frustrating that she couldn't fully do something as simple as drying her own hair. Every attempt resulted in a slight strain on her wound, causing the skin to fray a bit.

"Gently. You'll spill my brain out my ears," she grumbled, forgetting that his hearing wasn't human. *He* wasn't human, and he would be able to hear her just fine.

Pogue stiffened, but she was almost sure she heard a hint of a smile when he spoke.

"Sure there's any to spill?"

"Oh, har di har har, asshole... Just dry it gently. Like you're giving a massage or something. Please," she added, trying to keep the sarcasm from her voice.

He breathed out harshly through his nose but complied. *Bliss.*

Grace had always loved head massages. Against her will, her body bent forward, and rested her head on his broad chest. Grace had no idea how tall he was, but he was a hell of a lot taller than her. Her lips were facing his solar plexus. His hands moved the towel in slow circular motions, and with each shift, she leaned in closer and closer until she was flush against him. *How's that for desperate?!* She felt like an idiot trying to inhale the rather delectable scent of a man who A. was an asshole, and B. swung for the other team. Grace felt Pogue's breath on her head and tilted her head up, her eyes closed.

"Sugar."

"Excuse me?" His voice sounded strained.

"I smell sugar on your breath."

Pogue abruptly stopped and stepped away from her, turning towards the door.

"I'll be back. Take you to breakfast. Micah will drop by clothes for you."

And with that, he left.

Chapter 14

Pogue briskly walked back to his room adjacent to hers. His cat was pushing under his skin. It wanted to bite. To lick. Annoyed, he changed his clothes and headed to the gym. An hour later, he was still agitated, his body refusing to comply with his demands to calm the fuck down. Grace pissed him off to no end. Every damn thing about her got on his nerves, he thought while trotting down the steps from the gym on the second floor, his steps easy on the soft stones. The way she smelled, her sailor-like language, those stupid blue eyes, and those damn fine...

He froze, stunned by the fact that he was so captivated by her. Why was he so damn focused on every little damn detail about her?! He felt his cat stir in his mind. It wasn't shocked in the slightest. He pivoted towards the wall at the foot of the stairs and lightly tapped his head against it a few times. He glanced down at his crotch.

"Fine. Let's go see if Rosie's home," he told his treacherous baser desires. Pogue broke out into a run, hoping the short trip across the inner yard and into the forest to Rosita's burrow would at least distract him from...

He felt his phone vibrate in his pocket and plucked it out, looking at the caller ID. Cades. He flipped it open, stopping as he did so. He'd barely gotten five meters.

"What?" he asked as he walked briskly towards the well-lit area of the aeries-the treetop houses by the clinic, opposite the Den. The forest lay beyond that, and in it, the burrows.

"Okay, hi to you too. Look, I've just gotten a phone call from DeCoill. He's paying us a surprise visit. I've called for a meeting."

Pogue felt his hand clench around the phone.

"What?!"

They'd decided to keep Grace's presence under wraps until they were sure she was safe to be around and could confirm her veterinary nurse credentials. And, of course, there was the matter of dealing with the Challenge. He and Cades knew that Hannah and Nigel would need to inform the Academy, who would probably notify the Council as a routine matter. Still, Pogue and Caden hoped the Council wouldn't bother to fact-check the information, especially regarding when Grace had stumbled into their Pridelands and his life. As far as Pogue knew, they usually didn't.

On the other end, Caden let out a sigh.

"This is a problem. DeCoill knows she's here now, and he might know for how long she's been here... Pogue, that's a major offense if he thinks we purposely kept her a secret. Which we did." Caden said, worry radiating through the phone, even as Pogue felt his chest constrict. "She's not registered yet, and DeCoill is gonna shit a brick because we weren't the ones to tell him about her in the first place."

"I know, Cades. On my way." Pogue hung up and ran for the office. He almost ran into Micah by the door and motioned for him to follow him in as he opened it. They kicked off their shoes and walked inside.

Caden looked freaked. His brother didn't get freaked. The man was a rock; he always had been.

"Cades, stop. Look at me." Pogue stepped before Caden and grabbed his chin to look him in the eye. "This is not a big deal!" He was all business now. *What the fuck did they tell him to make him react like this?* Pogue wondered. Caden's eyes were all cat, and his fingers clawed as he stood in front of Pogue. *Nobody* got to wind his baby brother up like that! Yeah, Pogue and Caden were twins, but Caden had been slow as fuck, so Pogue was a whole minute older than him. He would forever be his brother's keeper.

This is where he excelled. Chaos and crises were his home ground. Caden looked at him and took a series of deep breaths as Micah went to the PA and ordered coffee and food.

"Just the Vigilia?" Pogue asked as Henley strode silently through the door. He nodded to both Alphas and Micah before retreating to a corner of the room.

"Reps, too," Caden answered. Sometimes, Pogue and Caden would invite the Submissives representative Liam and Maternal representative Juno to join them; it allowed them to check in on how their people were doing. As much as the Pride trusted their Alphas, some things were easier to talk about with someone of their own rank.

Micah and Pogue went to get an extra table from the small study next door.

Counting the number of chairs, Pogue told Beau to grab one more as the large Shifter greeted him in the doorway.

Beau turned around and headed back down the stairwell when Mehendi's tall, athletic form appeared around the second landing. He called out to her.

"Yo! Grab a couple of foldouts, will you?" They could hear her footsteps as she descended quickly again.

Ten minutes went by as Shifters filed in. Pogue greeted Juno as she kicked off her shoes by the door and walked straight to a beanbag chair to sit down, gently nudging Beau out of the way.

Juno was the Maternal representative. Maternals were defined by their animal's nature rather than their age or gender. The personality of the human part did not always reveal what designation they were, either. Juno, though, was Maternal in every way. A soft-curved, sweet-natured woman who oozed cuddles and cookies and even had a look to match, but Pogue pitied the fool who fucked with the Pride in her presence. She smiled as the Submissives representative, Liam, walked in. Pogue moved out of the way to allow the short Shifter to pass as Liam made his way to Juno. He bent to kiss Juno's cheek.

"Hey, mama," he whispered, his Irish accent pronounced, his smile soft.

"Hi, baby. You okay?" she asked.

"Fine, thank you. Claus sends his best," he answered, referring to his True Mate.

Dina fluttered in and settled on the back of Pogue's office chair, preening her feathers. She was just as social as anyone else but seldom chimed in during these meetings.

Pogue claimed the desk chair while Caden opted for a beanbag. Grayson arrived a bit late, offering murmured apologies as he leaned his sizable frame against the wall. He gestured for Mehendi to join him, and she eagerly nestled into his embrace, giving him a swift kiss on the cheek. Pogue and Caden had an ongoing bet about the nature of their relationship. While Mehendi was generally a playful Shifter, she wasn't as physically affectionate with the rest of the Pride.

Grayson, on the other hand, casually draped his arms around her, pulling her in close and playfully nipping at her ear. Despite only being a part of StormEdge for about six years, the large leopard Shifter exuded a quiet intelligence that didn't escape Pogue's notice. He had no doubt about Grayson's unwavering loyalty.

Micah propped himself against the corner of the colossal desk as they waited for Tari and the others. Pogue was on the verge of asking where the hell the damn lawyer was when said lawyer burst through the door. His t-shirt was on inside out, he was without socks and shoes, and his blond hair resembled a whirlwind. He abruptly came to a stop, scanning the room in a state of mild panic.

"I'm here!"

Juno laughed out loud, her deep voice booming as Beau whistled.

"Yes, hun, we *all* see that. You might wanna fix your shirt, baby," she leered at him.

He looked down at the t-shirt that was plastered to his slim body. He cursed a blue streak as he swiftly grabbed the hem and pulled it up over his head before putting it on the right way.

"Sorry guys, I was in the shower." A chorus of snorts and snickers sounded throughout the room.

"Of course you were," Mehendi snickered.

"And your hair dried 'cause you were running so fast to get here," Beau finished, much to Tari's chagrin.

"Also, ye kinda smell like sex," Liam added with a smirk as he casually crossed one leg over his knee.

Tari swaggered over to one of the chairs and flipped them off. Having a keen sense of smell could be aggravating, but it was hella fun right now, Pogue thought to himself.

Lucy, a young lioness Shifter, appeared moments later, pushing a rolling cart filled with drinks and snacks. She smiled and blushed when Micah winked at her.

"Thank you, darlin'." She quickly turned and almost ran out the door.

Caden and Pogue stood and faced the group, who were supplying themselves.

"All right," Caden began. "Earlier tonight, I received a phone call from De-Coill, and we've got some other news, too." The group collectively groaned. Grayson rolled his eyes.

"Yeah, I know. But to put it bluntly, we're in trouble," Caden said.

"Did he find a crooked twig and conclude it was our bloody fault now?" Liam quipped.

"Not quite," Pogue answered.

Caden took the floor.

"I'm gonna rip the band-aid off quickly. Keep your animals in check," he pointed.

The group nodded. Their Shifters were not volatile or unruly, but certain things would set off almost any Shifter, one of which was war. This was particularly true in a young Pride with Submissives and cubs to protect.

"One," Caden started. "The Challenge isn't going to be an Alpha Challenge," he said, absentmindedly stroking Dinas' wing. "IceFjord petitioned for a Turf War. The Council approved it. They attack on December twenty-fifth. Today is October twenty-seventh, so we have eight weeks and four days. Two. That's why we're keeping Grace. She's a veterinary nurse, and Micah has her credentials. She checks out, and she might come in very handy now."

The group, to their credit, kept relatively calm. Pogue noticed Grayson baring his teeth, his canines elongating. Tari hissed as his eyes shifted from his regular pale blue to the golden hue of his serval cat. Pogue started pushing out calming pheromones automatically to help them settle. His own hands fisted but for an entirely different reason. Grace. Caden pressed on, pulling Pogue back to the present, even though seething anger lingered just below the surface. The idea of anyone threatening his people stirred a primal urge within him - protect. Kill if need be.

"Three. The Council knows we have her. They're pissed we waited more than twenty-four hours to contact them, especially since Nigel reported the magic discovered at the crash to the Academy last week, and we haven't petitioned to keep her as a Pet." Tari was about to speak, but Grayson cut him off.

"Why would StormEdge Wielders inform the Academy in the first place?" Grayson asked quietly. He was twirling a coin through his fingers as he spoke. Mehendi stroked his arm, her head leaning back against his clavicle.

"You know they don't have a choice," Tari said. "The Academy does something to test them, to see if they're withholding information." He held up a hand when Pogue was about to ask him about it. "No, I still don't know what or how, and Hannah still isn't telling. Just trust me. They don't have a choice. But you sort of have a point, Gray. The Academy wouldn't normally have to inform the Council. It's more of a courtesy than anything else." Tari sighed and leaned back in the chair. Liam reached over to hand him a cup of coffee. Tari took it and nodded his thanks.

Caden took a breath and started again.

"So someone else must have made sure the Academy told the Council to look deeper into it. Another issue for another day, but it brings me to number four; they've summoned us for failing to notify, and five, DeCoill will personally visit tomorrow morning. He apparently wants to see her. " Caden frowned as he said it. Tari nodded to confirm that DeCoill did indeed have the right. Yeah, that was a lot to take in. Pogue and Caden had to repeat the whole thing twice.

"Has DeCoill given a reason why he wants to see her? I have never heard of that before. Is it a new procedure, Tari?" Henley asked.

Tari shook his head. "No, and it worries me. And on the not petitioning. I got a letter yesterday saying that our petition for a Pet has been approved. Except, as you know, I didn't file one."

Henley frowned.

"How can they approve a petition we didn't file? Is DeCoill messing with us?"

Tari shook his head and brushed his hair out of his eyes. He reached over to pour milk into Henley's coffee as he spoke.

"That's the thing, I don't think he is. The stamp on the letter was Council, but DeCoill always signs his, so I *know* it wasn't from him."

"Meaning someone on the Council knew we had taken in a human, decided not to say anything, but instead, what? Help us? Why?" Caden turned to Pogue. "This is exactly why we need to be more involved in local politics!"

Pogue rolled his eyes. Caden knew how he felt about it, and this wouldn't change his mind.

Beau looked up from where he was unwrapping his second sandwich.

"Does it matter right now? Take the olive branch, I say. Worry about the why and who later."

Pogue nodded his agreement as Tari went on.

"I'll put out a discrete feeler. I also think DeCoill is paying a visit specifically because he didn't approve anything. he's been left out of the loop, and it pisses him off." he shrugged. "Gives us a possible ally within the Council, but I'd like to know who it is," Tari finished.

"And he can't retract the permission because it would make the Council look weak. They can't have that with the mistrust Shifters are voicing these days," Caden added.

Pogue was well aware of the Council's tarnished reputation. Shifters were vanishing, yet the Council seemed more fixated on DeCoill's far-fetched vision of a pure Shifter society than on investigating the disappearances. In his mind, this made the Council obsolete and incompetent at best.

Pogue walked over to open the window, lighting up a cigarette. He nodded to Tari.

"What kind of damage are we looking at for not notifying?"

Tari furrowed his brow and reclined in the beanbag chair, letting his legs stretch out as he accepted the cookie Henley offered him.

"Depends on whether or not I can bring it down from a major offense to a misdemeanor. If I can't? At the bare minimum, they sanction us. Forced transfers, lashings, maybe land," Tari muttered as he went through his notes.

Growls emanated from around the room. Pogue heaved a deep breath and held up his hand, silencing them.

"Deep fucking breaths! Sounds like DeCoill's looking for a reason to take her to the Council. We could need her skills in the Challenge, so we need to make sure that doesn't fucking happen," he growled. "Any ammunition we can get our paws on, we take and we use! Worry about why he seems to want her later."

Perched on the minifridge with his feline grace on display, Micah spoke up over the growls and huffs. He'd been mostly quiet so far, but that wasn't unusual. He liked having all the facts before speaking, Pogue knew.

As he spoke, Micah walked over, wafting a hand at Pogue- or his cigarette, more like it.

"Do we know if there's magic in Grace? Might give justification for keeping her on the down low. It's not a stretch that we would question her, and to do that, she would have to be up for it physically. That would account for the time delay. Do we know when the petition we didn't file *was* filed?"

Tari shook his head. *That's a problem,* Pogue thought as he pointed to his water bottle. Caden grabbed it and tossed it to him.

Pogue noted Mehendi tracking the object with her gaze. A soft, chirping sound escaped her lips. Mehendi's cat had a very playful spirit. She blushed, bringing a hand to her mouth, and nestled her face into Grayson's neck.

Tari seemed to think about it before answering.

"If Hannah discovers magic in her, it justifies not killing her on sight, at least," he said, shrugging his shoulders. He turned to face Caden.

They were just about to move on to a little small talk when Caden snapped his fingers.

"All right, back to pressing matters. Well, more pressing for us anyway. We need to review the trade agreement with the Dahlings; Henley, take Tari and go tomorrow."

The Dahlings, a non-predatory Herd within StormEdge, had a trade pact. They provided gems and veggies; in return, they could live safely in StormEdge Pridelands. This ensured protection for both the Herd and the territory.

Henley and Tari both nodded. Pogue couldn't help but smile at how those two functioned like little old ladies, with their coffee and tea swaps, the cookie exchanges, and whatnot.

Beau looked up, a smirk on his tan face.

"Guess I'll be trying to persuade Oliver to not hang out in the Den when DeCoill shows up then."

Mehendi grinned and winked at Beau.

"I'm sure you'll manage. Your not very Submissive Mate sure does have a healthy temper when it comes to DeCoill," she wrinkled her nose as she spoke.

Grayson looked up from where his hands were twirling the coin steadily.

"Why would an Alpha, beaten thrice, choose this course of action? Why Challenge us again?" Grayson seemed to have skipped everything else, focusing on what he deemed the most significant threat. The Challenge. The War...

Pogue nodded to Henley. The fox knew what Pogue wanted before even asking.

"Do some digging. We've been wondering the same thing," he said, frowning.

Caden nodded solemnly and turned to Pogue.

"Stellan is cocky, but he's not dumb," Caden said, referring to the Alpha of IceFjord, who would be attacking them on December 25th. "There's gotta be more to it."

Pogue ran a hand across his face and nodded. Too much shit to deal with and too little time to do it. He then turned to Tari.

"Wanna go get Hannah? I want answers before tomorrow, just in case DeCoill does something we need a defense against."

Tari nodded and rose. He looked pointedly at Pogue.

"Wanna go get your human?" Pogue felt his chest vibrate as a soft growl formed in his throat. Fortunately, it translated as annoyance.

"Not my fucking human, and if she can't keep her sass this time, I'm gonna bite!" he stated. He barely caught Henley murmuring so low only Pogue would hear as he passed him on his way out.

"I do believe you would."

Micah followed him out and stopped him after the door to the office was closed.

"Pogue?"

Pogue turned around. He saw Micah's lion was close to the surface.

"What, Micah?" Pogue knew when to be gentle with Micah. His lion was savage, and if it was close to the surface now, something big was happening.

"Be gentle, no pushing. Keep her calm. She likes her hair stroked, leans in with your arm around her. She needs to feel safe. Micah glanced down, avoiding eye contact." *Tell me you didn't fall for her, kid.*

"You're never this impulsive, and your cat is prowling too close to the surface. Do you *want* her? Is that it?" Pogue asked, frowning, confused.

"Micah hissed, confronting Pogue. Swiftly, Pogue grabbed his throat and pressed him against the staircase wall. His inner feline emerged with a growl. This reaction was excessive considering Pogue's words. Micah was crossing the line." It took almost a minute for Micah to look away and turn his head, baring his throat, but the anger still poured off him in waves. Pogue released him.

"The fuck, Micah?!"

Micah looked down.

"I'm sorry. I know I'm all over the place right now, Alpha. Pogue. I'm onto something. Just need a bit of time, okay? Just trust me please?"

Shit, meet fan... again... Pogue sighed.

"One chance, Micah."

Micah looked up, took a breath, and nodded sharply.

"I'll take it."

Pogue seized the opportunity to avoid being in a confined room with the small woman.

"So, how about you go get her?"

"I can't. I think I need to breathe a little right now. Get my cat under control."

Pogue nodded, turned to leave, then paused, as a nagging thought entered his mind.

"Micah?"

"Yeah."

"Why would a human throw salt over their left shoulder?" It seemed like a waste, not to mention the subsequent cleanup.

Micah shook his head and sighed, a small smile tugging at his lips.

"Human superstition. Why?" Pogue just shook his head as he left.

Chapter 15

Grace was jolted awake by the sound of a door opening and closing. Must be night still, she thought. Grace had always been a light sleeper, and being in a strange place didn't help. She didn't register any footsteps, though.

"Wake up!" Pogue's' voice startled her, coming from right by her ear.

Her arm shot out without thinking, but she only met empty air. A sudden tightness gripped Grace's throat. Instinctively, she curled in on herself, feeling the familiar onset of cold sweat at the base of her spine—a sign that she wouldn't remember what would come next.

"Gaah! Wha-..?"

Pogue sneered.

"You heard me."

"Narngh...What time is it?" she asked, burrowing her head under her pillow. *Not now, please, not right now, brain!* She begged her system to calm down. Grace knew from experience that being woken up like this could quickly push her into a fugue. She took a deep breath, centering herself around Pogue's' scent, willing it to calm her nervous system. *Nice and steady*, she coaxed herself.

"It's after midnight," Pogue said as he picked up the towels she had left on the floor, sighing. When he looked at her, he angled his head, subtly lifting his chin to scent the air. Then he frowned. *I can't... I just can't with this right now*, Grace thought as she buried her head under the pillow and pulled the duvet over it.

"Not a morning person," he stated more than asked, though his tone was less grr than it had been a minute ago.

"Because it's fucking midnight!" she mumbled as the bed dipped. Pogue stayed motionless for a moment. Grace took advantage of this time to regain full control of herself. The second she had, Pogue lifted the pillow from her face and lightly tapped her forehead.

"Up." *Did he just thump me?! Motherfucking fucktard!* she thought, outraged, as she narrowed her eyes at him. Pogue's face was right beside her, his night-glowing eyes fixed on her. This optical phenomenon was known as tapetum lucidum, allowing felines to see in the dark. It was both eerie and super fascinating. Pogue continued to stare at her, unblinking, and raised a finger, probably to repeat the stupid thumping of her head.

Grace snapped her teeth at him, catching the tip of his index finger hard. He cursed as he yanked it away from her, something between a sharp growl and a yowl escaping his mouth. The Alpha should have scared her with his growling. He didn't, and she wondered why she lacked self-preservation skills in the presence of someone who could clearly snap her like a twig. He should have terrified her. Instead, the verbal sparring actually helped her focus.

"Fuck off, growly McSnape! Don't you people ever fucking sleep?!" she snarled at him.

Grace heard Pogue sigh before his head dipped close to hers again. Way close. For a second, she thought he was going to kiss her. Then she felt the sharp sting of teeth as he nipped her ear like she was an unruly kitten. She was about to go full-on Buckbeak when he bit Malfoy, when Pogue got off the bed and started towards the door.

"You'll get to see magic..." he stated.

That got her attention. Now, she just needed her brain to wake up enough to do something about it. Grace turned in bed, wincing, when the long gash on her back was twisted with the movements.

"Clothes. Light," she mumbled, her eyes closed and her face buried back in the pillow. Just for a little more rest, 'cause, you know. owies. Also, still fucking midnight...

"Hrmh!" Moments later, the door clicked open, then closed.

Grace had just drifted off when the door opened again. Still no light. *I swear, the fucker does shit like this just to aggravate me,* Grace concluded as she tried to force her dumb human eyes to adjust to the lack of light.

"Here." His dark, rusty, honeyed voice commanded more than stated.

Grace sat up in bed, hugging the duvet to her chest.

"Lights?"

She could almost feel the spite coming off him.

"Follow my eyes. I'll try not to blink. Much."

"How about I feel my way, hmm? Just hand me a couple of knives," she answered in a sickeningly sweet voice. *See how weak of a human you think I am with a carving knife up your nose!* Pogue hummed under his breath. A second later, a pile of clothes was thrust in her face.

A hoodie and a pair of sweatpants that were five sizes too big. Grace drew them beneath the duvet to put them on, remembering his night vision. Grace slid her legs forward until her feet dangled over the edge. Her nose picked up on smells of rain and snow, and she wondered for a second why those scents warranted the butterflies in her stomach. *Magic. We're looking forward to magic, that's why.*

She stood up too quickly, only to sway and sit down again. Pogue had moved with unnatural speed from the door, and she immediately felt two large hands on her waist.

"Head rush," she said on the breath of an exhale. "Probably didn't drink enough today."

Pogue cursed under his breath and unceremoniously picked her up.

"You don't have to carry me."

"No time for you to be human," Pogue replied tersely as he started walking. Grace decided to hell with it and leaned her head onto Sir Grump-a-lot's shoulder as they walked. He briskly moved down the hallway and up the stairs. She breathed through her nose, tilting her head slightly against his shoulder to catch his scent. And the Alpha of course didn't miss that.

"Why are you smelling me?" he rumbled softly.

"Am I wearing your clothes?"

"Yes."

"*Why* am I wearing your clothes Pogue?" she asked, deliberately using a complete sentence, just 'cause he didn't.

"Closest. We're here."

Pogue dipped to open the door. Grace blinked to adjust to the brightness of the room. The hallways had been dim, and the whole Pride- well, most, it seemed- were sound asleep.

"Why are we carrying my patient, Pogue?" Doc asked as he greeted Grace, just as Caden did too.

"Headrush evidently made me incapable of walking," she grumbled, taking in the packed room.

"Made you fucking slow," Pogue grunted. Grace tilted her head to glare at him.

Hannah, the eccentric Wielder, smiled at her before frowning as her eyes zeroed in on Grace's right ear. Grace could still feel the heat from where Pogue had nipped her. She just wasn't sure if the heat was because of pain or something else...

"Did you bite her, Pogue?" Hannah sounded outraged as she approached Grace, whom Pogue had placed on a foldout chair beside him. Nobody in the room appeared surprised. A nip was nothing out of the ordinary for them, Grace knew. Hannah, on the other hand, was not a Shifter, though it stood to reason she would know their culture and customs intimately, having grown up in this world. After glaring at Pogue for a full minute, Hannah seemed to concede defeat- mostly because Pogue just glared back. He was good at that. Having given up, Hannah turned her attention to Grace, a smile on her face.

"'K, so I'm just gonna poke you in the eyes real quick."

Grace winced.

"Yeah-nah." She turned to Pogue, narrowing her eyes, and pointed a finger in his face. "You duped me, asshole!" Pogue flashed her a flat stare before he bit the tip of her finger, leaving a small mark. Grace noticed several heads tilt to the side, their focus- and their heads, shifting between her and Pogue. It was a strange mix of unsettling and adorable, like those viral YouTube videos of five kittens tilting their heads simultaneously. As cute as it was, it didn't stop her from smacking his forehead with her free hand and reciprocating the bite, this time with more gusto. Pogue relinquished her finger and let out a frustrated growl. Grace couldn't help but giggle; she was too worn out to be serious at the moment, and he kinda reminded her of the Beast from "Beauty and the Beast" right now. All grouchy and shit. A few snickers and surprised gasps from around the room indicated that her behavior had caught them off guard. You weren't supposed to do that to the Alpha? Grace, again, questioned her lack of self-preservation skills and looked to Micah for answers. Pogue's' growl turned into a chuffing type of grunt before he leaned back on the foldout chair and averted his attention.

Caden grinned, answering for Micah, who sat there, not saying a word, slightly slack-jawed.

"If you stop biting the Alpha, he might stop biting you," he gently admonished.

"Or bite harder, Grace. It's good for him." Juno chortled, making Pogue glare at her.

Caden coughed into his hand, trying to hide a smile.

"All right, all right. Let's do this. Hannah's gonna hold a finger in front of your eyes and coax... Well, she's gonna pull out something, to erh.." He looked at Hannah.

"How do you do this again?"

Hannah's lips twitched as Grace quipped.

"Thanks, Dumble-not..." Hannah snort-laughed as she turned toward her and explained how she would extract a little bit of what she called her essence. She would then drip it onto a small iron pebble that worked kinda like a microscope, and that would tell them what they needed to know. "Try to keep them open as I look. It may feel cold, but it shouldn't hurt."

"What is it actually you need to know, and why?" Grace asked skeptically.

"If you have any magic in you, it'll help Tweedle-dee and Tweedledum keep you alive and them out of trouble when you meet the Council tomorrow. And it'll help the Academy of Wielders decide if you live, die, or get turned into a toad," Hannah said in a deadpan voice. Grace started to get up, but Pogue pushed her back down with a hand.

"Not negotiable."

"Fuck you, it's not negotiable, Sir Snapalot! I don't wanna die, and I sure as hell don't wanna meet the Council! And again, you're all throwing around words

like die, like it's a fucking hacky sack! I will not be the rice in your hacky sack!"
Pogue just glared at her, his human eyes surrendering to those of his cat. Everyone
else looked genuinely confused, though Micah seemed to feel bad for her. Grace
and Pogue then glared at each other for almost a solid minute before she threw
up her hands and slumped down on the chair, nodding to Hannah.

"Whatever, whip your wand out!" Hannah barked a laugh before she pointed
a glowing finger at Grace's eye.

"Hey, does this mean E.T. gets to phone home soon?"

Hannah's focus slipped as laughter bubbled up. Pogue playfully grumbled at
her, and she pretended to clear her throat before continuing. Grace felt something
cold touching her eyes, causing her to tense up.

A few moments later, Pogue's hand came to rest on her neck, his grip firm.
Grace noticed Micah subtly nodding in Pogue's direction, signaling him to do
so. She didn't miss the dominant move it was. She accepted it anyway, though she
wasn't sure why she was A. Letting him and B. It was actually working. And not
just a little. She used that trick on wild cats at the clinic where she worked. Scruff
them with a soft clamp, and about sixty percent became docile kittens. *Is he doing
the Shifter equivalent of scuffing?* Moments later, his grip loosened, and he started
tracing his thumb in a small circle on the back of her neck. This brought about
a completely different reaction, although she maintained a casual posture. Yet,
Grace couldn't ignore the sensation of his thumb, sending a warmth pooling in
her stomach. Unconsciously, she leaned into the touch, just a fraction. The subtle
twitch of his lips told her he'd noticed. *Well fuckery...*

"So, what's the verdict?" Grace asked, her voice coming out thready, as Hannah dropped small balls of light onto the pebble. Pogue's hand had curled around
her nape, resting there. The slight touch was setting her nerve endings on low-key
fire.

"Hang on. The test results are developing. It'll take a few mo- Oh, that was
quick." Hannah said almost immediately after and began to sing. "You've got the
magic in youuuu." Pogue shot up from his chair, causing her to be jolted off her
hers and onto a thick, soft carpet because the idiot forgot to let go of her fucking

nape! She cried out as her hip connected with the floor. Pain and surprise went through her like a low-key lightning strike.

"I've got the what now? I'm what, a-"

Hannah held up her hands in a placating gesture.

"I'm not saying you're anything, Grace. Breathe," she coaxed as Grace tried to get her bearings.

There were voices around her, all speaking. It was like she was underwater, the sounds coming out muffled around her as pressure built in her head and cold sweat started at the base of her spine. Pogue growling, Caden echoing him, her own voice asking questions she wouldn't be able to remember tomorrow. There was a lot of rustling, and then, all of a sudden, Micah was gone.

In his place stood a massive lion, growling at everyone as it stalked toward her. Everything inside and around her froze; her brain was momentarily shocked out of the most recent revelation and shock to her system. Every Shifter in the room scooted out of the way, letting him pass. They were clearly wary of him. Pogue adjusted his body to partly shield her from him.

Surprise turned into anticipation—well, more like a good distraction. Grace widened her stance and reached out for him, absentmindedly tapping Pogue's calf to signal him to shift. He surprised her by repositioning himself right beside her instead of in front. Now, he was in a low crouch with an arm outstretched in front of her.

"Grace, stay still," Caden cautioned.

She tilted her head to the side, not understanding.

"Micah isn't really home right now, Grace," Beau added as he shifted his feet a little. Grace was sure that he was preparing to tackle the lion.

Very gently for a big cat, Micah rubbed his massive head on hers, and she tentatively reached for his muzzle.

"Grace," Pogue said calmly, drawing out her name slightly. Grace assumed Micah would listen to his Alpha, but more than one Shifter had told her that Micah's cat was nasty. The cat hissed, baring his teeth at his Alpha, who did the same, though his human teeth were less impressive at the moment. She felt the weight of the lion's head as he put it between her legs and rolled over onto his back. *Big softie.* Cats generally liked her, and she, in turn, loved them back.

She felt almost giddy as she started running her hands over the paws and legs, his neck and face, smiling. She searched for the trigger points in his ears and started massaging them. Sure enough, seconds later, the tell-tell of a happy lion. A lowly moan akin to a purr but not quite rumbled from his throat. Wild lions couldn't purr, and it seemed neither could Shifter ones, Grace discovered.

"Woah..." Caden and Pogue said simultaneously, making her giggle even more.

"Soft kitty, warm kitty, little ball of fur," she began singing. Hannah started chuckling. Soon, the woman was a mess of snorting laughter as she slid to the floor, curled up in a fit of laughter.

"Stop, ohmygod, stop you're killing me!" she chortled.

Grace grinned.

"Happy kitty, sleepy kitty, purr, purr, purr," she continued softly, massaging the cat's ears.

"Love Sheldon," Hannah wheezed as she curled up on the floor, clutching her stomach. Beau gently picked her up, chuckling as he shook his head., while Doc checked on Hannah.

Liam was smirking and looked exceptionally relaxed; his body burrowed into one of the bean bag chairs. He pointed to Micah.

"Grace, Micah's cat is a nasty one, he is! You need to teach me that trick!" Multiple echoes from around the room.

Beau leered;

"Hey, seriously, will you teach me? It'll make life so much easier at home when Oliver's being a brat. Does it work on bears?" Grace nodded, allowing Beau to effectively break the tension in the room.

Pogue glared the man into silence as Caden threw up his hands.

"Right! Ok, Grace, we need to discuss this alone, so Pogue will whisk you off to bed."

The room filled with gentle chuckles as Grace scrunched up her nose and tensed when Pogue effortlessly scooped her up, holding her close. He paused shortly as Micah's low growls grew more distinct. Pogue glanced down at the lion, raising an eyebrow in question.

"You done?" he asked the cat. Micah's jaw tensed briefly before he relaxed and laid his large head back on the soft carpet. Whatever, Grace thought. She was too damn tired to deal with all this shit right now. Grace heard Beaus' dark voice as Pogue turned with her, walking to the door.

"We're really doing this, huh? We're gonna go to bat for the human?"

Grace looked over Pogue's shoulder, letting her cheek lean on it, to see Mehendi taking a deep breath before straightening up against Grayson, her chin defiantly rising as she whispered.

"Cry havoc! And let slip the dogs of war…"

Chapter 16

24 hours later

Morning rolled around too soon after a restless and short night's sleep. Pogue got out of bed, showered, and made it to the office by eight. Of course, Caden, Juno, and Doc were already there. Taruk, on kitchen duty, wheeled in a breakfast cart just as everyone else strolled in. Pogue gratefully accepted his travel mug. Hannah was the last to arrive. Her hair, once again, had changed color and now matched her shirt. He gave her a nod, and she settled in next to Micah, who gave her a high-five without really paying attention, just nursing his coffee. The guy was practically asleep on his feet, his messy hair nearly hiding his eyes as he lounged in the beanbag chair he'd commandeered.

Caden got up and opened the window, knowing Pogue would light up any second as he looked at Micah.

"Wakey, wakey, soft kitty," he snickered. Micah growled and flipped him off, the golden hue of his lion peeping out under his heavy eyelids.

Caden snorted and turned to the group.

"Let's kick things off before our guest wakes up shall we?" A chorus of mumbles and groans filled the room. Caden strolled over and kicked Micah's foot. Micah jolted up, nearly sloshing his coffee all over.

"I'm awake!"

Liam snorted as Juno chuckled.

"Sure, baby. Very..."

Pogue lit his smoke and started pacing slowly.

"Hannah, take it away," he said, waving the cigarette around.

"OK, so magic is definitely attached to her, but it's not a lot," she began. Pogue frowned.

"Dumb it down."

"Right, sorry. All right, as you know, all Wielders are born with a spark—that's what we call our magic, and all Shifters register with a bit of magic, too, right? Well, yesterday I got in touch with my old mentor. She thinks Grace's magic level is on par with having a Wielder or Shifter relative, probably going back to great-grandparents. She will never Wield or grow claws."

"She's already got claws," Pogue snorted and swallowed half the cup's contents. "So where do we go from here? Anything we can use to protect her from DeCoill without endangering the Pride? Tari?"

Their lawyer turned his body away from the Wielder to face Pogue.

"Yes, Alpha. In the many, many minutes, I have had to look through hundreds of years' worth of dusty old files," he glared back at Pogue. "Hannah is right, but I'll have to g-"

Micah cut him off.

"How do we *protect* her?" He was tense and smelt of anxiety and frustration. Given how attached his Beta had grown to the little human, it made sense. Knowing DeCoill would be around soon didn't help. Even Pogue's own cat was furious, and had been since he woke up.

Tari gave Pogue and Caden pointed stares. They simultaneously rolled their eyes as Caden made a zipping motion across his lips to Micah.

"As I was saying before Soft Kitty so rudely interrupted, I have to g-... Euuw!" He touched his cheek where a bun had hit him, leaving a chocolate mark behind.

"Fucking juveniles!" Pogue growled, trying not to smile, motioning Tari to get on with it." Tari grabbed the napkin Juno held out and wiped his cheek.

"I need to get the Academy to officially approve her results, confirming her magic, and then the Council to acknowledge it. If the Council would just agree to go digital, it wouldn't take so fucking long, you know," he scoffed. "I also talked to Summer last night. I mentioned I might have messed up the date on the Pet petition, trying to cover for not filing it ourselves. He confirmed we petitioned two days after we brought Grace home. So, we just need to account for those days, which is simple since she was mostly out of it."

Caden got up and refilled his coffee.

"All right, good job, Tari. In the meantime, we'll teach her to defend herself. Her being a human and all it might be smart. Pogue set her up with symbiotic training.

"I'm thinking, and Doc, correct me if I'm off." - Doc nodded - "Could she handle a quick tour around the Den? Pogue, stick by her as we discussed. It'll be a good gauge for everyone else. Seems like she's got everyone intrigued, and nobody's made any hostile moves yet."

"Try to be nice, Pogue," Micah told him pointedly.

"If you want nice, *you* take her," he grumbled.

Juno stood and walked over, reaching to flick his ear.

"You *will* be nice to that poor girl, Alpha! She's had to deal with a lot, and she's just a baby!"

"I'll keep the growling to a minimum," he quipped with a mock bow. You didn't want to piss off a Maternal shifter. Pogue might be her Alpha, but he knew when to tread lightly.

"How 'bout you bring her to our group meeting this afternoon? She's met most of us already," he suggested, referring to Grace's earlier visits to her bedroom.

"Sure. Just casual chatting?" Pogue inquired.

"Yes. Claus is in charge of grub, and we'll be doing some griping," Liam replied.

"I'll tell her when she's up and dressed. Micah, drop off some clothes for her so I can have mine back. We meet DeCoill at the end of the gravel road after breakfast."

Caden called the meeting to an end, promising to keep everyone in the loop. Pogue went to his own apartment to relax before picking up the human menace, who occupied far too many of his private fantasies.

One problem with that, though... The menace was missing.

Chapter 17

Grace barely slept after Pogue left her last night. The thought of facing the Council left her restless, piling on top of her existing anxiety. Meeting the Council was low on her to-do list today. She wasn't one to usually avoid her problems but in this case... *If they can't find me when the Council arrives, I can't meet them. If I can't meet them, they can't take me. Better the devil you know,* she reasoned. She also knew she'd only have a small window to slip out, likely between Micah leaving and Pogue arriving. Her makeshift hide-and-seek plans were cut short by a knock at her door.

"Come on in." She wrapped a towel around herself.

"Mornin' darlin'." Micah beamed as he entered. He stalked towards her, all masculine grace, a lazy smile on his lips.

"How's my girl doin' today? I got some clothes from Louisa for you. You're about the same size of small." He placed the clothes on the bed and leaned down to affectionately rub his cheek against her hair, a distinctly feline gesture she had grown to adore.

She flopped onto the bed, letting her head hang over the edge.

"Dress me, Cinna," she teased, referring to the stylist in the movie The Hunger Games. Seemed fitting. Micah started coughing, blurting out a string of 'uhms' and no thank yous. Grace looked at him, noticing his eyes avoiding direct contact with her.

He's finding this awkward, she figured, not really taking offense. But still...

"What am I, chopped liver?"

Micah laughed, a slight blush tinting his tanned cheeks. He gently cupped her cheek, the golden eyes of a lion slowly edging in on his usually baby blues.

"No darlin', you're decidedly not. You sure are a very well-put-together lady. But my cat's more likely to tote you around like a cub than claim you, so I reckon you're in the friend zone. I think my cat has sort of adopted you," he stated with care.

Grace couldn't help but grin.

"I'd like that. The friend part, not the being carried around. I think I might have adopted you too anyway," Grace giggled. "I seem to vibe with you, and I've never had a brother. Just Sophie... Oh fuck! Sophie!" Grace started to sit up when Micah gently pushed her back down and bobbed her on the nose.

"I spoke to her again yesterday. We like her," Micah said, referring to both of his halves. "She wants to talk to you, though. She's threatening to come out here. Would she do that?"

Grace didn't even have to think about it.

"Yup. If we don't have an actual conversation, I foresee Miss Sophie grabbing daddy's private plane any day now. Not that she'd know how to get here." Grace mused. Micah turned serious.

"I'm heading out soon. I'll see what I can do about getting you girls some facetime. OK, But in the meantime, let's get you dressed, okay?"

Grace started to sit up, feeling a slight tug in her back. The gash was almost healed, but the skin was still tender, especially when she moved a certain way.

"And before you ask, yes, the underwear is new. I had to guess your cup size, though; sorry if it doesn't fit. I'll get up now and turn around so you can get dressed."

Grace scowled at him.

"And I'll know this how?"

A few moments later, a gentle thud against the door. She chuckled. The hipster string fit just right, but the bra was too big. She was more of a C cup; this felt like a double D. They might not be huge, but if she wasn't being modest, she had fantastic boobs—sitting high and perky.

The thumping stopped.

"Micaaaah," she said in a motherly voice, turning around as she covered her boobs with a sweater. "Are you checking out my A's and B's?"

"Sorry, what?" he said, slightly high-pitched, his head facing the wall though his body was half turned toward her.

"Are you, mister friendzone, looking at my ass and boobs?!" she said mockingly.

Micah coughed, and his whole face turned red. He had the Grace to look utterly disgusted with himself.

"Sorry," he winced. "Friendzone and all, you really are a *very* well-put-together female. And you're not wearing the bra. Why aren't you wearing the bra?" he asked, his voice pitched higher than before. "I'll just go to the corner in shame now, OK?"

Grace's mouth twitched as she responded.

"So, apart from the odds not being forever in my favor cause I have to meet the doomsday squad, what's on the agenda? I can't just pamper you all day," she quipped, not completely truthful. She'd spent countless hours on numerous days tenderly massaging both his human and lion ears. The man would practically do cartwheels for her trigger-point massages. Micah groaned from the corner, thudding his head against the wall once.

Grace announced that she was ready to leave when a knock sounded on the door.

Micah opened it before answering her question.

"Ah, it's your tailor, milady. I'll shoot off to ring Sophie again soon," he said as Hannah strode through the door. In answer to your question, You get to level up on your self-defense skills. And you're not meeting the entire Council today. Just DeCoill." Micah growled a little on that last part, and Grace felt a cold sweat starting up at the base of her spine as Hannah stood before her, eying Grace up and down.

Micah frowned.

"I won't lie, darlin'. DeCoill's not a good man. But we'll keep you safe."

"From your rulers?" Grace asked. Because that seemed to be what the Council was. And they didn't strike her as a democracy. Micah nodded but didn't say anything else. His face said it all, though. *Yeah-na. Hard pass on meeting Mr.*

Coill, she concluded. Hannah took one last look at Grace's clothes and snapped her fingers. Grace felt her clothes move and yelped.

"Stop moving, lady! You're gonna make me lose my focus," Hannah laughed. Grace followed the instructions and marveled as her everyday attire morphed into vibrant red harem pants and a snug green Slytherin tank top. She stared in astonishment at Hannah, who seemed thoroughly pleased with her handiwork. She beamed at Grace.

"Not only do you get to do Symbiotic training. You get to hang out with the Submissives without the broodster hanging around!" Hannah laughed as she tossed three odd-looking protein bars to her. Grace ate as she hummed while swaying her body back and forth. *Skip the meeting, go straight to kick ass, and cuddles. Gotcha!*

Five minutes later, they left, promising her Pogue was on his way. Grace pressed her ear to the door. Another five minutes, she turned the knob carefully. Not locked. So far, so good.

Hiding, Grace was good at. She'd had plenty of practice, and knowing Shifters couldn't track her scent gave her a huge advantage. Micah had mentioned something about her not having one, which had struck her as odd at the time. But honestly, that detail got lost in the shuffle of information. The problem now, was that Grace didn't know the layout of this place. She peeked out and found the hallway empty.

"OK, where to go, where to go..." she mumbled as she snuck out the door. The well-lit hallway had walls hewn from smooth, polished stone. Next to her door, there were two bins. Micah had explained them—yellow for dirty, blue for clean.

Grace quietly moved down the hall, passing a neighboring door. In the large foyer, a grand sandstone staircase loomed to her right. It led to the third-floor office she'd visited. Next to it, massive metal double swing doors emitted sounds of people talking, so that option was out.

"Come on, come on, come on!" she urged herself. To her left was the sturdy, steel-reinforced front door and a dimly lit narrow hallway across from her.

Up. We go up. Grace swiftly crossed the foyer and ascended the stairs. On the second landing, she paused to listen. Silence. She proceeded down a brief hallway to a large wooden door and slipped inside.

"Of course... They have a gym..." The gym resembled a '90s high school setup, except for a conspicuously polished floor with a pole dancer's pole at the far end. Next to it was a huge mirror. Scanning around frantically, she located her hiding spot. Way the fuck up there...

The ceiling was crazy high, obviously for the avian Shifters. Hanging up, there was this odd little woven basket. She had no clue why it was there. But if she could grab onto those wooden supports on the right wall, maybe she could balance on that lower beam and shimmy across. Getting to the stupid beam took longer than she'd prefer. Grace wasn't usually scared of heights. That changed when she realized just how high up she was, and her body protested its soreness. Plus, that damn gash on her back was pulling and itching like crazy.

"Just a little more," she told herself as she reached the end of the beam. "Shit!" she cursed. As she lowered her upper body into the basket, Grace realized it was much smaller than she'd thought. She had to curl up tightly, and it didn't feel particularly stable as it groaned and swayed gently. "Well, here goes nothing," she muttered to herself. Peering down from the edge of the basket, she muttered, "Yeah, that's pretty fucking far."

Pogue

"Human!" Pogue roared as he concluded she was, in fact, not in her room. The fucking menace had disappeared on him! He'd phoned Micah and Hannah, only to learn Grace was with them when they left. Micah was now out canvassing, leaving Pogue to track down his brother and confess he'd misplaced the human. Mother of bad fucking timing...

Locating Caden in the dining hall, where he and Brody sat, strumming their guitars and jotting things down between chords. Caden glanced up as Pogue approached.

"What happened?"

Pogue was seething.

"We have a problem."

Caden tilted his head, a frown forming.

"Where's Grace?"

"That's the fucking problem, Cades!" he snarled. "She's gone, and seeing as she doesn't have a scent I can track, we're shit out of luck!"

Caden shot up. Brody wisely kept his head in the notes and didn't comment, though Pogue could see his lips twitching. How that man could keep his cool with the Council, basically up the entire Prides ass, was a mystery to him. Caden drew in a deep breath, calming himself.

"DeCoill is here in an hour. Micah's looking?"

Pogue nodded, confirming it.

"Hannah, too. We need to fucking find her! The fucking human will end me, and what the fuck is so funny, Brody?!" He looked at Brody, who was trying to focus on the notes. Brody looked up, his dark blue eyes piercing.

"Not a damn thing. But can I make a suggestion without you ripping my head off?" he asked carefully.

Pogue said no, as Caden answered yes. Caden glared at Pogue.

"Accept the help, bro. We need her found!"

Pogue threw up his hands.

"Fine! Talk!"

Brody smiled a little as he answered.

"Maybe find out *why* she's gone. That might tell you if she's running or hiding. If she's hiding, ask the cubs. She's about the same size." He shrugged.

Actually, not a shitty idea, Pogue thought. Brody, despite his hormonal whirlwind, was surprisingly sharp. He motioned for Oliver and Beau to join them. They were sipping coffee at a nearby table.

Oliver was adored by the Pride, but the man was a real piece of work when it came to being a Submissive. He seemed to thrive on getting Dominants riled up. Pogue swiftly filled them in on the situation. Oliver burst into uproarious laughter, so much so that Beau had to shield him with his own body to keep Pogue from slapping his Mate. Sadistic little shit.

"Dude, don't bother getting the cubs. Just get Gray to ask the door." Oliver smirked.

Pogue quickly texted Grayson. Grayson was the front door's caretaker, and the stupid thing responded more to him than any others for some ungodly reason. Yeah, magic was great when it worked. When it didn't? Depending on the day, you have a magical front door with personality and/or attitude.

"If she's not out, she's in." he mused.

"And if she's in, there aren't many places she could have run to. Why is she running?" Oliver asked.

Brody gave Pogue a pointed look. Pogue pinched the bridge of his nose as the reason dawned on him.

"She thinks the Council is gonna kill her. She's not running. She's hiding until DeCoill has been and gone," he concluded.

Brody nodded.

"She wouldn't have gone in here then. Too many Shifters."

"And she can't have gone to the Wielders' hallway. Nigel has it warded to alert him to her presence," Caden said.

What the fuck?

"Why the hell would Nigel do that?" Pogue asked his brother. Caden just shrugged. Technically, Nigel had the right to do it. By law, Wielders could take any precautions they felt necessary for their own safety when staying with a Community. Still, it irked him. He couldn't put his finger on why it bothered him so much. His inner cat was poised for a fight. To be honest, Pogue had never liked Nigel. But he did care about Hannah, and they were a team, so there's that.

A ping on his phone alerted him he'd received a text. He looked.

"The door hasn't let her out."

"So, not with the Wielders, not here, and not in yours or her own room," Brody concluded for them.

"Why the fuck would she be in my room?!" Pogue snarled at the giant bear Shifter.

Oliver grinned as he answered for his Mate.

"Cause she's hot, and you're obviously *sangry*?"

Pogue whipped his head around to face Oliver, who had sidled up against Beau's side, refusing to hide behind him despite Beau's obvious attempt to make him.

"*Sangry?*"

"Like hangry, but with sex," Beau explained, pulling Oliver closer and giving him a peck on the cheek.

"She's a human!" Pogue bristled.

"Methinks thou protest too much," Caden grinned. Pogue reached out to cuff the side of his head. Caden leaned back and out of Pogue's reach. "The office is locked, so that really only leaves-"

"The gym," Pogue concluded, shot up from his chair, and bolted from the room, Oliver, Brody, Beau, and Caden on his heels.

Grace

This was a dumb fucking idea, Grace concluded. The damn basket swayed slightly and started making noises she did not appreciate. The kind of noise wicker baskets make when you put too much in them. And now her legs were all tingly and asleep, so not moving was tricky.

She froze when she heard the door open. *Shit, shit, shit!*

"Come out, Gracie," a voice she recognized as Oliver's sang. She liked Oliver. His level of sadism matched hers, and they were roughly the same size. How on earth he managed to fit, both physically and in personality, with his Mate—who was about four times his size—was beyond her. But whenever she saw them together during their visits, they seemed perfect for each other. Beau seemed to balance out Oliver, and Oliver made Beau laugh. *I will not answer!*

"Human, you will do as you're told!"

Oh yay. The grump is here. She rolled her eyes at Pogue's none-too-gentle coaxing. By the way, Pogue was scanning the area; they had no clue where she was yet. She could just about spot him—rocking a pair of black jeans and a snug dark green T-shirt. He might be the embodiment of anger, but he was seriously easy on the eyes. And the ears, too. He had a damn good voice, she thought, as a triumphant sound came from below.

"Gotcha!" he called, with evident satisfaction as he looked up at her. "Down! Now!" he ordered.

"Uhm, maybe a little less ordering and a little more asking Alpha?" A tall young man with wild brown hair suggested carefully. Brandon? Bray? Brody! Ah, yeah, Brody. Tiger, she remembered. *Sage advice, kitty, but no dice*, she smiled to herself. She looked at Pogue, pointing to the door while looking at Brody. Brody shrugged and quietly left, though he did wave at her. Grace raised a hand and waved back. They all knew where she was, so why not? But no way was she coming down. And not just because she was unable to move now due to sleeping legs. She would not, on pure principle. And it kinda felt like she was up higher than before.

"Come on down, sweetheart. He's not as pissed as he sounds," Oliver tried.

"Lying is a sin," she told him softly.

"Yeah, well, the alternative is telling you he's gonna bite you again," Oliver grinned. *Damn, shifter hearing!* She kept forgetting they had an almost batlike hearing.

"Out!" Pogue ordered Oliver. Beau grinned, slung Oliver onto his back, and left.

"Traitors," she yelled.

The sound of the couple laughing was her only answer.

"You deal with her; I'll go stall," Caden said and left as Pogue stood directly below the basket, his hands on his hips.

The door slammed shortly after.

"Down, Grace!" Pogue called up to her.

"No!"

"Not optional!" he barked.

"Fuck you, Sargent Fluffball!"

She heard him growl and watched as he shook out his arms and took a deep breath.

"Do as you're told and stop pissing me off," he said in a sickeningly sweet voice.

Grace snorted and tried to adjust herself. The basket groaned.

"Stop moving around!" he ordered now.

"You're always pissed off. I'm staying here, thank you very much!"

"Why?" he asked, a little calmer now. "And stop fucking moving!"

"I'm not fucking moving. The damn basket is!" Grace shouted, making it move more. "I'm not letting you hand me over to the Council!"

Grace looked down to see him pinch the bridge of his nose.

"You're acting like a cub." *Am not,* she thought. "Grace?" he prompted when she didn't answer.

"I may or may not, like a rational fucking human being, be a little worried about a Council who rules you furballs human-kidnapping me, yeah?! They can take me away or turn me into a toad or whatever. So sorry if I'm not just all happy-go-lala about it!"

"We're not handing you over," Pogue said. He sounded almost normal, his voice exuding a reassuring authority that Grace couldn't help but find comfort in. Pogue had this aura of power about him, and when she wasn't angry with him, she had to admit, that untamed, raw sense of protector vibe eased something inside her. "But if you don't get down, I'm gonna put you over my fucking knee!" *And there's a different picture,* Grace concluded as her thighs clenched automatically.

"Fuck. You!"

"Right, that's it!"

Grace looked over the basket edge to see Pogue pulling out ropes fastened to a suspended ceiling rail system. She watched in mixed horror and fascination as he pulled himself up by his arms in under five seconds, his biceps bulging as he easily maneuvered up the rope. The look on his face was thunderous as he hung there, directly in front of her. His cat was looking out at her. She liked his cat.

"I'm gonna pull you out of there, and we're gonna go see the fucking Council man, got it?"

Pogue grabbed the side of the basket. Grace tried pushing herself away from him, but the basket was too small, and her legs were still asleep. She yelped as one of the wicker strands snapped as she moved.

"Stop moving, Grace!"

"Well, I'm sorry if my wanting to live is inconvenient for you, mister Alpha sir!" she shouted in his face.

"I will not hand you over to them, dammit. Will you just listen to me?!" Pogue snarled back. "That basket is old as fuck and dry as hell. Stop! Moving! Now!" he ordered sternly.

Grace froze. Yeah, *maybe the old broken basket suspended way up high wasn't the brightest idea I ever had.*

"How do I know you won't let them have me?" she asked, her voice becoming smaller than she'd like. She would never admit how scared she was, but she was tired.

Pogue sighed, adjusted his grip on the rope, and made a loop to stick his foot in. He slowly reached for her. Instinctively, she pushed herself back. Another strand snapped, and she couldn't help the small whimper. Pogue stopped his momentum toward her, holding up his hand, palm out to her.

"Grace, I won't hand you over. Look at me." He ordered more gently. She looked him in the eyes as he repeated himself. "I won't ever let them have you."

Pogue

Pogue felt his cat sit down on its haunches inside him as he said the words. *What the actual fuck?* He could feel his cat's steely determination overruling the man's logic. Shifters didn't have relationships with humans. They didn't claim them as their own. He shook his head sharply, trying to force his cat back down. *She's human, and she's not staying,* he reminded his dumbass feline self. He could almost feel it hissing at him. He couldn't scent fear from her, and it pissed him off. No scent markers. She just smelled like wildflowers to him. But her body language told him she was scared. Her very nice body, he would admit as much. She was fit but shapely, though she was kinda pint-size.

"Grace, are you afraid of heights?" he asked more carefully.

"No." Her electric blue eyes flashed at him, the yellow specs dancing.

Stubborn woman.

"Grace, are you lying?"

Grace looked at him defiantly.

"Well, I wasn't before I climbed up here. And my legs really are asleep," she mumbled.

He raised a brow at her.

"Not your brightest moment, huh?"

"Fuck. You. Pogue!" she snarled.

If it wasn't for the fact that the damn basket was about to fall apart, he'd find this amusing. But it was, and so he didn't.

"You gonna fight me if I reach out and grab you?"

She seemed to think about it, obviously weighing up her options. *Patience*, he reminded himself. He wanted to just haul her out of there. Finally, she shook her head.

"Don't drop me!" she ordered.

He snorted.

"Don't insult my cat. Arms around my neck." She carefully leaned forward and slid her arms around his shoulders. "How asleep are your legs?"

"I'm not sure they can grab on until I shake them out."

Pogue nodded and used an arm to press her tightly against him as he pulled her out. She tightened her arms around him, burying her face in the crook of his neck. *Yup, scared of heights,* he concluded as he felt her body mold itself to his. He breathed through his nose, slow and rhythmically. She'd think he was trying to calm her. In reality, he was trying to ignore the lightning strike of lust that welled up in him the second she was flush against him. He hated that she had this effect on him. *Basic biological instinct. Female equals sex. Nothing more.*

"Ow! Motherfucking pins," she groaned against his neck as they hung there. She weighed nothing to him, and not just because she was slim. Shifters were more robust than humans, and Pogue was an Alpha. He was stronger than most Shifters in his Pride, the bears excluded. They might be klutzes, but you did not want to get pinned by one of them. Grace hissed, and he felt her tense up.

"Hurt?"

"No, it's like a wellness massage on my legs," Grace commented dryly. She moved her lower body around, trying to shake some feeling back into her legs. The motion swiftly woke up a part of him that really needed to stay the fuck asleep right now. *She is human, for fuck's sake! I don't need a human! I need a strong fucking Dominant Shifter. Not that I need a mate at all.* He wanted to slap himself out of his inner monologue. *When did I become so fucking unhinged*, Pogue wondered.

Finally, she wound her legs around his waist. Surprisingly strong legs. They would feel so- *STOP! Dirty socks, peas, hippo shit, mom's spaghetti...*

He descended the rope almost as quickly as he had climbed it, dropping the final two meters. He sat Grace down on the gym floor and stared at her, a hand on her waist to steady her as she swayed slightly, trying to re-establish feeling in her legs. Yeah, that was totally the only reason. If he hadn't been good at reading body language, Pogue wouldn't have noticed the slight twist of her hip, indicating she was about to run. The moment she turned, he grabbed her upper arm.

"Nu-uh!" If looks could kill, he'd be dead. "We're gonna go talk to the Councilman."

No response. He looked down at the small human. She was making a weird motion with her fingers by her hips. It almost looked like she was playing the piano, but her fingers were pointed toward the floor. She touched her index fingers to her thumbs as he looked at them. His cat crouched. Something was wrong. The scent of wildflowers turned into something like rotting flowers. *Wrong! All wrong.* He couldn't figure out what it was, and her eyes looked almost glazed over. *What is this?* Was this related to what Micah had told him earlier? Some kind of trauma response? He leaned down, carefully nipping the tip of her ear to snap her out of it.

Grace jumped. She looked around the gym for a second, panic evident on her face. She then looked up at him and let out a little human growl.

"Ow! Why the fuck did you-" She didn't finish the sentence, instead stepping into him and biting him just below his nipple. Hard. Judging from the blush on her cheeks, she must not have realized where she'd bitten him until it was done. Pogue had to fight the answering growl lingering in his throat, which had nothing to do with her action and much more to do with the reaction it sparked in his body. Pogue swallowed it down and took a deep breath as Grace, her face the shade of a damn tomato, tried to explain.

"You bite me, I'll bite you. And I can't reach your ear. Asshole!"

Smiling despite himself, he bent down, a sense of satisfaction spreading in his chest as she held her breath when his lips were by her ear.

"You don't bite the Alphas' ear, human. One day, the Alpha might bite you back for real," he purred. He might not be able to have her, but the close proximity and a little sensual playfulness seemed to distract her from fear. And that, Pogue, could do. Shifters thrived on touch, but he needed to be very careful here. One wrong step, and he'd be in a rabbit hole that could quite possibly swallow him whole.

Grace finally sucked in a breath and settled her face into a frowned.

"Can't you bring out your cat instead? He's a shit ton easier to be around!"

And here I am, trying to be nice and shit...She wants the cat. Fine. Cat it is, he thought as he shifted where he stood, knowing he'd destroy his nice jeans and new t-shirt. *Fuck it!* Pissing her off was a bonus. Or it would have been, but how she looked at him the second he was in his fur made him stop. *Does she not understand I'm the same person? She must not,* he thought as Grace leaned into his large head and, honest to God, nuzzled him.

"Hey, kitty cat. Your human is a dick." She said into his fur. He rumbled a little, just on principle. "I know you like him, and he's probably not all bad, but you're easier to be around. That's the thing, kitty. Animals don't lie. You, I might trust. I know you know where we have to go, and I'll go with you. But can you please make sure the Council doesn't get me? I haven't got much energy left, and I'd really like to save some brain power for when the police find my stalker," she smiled tightly.

Pogue nuzzled her neck and gently nipped her jaw. He gently closed his jaws around her wrist, pulling lightly to make her follow. He wasn't a complete dick, and he could hear she didn't need to be pushed more. At least not right now. Micah kept reminding him not to, as well.

"I'll follow. You can let go," Grace said, stroking his neck.

So he let go and led her out from the gym, down the stairs, and to the front door. *Oh, for fuck's sake*, he thought when the damn thing wouldn't open.

Because she's wearing gym clothes and no fucking shoes... Of course. Having a front door magically reinforced to the point of having developed something akin to a personality had its bright moments. Right now, however, it was just fucking annoying. Pogue gently butted her with his head until he got her backed up to the staircase and pushed her down to sit with a paw. He huffed at her. She frowned.

"We need to go up?"

He shook his head and tapped the stairs. She seemed to think about it for a beat, then nodded, a smile spreading on her face.

"You want me to stay?" He nodded. "OK."

Yeah, I don't trust that, he thought as he turned and ran back to his apartment. The second he was inside, he shifted and threw on a pair of grey sweatpants and a hoodie, pulling on socks as fast as he could. He grabbed the nearest hoodie for her and slammed his feet into his winter boots, not bothering to lace them up.

When he returned, Juno was standing with Grace, rubbing her shoulder. Grace's head was down, and he could hear Juno consoling her.

"Pogue!" Juno exclaimed as he approached.

Grace looked up just enough for him to see the small smile tugging at the side of her lips. *The little devil!* Juno looked pissed, and Grace was fucking fine! He stopped in front of them, looking at Juno. The woman was only half a head shorter than him and obviously a bear. Broad shoulders, wide hips. Her black hair was impossibly thick and curly. She stroked Grace's shoulder again.

"Why would you threaten her?!"

Great. Mama Bear is out. You did not fuck with the Maternals. They had honed the art of telling people off to perfection. He could almost feel his ears burning, and she hadn't even grabbed them yet.

He planted his hands on his hips. *I am an Alpha! I will not be treated like a fucking juvenile!*

"Juno, I didn't threaten her. The menace is pulling your leg."

Juno gently tipped Grace's face up, and damn it if her eyes weren't red. Had she been crying? No, no, she was acting. He was almost a hundred percent sure. Almost. Grace leaned into Juno.

"It's OK, Juno, really. I'm sure he'll make it quick." She sniffled.

Make it quick?!

"I didn't fucking threaten you, female!"

"You didn't tell her there was a spanking in her future?!" Juno rumbled, her eyes bleeding to near on black- curtesy of her bear. His own answering growl cut her off abruptly, but Juno didn't back down, though she tilted her head to expose her throat. She knew he was more dominant and was doing her best to balance her need to protect a weaker person and still appease her Alpha.

"What? No? I-"

"Alpha, you cannot threaten the human."

Pogue was outraged.

"That is out of context, Juno! I don't have time for this!"

Pogue knew Juno sensed Grace needed support and distraction. He also knew Juno trusted him not to harm a weaker female. It frustrated him that Grace trusted his cat more in this situation. He reminded himself to talk to Grace about not pitting Shifters against each other, especially an Alpha. It wasn't fair to their animals. Juno would need comforting after this, reassuring her bear that everything was okay.

But Juno stepped away from Grace and, like a true mama bear, she grabbed Pogue's ear. He knew better than to tell her off for what she believed was protecting someone weaker. One he knew, she viewed as a baby still.

"You will apologize to her gently and carry her to this meeting so she doesn't freeze her little feet off! And give her something warm to wear!" Juno ordered. Juno was generally a loving, sweet, calm bear. Right now? Not so much.

"Release, Juno," he gently urged. Though his dominance was evident, he kept his gaze low to show he'd comply. Juno released her grip, allowing Pogue to approach Grace. He crouched in front of her, tenderly wiping her cheeks and draping his oversized hoodie around her. Then, Sighing, he tipped her head up, swiftly brushed his lips across hers. When Grace didn't acknowledge his apology, he added.

"That is how Shifters apologize." He then turned to Juno and pulled her into a tight hug, letting his pheromones soothe her animal. He brushed his lips across hers gently.

Juno nodded first to him, then to Grace, before turning around and leaving.

Pogue didn't bother asking before scooping up the human.

"We're gonna talk about manipulating my Pride later, Grace," he informed the lithe bundle in his arms. Pogue looked down at her. "Fucking menace," he muttered under his breath, though he couldn't help the twitching of his lips. She made life interesting. Frustrating but interesting.

Grace said nothing as he carried her out of the Den and started walking down the long gravel road. She winced as he started jogging, making him stop.

"What?" he snarled. DeCoill would probably be waiting, and he, like most of the Council, didn't take kindly to being kept in suspense.

"It hurts my back when you jostle me around like that." She muttered. "And I'm cold."

He put her on her feet and whipped off his own hoodie, swiftly helping her into it before picking her up again.

"Satisfied?"

"Whatever, cuz. Sorry about the thing," Pogue heard her mutter as she burrowed into his chest.

"Acknowledged," he responded. He then set a brisk walking pace down the gravel road.

Chapter 18

G race was snug in Pogue's warm clothes, though her toes were still freezing. Much to her irritation, she couldn't help the dragon-sized butterflies that had taken off in her stomach when he stripped off his hoodie to reveal a tight black t-shirt underneath. Even more annoying, he smelled so damn good, and his five o'clock shadow was annoyingly sexy. Grace knew perfectly well he'd been sarcastic in apologizing, and she knew, he knew she'd been playing him. But his human eyes held something more when he looked into her eyes. Something she wasn't sure what was. Maybe a promise of something more to him than just being a dick. *A gay dick*, her brain reminded her. It just didn't really fit, she thought. She usually had a pretty good gaydar, but maybe it was warped, what with him being a Shifter and all. Oliver, though she hadn't interacted much with him, didn't come off as gay, but she knew he was. Wasn't Pogue dating Brody though? *Maybe he's bi*, she mused before slamming a steel door in front of that thought. *He's an asshole, and we don't like him!* But his eyes were beautiful, not that she'd ever admit it to him. Pale green.

The wind had picked up, but at least no rain or sleet. Not that her feet cared. They were popsicles by now. She'd put up both hoods and drawn them close around her face. The gravel road Pogue had walked down carrying her was long, and they walked for almost ten minutes before arriving. Two Shifters stood in front of

Caden. Caden stood beside a tall, quiet shifter who unnerved her almost as much as Mehendi, the Indian cheetah. She had seen him multiple times, but he seemed to always be in the background, trying to blend in. Not that he could- he was as tall as Pogue and Caden and as broad across the shoulders as Pogue. She couldn't quite place his heritage. Best guess was Middle Eastern, but his short-cropped hair was a muddy brown and not black. He would be attractive if it wasn't for the air of... Well, danger that surrounded him. Grace had a feeling this Shifter wouldn't blink if he took a life. The quiet Shifters eyes took her in, the pale yellow telling her his cat was looking at her. When Pogue stopped, he walked over and closed his hands around her feet, warming them instantly. The shock of the gesture and the surprise of his gentle hands contradicted her initial thoughts of him. Grace smiled at him in gratitude, even as she noticed Pogue roll his eyes and greet his brother and the quiet Shifter. Grayson was his name.

Opposite them stood a thin man with thin blond hair, beady eyes, and a nose that looked like the one witches had in all the stories. Despite the cold, he looked like he was sweating. She couldn't tell what he was wearing, as a thick green cloak was wrapped around him. Not meaning to, she pushed into Pogue, pushing her head under his chin. Grayson kept hold of her feet but stepped closer to her, his side to the Councilman, Grace had decided the new Shifter must be.

"This is Myla DeCoill, Grace," Caden said. "We're just waiting for-"

"Oh, that won't be necessary. I am the Primus, after all," DeCoill cut Caden off, a thin smile appearing on his pale lips.

Grace felt Pogue's' arms tense and noticed Grayson angling his body slightly to partially hide DeCoill's view of her. Caden inclined his head toward DeCoill.

"Even so, we will wait. We don't want to offend the Council by leaving out a member," Caden replied smoothly. "Though I might add if we had known you were bringing a colleague, I would have arranged for shelter from the weather." It didn't take a genius to deduct that Caden just told DeCoill how little he warranted StormEdges hospitality. She liked the Alpha for that, but right now, she only wanted to not be here. Pogue had turned to granite as he held her. She could feel the tension in his muscles, making her more nervous.

DeCoill was about to respond when Grace spotted someone popping into thin air a few meters behind Caden and DeCoill. Hannah had briefly explained how Wielders and Shifters could travel via portals or being.... She couldn't remember the word. *Disportaled?* A tall, slender blond male with long hair and a soft smile quickly approached them. He, too, was wearing a cloak, this one blue. A figure as big as Pogue followed him. Grace wasn't sure, but it almost looked like it floated. She thought it was because she could see black boots under the hooded gray cloak, but she wasn't sure they were actually touching the ground. Something was wrong with the hood. It was wide and deep but not so much that she shouldn't have been able to see the face of what must be a Wielder. Except she couldn't. She averted her gaze to the blond man as he spoke.

"I apologize for my delay. Alphas, Primus." He greeted them with nods and a smile before looking at her. Grace chanced, looking directly at him. He had a nice smile and laugh wrinkles around his eyes. People who laughed tended to not be serial killers. She relaxed a little but kept herself pressed against Pogue. "Greetings, human. My name is Daffid Summer. The ominous-looking chap in the cloak is a Regulator. Worry not, I just need him for a separate meeting afterward." He spoke the words seemingly to Grace, but mentioning the Regulator, his gaze switched to Pogue and then Caden. Grace felt Pogue relax a little. "Have we begun?" Summer asked, looking to DeCoill.

DeCoill's lips thinned, and Grace could see his jaw tightening.

"I don't believe I asked for your presence, Summer."

Summer smiled.

"I received notice my presence was requested. Shall we?"

DeCoill seemed to debate it but shrugged lightly and looked to Caden.

"You have an unsanctioned human on your Pridelands."

Caden quickly took the rolled-up piece of paper Grayson handed to him.

"I believe the Council approved our request to keep a Pet. You'll find everything stamped and approved." He handed the papers to DeCoill, who snatched them from him, quickly reading through them.

"I am the human liaison, and I did *not* approve this and-"

Summer cut him off before he could say whatever he was about to.

"But of course, as Council, we stand by the overall decision. There must have been some miscommunication at the office."

DeCoill snapped his eyes to Summer, looking at him sternly for a minute before plastering an obviously fake smile on his face.

"Yes, of course. I will review the human now. Place her on the ground, Alpha." He ordered Pogue. She held on to Pogue, not wanting that vile man anywhere near her. Pogue sighed and looked at the Councilman.

"She has no shoes."

"I don't care!" DeCoill screeched. "I will see her!"

Pogue gently disentangled Grace's hands and set her on her feet. She hissed when her cold feet touched the frozen ground. Next to her, Grayson started growling, and she instinctively stepped to the side, putting her up against Pogue's' side.

DeCoill evidently didn't take kindly to the growling.

"You will control your Vigilia!"

Caden placed a hand on Grayson's shoulder. *Right, Vigilia. The soldiers,* Grace vaguely remembered being told.

"Apologies, Primus. He is very protective of Submissives."

DeCoill took a step forward, reaching out to Grace. Grace pressed herself to Pogue, grasping his shirt and looking up at him, pleading silently. *You promised you wouldn't let him take me,* she screamed in her head. Something about this Councilman told every fiber in her to run and hide. Pogue, the fucker, just stood there! He just looked at her; his eyes had gone completely cat, the pupils blown, and his hands fisted so hard around her wrists, she was sure she'd bruise. *Keep me safe, my ass.* DeCoill started to pull at her when Grayson grabbed her from Pogue and instantly wrapped an arm around her shoulders, pulling her flush against his broad chest. *He let me go...* For some reason, the fact that Pogue had just allowed Grayson to take her hurt so much more than she thought it would. She barely knew him. The cold sweat started up, and seconds later, she felt the fugue take her under.

Pogue

130

Hunt, catch, kill... His cat was roaring inside Pogue. The second Grace had latched on to him, her eyes pleading, the human part of his brain had almost shut down. Pogue knew attacking a Council member was a death penalty for him and disbandment for the Pride. He couldn't act. But he had promised her he wouldn't let DeCoill take her. All it took was one look at Gray while Caden distracted the Council members with an apology. Although Gray had only been with StormEdge for six years, Pogue knew this Vigilia well enough to know what he would do. Grayson would take the blame and, if need be, run with Grace. Because that was just who he was. When Grayson Reza, six years ago, had told Pogue and Caden he would die for StormEdge, he meant it. And today, he proved it.

DeCoill was livid. Standing silently beside Summer, the Regulator didn't seem to move at all. Floating just above the ground, like a silent shadow. The Council hunting dogs, Oliver likes to call them.

"You will let me see her, or I will take her into custody. I *will* document every human in my region!"

"You don't need to touch to see," Grayson said, keeping his voice neutral.

"Really, there is no need for this to be difficult." Summer cut in. "May I?" He asked, looking at Grace. Much to DeCoill's irritation, apparently, Summer didn't speak to the Shifters. He spoke to her. The scent of rotting flowers reached Pogue's' nose. His head whipped to her. His cat was roaring under his skin, and he felt his claws trying to break through his skin. *Wrong. She's not here. Where is she?* His cat was frantic, though anyone looking wouldn't see a muscle move in his face now. He had learned long ago how to lock down his scent trail, coming across as neutral when, in reality, he was screaming on the inside. Shit! Bad fucking timing menace, Pogue growled inside his head. Summer stepped closer and gently pulled down her hoodie to reveal her whole face.

"Hello, young lady."

Grace looked up at him. Her face was relaxed, and she was smiling softly. A complete U-turn to her behavior mere seconds ago. Thankfully, Summer didn't seem to notice.

"Hi," she said.

Summer didn't seem aggressive, not like the other Councilman.

"May I ask, are you here of your own volition?"

Grace frowned.

"What's a vol-whatchamacallit?" She sounded almost childlike to Pogue.

Caden smirked as he responded.

"Of your own free will."

"Yup. We're gonna have lasagna for dinner, and if I'm good, I get the strawberry ice cream too," Grace beamed at Summer. She then looked to DeCoill. There was something in his eyes she didn't like because she frowned, turned around, and looked up at Gray.

"Up."

To his credit, Grayson didn't bat an eye but swiftly picked her up, allowing her to wind her legs around his waist. Pogue looked at DeCoill. He looked... Hungry was the best word for it. DeCoill smiled wide, his canines elongating slightly. The Regulator floated closer, but to Pogue's surprise, it seemed to move closer to DeCoill. DeCoill didn't need protection. So why, Pogue wondered.

"You have failed to notify within a reasonable timeframe. Yes, you filed and have been granted approval, but gentlemen, we must follow all the rules. You should have notified me the moment she stepped inside the Barrier."

"Tari will gladly go over the semantics with you, DeCoill," Caden said, referring to the Pride lawyer.

DeCoill snorted and wiped his sweaty brow.

"I am the human liaison. I know every rule, Shifter. I wrote most of them, you know. Now, I can take her today, and there will be no consequences, or I will summon you to court to answer for your offense as you've already received notice about." His words were hurried, and he looked like he was fighting to keep his hands from reaching out to grab her. Grayson must have concluded the same thing. He took a step back with Grace.

"She stays," Pogue said, his voice flat. Caden echoed him.

"I'll take note of that," Summer said calmly, taking a step back when Grayson growled again. Summer was a Maternal Shifter, Pogue knew. It made sense that he wouldn't want to upset an anxious, weaker being. DeCoill, as a Dominant, should have wanted to protect her, but Pogue was well aware that there were bad Shifters, just as there were bad humans.

DeCoill snarled at Pogue.

"You have a Challenge coming up. She moves so much as a finger toward a Shifter, I take her in to answer for her crimes under the laws governing Pets. Otherwise, I will see you at your summoning." DeCoill said, as a very much not fake smile spread on his lips.

"Accepted," Pogue responded. "We done?"

DeCoill smiled again. The creeper.

"Summer, take a picture. I will draw a blood sample." Grace whimpered and hid her face in the crook of Grayson's neck.

Caden intercepted him, holding up his hand as he fished another piece of paper from his pocket. This one was on purple paper.

"My Wielder has instructed me to hand this to you. As you will see, the Academy claims any and all things relating to the magic inside her."

"I don't need it for magic. It's a blood sample for DNA testing only," DeCoill snarled and reached out again, only to find his hand grasped by the cloaked figure. DeCoill froze. *Scared of Regulators*, Pogue noted with a not-so-small amount of glee. The figure floated up to Grace, and a slender hand reached out through the cloak. Caden had to place a hand on Grayson's shoulder, keeping him calm. The Regulator barely touched Grace's neck, but it was enough to make her flinch, and Grayson literally snapped his teeth at the hand. Thankfully, the Regulator took no offense- at least not one it was willing to share. It turned to DeCoill, and a voice so neutral, Grace couldn't figure out if it was male or female said,

"I will deliver this to the Academy. They will DNA test it. This decision is final, Primus."

Pogue could tell DeCoill was seething. DeCoill abruptly turned and walked away. Summer looked first to Caden, then Pogue.

"I believe this concludes our meeting. I thank you." He turned to leave but thought better of it and turned back, looking at Pogue. "Might I suggest footwear, young lady?"

"Noted," Pogue grated out. A few seconds later, Summer and DeCoill, along with the Regulator, disappeared as though they had never been there in the first place. The second they were gone, Pogue let go of his composure and damn near ripped Grace from Grayson, holding her tightly to him, bridal style. Grayson grabbed her ice-cold feet, hissing as he guided them under his warm sweater to press against his taut abs.

Caden let out a heavy breath and clamped down a hand on Pogue's shoulder.

"Breathe, bro. Shit, for a second, I was worried you were gonna remove De-Coill's head from his body."

Pogue didn't listen to anything Caden was saying. He bent his head and nipped her ear. It didn't work, save for making Gray growl. He didn't bother to growl back. He put his lips by Grace's ear.

"Come back, Grace."

"That could have gone worse." Caden was telling him, though the words sounded far away.

"Come back, Grace. Now!" Pogue ordered more sternly. Grayson had stopped growling and now just looked at her. Caden must have been stressed because he wasn't catching any of this as he continued.

"We owe Hannah. She caught me at the last minute to hand me that paper-work. She must have suspected the Council would try for a blood sample."

"Why is that bad?" Grace suddenly asked.

Pogue could feel her shaking against him, but the scent of wildflowers was back, the rotten smell receding. He looked down at her, a brow lifted in silent question. He caught the barely there shake of her head. Pogue sighed and nodded just as discretely. He would let it go for now.

Grace didn't speak for the entire walk back, and Pogue didn't press it. Sometimes, you needed a little quiet. Decompress. Just be.

Chapter 19

P ogue pulled himself out of the shower and dried off. Like his wild counterpart, his jaguar liked water. Most days, he would draw a bath, but tonight,
even the shower annoyed his cat. The second he'd dropped Grace off in her room
and texted Mehendi to stand guard, he'd hopped into his large shower stall to
wash off the scent of the little menace. His cat hissed at him the entire time - it
liked her scent on them. He told his cat to put a cork in it.

"We don't need a human in StormEdge. What the hell are we even gonna do
with her here?" he muttered as he pulled on his boxer briefs. He had a little time to
kill, so he opened the door to the only place in his home that looked like Micah's
whole aerie did. Messy. Yes, the aeries were large tree houses, but that didn't mean
one should live like a cub. Not that he'd ever tell Micah that. What the male did
on his own turf was his, and only his business.

Pogue entered his own messy space and sat down on the wooden stool, and
pulled out a fresh piece of paper and a charcoal pen. Doodling always helped him
calm down. He'd been wound too tight since Grace had crash-landed into his life,
fucking everything up. He was fine before! His life had order. It was organized,
categorized, and compartmentalized into neat boxes. Caden was naturally calm,
but Pogue had always needed to instill order for himself- because, unlike his
brother, Pogue was not calm. Of the two, he was the naturally aggressive one.
Now, he went to sleep and woke up restless, tossing and turning throughout the
night. He'd put on one shirt and then stop as he opened the door, turn around,
and change it. Not because it mattered what she thought of his clothing, nope. He
was just indecisive for some reason that had nothing to do with the little human,
he thought as his hand, of its own accord, attacked the paper with a vengeance.

He had to give it to her, though. She had taken to all of this better than he thought she would, and much as he hated to admit it (and never would publicly), he really didn't want to kill her. Much. Maybe bite a little.

"Grow a fucking backbone, Pogue," he told himself as he got up, throwing the pencil down on the drawing. He cursed himself as he recognized the jawline and lips he'd been drawing from three different angles. *Nope! We're not doing this!* Pogue got up and got ready for the Vigilia meeting he was attending before doing the symbiotic training session with the damn human. She would probably take multiple sessions to get the hang of it, he mused, exiting his home, nodding to Mehendi as he turned down the hallway.

"Aherm."

He stopped and looked at Mehendi. Her heritage was Indian, though she was much taller than most he knew of, standing at almost 1.8 meters. She was a good Shifter. Strong and loyal. As a woman, she was attractive to many males he knew.

"What?" he said, annoyed to delay himself.

Mehendi let out a soft chirping noise - her cheetah was laughing at him. Mehendi, like Grayson and, to a lesser extent, Pogue himself, had always carried her cat close to the surface. It was a very playful thing, her cat. Until it got hungry or angry. Mehendi could brawl with the best of them.

"You seem to have forgotten something, Alpha?"

Pogue thought about it. Put laundry in the basket, washed my hands, turned off the coffee machine, rinsed out cup. We're good.

"No?" he asked more than stated.

Mehendi waved a finger, motioning it up and down before him. He looked down. Fuck my life. He nodded sharply and went back inside to put on his pants.

Pogue arrived as the last one there. Caden was relaxing in one of the beanbag chairs, his acoustic guitar resting across his thigh as he plucked the strings, the guitar pick firmly clasped between his teeth. He looked up and smirked as Pogue entered. Pogue went straight for the travel mug waiting for him on the large wooden desk next to Micah, who was leaning against it. Micah, who, Pogue now noted, was smirking too. He turned to the rest of the Vigilia. Grayson was, as usual, leaning up against the wall by the door, twirling his coin between his fingers. The Vigilia were all strong males and females. Loyal members who would defend the Pride with their lives. Pogue loved each and every one of them. Even when they were all looking at him like he'd sprouted a unicorn horn.

"What?" he snarled and took a sip of his coffee, looking around. Henley was chuckling now, and Tari wasn't even looking at Pogue, his blond hair covering what his hands didn't of his face.

"Seriously? What?!" he said, a little more forceful.

Tari held up a finger, got up, and walked out the door. He returned a couple of seconds later with three pairs of jeans. He laid them before Pogue and stepped back to retake his seat.

"Fucking hilarious," he muttered and kicked the jeans. "Don't you have anything else to do? We have a serious situation here!

"Very. Our Alpha is becoming senile," Henley said, his tone serious.

"Or he has run out of pants. It's ok, big guy, I got you." Tari quipped, his lips twitching furiously.

Beau frowned.

"Dude, no way will he fit your clothes. You're closer to Grace's waist size than Pogue's."

"Juveniles," Pogue grumbled. "Cades, get it started," he ordered his twin.

Caden got up, handing his guitar to Micah, who put it back in its case.

"Right. Let's do this. Pogue, you'll borrow my pants until you either get new ones or Doc declares you unfit, and I'll have to cart you up to Mom and Pops for retirement."

Pogue didn't waste a second, closing the distance to his brother and putting him in a headlock.

"I'm not fucking senile!" he roared as he punched Caden in the stomach. Caden returned in kind, landing a solid blow to Pogue's kidneys, freeing himself from the headlock. Yes, we're being this adult right now, Pogue thought as he stomped on his brother's foot, making Caden howl before he pulled Pogue's ear.

They tussled for a few minutes, the Vigilia taking bets on who won this time. Pogue did. Caden groaned as he started the meeting by relaying what had happened during DeCoill's visit.

"So, he's standing by the Summoning?" Beau asked.

Tari answered before anyone else could.

"Not just that. I received the date for it just before I came in. We have to appear on December twenty-sixth."

"The day after we've gone to war?! Can you appeal?" Caden asked, outraged.

Tari shook his head.

"It's the Council. The laws are so outdated I don't even know where to begin. I'm telling you; this is why we need either a new Council or none at all!" he fumed. Tari was adamant the Council would be better if it just weren't there. Pogue agreed with him because there weren't enough Shifters left to warrant a ruling body that refused to change.

Between low birthrate and high mortality rates, Shifterkind's numbers were, declining. True Mates were few and far between, meaning even lower odds of breeding. Shifters could enter a mating agreement, not unlike the human versions of marriage. But, the odds of A. conceiving and B. the female carrying to term and actually surviving giving birth weren't good. The odds were even worse for those who chose to mate with a species not their own. Then, there was the fact that most of the Council's laws were stuck somewhere in the Middle Ages.

Pogue liked simplicity as a general concept and didn't love change. Still, even he admitted that some was needed to keep up with times. StormEdge was cutting edge in more ways than one. Taking in every species, not caring about their sexuality, and allowing, albeit secretly, that some Pride members had a real connection to the human world was a big deal.

"I know, Tari, but we must focus on the here and now. So," Caden sighed, "we'll have to show up. That's a problem more than three months away. We need to start preparing the Pride for a Turf War. We have to decide some parameters for Grace if she's going to stay. I want to touch in on Nadya and Doc too."

Pogue nodded and started talking as he grabbed his cigarettes, lighting one.

"Micah, start planning a training schedule for the Dominants. I want you all in units. One Vigilia member to lead each unit, and then we divide Dominants according to skill. Ideally, Henley, I want you to run a shadow unit. Start looking at who would be best. Pick the ones you feel are best in terms of speed and stealth," Pogue said, looking at their tracker. Henley nodded his agreement.

"I don't want the Submissives fighting. I'm placing Nadya beside the clinic." Grayson said quietly, not looking up. Pogue growled at him, forcing the leopard to look up. Grayson was highly protective of the Submissives, Nadya especially. She was like a kid sister to him, always following him closely, not to mention her being lowest ranked in the Pride, just above the cubs. Grayson looked up, meeting Pogue's eyes. He was fifth in the hierarchy, just below Tari. However, the lawyer held no official rank due to his job as their lawyer.

Pogue huffed.

"Not your call, but I agree." Pogue held his gaze a little longer until Grayson lowered his eyes and tilted his neck the slightest. "Beau, talk to Juno and get all the Maternals assessed in their fighting skills."

Caden took over.

"We need to know exactly what everyone can and cannot do within the next two weeks." From there, we'll begin planning and training, and I'll develop defensive and offensive strategies. Pogue will run three or four smaller scenarios to have a backup plan if we need to deviate from the main ones." Pogue took a long drag on his cigarette as he assessed his Vigilia. Steely determination emanated from all of them.

"Doc is already making up a list of supplies he needs. We'll have to get the finances together. Micah, can you do another run when the Dahlings come through with more gems?" Caden asked. Micah nodded and wrote it down.

"You're all going to have to rotate your extracurriculars. We'll need you to double up on the patrols. We've been lax the past year," Pogue added. "Questions?"

With no one asking questions, Pogue went on to do a status on Nadya and Doc. They were the only Pride members who could walk in both worlds. Nadya's best friend, Brody only accompanied her and remained by her side. He didn't have his own thing in the human world yet, despite Pogue knowing he'd been asking questions for months. Nadya was doing well in school and had a lot of studying from home days thanks to some new human virus, Covid-something.

Doc had recently begun volunteering at an Ontario hospital clinic in order to maintain his medical knowledge and learn more about humans. Doc was a sound healer who insisted on learning everything he could. Humans and Shifters had very similar physiology, according to Doc, but there were clearly some differences Doc wanted to know about.

Next up was the subject of the one person he really didn't want to discuss. He put out one smoke with a new one. Yeah, chain-smoking was a thing today, he accepted as Caden glared at him before asking Micah for his assessment.

"Honestly, she's doing really good. The questions she's asking are very..." Micah bit his lip as he tried to find the right word. "Practical, I guess? I mean, she doesn't seem to care about the larger questions, origin, and all that. It's much more along the lines of, whether it hurts when we change, does a wound inflicted on our animals carry over to our human form and stuff like that," he said, walking to the small minifridge in the back of the room to grab a water bottle. "From what I'm learning, she's had a rough start. She was left in a dumpster as a baby, multiple fosters, uhm, that's humans who take in kids no one wants," he explained when he noticed the confusion in the room. Grayson covered his growl with a cough and motioned for Micah to go on. "It's left her with some pretty psychological scars. I'll let her tell you when she's ready, but if you find her wandering, just call me, and I'll deal with it. Don't try and stop her unless she's in danger. She'll probably interact, but you might find what she does is weird and-"

"She won't wander because Pogue is glued to her," Caden said sternly. "And I need to know more about these mental scars you're talking about. If you can't tell me because you promised her, you're going to have to give me something close enough to whatever it is. Also," Caden fixed a glare at the Beta " we're gonna talk about you not telling your Alphas."

Micah nodded and continued. He knew you didn't keep shit from the Alphas. "Think of it as sleepwalking. Acceptable?"

Pogue looked at Caden, who mulled it over for a beat before nodding. Sleepwalking was acceptable to Pogue, too, and it didn't sound dangerous to the Pride. He motioned for Micah to carry on. "She says she's good with a bow and has agreed to stay and assist Doc during the Turf War. All we have to do is not kill her and help her locate whoever is stalking her in her hometown. I know the bow won't help, but I think the Pride will appreciate her not being completely clawless." Micah uncapped the lid on his water bottle and took a long drag as Henley stood to stretch his legs.

"And how are we going to do that, Micah?" Henley asked, sounding skeptical. With good reason, Pogue thought. They couldn't just set up a camp in the human world. Humans had their own police.

Micah didn't look up as he answered.

"The not killing? Uhm, well, just you know... Don't? Micah said, shrugging. Mehendi cuffed Micah upside the head from where she was leaning against Gray. Micah shifted his gaze to her before giving Henley a more serious response. "Honestly? I'm hoping she doesn't want to return. I think having her here is healthy for the Pride."

"How the fuck can that human be healthy for anyone here?" Pogue asked, outraged enough that he started coughing as the smoke went down the wrong pipe. Henley grabbed Micah's bottle, uncapped it and handed it to Pogue.

Micah shot him an annoyed look and slammed his hands in his pockets.

"She's gonna teach us a lot. You just have to give her a chance. And stop threatening her all the time."

"I did not threaten her!" Pogue felt his jaw tighten so hard he was surprised he hadn't broken a tooth. He knew Caden and he had told the Vigilia that the office was neutral ground and everyone could speak how they wanted. But damn if he didn't wish his subordinates would act the part right now. This human made him feel less in control than he ever had, and he did. Not. Like. It!

"I heard Lucy saying you'd told her you were gonna rip her arms off," Beau commented.

What?! Pogue turned to the giant bear Shifter.

"No!"

"You didn't tell her you would smother her in her sleep after you put her over your knee?" Henley asked, his tone light. Clearly, he was pulling his leg.

"I didn't fucking threaten her! What the fuck is wrong with you?!" Pogue roared.

Caden smirked, pouring himself another cup of coffee, answering while handing Henley a spoon to stir his tea.

"Rumor mill at work. You have been a lot more tense since she got here. She seems to be quite adept at pushing your...." Caden trailed, smiling wide.

"Buttons! Yeah, she fucking does. She doesn't belong here! We're heading into a fucking war! It's dangerous and... Well, she... And she's fucking insolent!" he ranted. Micah set his jaw. The Beta could be as stubborn as a mule when he set his mind to it. But so could Pogue.

Micah lifted his chin, saying,

"She will be an asset. She's agreed to help Doc. And Soph works for a major security firm her dad owns. She can get her hands on some things we can use." He said, making air quotations as he spoke. "And she says she'll be happy to send over things for Grace too!"

Pogue smiled in spite of himself. The Beta just turned the fire on himself.

"Who's Soph, Micah?"

Micah blushed and stood up, returning to the fridge and taking the empty one from Pogue to place in the reuse box. He grabbed a new bottle and uncapped it, taking slow gulps.

"That bottle will run dry at some point, Beta," Caden smirked. Micah rolled his eyes and gave up. He threw his hand up and answered.

"Sophie is Grace's best friend. I keep her updated. She thinks Grace crashed near the wildlife sanctuary. Grace says she's a stubborn female and that she'll come looking if she doesn't get to talk to Grace soon. I believe her. Look, I vouched in every way for Grace. If you won't trust her, trust me. Pogue, I know she pisses you off, but I'm telling you, just let her have a little longer rein, and you'll see a different Grace. She doesn't react well to feeling trapped and controlled.

"She *is* trapped and controlled. Mostly." Pogue muttered as he put out the cigarette and closed the window.

Beau shrugged.

"What harm can she really do? Oliver likes her, and he's usually pretty reserved around new people," That was true. Oliver, Beau's mate, did not trust easily.

"He would. Their aggression levels match," Henley smiled, crossing his legs. Beau tossed a sugar cube at him. Henley caught it and returned it so fast it caught Beau on the forehead. The large bear shifter ran his fingers over the small mark, scowling at Henley, who just smirked at him.

Caden looked pointedly at Pogue.

"Loosen the reins a little bro. Take her to the Submissives meeting after training so she can socialize. See how it goes, yeah?" They glared at each other for almost a full minute before Pogue finally rolled his eyes.

"Postpone the Submissives meeting until tomorrow, and I'll take her out and show her around today, but first symbiotic training." Pogue nodded to his brother.

Caden stood up.

"Mhm, you show her, Pogue."

Chapter 20

"**W**hy are we doing this again?" Pogue asked as he and Caden climbed the stairs to the second-floor gym after having changed in his lair. He'd put on a pair of worn kickboxer shorts and a tank, knowing they'd be working out for hours. Caden rolled his eyes and hitched up the equipment bag.

"Because, Pogue, for the third time, we need her to be able to defend herself on a basic level. What if she gets into a brawl? Her temper is as loose as yours these days, and she doesn't have the claws to back it up."

Pogue nodded. Logically, it made sense. He didn't know if it was the fact that they had to spend the time teaching her that pissed him off or the fact that his cat got pissy when they thought about Grace having to defend herself.

Grace and Hannah were already in the gym when they arrived. Hannah wore pants that looked like a skirt and a green top with a black snake. Grace was in a pair of harem yoga pants and a tank top. Her red hair was gathered in a braid over her shoulder, the burnt ends sticking out everywhere. She frowned as soon as she saw him. His cat huffed a little. It wasn't the reaction it wanted. He told it to shut up.

"So, what is it we're going to do again?" Grace asked, scrunching up her nose.

Hannah grinned at her.

"Symbiotic training. I feel like we've had this conversation ten times, Grace," Hannah grinned.

"And we're doing that why?" Grace asked, her lips set in a tight line.

"Because yoga won't help you defend against a wolf," Caden said solemnly as they approached the women.

Grace stuck out her tongue at him.

"And my bow is what? A stick for fetch?!" She huffed and glared at Pogue. He stared right back at her as she switched her focus to Cades. "What's *he* gonna do? Teach me to glare someone into submission?" Caden beamed as he grabbed Pogue's arm and pushed him in front of Grace.

"Meet your instructor," Pogue grumbled at Caden like an unwilling cub getting punished, then turned to Grace, who sighed and rolled her eyes.

"I'm gonna die after all."

Pogue turned to Caden, pinching the bridge of his nose.

"*Why* can't you do it, Cades?"

Caden and Hannah answered in unison.

"You're the knife guy."

Grace

"Alright, kids, let's get this party started. Look, Grace, time is short. Symbiotic training teaches your muscles movements that your brain would take years to learn. It does it in a couple of sessions instead of twenty years. You're basically going to suck out some of Pogue's," Hannah paused long enough for Grace to kick her shin.

"Knowledge," she sniggered. Grace hoped the warmth she felt in her cheeks didn't show on her face. It pissed her off to no end that her body didn't understand how much of an asshole Pogue was. The chauvinistic and overbearing male who thought his word was law. Well, technically, it sort of was here, but still. *But he smells so good*, her brain started. *Still an asshat, and we don't like him. Not even a little. Not even at all*, she thought as her eyes roamed his large body. *Does he have to show off his arms?* And she could damn near count his abs through the fabric of his sleeveless t-shirt. *His very gay abs. And arms. And everything else*, she reminded herself, feeling not just a little dumb for thinking about him that way. *How desperate are you, Grace?* She asked herself internally. Granted, it had been... *Oh my god, it's been almost a year. Urgh.*

Caden coughed and motioned to Pogue, shocking Grace out of her thoughts and dragging her eyes away from Pogue.

"Let's measure you up, big guy," Caden said. Pogue sighed and walked around to stand behind Grace. It took only a second for everyone to realize that the height difference was too big for whatever this was, and Hannah went to get something called a wobbler. It turned out to be a metal stick with a saddle seat. She pushed it into a small metal cover on the gym floor and locked it in with a pin. Pogue sat down and put it to the test. As he moved his legs and hips, it rotated.

He motioned for her to step into the V between his thighs so they could adjust. She did as he asked, feeling her spine stiffen up as she felt the heat of him behind her.

"Ok, next part is gonna feel a little odd, but trust Pogue on this, Grace. He knows what he's doing. He's been teaching the submissives like this, too." Hannah said sternly, though Grace could see she was trying not to smile. "Lean into him and hold out your arms. Pogue will be placing his arms and hands on the outside of yours." Hannah frowned and pointed at Pogue. "Pogue, you need to be a little lower. Damn, Grace, you're pint-sized," she grinned.

Caden adjusted the seat slightly lower, and Pogue grumbled. Pogue shifted his larger hands to align his fingers with Grace's smaller ones. They tightened the swivel chair again when he could rest his chin on her shoulder. Grace winced as small yellow ribbons snaked around her arm, tying it to Pogue's in several places, down to their fingers. Caden frowned and stepped around Pogue.

"Grace, can you tilt your hips back more? You're not flush." Pogue tensed before taking a slow breath as more yellow ribbons wrapped around their torsos. His chest vibrated slightly, and she wondered for a split second if he could purr like Grayson had earlier. If looks could dismember, Caden would be missing the hands he was using to gently coax her hips and stomach back until she was plastered to Pogue.

"Yeah-na, don't like this," Grace mumbled. She tried to move, only to find Pogue's more muscular arms holding her in place. She slowly felt her strength ebb, probably compliments of the ribbons, making her panic rise.

"Guys, I'm not sure I can do this. This is not comfortable! Nope!"

"Blindfold her," Pogue ordered calmly behind her. Grace tried to turn her head to his.

"The fuck you are, kink meister! I can't fight what I can't see, dipshit!"

Caden chuckled as he answered.

"It's not a bad idea, Grace. You're all...." He waved a hand around. "What did Micah call it. You're all Predator right now. You'll try to be in charge as long as you can see. This only works if you relax and let Pogue steer. Trust him; he's *good* at this. You'll know it's taking when your muscles start anticipating the moves."

"How the fuck am I gonna know that?!"

"When you stop fighting me," Pogue said simply.

But if I can't see, I'll have to feel. Really don't wanna go there, she whined internally. Caden held out two curved knives the size of her underarm. Pogue took a deep breath as he reached for them, forcing Grace to grab them as he controlled her hands now. *I can't do this... Not like this, I can't,* Grace concluded.

"Fine! Fucking blindfold me, but if this is some kind of sick joke, I will fuck you up and-"

"Yes, yes, entrails, extrails, and a world of owies," Hannah muttered as another yellow ribbon blinded a cursing Grace. "Do some breathing exercises first, maybe, Pogue?"

He just grumbled. Footsteps soon told her they were leaving. She heard the doors slam not long after.

"Pogue?" she asked tentatively.

"Breathe, Grace. The others just left. Match your breathing to mine," he said, starting a deep breathing exercise she recognized from flow yoga. She felt a shift in him as he seemed to put away his dislike for her and become a teacher.

So, Grace tried to match her breathing and follow his. Except she was having real trouble matching anything right now. Her stomach tightened, and all she could think about was his larger body encasing her and his skin touching hers. After a minute, Pogue gently placed her hand—and his larger one—just under her breasts.

"Focus, Grace," he whispered just before his teeth nipped the top of her ear.

I am fucking focusing! Just not on breathing, she screamed internally. Another minute, and he nipped her ear again, like the feline he was.

"I fucking swear if you keep biting me-"

"You're not focusing. Lean back properly and breathe.".

Grace knew if she could just try a little harder and not focus on the granite-like muscles encasing her, this would help her. *This is just another lesson, another weapon in your arsenal*, she reminded herself as she leaned into him and focused on matching her breathing to his. Pogue began moving her hands, then her arms, in a well-practiced sequence of movements. He moved her slowly.

"Stop fighting me, Grace." She heard his voice by her ear and felt his lips against her skin.

It took her ten more minutes to actually relax into him and allow him to take complete control. As much as she hated the thought, actually doing it wasn't as bad as she thought.

Slowly, Grace got used to him controlling her arms and just following him as time passed by, and she got lost in it all. He moved faster and with more body movement, tilting her to the sides and back and forth as he shifted her in various sequences. Somehow, at some point, the grumpy Shifter had managed to relax her body and mind more than she had been in the past year. She found herself smiling and having fun.

Somewhere in the fun, a part of her she'd been trying to deny woke up the hell up, too. The smell of Pogue's' skin embedded into her pores and the feel of his chest made her think of how that same broad chest would move in a more intimate situation. Heat pooled in her stomach, and she felt his thigs tighten on the outside of hers. In response to her? She could feel his nose by her ear as he mumbled, and damn it if his voice didn't make all kinds of sexy thoughts appear in her now rapidly evolving fantasy. One where Pogue wasn't gay or bi or whatever, and she wasn't broken, and he just wanted her the same way she wanted him right now. Oh yeah, and he didn't have a fucking boyfriend...

"There you are. Good girl." Pogue's voice rasped by her ear, his nose tracing the shell as he breathed in.

Did he know how damp her panties were right now? Grace stiffened as she felt him move back, creating a sliver of space between their hips.

"Huh?" she exhaled softly.

"Wildflowers Grace. Fucking wildflowers" He nipped her ear again when her breathing hitched. Her ears had never been this sensitive. *Well, they sure as hell are now*, she concluded.

Pogue abruptly stopped as the doors opened, and Hannah walked in with Henley in tow. She hadn't spoken much to the fox shifter with the dark blue eyes, but she had the impression that he wasn't much of a talker. He was pretty attractive in a Sean Connery kind of way. He appeared to be in his thirties. He nodded to her, shaking his straight black hair out of his eyes.

"Hey, guys. Good to see you're both alive." Hannah smirked. They both flipped her off simultaneously, making Henley's lips twitch. "Ok, so I talked to Caden, Pogue, you're too big for her to do the body symbiotic. Henley volunteered. Caden wants to talk to you anyway," Hannah motioned to the door. Like the feline he was, Pogue silently padded out without saying a word.

Henley turned out to be highly skilled in martial arts, though what he was teaching her now was basic self-defense. He was also similar in size to her. They went through the motions again, but this time with less anger and nervous- and definitely less turned on. Grace discovered that Henley was easy to follow, and soon Peter was squealing with delight as she flipped, jumped, spun, and kicked around the entire gym, laughing. Henley didn't say a word, but she could feel his smile as he whirled her through routine after routine.

Chapter 21

24 hours later

Grace woke up feeling sore as hell and welcomed Grayson not long after. He didn't speak much as he loosened her muscles, and she was still trying to wake up. An hour later, she felt loose and limber again and would forever be grateful for Grayson and his hands. He escorted her to breakfast when she was dressed. She'd put on the clothes Pogue had left, not bothering to ask Grayson why he frowned when he looked at her as he led her down to the dining hall.

Nadya joined them shortly, with Beau and Oliver in tow. Oliver, a savior among gods, handed her a steaming cup of coffee, just how she liked it. Grace wolfed down her breakfast, glancing up as Pogue gestured from the dais. He didn't need to say a word; she knew to follow." Shit, it's time already?" Oliver asked Pogue. He grunted. Grace watched as Beau clasped Oliver's nape and hauled him in for a long kiss, smiling the whole time.

"Be good, babe," Beau teased with a faux stern look as Oliver stood up. Oliver shot him a smirk and ruffled Beau's newly dyed hair. It was now a bold black with vibrant purple tips." But you like me so much better when I'm not." Pogue rumbled again. Nadya stood, smiling as Oliver and Grace rolled their eyes at the Alpha. As they approached the front door, Pogue halted her. It had been slightly open, but it slammed shut just as she moved towards it. It nearly hit Nadya, who jumped back with a frown, giving the door the stink eye.

"No shoes," Pogue said before lifting her in his arms. He moved towards the door, but it refused to budge. With a puzzled expression, he gave it a light kick. Then, he gently set her down, heaving the mother of all sighs.

"No jacket," he stated as his brows knitted together.

150

"Yeah-nah. Still don't have that. Can Sophie send me clothes soon? Shoes, specifically, would be a real treat. Just sayin'." Grace wiggled her toes, feeling a little dumb. Pogue grunted but didn't answer her question. Seconds later, a warm knit sweater was pushed into her arms. She looked up to see Pogue without his. It took her brain a few seconds to form a coherent thought and force her eyes up toward his eyes and not his pecs. *I think I wanna lick that*, brain commented. She told it to shut up. The man was mean, not to mention batting for the other team. *Get a fucking grip*, Grace, she chided herself as her mouth opened to ask.

"Won't you be cold?"

"He runs hot," Oliver commented from behind them. *Dammit! You knew that, dummy!* Pogue must have caught her looking at Pogue, judging from the smirk on his damn face.

As people spilled out of the dining hall, a few whistles echoed in the large foyer toward the front door. Pogue grumbled and gestured toward Brody, who entered with a mischievous grin, wagging his brows playfully. One look from Pogue, though, and he turned on his heel, hands up, and walked back where he came from.

Pogue crossed his arms over his chest, impatiently tapping his index finger, signaling her to hurry up. She hadn't realized the sweater had yet to magically go from dangling in her hand to covering her body. When it was on and drowning her, he easily lifted her again and went off to the group meeting. Oliver and Nadya ran ahead of them, talking as they jogged. Pogue walked in slow, calculated strides.

Grace's face lit up with a wide grin as the cool breeze tousled her hair and brought with it a delightful surprise - snow! She couldn't help but feel a childlike wonder and joy. Snow was a rare sight she'd only experienced a few times. After all, Wellington was known more for its blustery winds than winter flurries.

"Pogue, will you stop for a minute?" she asked, tapping his shoulder with her palm. *Be nice.* To her surprise, he complied. She stuck her tongue out to catch the snowflakes. She was almost sure; she felt his chest vibrate with silent laughter.

"The fuck are you doing?"

She tilted her head to look at him. Sure enough, a smile was tugging at his lips.

"If I ask you to do something, will you please just do it, even if it's silly? Then I'll never ask for anything else, and I might even try to be less of a pain in your ass," she tried her best innocent smile.

"What?" He deadpanned, suspicion in his voice.

"Will you spin me around? Like they do it in the movies. Seems like the thing to do in the snow," She shrugged lightly.

"Seriously?"

Grace tried to give him puppy dog eyes, but the snowflakes kept making her eyes blink. And then she was spinning. Slowly, Pogue spun them around as she caught snowflakes with her tongue, her arms up. For a moment, just a little moment, she let go of where she was, her whole messed up life and everything in between, and just let herself feel free.

"Woohoooo," she laughed.

Three times, then four, then five, and six. Then she heard a sound she knew she recognized but couldn't quite place. Pogue came to an abrupt halt, his gaze fixed on a guy in his mid-twenties, decked out in what could only be described as the fluffiest snow suit in the world. He resembled a marshmallow in that ankle-length, puffy thing. The guy flashed a wide grin and deftly stashed a Polaroid camera back into his backpack.

"Fuck off, Sulis!" Pogue muttered and started walking, shattering the moment. Sulis followed them.

Pogue excused himself when they arrived at a small wooden log house, having reintroduced her to Claus, one of the cooks. Claus led her into what appeared to be a single large room. A small kitchenette was in the far corner, and mismatched sofas and chairs were scattered around the space. Large leafy plants covered nearly one entire wall, and there were a couple of sewing tables. The ones that could have their height adjusted. The Submissives had formed a semicircle by dragging some sofas together.

Claus settled her into a cozy chair, draping a warm blanket around her shoulders and tucking another around her feet. He flashed her a friendly smile. He then reintroduced her and mentioned that the meeting was a casual get-together. The Pride's Submissives gathered weekly to catch up and chat about whatever was on their minds. It was like a gossip session for the eleven Submissives in the Pride. So Grace simply sat back, observed, and listened. She watched every little detail: Lucy's fidgeting, Brody absentmindedly playing with her ponytail to soothe her, Sulis's reaction to the hot tea, and Ava's quick response with an ice cube, even though he hadn't requested it. They were like a small, tightly-knit family within a larger, more protective one. Yota and her Mate Luna snuggled close, leaning on Magnus, a large tiger, while they discussed the latest updates from other Communities. It felt... homely.

Oliver was like everyone's very snarky kid brother, and she really liked him. Maybe it was because they seemed to share the same sadistic humor. He had coaxed Grace into a trigger point massage in less than five minutes.

"So, Grace, apart from almost dying and being injured, how are you doing?" Liam asked her as he reached for a cookie.

"Thanks, cuz. I'm..." Grace thought about it for a bit. "I think I'm ok. Honestly, it feels like I stepped into a very aggressive version of Harry Potter and the Furries," she shrugged. "Apart from Pogue, most of you seem nice, and.." She took a breath. "I guess... Look, I know it's not like anyone chose to have me here, but I really do want to help. I do. You seem like this effortless family. You have no idea how attractive that is to someone like me." Grace felt a bit deflated, realizing that she, yet again, was on the wrong side of the window, looking in on something that looked really nice. Suddenly, the blankets didn't feel so warm anymore.

Nadya, who sat beside her on the three-seat sofa, gently touched her shoulder.

"I know some of the people aren't lovebugs, but please don't feel like you're not welcome." The group nodded sincerely as Brody gently ran his hand over Grace's hair before bending down to nuzzle her neck. She let him. She repeated to herself what had become a mantra: win the Pride, win the Alphas.

"And Pogue can be a little... Well, grouchy," Githa, the youngest Submissive in the Pride, said with a twinkle in her eye. Githa was as quick as a whip and didn't take crap from anyone - and she was still a cub at age sixteen. Githa had explained during one of her many bedside visits that knowing her wolf was cared for and protected made it happy. She was helping roster everyone in the kitchen and loved it. She had emphasized that she was no less valuable than a Vigilia member. She just didn't need to whip her claws out at every turn to prove it.

"You are *more* than welcome here," Brody flashed her a wolfish grin, causing Claus to cuff the back of his head as he wrinkled his nose. Brody glared at him and tried to fix his hair as he sheepishly grinned at her. "Sorry, my cat is... I guess, in human terms, I'd be a teenager. A little hormonal."

Sulis, who had emerged from his marshmallow suit as a small, pudgy man, snorted.

"Dude, you're in fight-or-fuck mode. Own that shit."

"Cool vintage you got there, cuz," Grace nodded to the camera.

Sulis tilted his head.

"Vintage?"

"Yeah, they were all the rage in the eighties, before digital won and camera phones," Grace said offhandedly. Sulis kept staring at her, still confused. Grace took pity on him. "I'll give you my old one if I can convince the Alphas to let my best friend send it here. It's digital. Takes better photos."

That seemed to make him smile.

"Yeah, from what Micah is saying, our technology is kind of outdated, right?"

Grace nodded as a question popped into her head.

"Hey, what's a Pet? Pogue said I'm a Pet here, but his grunts and snark didn't come with an actual explanation."

Grace noticed how they all looked to Liam. *So, he's the strongest Submissive,* she concluded, as Liam leaned forward to answer, resting his elbows on his knees.

Liam stood out among the Shifters for his shorter stature. She knew he was mated to Claus, who resembled a Viking with his tall frame, short blond hair, and piercing blue eyes that complemented his fair complexion.

"Grace, we do *not*—and I mean that - subscribe to the traditional ways of owning a pet. Crudely put, a Pet is a human slave." He held up a hand when she moved to speak. "In your case, it's purely a case of paperwork and technicalities. Pogue and Caden have made it clear from the start that anyone with that backwoods mindset does not belong in StormEdge. As I see it, you're an opportunity for us to learn and grow. I'm hoping you'll use us much the same way. When you're not working your way through the waitlist for massages, that is," he grinned.

He elaborated, probably seeing Grace's confusion. He mentioned that word had spread quickly about her talent for animal massages. He recalled her work on Micah, in which she described her specialized training in feline trigger point massages. Her goal was to provide cats with gentle, stress-free handling, so she studied every technique that could help them.

It seemed Grace would have to learn about wolves, foxes, and bears too, she mused. Maybe then they'd let her stay. *Do I want to stay?* She wondered as Brody shrugged and got up to grab some coffee from the kitchenette.

Nadya still sounded worried as she stroked Grace's hair.

"Anything we can do to help you feel welcome? To help you understand us, maybe? Maybe Lucy can fix your hair? She's really good at it."

Lucy jumped at the opportunity. Lucy would be a heartbreaker if she wasn't already. She was a true beauty, with her flowing brown hair and captivating hazel eyes framed by enviable lashes. As Lucy ran her fingers through Grace's hair, it was clear that she was endowed with natural Grace and charm. Lucy was a lioness, and as Micah had predicted, she would transition soon.

"I was thinking just do some layers and hide the clumps missing... And the burnt ends," Lucy winced a little as she said it.

"Yeah, if you want." Grace shrugged. *First world problems, Grace, jeesh,* her brain retorted. But getting her hair done would do a lot for her self-esteem, and besides, it was their suggestion, not hers. While Lucy was cutting, Grace found herself chewing on her lower lip, sorting through the slew of questions she had and somehow prioritizing them. One thing that irritated her was her lack of understanding of Shifter social interaction. She had tried to soak up as much information as possible, but some things didn't make sense.

She'd noticed a clear hierarchy in terms of who interacted with whom, which was frequently guided by scent. Discreet head rubs were exchanged among the Pridemembers, whom she suspected were cats. The Maternals, similar to parents, were affectionate but mostly to the Submissives. The Submissives, on the other hand, appeared to enjoy any type of physical contact. The Vigilia seemed extremely picky but didn't deny anyone comfort. They just seemed to wait for the Maternals to come to them, rather than approach.

And then there were the Alphas. Occasionally, a Pride member would come up to them and stand there until they pulled them into a hug, clasped their nape, or even gave them a light peck on the cheek or lips. It looked intimate; she recalled Brody and Pogue's interaction. *Hmm, maybe Brody isn't Pogue's boyfriend?* She noticed how every touch seemed to precede or follow them, scenting the air. They sensed each other so differently than humans. Grace was particularly intrigued by one thing. In a conversation with Micah at her bedside, he mentioned a play drill they were planning. It involved everyone in the room closing their eyes. Then, someone would enter, walk up to one of the shifters, and allow them to run their fingers down their face. It seemed like a very gentle, almost fleeting touch. Surprisingly, from this brief contact and a subtle scenting of the air, they could tell exactly who was in front of them. Nifty skill to have.

Grace craved some of those abilities, not just scenting and feeling things. She wanted to soak up this new world and absorb its knowledge. It might just make everything a little easier to cope with. Much to her surprise, Grace realized that she genuinely wanted to make things easier. She wanted to go deeper into this world where tangible actions backed up protective words. A world where hanging out with pumas, tigers, and humans seemed like the most natural thing.

After thirty minutes and copious amounts of talk and laughter, Lucy pronounced her done and pretty. Grace thanked her, finally having worked up the courage to ask her about it.

"I can't see you like you see each other. Social cues are hard for me around humans, but it is extra hard here," she admitted, slightly embarrassed. "And I really fucking wish I could do the scent touch thing. Waking up in the middle of the night and knowing who's hovering in front of my face would be nice, you know?"

Liam frowned and looked at her.

"Someone is hovering by your bed? While you sleep?"

Grace thought back to Pogue's glowing eyes. *Yeah, better not mention the nighttime wakeup call,* she decided and shook her head, dismissing the subject as nicely as she could. Thankfully, oblivious to Liam's continued frowning, Sulis clapped his hands and distracted them all.

"But you can! I think, at least. You have a little magic in you, so it might work even though you're not a Shifter!" Sulis said excitedly. "We can show you how we imprint, how we--" he waved his hand around, unsure how to explain when Brody elaborated,

"It's like you take in the essence of your Pridemate. Basically, means you own their scent. They get imprinted in your brain, kinda. Also, it's a great excuse to feel up people," he leered, making her laugh.

"*Can* I learn that, though? I barely have any magic in me, from what Hannah says."

"Of course you can! Even humans without magic can, "Sulis snorted.

Claus nodded and took a swig of coffee before pulling Liam's feet onto his lap.

"Humans who are born without sight or lose it early do something similar to it. Touching a face, using specific points of reference, paints an internal picture for them."

"Huh, didn't know that," Grace commented. "How do you know? I thought you guys didn't really interact with the human world?"

"Most of us don't. We're not allowed, by Council law. But our Alphas are more..." he bobbed his head from side to side.

"Forward-thinking," Liam supplied. Claus squeezed his foot in thanks and looked back to Grace.

"Yes. I do volunteer work at a school for disabled kids. It's just an hour a week, but it gives me purpose. The point is that you can learn." He looked at Liam pointedly. Liam raised a brow in question at his mate. Claus continued, "By the way, don't you have something to say, Liam? As the Submissives' representative?"

Liam facepalmed.

"Oh my god, I'm so sorry. I don't know where my head is today."

"Still in bed," Claus mumbled, his lips twitching. Liam smirked and turned his attention to Grace.

"The Submissives are, as a group, vouching for you. I'm telling the Alphas today."

Grace was stunned and confused at the same time.

"Thank you? But, uhm… Why?" she asked, unsure what a group vouching meant. Brody grabbed her and wrapped her in a hug.

"Submissives, well at least us," Brody gestured around the room to the group, "we just kinda know. I can't really explain it. But we wanna keep you. Honestly, I think, for me at least, I like how you don't just take shit lying down, and though I'm never gonna admit it to his face, I like that you fluster our Alpha," he grinned. "Vouching means we, as a group, will do what Micah is doing for you now. We will put ourselves on the line. Now do me first," Brody demanded as though he hadn't just blown up her whole world in the best possible way.

They want me here. But do they really? A small voice in the back of her mind questioned. Claus playfully cuffed the back of his head once again while Nadya did the same. Grace couldn't help but burst out laughing. This, right here, was exactly what she'd been searching for. Micah had asked her to stay, and now the Submissives were saying the same thing. They wanted her here. There was a potential future to be built. It was overwhelming, but it felt so good. Now, if she could just win over the Vigilia, Dominants, and Maternals. And the Alphas. The gods damned Alphas. Caden, she wasn't as concerned about. That man seemed to roll with it like it was his job. Which it kinda was. But Grace wondered… She shouldn't even think about it, let alone ask. Her mouth, of course, hadn't adapted a filter.

"Do you think I could try the imprinting thing with Pogue?" she asked, hoping they wouldn't see through her. She had this ridiculous need to touch him, and she had no idea where it came from or how to get rid of it.

Nadya looked apprehensive and leaned into Liam a little. He leaned over and kissed her cheek.

"He is extremely picky with touch…I mean, he'll never deny a Pridemember, but I'm not sure he'd allow imprinting. It's kind of a big deal to a Shifter. He owns all of our scents, of course," Nadya gestured around her. "And he can read anyone in the Pride even if he didn't know us by scent, uhm…But… I mean, Caden is much more open."

Grace looked to her right, to Liam - mainly because all the Submissives in the room, except for a snoring Magnus, did the same. He seemed to think for a bit, then gave her an impish smile.

"He needs his fur ruffled, and you, my dear, appear to be the perfect brush."

Claus smiled as he smoothly shifted positions to slide down behind Liam. He draped his arm over Liam's shoulders, gently nipping at his neck. In response, Liam smiled and clasped Claus' hands, turning to give him a quick kiss.

Grace stared. They were perfect together.

"You look too freaking adorable." She smiled wide. "Married?"

Liam turned to steal another kiss before answering.

"True Mated."

Grace felt a tugging sensation in her chest at the word. Mate... she tested the word on her lips without looking at them. When she finally did look up, she found Liam flaring his nostrils. Claus tilted his head as Nadya echoed him. One of the lynxes hopped off and padded over from behind her on the couch, tilting her head quizzically up at her.

"We can't scent you, but your pupils just blew up like someone fed you catnip," Liam said. She'd say the man looked smug if she didn't know better. Grace was about to say something when the door swung open, revealing Pogue. One of the lynxes, Yota, moved to the sofa and draped herself over Brody, who immediately started rubbing her head. Meanwhile, Liam guided Grace through the process of mapping a face while Nadya explained the significance of each point on the face for creating a mental image of someone.

Liam acknowledged Pogue with a slight lift of his chin, then turned back to Grace. She shifted her gaze to meet Pogue's. He'd been lingering silently in the background, in his classic brooding stance.

"Try, Pogue."

"Excuse me?" Pogue asked, his irritation evident as he wiped his feet on the doormat and joined the group." Try Pogue *what*?" Pogue repeated slowly.

"We're teaching her about imprinting," Liam said as Sulis led Grace to the sewing table. As soon as she hopped onto it, he raised the table so her feet dangled off the floor.

"Uh, smart," Grace grinned as he raised her up.

"I realize it will take her a wee bit longer than a Shifter to learn, but to do so, she will, one could assume, need to practice," Liam smirked.

"Come on, sugar, let's feel your grumpy face." Grace wiggled her fingers in his direction, feeling giddy after a fun couple of hours.

"No," he replied, even as he approached her.

"Why not?" Grace pouted.

"Yeah, Alpha, why not? Exceptional educational opportunity, remember?" Liam prodded.

Pogue sighed as he rolled his eyes, nodded, and approached her, his scent now easily recognizable to her, no imprinting needed. Not that it was gonna stop her. *Nope, today, we get to just have fun,* she thought.

"She won't learn shit."

"Shut it," she said, grinning as she took him in.

His hair, a rich auburn, was kept short on the

sides but left a bit longer on top like he put some effort into styling it

daily. Unlike the rest, he, along with Nadya and Micah, didn't sport patched-up clothes. His stubbles, a mix of auburn and dark brown, framed his face. As she checked out his hands, she noticed smudges of black on his thumb and middle finger.

"Can't reach properly. Step a little closer?" Grace asked, reaching for his face. He stepped close enough to bump her knees and push them against the outside of his thighs.

Grace closed her eyes, as the others had taught her, and ran her fingers over his brows and forehead, inhaling deep and slow. Smiling, she brushed her thumbs over them, trying to erase the frown.

"Scar?" she asked softly, referring to the difference in his eyebrows.

"Mhm," he responded. Grace felt him tilt his head down a bit, giving her better access, like a cat, knowing it was about to be petted.

"Close your eyes. Don't want to poke them out."

He obliged, and she carefully traced her fingers down his eyelids, over his sharp nose and chiseled cheekbones, and down to a tight jaw that felt like it was due for a shave. The five o'clock shadow seemed more like eight.

"You need a shave," she whispered, breathing rhythmically slow like they'd taught her.

"I know," he replied softly. Grace gently traced his full lips, noting the pronounced cupid's bow. Pogue leaned in closer, positioning himself between her thighs, and placed his hands on the table as he leaned in even further. She could feel his warm breath on her forehead, and he subtly followed the path of her thumb as it moved from his lips to his cheeks.

"Smile," she mumbled. Again, Pogue obliged, and Grace was delighted to feel dimples. She giggled. She loved dimples. *Gay. He. Is. Gay, Grace!* she wondered. She flattened her hands and ran them down his neck, letting her thumb gently graze his Adam's apple before descending over his broad shoulders, to his firm biceps, and further down his tense forearm. Grace knew perfectly well she didn't need to feel anything but his face, but he wasn't moving, and she wasn't ready to stop.

"You cut your hair," he murmured, referring to the slightly shorter, now layered hair. It still reached almost to her waist, though.

"Nice?" Her only answer was a low grumble; she wasn't really sure what that meant.

She moved slowly up to his shoulders, then across his collarbone and taut pecs. She heard a short, almost silent hiss from him when her pinky accidentally scraped across one of his nipples. Pogue's chest was covered in a fine layer of hair. She drew her hands back slowly, her fingers trailing over his well-defined abs, which dipped into a prominent V.

Her fingers came to a halt as she reached the top of his jeans, and his breath caught. "Magnificent," she whispered before she could stop herself.

It was as if the world had stopped breathing. Grace became acutely aware that the room had become silent, and Pogues' breaths came out in short bursts as his entire body tensed. Grace sat back, mortified.

"Enough!" he hissed as he took a large step back.

161

The bitter taste of humiliation and rejection settled in her mouth like an overripe lemon. The fact that it was Pogue, specifically, who rejected her made her heart clench. The fact that the entire room had gone eerily quiet and everyone was now staring at her with wide eyes didn't help. She felt hot tears filling her eyes and making their way down her cheeks as she sat there, her eyes closed, hiding as a child would. Public humiliation never failed to cut her off at the knees.

Micah arrived not long after Pogue had left. He picked her up, kissed her on the cheek, and carried her to her room, no questions asked. Her body was finally catching up with her brain as exhaustion caught up. Grace's nemesis was public humiliation. She was a proud woman. Right now, *was,* being the operative word. Her head was in Micah's lap when she woke up. They were in her room. Micah didn't say anything, just stroked her hair as she sobbed quietly. She was grateful for his understanding. For his silence.

Chapter 22

Council

A^{rcher}

"Are you absolutely positive?" Archer asked one of his most trusted people on the other end. Freshly out of the shower in his cozy home, Archer's call was met with a patchy connection, his contact's voice crackling through. Being aware of DeCoill's watchful eyes, Archer strategically maintained three residences worldwide. One in Homer, Alaska, another in Ronda, Spain, and the one he was utilizing this week in Sohag, Egypt. Although he personally favored his den in Homer, his wolf had an affinity for colder climates. Nevertheless, he opted for safety over comfort.

"I am. I thought I knew the scent from somewhere. As soon as I ran into him last week, I started digging. DeCoill is hunting the human. Probably has been for a long time. It's a miracle she's still alive," he said.

"More luck than anything else, I'm afraid. I have her, so no need to worry about that part. Have you any news regarding the Challenge set out by IceFjord?"

After a brief pause, Archer shifted around to find a better signal. His Den in Sohag was situated on the city's outskirts, and he relied on an antiquated phone. It was a necessity; the newer models were more susceptible to tracking, or so he'd been informed. He couldn't afford to take the chance.

"DeCoill has the Alpha's son. I can't figure out where, but I believe he is the one who pressured IceFjord into making the Challenge," his contact said.

"It makes sense. DeCoill is blackmailing them. Find proof if you can."

"Working on it. I have to go."

The phone line went dead. Archer immediately made another call. He needed to get a message to StormEdge.

Chapter 23

Pogue left the building, his hands shaking, and he knew his cat was in his eyes. He stopped under a large overhang outside, trying to get his breathing under control.

"Damn... I probably startled the Submissives all to hell," he cursed as he stood there trying to regain some semblance of control.

Getting aroused wasn't anything to be embarrassed about, but Alphas gave off extremely potent pheromones. To a Submissive, it would feel like having their senses burned, triggering a flight or freeze reaction, precisely what happened.

As he turned to them on his way out - with a cock threatening to geld itself on his zipper – he was so hard; he saw them frozen, their eyes downcast. He'd lowered his gaze to avoid aggravating matters and raised his hands reassuringly. Liam, the only Submissive who seemed to be able to breathe through it, had managed to smirk at him. Besides the cringe-worthy embarrassment of the moment, the issue was that Submissives had keen survival instincts. They noted small changes.

They'd pick up on it way earlier than the rest of the Pride—the swift transformation in his scent, not just the pheromones. This shift happened for three reasons: death, pregnancy, and when a Shifter altered his scent to align with his Mate's preferences. *She is not our Mate!* He steeled himself. He didn't need nor want one; if he did, it wouldn't be a smartass human who pissed him off. He wasn't even sure if a human/Shifter True Mate was a real thing. He'd have to meet with the Submissives later and talk it out. But for the time being, he needed to get away from the human who smelled like wildflowers and into the office that smelled like coffee.

Caden met Pogue in the hallway outside their office. His face held a mixture of worry and anger.

"Are you ok?" he asked harshly.

"I'm fine. What's up your ass?!" He snapped.

Caden stepped close to him, sniffing.

"What's happening to you, Pogue? Your cat is acting erratically, and you've been tense as hell for days now. What did you do?"

Pogue pushed him away.

"Nothing, and stop fucking smelling me!"

Caden took a step even closer, his cat looking out at Pogue.

"Then why did I have the weirdest feeling just before getting a text from Liam saying, and I quote: 'I'll get them settled,' and a call from Micah saying he'll, and I quote, 'respectfully kill his Alphaholeness Pogue the asshat'?"

Pogue took a couple of deep breaths before answering.

"I'll take care of the Submissives. What exactly did you feel?" Pogue asked, referring to the tight connection they had as twins. Caden blushed. Caden didn't blush, so whatever it was must have been potent.

"We'll talk about it later. We're in session now without our Beta and Submissives rep!" He turned around and walked into the office. Pogue followed him silently. As he entered, he looked around to find everyone there quiet. The Vigilia stood silently against the walls as the rest had taken up spaces on beanbags and the soft carpet. They'd barely entered the office when Caden started.

"IceFjord is being blackmailed," he said, his voice terse. "And I've received a message urging us to keep Grace on Pridelands. It wasn't signed, but I had Henley track it. He says it might be from the Council or someone in it." Pogue looked around. The Vigilia all looked stunned, and no one said a word. Grayson growled as he kicked off from the wall he was leaning against, his large frame looming over Tari, who sat on a beanbag in front of him.

"Grace stays here then. Keep her safe here," Grayson said quietly as he reached into his sweatpants for his coin, twirling it through his fingers. Pogue could smell his irritability and confusion.

Tari gently yanked on Gray's T-shirt until he was right behind him, his thighs brushing up against Tari's back. Tari rubbed his hands firmly up and down Grayson's legs, coaxing his cat to calm down. Mehendi silently followed Grayson and pressed herself against his back, her toned arms encircling his waist.

"Deal with the blackmail later. We can't do anything about it right now, but it's good info to have," Caden said. "Tari, go over what you have. You got word earlier, right?" Pogue noticed Henley frowning as Caden dismissed the information.

Tari nodded and got out his notebook from a small hemp satchel by his feet. Pogue held up a hand.

"Henley, what can we do with the info?"

Henley blew out a harsh breath.

"Chew on it. Could mean someone crashed the plane but kept her alive, but it's all just speculation. I believe what we *can* do right now is focus on preparing for this dammed war and ensure our guest is safe as we do so! There are too many moving parts between Grace, why someone wanted her stashed here, Blackmail, war, and Summoning," he said, clearly frustrated.

Henley ran his hands through his hair multiple times before Beau grabbed him from behind and bent to nuzzle his neck. Henley growled at Beau, though. He let him go. Pogue cocked a brow at the Shifter.

Henley threw up his hands.

"I am dealing with a personal matter on the side. No, I wouldn't appreciate the meddling, so please just leave it be. I'll be fine."

Pogue narrowed his eyes at the tracker, signaling that he'd let it go for the time being, but he'd keep an eye on him. Henley huffed a breath but leaned back and reached for a cookie, which Tari quickly slapped into his palm.

"All right. Tari?" Caden prompted.

Tari cleared his throat and faced the room.

"The Summoning. Right. So, as you know, they're pulling us up for failure to notify. The Council we'll face at the Summoning is DeCoill, Hayfield, Summer, Archer, and Mayflower. I'm not worried about Archer and Summer. They're progressive and known to be objective. Mayflower can go either way - depends on his mood—and Hayfield tends to follow the majority. DeCoill, we know, wants to see us burn."

"What are we looking at?" Pogue looked to Tari. He noticed Caden rubbing at his solar plexus before turning his attention back to their lawyer.

"Assuming we win the Turf War, they'll almost certainly demand forced transfers, possibly ten or more. If Grace survives the Council's 'tender care,' DeCoill will twist old laws to get her whipped," Tari sneered. "Don't worry about the red tape. As Henley pointed out, concentrate on the Turf War and leave the trial to me. It would be a game changer if we could find proof that DeCoill was coercing IceFjord into this attack, but I'm not holding my breath for that to happen anytime soon."

Culling, or forced transfers in layman's terms, was an easy way to punish Communities. Take away their people and diminish their collective strength. It was a quick way of weakening a strong Pride like StormEdge. As for the lashings, the Council was adamant about keeping lashings as part of the punitive system. He and Caden agreed it was archaic and unnecessary, so they banned it from their Pride. Many laws regarding magic and Shifters were woefully out of date.

They talked back and forth for a bit before ending the meeting, agreeing to inform the Pride of everything tomorrow. They moved up the timeframe for assessing the factions to start a strict training regime as soon as possible. As the Vigilia left, Caden motioned for Pogue to stay.

Pogue glared suspiciously at his twin as Caden stepped closer, sniffing again, his cat obviously distracted.

"What *is* that smell?" he asked, tilting his head to the side.

"What smell?!" Pogue snarled, stepping back. Caden stalked him.

"That smell." Caden started sniffing a little too close for comfort, and Pogue pushed his head away.

Caden's eyes had gone cat.

"Holy shit, Pogue!"

"What?!" he hissed, throwing up his hands and backing away. He quickly grabbed the cigarettes and lit one as Caden stalked him around the large desk.

Pogue blew the smoke at Caden, who wafted a hand in front of him to clear the smoke.

"You smell like your cat recently released enough pheromones to attract every female in the Pride, and it's changing! Rosie? Tell me it's not Rosita," Caden asked, his eyes wide, referring to a female, a Pridemember Pogue had an understanding with. He got off, and she got to fuck an Alpha because that was her thing, apparently. They didn't even like each other, and both knew they were only scratching itches.

Pogue shook his head. *Yeah, this is about to get awkward*, he groaned.

"So *that's* what that feeling was," Caden said - still stalking, by the way - his voice bright with wonder as he rubbed his right pec. "But you were with the Submiss-..." he trailed off, stopped in his tracks, and whipped his head around to Pogue so fast his neck cracked, as a wolfish smile spread across his whole damn face. Pogue hung his head. *Kill me now...*

"No!?" Caden started to grin, but then the smile faltered. "Shit, bro, your timing sucks. Did you-" He mimicked, biting, holding up two fingers in front of his mouth like fangs. Pogue walked over and smacked him on the forehead.

"No, you dolt, I didn't fucking mate her!" he snarled. "Or mark her, for that matter! She pisses me off! Also, we're not fucking snakes, Cades. We don't do the fang thing." he added as an afterthought. Then he had another thought: "I don't even know her, or if she likes me. Hell, I don't even know if I *like* her," Pogue trailed, trying to convince himself as much as he was his twin. Grace not having scent markers made it really fucking difficult for him to be sure of anything. "And it doesn't matter anyway. I don't need or want a Mate."

"Well, you might have to change your mind 'cause it looks like the Pride is playing for keeps, and your scent doesn't just change for shits and giggles Plus, the Submissives are vouching for her as a group. I mean, shit, bro, you know how rare that is? They barely know her. She hasn't even been here a month." Caden said excitedly as he walked over to open the window...

"And don't give me the 'I don't need a Mate' crap," he made air quotes as he spoke. "Even if you don't like her, your cat does, and not just a little bit. Don't think I haven't noticed you tracking her every movement. And I see how you look at Gray when he brings food. She rocks your boat, and you don't like *that*, but bro. You kinda like *her*," he beamed.

"Thanks, Cades, good looking out," he snarled sarcastically. "Look, I don't know anything right now. Rosita is gonna bite my balls off if I dump her for a human. I don't need or want a human Mate, and I sure as fuck don't need you trying to push anything. She pisses me off. I just need to get some decent touch, that's all. And we've got too much shit going on," Pogue ranted as Caden guffawed and sat down in his bean bag. She was like a chaos ball rolling into his very structured life, and now, not only did his Beta want to keep her, the damn Submissives too?! This was not the kind of order Pogue was used to.

"Yup. Getting laid will solve everything... So, you wanna sit Grace down and tell her the Alpha Jaguar is crushing on her and has like five drawings of her hidden in his desk drawer?" Caden said, his lips twitching, earning him a dirty look from Pogue. Pogue knew his brother was a hopeless romantic, and he'd love nothing more than to see Pogue settle down with anyone but Rosita.

"Yeah. No! What?! Fuck you, Caden, this isn't funny! And stop going through my desk drawer, or I'll tell Maude about the teddy bear in yours! Hear me, Caden. I. Don't. Want. Her!" Pogue tossed a pen at his brother, who caught it midair as he stuck out his tongue at Pogue. *Fucking juvenile.*

"All right. But, Pogue, maybe try and get to know her at least. Scent doesn't lie." Caden held up his hands, shrugging.

"She doesn't give out a scent, and she bites more than any fucking female I've ever known. When she's not pissing me off just to spite me, that is," he added with a frown. "What's to know? I mean, she did prefer me over Micah with the back thing, and she seems to like it when I read to her," he shrugged. *Why am I still having this conversation?! Stop talking, Pogue*, he chided himself.

He noticed Caden's whole body was trembling as he was laughing silently. The idiot was grabbing his sides as he tumbled to the floor.

"What the fuck is so funny about that?!" Pogue asked, thoroughly irritated with the whole stupid situation. He walked over and lightly kicked Caden, who just laughed harder, wheezing as he tried to draw breath. His entire face was turning red.

"Caden!" Pogue roared at him.

It took another three minutes for Caden to finally be able to speak. Pogue knew. He timed it. Tears streamed down Caden's face, and he still held his side.

"She friend-zoned Micah so hard, and she not only thinks you're gay but that you're on mood-stabilizing drugs!" he started up again, but this time, Pogue bent down and grabbed Cades by the collar.

"Who?!" he growled, his cat suddenly angry that Grace might think he was gay.

Caden shook his head. He wasn't gonna say.

Fuck my life...

Chapter 24

A s evening rolled around, Micah shifted back and quickly dressed. He'd been spending the whole day with her, only leaving to grab them food and some psychology journals. He'd been switching between his forms for the past couple of hours. Grace recognized the signs of him being restless by now. Grace knew what Micah was reading up on. He'd promised not to tell anyone about the fugues but made her promise she would when ready. Ready, being kinda soon from what she'd gathered. He'd told them just to call him if she did anything weird. Grace stole a look as he dressed. Micah was a little softer to look at than Pogue and Caden, but he was no less appealing. Well, he would be for most females, she mused. But Micah, to her, felt like a friend more than anything else.

"Micah?"

He looked up at her as he was pulling on his socks. He must have seen something on her face because he dropped the T-shirt he was holding on the floor and crawled onto the bed, grabbing her to pull her onto his lap.

"What's up, darlin'?" he asked, gently nuzzling her neck. She noticed him breathing out on her skin. He did that a lot.

"Why do you do that?" she asked, procrastinating from what she really needed to talk about.

"Do what?" he asked as he settled her against him and started giving her a head rub.

"Breathe on me. I've seen many of the others do it, too. Not so much to me, but each other."

"Mhm. It's scent embedding. I leave my scent on you because my cat needs to keep you safe. It's like a marking. Not a mating mark, don't worry. It's more of a family thing, I guess." Grace felt her eyes sting. *I have no family*, she thought.

"Darlin', if I asked you to stay, not just for the Turf War, would you consider it?"

That caught her off guard enough that she sat up abruptly and turned to look at him.

"Why would you ask me that?" *I want to stay.*

Micah started fiddling with a loose string on her hoodie. Pogue's hoodie. He looked so small, sitting there. She gently rested her palm on his lightly stubbled cheek. "Micah, I don't do well with hints. I need you to talk in straight lines to me."

He looked up at her, placing his larger hand over hers, and looked her in the eye. His cat looked back at her.

"Because *I* don't want you to go. There is no ulterior motive, Grace. I just want you to stay. Not with me, not like that," he frowned."

Grace grimaced.

"You want me to stay with someone else?"

Micah huffed out a breath.

"That's the thing, darlin'. My cat hates the idea of you with another male, but at the same time, I think I wish you would form a connection. If it would make you stay. Will you at least consider it? If I can get you a phone call with Sophie, maybe?"

Grace wasn't ready to admit it, but butterflies were soaring in her belly. This place, these people. They had gotten to her so bad.

"I'll think about it. Let's see if I can convince that overbearing Alpha first," she snorted.

Micah mumbled something she didn't quite catch. Before she could ask him about it, his phone buzzed. He looked at it.

"We have to go grab dinner. Do me a favor. Stay close to Pogue, darlin'. We're gonna tell them about the Turf War, and I need to be able to assess them."

"And you think I'll be safe with that sour piece of meat?" she asked incredulously. "And why do I need to be safe? I thought I was safe here?" Grace sighed, hand brushing her face. Being near Pogue would only serve as a reminder of her silly reaction. But Micah didn't need to know how embarrassed she felt.

"Yes," Micah said seriously and got up. " Yes, Pogue will keep you safe, and no, you don't really need it, but Grace, I do, OK? I know it's really weird, but I need to know someone has an eye on you. My lion has an attachment to you, and I'm still trying to figure it out. Can you please bear with me, just for a little while?"

Grace gave Micah a long, thorough once-over. Moving past his captivating blue eyes, chiseled jawline, and distinctive features. Past his slightly unkempt wheat-colored hair and the smattering of freckles on his nose. She honed in on the subtle crease between his brows, the tension in his jaw, and the strain in his smile. A wave of tenderness washed over her at his obvious concern for her well-being. So, yes, she figured she could bear with him. At least for a bit longer, she decided.

They quickly made their way to the dining hall. Pogue was waiting by the door. He nodded sharply to Micah, who squeezed Grace's hand quickly and left her to wind his way through the crowd. *I really need some fucking shoes,* she reminded herself as they entered the large room. Her feet were a little cold. The sandstone floor wasn't actually that uncomfortable. Come to think of it, the whole Den was pretty comfy. She guessed there were around forty, maybe more Shifters, in here. Pogue looked down at her.

"Stay close," he ordered.

Grace glared at him, trying to cover up the unease and strangely sad feeling in her chest. When she didn't immediately respond, he leaned down, nipping her ear hard enough to leave a mark.

"Ow! You overgrown housecat! What the fuck did I do now?!"

Pogue looked like he was about to answer when another did it for him.

"Our Alpha has no patience, but we love him anyway." A lean man with softly curled hair and piercing gray eyes appeared. He was dressed casually in a lumberjack shirt thrown over worn-in jeans.

"Oliver," she said, smiling back. Oliver was quickly becoming one of her favorite people. He couldn't care less about Pogue's complaints and grumbles, and Grace adored him for it. Pogue stood silently behind her, watching the crowd. She couldn't help but notice his protective stance and the sharp glares he shot at anyone who got too close.

"Come on, I've saved you a seat," Oliver said excitedly. She heard Pogue growl low in his chest. "By the dais," Oliver added, shooting the Alpha a pointed look. Pogue cleared his throat and nodded. *Well, thank you, Your Majesty.* Grace scowled at him.

They advanced through the crowd. She could feel several Pridemembers staring at her, which made her wonder why. Why the stares? They'd seen her before. She instinctively folded in on herself. Oliver had wrapped his arm around her waist and seemed to be watching everyone. Doc greeted her as she sat down at the round table. As Oliver pulled out a chair for her, he leaned down to whisper,

"The Submissives vouched for you, and our Alpha looks ready to chew off the head of anyone who gets near you. That's why they're staring." He winked at her and grabbed a seat, his arm still slung loosely around her shoulders. *Yeah, and why the fuck is that? He's gay! Right? Micah said so,* she mused.

Oliver cradled the side of her head, drawing her near, and murmured, "Liam made it clear to our entire faction that we need to keep this under wraps. We usually chat like gossip-hungry grannies, but he's drilled it into them that discussing this would only hurt you. Plus, everyone's busy speculating why we were summoned for a mandatory Pride gathering. But, sweetheart, you and I are definitely going to have a serious chat about that whole foreplay episode real soon." Oliver kissed her cheek just as Juno approached the table.

"Hello, sweet child," Juno's deep voice greeted her as she basically ripped her out of Oliver's hold for a bear hug. Grace would recognize that voice anywhere. *Sweet child? Is she drunk?*

"Juno!" Grace leaned back and looked at her. "You look incredible today!" She took in her round, soft body, big brown eyes, and gorgeous black wavy hair. She wore jeans and a fluffy beige sweater with small flowers. She appeared to be in her forties. Juno blushed as she gently patted Grace's cheek.

"Oh, you shush now! Can't go around sayin' stuff like that," she gushed, fluffing her hair. "Now, my dear, let me look at you. You like the clothes we sent, I hope?" Juno lifted Grace to her feet, twirling her like a dancer before pulling her close and taking a deep breath near Grace's neck. With a soft touch, she smoothed Grace's hair behind her ear, her broad palms cradling Grace's head. Her eyes deepened, mirroring the intensity of her bear.

"Honey, you stay here for a minute. I'm just gonna go have a word with my Alpha," she smiled a little too sweetly for comfort. "Doc will fix that right up for you, won't you, Doc," she stated more than asked before getting up.

Doc, engrossed in his food, motioned for her to lean over. Absentmindedly, his hand healed the bite. Grace hadn't even checked for blood. It didn't hurt anymore. It struck her how routine it all felt, almost like tying shoelaces. Juno approached Pogue with a feral smile on her lips. She grabbed his ear and pulled his head down unceremoniously, faster than Grace thought that woman could move. He didn't have to bend all that much. Juno was quite tall. Pogue looked thunderous and about to say something when she hissed something in his ear.

Caden, who had just taken a bite of bread, almost choked on it. Then he winked at Grace before leaning back in the worn chair, a satisfied smile on his face. Caden, she noted, was more laid back than Pogue. He always seemed to roll with the punches. *His compartmentalization skills must be off the charts*, she thought. And he just seemed like a happy person in general.

But, while Grace admired Caden's calm demeanor, she was drawn to Pogue's wildness. She admired his ferocity and, though she'd never admit it publicly, his stereotypical male dominance. She felt safe with him, and Gods, she liked the banter. *No, no, I do not! He is bossy, overbearing, and arrogant*, she tried telling herself. At this point, Grace was pretty sure she was lying to herself, but no way was she going to admit to herself she was crushing on a gay man who hated her guts.

Pogue went from looking like he was gonna blow to a five-year-old in a split second. He looked at Grace and mouthed sorry. Juno let him go, her warm smile back on her face. Grace just stared at him, stunned. He had actually apologized. *The power of the Maternals*, she thought in complete awe.

Tari, sitting next to Grace, had been staring at her for the past five minutes. He looked like a fusion of Tilda Swinton and Jamie Campbell Bower—absolutely stunning. Tari was the type of man you'd see walking the runway. His presence embodied both femininity and masculinity, exuding an air of complete confidence. But it was his eyes that stood out the most. They looked pale blue at first glance, but looking closer, Grace noticed a ring of green encircling his iris.

She gave him a warm smile as she turned to face him.

"Whatcha' lookin' at?"

Tari blushed before answering.

"I'm sorry; it's just... On a selfish level, it's nice that everyone is looking at someone other than me for a change," he grinned.

"Well, you're kinda hot, so I get why they'd stare at you. Not like you imagine humans look in general?" Grace was curious.

"You're very different from us. Not so much looks, though you're bite-sized. But your demeanor," Tari trailed.

Grace tilted her head to the side.

"Cause I'm prickly?"

Tari barked a laugh and laid his arm out over her backrest, pushing Oliver's arm off. Grace didn't miss the gesture. *Tari is more dominant.* She filed away the information.

"Have you met Pogue? No, I mean... For starters, I've noticed you make a lot of eye contact. Our animals are rank conscious—instinct—they want to submit to the more dominant animal. I see you looking Caden in the eyes and scowling at Pogue. Most here couldn't hold that contact for more than a few seconds. I think you're either very dominant, or it's a lack of self-preservation skills," he grinned as Grayson walked by, placing a tray of food in front of her, and walked on, not even looking at her. *Ookay...* She shrugged and dug in immediately giving Gray a thumbs up as he walked away.

"And your scent doesn't change to us," Oliver added. "Normally, we can tell a lot by scent, but you just smell the same all the time. Delightful, by the way," he grinned and added, "though I see Micah and our esteemed hissy cat are marking the shit out of you."

Grace raised her eyes to Pogue. He was chatting with Hannah, who was dressed in a pink tulle skirt and black leggings, near the dais. As his gaze swept the room, Grace noticed it lingering on her for a moment before returning to his conversation. As she stared at the green cup, her mouth watered. It was silly, really, but she liked Pogue's cup. Reminded her of the keep cups they had back in NZ, and it brought her a resemblance of familiarity in what felt a little bit like limbo.

Caden and Pogue stood up, their movements eerily similar.

Caden raised his hand to silence the crowd.

"I appreciate everyone showing up on such short notice. As you know, we've had a human here for a while." Grace sagged in her chair as eyes turned to her. "She's gonna assist us during this next Challenge in exchange for us saving her life." The audience started murmuring. "Something big happened, which is why you're here now."

"She staying for good?" someone in the back asked.

"He'll get to that," Pogue said as he stepped down from the dais and walked over to Grace's table, placing his cup on the edge.

"That's what, two Challenges this year alone? "A voice, she recognized as Nadya asked.

"Less talking, more listening," Pogue told Nadya, effectively shushing the whole room.

"It's not an Alpha Challenge, Nadya," Caden answered.

Caden took a step forward and continued.

"The IceFjord Pack, whom you all know cause you watched Pogue beat the shit out their Alpha, three times before - has petitioned for a Turf War."

"Their petition was approved," Pogue added in a dark voice.

And that's when it all went to shit.

Chapter 25

S everal shouts erupted. Grace's body tensed as chaos erupted around her, her gaze darting around in an attempt to make sense of the pandemonium. She saw Pogue shift in front of her as a man she didn't remember the name of shifted into a huge black bear, and she heard Caden call out to Pogue to come grab Githa. Pogue bodily grabbed Grace and pushed her under the table as the room erupted. She didn't fight him. Most of the Submissives seemed to respond instinctively, shifting in their seats. In stark contrast, Oliver remained seated, retaining his human form, despite palpable waves of tension emanating from him, as he calmly crawled under the table with Grace. A shrill yelp drew her attention to Nadya's position. Grace almost missed the bright flash as Nadya shifted. Predators snarled, whimpered, and growled in the places where Submissives and a few Maternals she recognized had been. Keeping her cool required every ounce of Grace's self-control. She knew how to handle scared animals, but these weren't wild animals, and she wasn't sure how to react. Grace concentrated her attention solely on Nadya. She was hiding under a table. She stood up without thinking and crept towards the wolf on her knees.

"Nadya?" she coaxed, keeping her movements slow and deliberate. "Cuz, you in there?"

As she shivered in fear, the wolf nodded a very human movement.

"Can you let me come to you and help you relax?" Grace crept slowly towards Nadya, aware of the animal's low growl and tight muzzle, even as Oliver hissed at her to stay put. Grace was betting that the trigger points on a wolf and a cat would be identical. She scooted up close and gently rubbed a pressure point in Nadya's soft ear. Nadya continued to growl but didn't move. Grace then ran her

179

hand over a paw for another trigger point before leaning into Nadya. Minutes later, the wolf was calm, its head in Grace's lap as she murmured "Soft Kitty" to her.

"Well, I say!" She looked up to see her worst nightmare. Doc was squatting about five meters from her. That wasn't the bad part. The whole fucking room was gathered around, looking at her with shocked expressions. This was another version of what happened at the Submissive's meeting but on a larger scale. Everyone was staring.

For a second, she was wondering why they weren't closer. But then her eyes caught a huge, very agitated melanistic jaguar. *Pogue...* He was pacing around the table, growling and swiping at anyone who got too close. Nadya shifted back, tears streaming down her face.

"I am so, so sorry, Grace. Gods, I didn't mean to scare you. Urgh, this is so embarrassing", Nadya whimpered as she tried to cover herself up. Grace gently rubbed Nadya's back, puzzled by her distress, until she followed Nadya's gaze to a large, motionless black leopard. It held a fixed stare on Nadya, causing all the other Shifters to give it a wide berth. It only stirred when Caden gently grasped the loose skin on its neck, emitting a deep rumble from his chest.

"Guessing the whole 'nudity doesn't faze us' thing kind of goes out the window when the boyfriend's watching, huh?" Grace whispered, attempting to lighten the atmosphere. It didn't work. Nadya looked horrified and curled up more. "We'll fix it," Grace reassured her. "Someone pass me a sweater or a blanket or something?" she called out.

Doc looked at her from where he was standing, securely away from her, and chuckled.

"We would love to, but it seems our Alpha has decided against any and all movement toward you two." Oliver handed a sweater and a pair of sweatpants to Caden, who walked towards the table unconcerned. Pogue, still shifted, hissed at him and swiped close to his thigh. Caden looked at him, his eyes narrowing.

"Seriously, dude?" The cat growled. "Pogue..." he said, his voice low, warning.

Grace could practically feel the power exuding from Caden. Pogue shifted his stance, placing himself between them and his brother. His tail whipped back and forth as he silently revealed his teeth to Caden. Caden, while rolling his eyes, refrained from advancing. It seemed he was in no rush, choosing instead to wait it out.

"Nadya, will you be OK? I'm gonna calm his ass down."

Nadya stared at her, eyes wide.

"Grace, no! Pogue's cat is not laid back at all!" She gently grabbed the sleeve of Grace's sweater.

"He won't hurt me. His cat and I have an understanding." Grace winked at her and slowly got out from under the table, dislodging Nadya's hand as she went.

Caden glanced at her, still focusing most of his attention on his brother, while tapping his foot impatiently.

"Slow, Grace. His cat has a mean-ass temper, worse than Micah's." She vaguely heard Micah protest in the background.

Someone chuckled, and she heard definite agreements. She cast a glance around the room from beneath the table. Most had shifted back to human, though many hadn't bothered to dress. They were staring at her, waiting to see what she'd do. She didn't get the impression that they were concerned as much as curious. Grace stood and approached the cat. She wasn't scared. He wouldn't hurt her.

"Hi, kitty cat." The large predator lowered his head to look at her. His tail twitched but was no longer swishing. She slowly raised her hand, palm out, for him to sniff. He let out a soft, coughing roar. He wasn't impressed that she'd left the safe spot, she concluded. That irritated the hell out of her. *Why the fuck are you warning me off? You like me, you idiot!* She rolled her eyes and planted her hands on her hips, glaring at him. She was pretty sure that though Pogue didn't think much of her, his cat had no such reservations.

"Don't make me sing 'Soft Kitty' to you!" She threatened him, pointing her finger at his nose. A barked laugh told her Hannah was probably somewhere in the crowd. He rumbled and made a snort-like sound. She grabbed his jaw, her grip firm even as her thumb caressed his muzzle. "Do not sass me!" Several gasps were heard throughout the room. Grace let her eyes stray from Pogue just long enough to see Juno give her a big grin and a thumbs up.

181

Pogue leaned into her, the weight of his head causing her to stumble back a step before she got her footing back. As she started massaging his ear, he blinked slow and a low rumbling sound poured from his throat.

"You do purr!" She stated, ecstatic that he could. Wild jaguars couldn't purr, she knew.

"Honey, I'll purr for you, too, if you do that to me!" Brody leered from where he was crouched in her line of sight. She couldn't see him, but she saw Caden drop Nadya's clothes and walk toward the voice. Oliver picked them up and tossed them to Nadya, who swiftly dressed but stayed where she was. Pogue had stopped purring and had resumed the growling, his teeth bared. Grace nuzzled the side of his head with her cheek.

"S'ok. Walk me up to the table. It's fine, kitty cat, it's OK," she whispered. Pogue turned his head to meet her gaze, offering a nod before walking beside her as they made their way back to the table. He lowered his head and very gently nipped her ear, a clear signal from his feline side to stay put before he departed. Again, Grace marveled at how much larger Pogue appeared in his shifted form compared to his wild counterpart. He was easily half, if not double, the size. Grace was pulled out of her not-so-casual and, to her horror, too-obvious appreciation of this particular large cat as Caden started speaking.

"Now that we've all had coffee and a show..." He rubbed the back of his neck with a sheepish look.

"Firstly. I know it's gonna take some time to settle our animals, but try and hold it together through this meeting, and then we'll do some R n' R." The crowd didn't look calm or able to make it through the next ten minutes, let alone however long the meeting would take. But it was a testament to the Pride's trust in their Alphas that everyone seemed to adjust where they were sitting and nodded their acceptance of Caden's request. Grace noted that most of the Submissives were cuddled up to Dominants, some of which looked shook up too. The Maternals, the ones she recognized anyway, seemed to have gone into care mode, handing out blankets and warm drinks, though some of them were shaking themselves.

"The next two days will be fighting assessments of all of you. Those of you who haven't been doing hand-to-hand combat training recently report to Pogue in the gym tomorrow morning. I'll set up exercises to get our animals in tune, and Micah will prepare the actual Den and surrounding areas. I'll set up a shooting range for you, Grace. Yes, that means you're free to roam, and we'll get you some of your stuff," he added with a smile." And Games Night has been rescheduled. Check the message board."

Pogue was making his way through the crowd again; Grace noticed out of the corner of her eye. He was dressed in dark blue cargo pants and a black T-shirt. He walked right past her on his way to get his coffee. He then turned around and placed the keep cup in her hands, his fingers lightly brushing hers, despite him undoubtedly being pissed at her for publicly chastising him. *A thank you, maybe?* She thought. Grace had started to notice that whereas Caden's cat seemed generally content and quite civilized, Pogue's cat seemed closer to the surface at all times and was more... assertive, for lack of a better word.

Chapter 26

24 hours later

Grace relaxed on her bed, enjoying a break for her mind after a yoga session following lunch. The previous evening had been eventful, and she had turned in early. Grace was well aware that her mental energy was running low, to say the least, but it had been worth it. With the freedom to move about now, she discovered a liking for her room. *Ironic that,* she snorted. Overall, she felt she was doing pretty well. Even though she was well aware Shifters were powerful and could be dangerous, they mostly came off as quite civilized. There had been no fights, and no one had tried to eat her. So far, so good. Still, it was a lot to take in, and she knew herself well enough to realize she needed to give herself quiet time to let her brain catch up.

A knock on the door had her uncross her legs from the meditative pose she'd adopted to wind down.

"It's open," she called softly.

The door opened to reveal Caden, Hannah, Tari, and Micah. Micah looked tense, she noticed, as she took him in. Today, it seemed, was eighties band day. He was wearing his usual low-hung jeans and an Ozzy Osbourne T-shirt. He pushed his flaxen hair from his eyes, gesturing for Hannah to go in first. Today, Hannah was all about Ravenclaw, rocking a long flowing cape in blue and bronze with the eagle emblem in the middle. It was safe to say she was a bigger Harry Potter fan than Grace. A grin spread across Grace's face as Hannah bounded onto the bed beside her, her excitement matching that of Tari, who had sat beside her. Seriously, only Tari could rock a fucking kilt, she smiled to herself. Caden walked over, his black blazer looking kinda snazzy with the blue jeans. He bent and nuzzled her in greeting. She tried getting used to it but pushed his head when he sniffed her.

"Cuz, get off," she laughed.

He looked at her, his head cocked.

"Still weird?"

Micah pushed him out of the way to engulf Grace in a hug, repeating the nuzzling quickly before looking up at his Alpha.

"She'll learn."

Grace looked from one to the other and then to Hannah.

"Why are you here? Not that I mind," she added.

Caden turned serious.

"Seems you're winning over the Pride. The Submissives are serious about you." He smirked. *Well that was sorta the plan I guess,* she thought as she felt a blush on her cheeks. "But before you get too cocky, remember that Pogue and I have the final word, and half the Pride still aren't sold on adopting a human." Before Grace could protest, Caden blurted, "And Micah has something to tell you." Tari snorted at the Alpha as Micah got off the bed and sat down on the floor. The snort earned Tari a head slap from Hannah, who glared at him and crossed her arms. Micah cleared his throat.

"Pogue was supposed to...-"

The door opened, revealing Pogue. He looked like he'd just returned from a run. His green T-shirt and gray track pants were both stuck to him. It was either raining, or he'd just returned from a run. Maybe a combination, she figured, as she wrenched her eyes from counting his abs through his T-shirt. He scowled and leaned against the door, not bothering with a greeting. He seemed more tense than she'd ever seen him. His nostrils flared as he glared at her, and he clenched and unclenched his fists.

"Why are we here?" he asked sternly. Hannah shrugged, still staring daggers at Tari for some reason. Tari pointed at Micah.

"Gonna guess he's about to tell us."

Grace looked around. It seemed no one knew from the looks on their faces. She felt a wave of nerves as her brain screamed at her. There wasn't a lot of energy for new mind-blowing information right now.

Pogue

Fucking wildflowers, Pogue cursed as he ground his molars into dust. The menace was staring at him, and how her eyes traced his stomach every time he took a breath made him want to lick her and flee the room simultaneously. *Humans and Shifters don't mix... You know this,* he reminded himself. Though for all the reasons he could usually list, right now, looking at her, he was having trouble coming up with even one. *You could kill her if you mated her.* The thought alone was enough to shore up his defenses once again.

"So, uhm, the Alphas know I've been doing some digging," Micah stated. Pogue and Caden nodded in agreement. Maybe Micah had discovered something in the human world that could be a game-changer in the war. Pogue remembered Micah becoming increasingly fixated on the human world many years ago.

Pogue and Caden wondered if the fixation was because Micah thought his mother was there. Micah was a rarity in their world, being half Shifter and half Wielder. From DeCoill's point of view, worthless. To StormEdge, he was invaluable. Micah took a deep breath. "As you know, my dad is half Wielder." Pogue nodded at the lion once more before rising and beginning to pace the room, his steps deliberate. "Well, I stole some of Grace's blood when she was in the clinic and-"

Pogue felt his inner cat surge so strongly that he didn't realize he had moved from his spot by the door. When he blinked, Micah was suspended off the ground. Pogue's arm was fully extended to support him as he emitted a low, menacing growl.

Tari was on his feet instantly, his posture stiff as he moved to stand in front of Hannah, who had stepped in front of Grace. Micah raised his hands and turned to Caden, who approached slowly, his eyes noting where everyone else was.

"Why?" Pogue asked carefully. His cat was right there with Pogue. Micah shook his head. Caden put a hand on Pogue's arm. Pogue lowered Micah to the ground but didn't let go.

"Now of all times? What did you do, Micah?" Caden asked.

"DNA test," Micah said quickly. "Just a test. Humans use it to determine a lot of things. Ok, man, can you let me the fuck go here?" He was, Pogue knew, *not* amused by Pogue's cat right now and dominant enough to do something about it. But Micah was on good behaviour right now. The cat didn't care, but Pogue let him go and glared at him as he realized everyone in the room, Grace included, was staring at him, her head ducking around Hannah and Tari. *Overreacting much?!* Pogue wanted to facepalm; he felt like such an idiot.

Micah slumped down on the ground. Pogue watched as Grace got up. She probably didn't realize, but she had placed herself between the Alphas and Micah. That would have been a bold move if she'd been a Shifter. A protective one. Grace sat down in front of Micah and gently cupped his cheek, and for some ungodly reason, that annoyed the hell out of Pogue.

Micah took a deep, slightly shaky breath.

"Darlin', there's a reason my cat latched on to you from the beginning. He knew you from the start."

"knew me how? I don't understand."

Micah shook his head.

"You do, though. I just thought I could smell it because Pogue told me. You smell like wildflowers," he smiled. "And me. And a little of Pogue, but that's 'cause he'd been your handler." Micah frowned at her.

"Okay? Uhm. Thank you, I think? Still not understanding tho'," she started carefully.

"You're my half-sister, Grace."

You could hear a pin drop. Grace stopped breathing for a beat, and Pogue damn near held his own breath for the entire ten minutes she just sat there. Every time one of them made a move, she'd hold up a finger and shake her head. Pogue noted every breath she took. Every twitch of her lips and every time she frowned.

Then, suddenly, Grace vaulted from her position in front of Micah and into him, knocking him onto his back. She proceeded to slap the ever-loving shit out of his chest.

"How could you not tell me sooner? How fucking dare you spring this on me?!" she screeched. Micah delved into his pocket and retrieved an official-looking document, ensuring she didn't slide off his stomach, where she was pressing her knees. Pogue couldn't help but smile to himself as she accepted the paperwork and shifted to sit cross-legged on Micah's chest, scrutinizing it closely.

No one in the room moved except for Hannah, who jumped onto the bed and got comfortable. She'd probably go straight to the Academy. She had to, he knew. Every time Micah tried to move, she bent over slightly and slapped his forehead without looking at him. *Fucking adorable,* Pogue thought, watching her slap his Beta every minute or so, almost automatically.

Micah seemed to get the picture after about six slaps to the forehead and a heel to the chest. He accepted defeat, crossing his arms behind his head and raising his legs a little for her to rest her back against.

The longer Pogue observed them, the clearer it became. He and Caden had shared the same dynamic when they were kids. How had he missed noticing how effortlessly those two interacted? How rapidly Micah had formed a bond with her, and how at ease she had become around him? He shook his head, a smile tugging at his lips. Micah deserved this. Losing his mom at such a young age and then having his dad vanish without a trace...

Grace was now going to learn what having an overprotective brother meant. *She'll stay,* a small voice in the back of his head said. *And her world will get so much more dangerous,* he told it.

Pogue knew that should anyone dare to cross her, Micah would become the apex predator he truly was beneath that friendly exterior. Deep down, Pogue was equally sure that Grace would never abandon her brother. She wasn't the type to walk away. This realization stirred conflicting emotions in him, a mixture of elation and bone-deep fear. She could die here.

Almost fifteen minutes later, she seemed to have read and reread it enough times to understand it. Then the chuckling began... Not long after that, she rolled off Micah, clutching her stomach, wheezing as tears ran down her cheeks.

Hannah snickered from her spot on the bed.

"Yeah, see how you like the cramping stomach. Soft kitty, my ass!" Pogue chuckled to himself, remembering how Hannah had been in the exact same position not so long ago when Grace had first sung Soft Kitty to Micah. As beautiful as she was, she couldn't sing to save her life. *Where the fuck did that come from?!* Pogue shook his head to clear the dumb pop-up thought. Micah crawled over and picked up his shaking bundle of laughter, stroking her back up and down.

"Grace, can we use words instead of snorts here? I'm a little worried," Micah said. Tari had the same worried look on his face. Hannah just chuckled.

Grace looked at Hannah and tried to speak, but the laughter kept her from forming full sentences. Pogue could only make out, "He... and then... with the... and the clothes," before Hannah joined Grace in a laughing fit.

Micah looked horrified as he held up his hands, palm out.

"I... oh stars, I checked out my own sister!" he groaned as he put his head in his hands. Grace was wheezing away but managed a thumbs up. "I told her she was a well-put-together female! I'm gonna go to the special hell...." Micah was mortified. Pogue looked around to find Caden holding in laughter. He tossed a pillow at him, setting him off too. Soon, he was curled up in a fetal position next to Hannah.

"She's turning blue, might wanna get her up and standing Pogue," Tari smirked, pointing to Grace.

"Enough, Menace!" Pogue told her. He lifted her to her feet and turned her away from the circus in front of her. Suppressing his own laughter, he held Grace snugly against his chest and coaxed her breathing back to normal. When she indicated she was alright, he stepped back just in time to catch the pillow Caden tossed his way. Pogue casually settled onto the floor, placing the pillow in his lap. He hoped Grace was too preoccupied to notice the reaction the rest of the room hadn't missed.

When everyone had finally calmed down, Grace said her first hello to her brother. Micah would be on cloud nine for the rest of his life.

"So, this basically explains your tiny amount of magic, Grace. If you and Micah share a dad, you're... Micah, remind me again?"

"My mom is pureblood Shifter. Dad, Avery. Grace, your dad's name is Avery," Micah said, a huge smile on his face. "Yeah, so dad is half Wielder and half Shifter. So that would make you..."

"A mudblood," Grace commented with a smirk.

"I will wash your mouth with soap for cussing like that!" Hannah told her sternly, though her lips were twitching.

Micah just looked confused.

Pogue's head felt like it was about to explode. Discovering Grace was Micah's sister was one thing; considering the implications was another. If she stayed, she'd be entering a world where some, like DeCoill, made it clear how little they valued anyone who wasn't pure blood. Sending her back to her own world, where she apparently had a stalker, didn't seem much safer either. Then there was the Turf War, Summoning, and the fact that Pogue was becoming increasingly unsure if he could let her go, no matter how rational doing so was.

Grace's giggles abruptly interrupted his thoughts. Everyone in the room cocked their heads, puzzledly looking at her.

"No more spoons left. Only knives left," she sighed.

Pogue looked at her again and wanted to slap himself. If this was a big revelation for him, how the fuck would she be feeling right now. Exhausted. She's exhausted, he knew.

"Only knives, darlin'. That's good, though. We know how to use them. We got you," Micah told her, a solemn promise. His claws shot out, and he wiggled his fingers.

Alright, Micah... Only knives left. She was Micah's, and that made her StormEdges.

190

Chapter 27

Grace was left alone not long after. The rest of the day flew by in a haze as she struggled with information overload. Her brain felt like it had been through a blender, and she was running on empty. She needed to decompress, and with Micah apparently having to leave, she felt incredibly alone. Micah kept his word though and gave her a crash course in what not to spill, leaving her with an almost ancient smartphone. At least Grace could send and receive photos, but that was about it. The day became evening before Grace felt ready to tackle what was sure to be a huge conversation with her ride-or-die, Sophie. She sighed, dialed Sophie's number, and waited.

"Hey, Sophie, girl!" Grace started when Sophie picked up.

A high-pitched squeal was her answer, followed by a series of curse words in random order before her best friend seemed to have run out of steam.

"Grace, you absolute twat!" How could you possibly do that to me?! It's been weeks!" She exclaimed.

"Uhm... well, the plane crashed and-"

"Yes, I know. Micah has been updating me, slash attempting to interrogate me," she deadpanned.

"Oookay."

"I, uhm... Well, I quite enjoy talking to him." Sophie's British accent was strong now. "Turns out we have a lot in common." Sophie was in every way a daddy's girl, including following in his footsteps in the security world. There wasn't time for men. Usually, at least. "But Grace, I'm worried, and so is daddy." Sophie sighed. "I need to know you're safe, and I would very much like to know where you are."

Grace bit the skin on her thumb.

"Micah didn't tell you?" Micah had told Grace that all he'd given Sophie was the name of the nearest town called Fawlks.

"Oh, he did, but the town doesn't exist on any maps Grace. So I'd like you to explain, Grace. Are you alright, and where are you?" Sophie's voice didn't leave room for doubt; she would accept nothing but facts.

So Grace gave her facts. Sort of. Grace spent the next hour and a half explaining everything that had happened since the plane went down, omitting the whole animals-to-humans and magic ordeal. StormEdge, according to the script, was a military training facility for international troops. Grace wished Micah had asked her about that part of the cover story. Sophie would gnaw on that story like a dog on a bone. Sophie's father had military connections, though Grace wasn't sure how deep they went, and Martin, Sophie's father, was as protective of Grace as Sophie was.

"I want to fly you home, Grace. Micah says you're doing better, so I assume you can safely travel?" Sophie sighed.

Grace knew she should just say yes and figure out where the nearest airstrip was. But the words wouldn't come. She couldn't and wouldn't abandon Micah. And he wouldn't leave StormEdge. Not with a war on the horizon. But even if he did, would she be able to leave? Did she really want to? Images of Pogue flooded her mind, and no matter how hard she tried to push them away, they remained.

"Soph, uhm... There's something else too," Grace started.

One hour and fifteen minutes later, Sophie had practically dissected the news about Micah and Grace being related. She insisted on Grace sending over a copy of the DNA results. It took some serious convincing and a well-timed distraction (the subject being Pogue) to guide Sophie away from the topic.

Eventually, Sophie agreed to let it go for now. Thank fuck. Lying to her best friend was not Grace's idea of a good time.

"I have to say, I'm impressed you haven't crashed. What are you doing to decompress? Any episodes?" Sophie had become something of a temperature gauge for Grace over the years. She knew how much pressure Grace could tolerate and how to recognize when she was slipping.

"I've been bedridden for most of the time, but yeah-na. I know I need to get back into yoga, and I should be doing more yoga to ground myself Micah said I've had a few episodes, but nothing major. I don't know, Soph. It's almost like, here, I can take it. I feel oddly safe here. I don't know, maybe this place heals?" Grace chuckled.

"Pogue?" Sophie guessed.

Grace sighed.

"It's so fucking dumb cuz. He's gay! Or bi or whatever. I don't even like him. He pisses me off!" But she kinda did... She liked his growly, scowly personality. She liked his little displays of dominance and how he kept track of her.

"What makes you say bi?" Sophie asked.

"I don't know. Maybe I'm imagining it, but sometimes it actually seems like he's almost flirting with me. Or... Well, sometimes he's less snarky and looks at me funny. Urgh, I am a grown-ass woman, Soph! I should know men. He is men!"

Sophie chuckled.

"You're a bit in the dark about men. I adore you, Grace, but let's be honest: your flirting skills are a smidge... well... You might come across as a bit aggressive, yeah? Try dipping your toe in the water first, hmm? Have you thought about approaching him about it? Nicely." Grace thought about it.

"Well, I guess I've mostly just snarled at him."

"Bloody hell, help me with this one," Sophie grinned... "Use your words, Grace. God, This is a lot, even for the most balanced person. I think you need to talk to someone, maybe Micah, seeing as he's qualified?"

Grace sighed, knowing she was right about everything.

"Yes, mom. I'll see if I can find Micah, and then I'll decompress, okay?"

"All right, love. Uh, there is something else while I've got you. I don't want to add to your plate, but I actually think this might be good news for you. It might even take something off the plate."

Grace sighed. *Sure, lay it on me...*

"Out with it."

"I've been working on a new facial recognition system. Grace, please don't be cross with me," she sighed. "I have been trying to find this stalker of yours for quite a while now. Uhm, I will send you a couple of pictures on your phone. I got him, Grace. I finally got him," Sophie said, elated.

"You've had me followed?! That's an invasion of privacy, Sophie!" She tried keeping her voice calm, but the thought of Sophie having her followed was icky.

"No, no, love, I haven't. I set up a camera in the hallway by your apartment. You know that sticker on the wall?"

"Yeah?"

"Yeah, there's a camera looking out of the possum's eye. I caught a man on camera months and months ago. I thought nothing of it because he was just standing there. But then I ran his face through this new program, and he popped up outside your school and by the scene of the car crash, too. I even have a picture of him next to some cargo box in Africa."

"Just send me the pictures. And I'm not mad. Just... this is a lot right now, but I'm thankful for your help."

"I just did. Grace, I'm sorry. I was just worried about you. Call me later, yeah?"

Grace agreed, and they hung up.

She sat back and waited for the photos to come through. They did.

"He was at my home...." She whispered as she looked through the photos. He was standing beneath a street sign, looking at her former workplace, the vet clinic. And there he was, looking down at a wooden box, grinning. It appeared to be an airport. Her insides were frozen by the last image she saw. He stood directly beside her almost mom's car at the crash scene. He was the one who attempted to remove her seatbelt. Memories rushed back in a blur.

"He was in the car with the drunk driver!"

She felt her pulse speed up. Grace remembered someone trying to cut her seatbelt off, attempting to get her out. They'd accidentally stabbed her with the knife they were using. *He wasn't trying to get my seatbelt off,* she remembered now. He hadn't stabbed her stomach with a knife by accident *Not a knife. Claws. Not an accident.* She realized that now. Grace lifted her shirt and touched her hand to the almost invisible scar on her stomach.

She would recognize those beady eyes anywhere.

I'm being hunted by a Shifter. The Councilman.

Grace felt nothing as darkness consumed her. She knew what was happening. *I have a brother, and my stalker is DeCoill.* Her last thought was that she'd rather be trying to make lasagna than be awake and know these things right now.

Chapter 28

"Pogue!" Liam burst into the room, swiftly shutting the door. Pogue straightened in his plush office chair, irritated by the interruption. He had been engrossed in a drawing for Claus, Liam's Mate, making this a less-than-ideal moment. Swiftly, he covered the work in progress with a fresh sheet of paper and reached for a cloth to clean his hands.

"Liam?"

Liam shifted his weight from one foot to another, looking uncomfortable.

"What?" Pogue asked, keeping his tone neutral.

"I called Micah. Sorry, I didn't know he was out of the Pridelands. He told me to follow her and make sure she didn't hurt herself. It's Grace."

Pogue's cat went from snoozing to hissing in a second flat.

"What's wrong with Grace?"

Liam shook his head.

"I don't know, just call Micah. I followed her to the dining hall. She went into the kitchen and turned on the stove, but then she just left again." Liam said in hurried words. "Caden's with her now, but she's still walking. Something's wrong, Pogue."

Pogue grabbed his phone and dialed up Micah. No answer. Growling, he dialed Caden instead. He picked up on the first ring. "Call Micah!" Pogue said and hung up as Liam opened the office door again, leaning out to look. He called out over his shoulder to Pogue.

"She's heading up the stairs. Micah told me to not disturb her movements."

Pogue stood up and walked over to one of the beanbags to put on his boots in case he had to follow her back out. Grace walked in barely a minute later, Caden right behind her. Liam slipped out quietly and closed the door behind him. Pogue knew something was seriously wrong. She was awake, but something told him she wasn't there. Her eyes were almost vacant, and she smelled wrong. Like rotten flowers almost. His cat was spitting and growling. She was in trouble, and it was well aware of it. Pogue felt the tip of his incisors lengthen in response to his cat's distress.

"Calm him down, bro," Caden said softly as he sidestepped but lingered by Grace's side as if afraid she'd fall. She didn't. She walked around the desk and threw the pack of cigarettes he had lying on the edge of the large wooden workspace into the bin, a frown on her face. "Seems she doesn't like you smoking either." Caden smiled tightly.

"Does she interact?" Pogue asked, keeping his voice low.

Caden nodded.

"She told Oliver to go shopping for lasagna sheets."

"We fucking needed Micah *here*."

"I know. But someone had to find a safe haven for the cubs, and you know our Beta is the best one for the job. I know, alright. I shouldn't have insisted. Micah was pissed too." Caden was right, though. Micah was the best one for the job. The Beta could talk the fur off a bear.

Grace was now directly in front of him.

"You in there?" Pogue softly asked, widening his legs slightly as she stepped forward, pushing her small form between his legs, her toes digging into the beanbag he was sitting on.

His hands itched to reach for her. Touch was a vital element of Shifter culture. Touch grounded you. Touch was a natural way to offer comfort, show care, and assure someone that you would keep them safe. But Grace wasn't a Shifter and wasn't here right now. Pogue knew it was just her body as his nose twitched at the stench of rotten flowers.

Grace just kept looking at his hand. He hadn't even realized he had reached for her. *Fuck it...*

"Grace..?" he allowed himself to carefully touch the tips of his clawed fingers on her hips. Her eyes were empty, almost glazed over. *Where are you, Grace?* He thought as he felt his chest constrict.

"Why? Because your boyfriend's gonna come beat me up, and you want me to stand up for the punches?" she grumbled. Pogue gave her a tight-lipped smile, not knowing what to say. Pogue was gonna strangle whoever thought it would be hilarious to tell Grace he was gay!

Caden quietly pulled up a chair, beside Pogue's beanbag chair, curling his fingers into the carpet.

"Your cats going crazy?" Caden asked softly, not looking away from Grace.

He just nodded, tracking Grace's eyes as they looked him up and down as if categorizing every part of him. Caden smiled. "She really is gorgeous. Human and all," he added.

Pogue felt his smile deepen until his dimples were probably showing, though he didn't offer his brother an answer outside of a soft snort. Caden gently bumped his calf with a closed fist. Why Caden was so damn insistent on Pogue getting to know Grace better was beyond him. His cat roared inside his skull at the thought, the word Mate ping-ponging around in his head like a damn moth in a glass jar.

"Not the time, Cades." She was, though. Her eyes were the deepest blue he'd ever seen, with yellow flakes that looked like they'd been sprayed on with angry whips of a paintbrush

He barely noticed Doc enter, then quietly leave, confirming she was physically fine as long as she didn't look pale or like she was about to faint, and just to let her go through the motions. Grace didn't move much. Pogue could feel her toes curling into the beanbag now and then, and she'd shift her fingers, lightly tapping her thumbs against her index fingers. Aside from that, she simply observed. Her head was slightly cocked. A small smile crept across her lush lips as he mirrored her. She tilted her head in the opposite direction, her smile growing wider when he replicated the movement. But she still smelled fucking wrong, and it creeped him out.

Caden left, saying he'd give them some space, leaving Pogue to keep an eye on Grace. She'd been there for an hour and was still just standing there. Looking at him.

"Grace?" *Gentle. Be gentle.* His voice came out more growl than human speech. *Fuck! Gentle dipshit. Growling isn't gentle*, Pogue cursed inwardly.

She looked down at him and, much to his surprise, shifted her position to slowly straddle him, looking him in the eye.

"Is this okay?"

"Yes," he murmured as his cat rose to the surface, his nails claw-tipped on her hip. *Shit!* He wasn't sure if he should try and snap her out of it. He remembered Micah mentioning something about not shocking her - kinda like if someone was sleepwalking. *Go through the motions.* Easier said than done. She'd shit a brick if she came back to her astride him.

"Will they hurt me?" She put a hand on his chest, her face angled to look at his clawed hand.

"Never."

Grace smiled at him and leaned forward, her knees digging too deeply into the beanbag, causing her entire body to tilt forward. His hands tightened on her hips, steadying her. *Not good*, he thought as the apex of her thighs pressed against him. He discreetly adjusted his position to put a minute amount of space between their bodies.

"Can you see in the dark?"

"Yes."

"Would you purr for me?"

Pogue chuckled despite the whole situation. The vibrations of his chest seemed to delight her, judging by the smile on her lips.

"If you're good."

Pogue then watched as she carefully took his hand and lifted it in front of her face, pricking a talon with her index finger.

"Ouch!" She withdrew it quickly as a small bead of blood appeared. "Sharper than I thought," she giggled, her eyes slightly more focused, though she still wasn't with him. He could feel it. "You said they wouldn't hurt," she accused.

"Stop playing with them then."

Pogue kept tracking her eyes, fighting the urge to pull her flush against him. Grace cupped his jaw, making him tense up even more. *Grace, you need to snap out of this,* he mentally groaned at her. He felt his entire body turn to stone as she leaned down and sniffed him, her nose buried in the crook of his neck, slowly traveling up over his jaw and into his hairline before straightening up and looking at him, her blue eyes sparking - almost as if she was fighting her way back. Anchoring herself using him, maybe? Pogue found he liked that. Wanted that. He demanded his breath to settle down along with the world's most inappropriate hard-on. Grace pulled his attention back to her words as she exclaimed,

"It's... That's you! That's your actual scent!" She seemed delighted about that. Pogue shrugged lightly.

"I wouldn't know. Pheromones smell different to everyone. Grace, you need to come back now," he softly ordered.

"But you smell so *good*," she moaned. "You smell safe. And sweet and like rain. I don't wanna come back," she told him resolutely, a small pout on her face. And then she bent and nipped his lip hard enough to break the skin. He couldn't have stopped the growl that tore through his human vocal cords or the involuntary bucking of his hips if he'd tried.

"Shit! Okay, you really need to snap the fuck out of it," he whispered harshly. Every human part of him knew she needed him in control and rational. But Pogue wasn't entirely human; his other half was chafing at that human control now. Wanting to stop talking and start doing. To bring her back with what came most natural to him. Touch. *Nip her back,* his cat urged. Deciding to listen to his other half, Pogue gently grabbed the back of her head and pulled her closer to nip the top of her ear. No reaction. He did it again harder, allowing his voice to deepen as he ordered her none too gently.

"Grace, come back. Now!"

He felt it the second she snapped out of it. Her whole body tensed up, and she scrambled away from him fast and hard enough to smack her head on the edge of the desk. She let out a surprised yelp and held her hand to the back of her head as she looked around, the panic visible on her face.

"You're fine," he told her quickly. Pogue slowly made his way to her. He would do whatever she needed to calm down. Right now, he would do nice. Grace was hyperventilating. *She's gonna pass out*, he knew. Changing tactics, Pogue grabbed her around the waist and stood to settle her on the desk. Aware of his height and build, he grabbed a beanbag chair and used it to kneel on, putting him roughly at face height with her as he ran his hands up and down her arms and shoulders with a firm touch.

"What did I do? How long was I out?" The words came hurriedly, and her breath burst from her in small, choppy movements.

Pogue chuckled, trying to lighten the mood and calm his own ass down.

"You sent Oliver out to get lasagna sheets and turned on the stove in the kitchen. You made Liam and Caden follow you around for a while and asked me about the boyfriend I don't have. You also bit me a little, but seeing as you also told me I smell sweet, I'll let it go," Pogue forced a smirk and pointed his finger to a small cut on his lower lip. "You've been... gone for about an hour. Breathe deep, Grace." He emphasized his order by placing one hand just below her throat, grabbing her smaller hand with the other, and placing it on his chest. "In and out, Grace."

"What else?" she demanded, her tone harsh, the words panicked. But she did start to follow his breathing - most likely, her body reacted to him on a subconscious level.

Grace

Please tell me I didn't just humiliate myself, Grace thought as the panic roared through her head. *Please tell me I didn't make your lip bleed...* She felt her eyes well up. *No! No I will not fucking cry!* The anger she could do. Anger was easy. Feeling vulnerable was the worst feeling in the world. Even worse, Pogue, of all people, seeing her like this. Pogue, who had his large, warm, clawed hand on her chest. Pogue, who gave her orders, and all she wanted to do right now was to follow. Pogue, who smelled like rain and safety and home...

All she wanted was for the entire world to vanish right now. To simply succumb to Pogue's scent and the touch of his hands. She just wanted to pretend he was someone who cared, that this was all on purpose, and that she was fucking normal. When she was in a fugue, she wasn't normally promiscuous. Most of the time, she just did mundane tasks, like making lasagna. She stared as Pogue touched a finger to his bloodied lip, drawing her eyes to the blood and the fullness of his lips and the prominent cupid brow.

"Wanna explain this?" His beautiful pale green eyes gave way to the darker and sharper ones of his cat as he looked at her.

Grace groaned softly.

"Nope. Wanna explain how Brody isn't your boyfriend?"

Pogue looked thoroughly confused.

"Nothing to explain. Brody isn't my boyfriend."

I got it wrong? She wondered, trying not to shiver every time his hands traced up and down her arms, using Pogue as a distraction, an anchor to the present. His firm touch had softened into a languid caress, his thumbs drawing unhurried circles on her upper arms. *Huh, never knew arms were sensitive like that,* Grace thought.

Pogue scowled at her.

"If I were taken, Grace, I wouldn't have let you crawl all over my lap. And, if I were in a relationship, it would be with a woman," he said, a sly grin on his lips. *Hang on, what? Crawling on his... We were making out?* Pogue noticed her zoning out a little as she tried to force memories back. He stepped into her and gently nipped her nip. It was forward, more than he would normally be, but he needed to make sure she didn't zone out again.

"Stop. You're overthinking. You did nothing wrong, Grace." Looking into his eyes, Grace saw the truth in them. Pogue didn't bullshit. He would have told her if she fucked up. Despite his provoking demeanor, he was honest as far as she knew. His newfound friendliness, ironically, irked her right now. He spoke to her like a scared animal, making her feel less somehow. It made no sense. Grace should be grateful that Pogue finally showed kindness. But, strangely, she found herself wanting the grump back. This Shifter set her blood on fire with his intense brooding (and the man was a master brooder). It was as if a switch had been flipped inside her. *I want Pogue to want me,* Grace realized. *I like the prickly bastard! How-*

A sharper nip to Grace's lower lip jolted her thoughts. Without missing a beat, she retaliated with a quick nip of her own, surprising herself. He didn't have time to speak. Fueled by borrowed courage, Grace threw caution and maybe a bit of her dignity out the window.

Grace grabbed the front of his T-shirt, drew him in, and kissed him.

His breath hitched as a deep growl vibrated in his chest. Without warning, he stood and effortlessly carried her over to the door, setting her down with her back to it. He wasn't smiling but looked so... Well, hungry, for lack of better words.

"What was that?" Pogue asked her softly. Dangerously. He seemed to debate stepping back, but he didn't move, his large body towering over her, caging her in. The crushing weight on her chest seemed to give way to something else as his body shielded her from the rest of the world. The weight made its way down, settling between her legs. She squeezed them together, surprised when a small whimper escaped her lips. Pogue seemed to zero in on that sound as he crowded her further, his body almost flush against hers as his large hands braced on the door beside her head.

"Words, Grace," Pogue ordered.

Grace snorted.

"Big ask coming from you. What does it look like I'm doing?" *Please don't reject me now, Pogue. I really fucking need you to work with me here,* she prayed silently as she boldly yanked at his jeans until the top button popped.

"Looks like you're panicking."

She pulled down his zipper as fast as she could and reached into the waistband of his boxer briefs to find him hard. And large. *Woah, that's a lot of man right there,* she thought as she wondered how the hell that thing would fit inside her. A groan slipped his lips before he cut it off and resumed glaring at her. But she did want him inside her, his domineering Alphaholeness be dammed. Right now, that's exactly what she wanted. What she needed. Pogue tried to step back, but instead of releasing him, she squeezed his hard length in warning.

He lowered his head and snarled, his hip pressing into her hand.

"We are not fucking doing this! Grace, you were just gone. In your head!" his voice was a whip against her senses.

"And now I'm back." She whispered harshly, tears running down her cheeks despite every effort to stop them. *When the fuck did I start crying?!* She needed to forget everything and just feel something good. "You use touch to anchor each other, don't you? Did I get that part right? So fucking anchor me!" she spat. *Make me feel safe...*

Pogue growled at her words, ripped open the front of her jeans, popping the button, and jammed a hand in her pants, cupping her with raw intimacy, his eyes boring into hers as he lowered his head.

"This what you want, huh? You want some meaningless fuck, because you're scared?!" He snarled even as he speared her with two fingers, his claws instinctively retracting. She was embarrassingly wet, and she knew it. It didn't lessen when he pushed his fingers into her, hooking them up to stroke that spot inside her. All men knew women had it, but none could actually find it on her. But he did. Of course, he fucking did, and he probably did it just to spite her. Frantically, she pulled at his jeans until she had them halfway down his thighs, along with his boxer briefs.

"Grace," he said, his anger fading. His fingers slowed, and he bent to rest his forehead against hers. She could almost hear him say 'no' again as he shook his head, though his thumb was still rubbing gently against her clit. She lifted his T-shirt and closed her teeth around his nipple, earning her a sharp hiss as he bucked in her hand. She pulled at the offending piece of clothing, wanting more skin, and let out a frustrated huff when he refused to cooperate. Huffing angrily, Grace yanked off her sweater. She still hadn't found the right bra, so she was "free-flying," as they say.

Pogue

As Grace's sweater came off, Pogue's mind froze. She was fucking flawless. *I can't do this!* Pogue's mind raced. *We can't fucking do this! This is so wrong on every damn level! We don't mix with humans!* He mentally listed all of the reasons. They were damn good reasons! A Shifter cub was less frail than a human female. Shifters were built tougher, stronger, and bigger. He could seriously hurt her. But in the condition he was in these days? She could annihilate *him*. She was his polar opposite. His order was disrupted on every level. Despite this, he felt like he needed her more than air. His cat didn't understand all his reasons. All it saw was black and white. *She hurts. We can fix it. Anchor her.* To Shifters, sex was a lot more than just that. It was the ultimate scent sharing. It was providing safety, comfort, and love. Shifters were sensual creatures. Pogue's top brain had the best of intentions. He wanted to back away and help her dress. He'd walk her to her room, and then he'd go pound the fuck out of Rosita and try to forget this human.

And that was a great plan until she grasped his cock again and pumped it firmly. He withdrew his hand from her jeans in shock. *Payback's a bitch,* Pogue thought to himself. He'd zoned out, just like her. He hadn't even noticed her shrugging out of her jeans. But his hands were clawed, and her panties were shredded on the floor…So yeah…He snarled and lifted her to brace her on his arm, poised above his erection. He held her there, braced on one arm, as his other hand splayed out on her chest.

"Tell me to stop," he told her, his breath coming out harsh as his heart picked up speed and he felt his control slipping. *Don't do this. You are not this much of a dick,* he chided himself. *Nothing can come from this, you fucking idiot!* Pogue was usually good with his control, but Grace seemed to have the opposite effect on him. "You're being irrational, Grace."

"Kiss me," she demanded. And dammit, if Pogue didn't do just that. *If there's a shifter hell, you're going straight down,* he told himself as he took her mouth, nipping and licking, dominating her the way he'd fantasized about so many nights over. He kissed her like it was the end of the fucking world and took every moan and whimper she gave. *I'm an asshole,* Pogue thought as he lowered her painstakingly slow onto him, to let her get used to his size. Her eyes drifted closed. *Hell fucking no you don't!* he thought, annoyance flaring up inside him. He shook his head and grabbed her chin between his thumb and index finger.

"No! You want this; you fucking look at me, menace. You show me you're here!" Grace opened her eyes and looked him dead in the eye. Pogue repeated his question. He wanted no blurred lines. "Do.You.Want.This?" he bit out.

"Yes," she whispered.

"Then you will fucking keep your eyes on me. Do you understand?"

"Yes." Her voice came out breathless as she squeezed around him. Seconds later, she gyrated her hips and bit his lip. He lost it, as the last semblance of human control broke, and his cat took over. He grabbed her wrists with one hand and slammed them against the door above her head, mindful of his strength. Then he snapped his hips in firm movements, angling to keep friction on the right spot inside her. He kissed away the tears on her cheeks and let her hold on to him as he rocked against her. Her eyes seemed to deepen in color, and the tears dried as his movements became harder. Pogue ground his jaw so fucking hard he was sure he cracked a molar. This was wrong on every goddamn level, but the moon itself couldn't take him away right now. But he would not fucking hurt her!

He felt her inner muscles contract around him seconds before she came with a strangled scream loud enough by his ear that he felt the blood seeping from it as his eardrum shattered. Shifters might be built tougher, but their hearing equaled that of their wild counterparts and then some. And the woman could scream like a banshee, it seemed. The hook, a part of his anatomy that would lock him in her, released before it had properly formed, spurred by his baser instincts to deal with the perceived danger.

Grace stared wide-eyed at him. Pogue ignored her shock and retook her lips as he chased his release at a frenzied rate, his breath coming out in hard grunts. It didn't take long.

Shock vibrated through him as he felt his cat bending its head to bite her shoulder, marking her. For the first time in his life, his cat had overridden him. He stilled, breathing hard as he looked at her and the small amount of blood coming from the bite. *Fuck!* he cursed himself silently, wiping his mouth with the back of his hand. *Why the fuck did you have to fucking bite her?!* He mentally smacked at his other half. The cat didn't see the problem. She was theirs to mark.

He was still holding her hands above her head, trying to gather his thoughts and level out his breathing, and still hard. It would take more than once. It did for most Shifters. He could hear her speaking but couldn't make out the words. He let go of her hands when she pulled. She palmed his cheeks, looking at his blood, and her eyes welled all over again. She said something to him. He focused on her mouth. Claus had been teaching everyone in StormEdge who wanted to learn how to read lips and sign language. He caught something he thought meant down.

"Fuck!" he snarled. Then, softer, he mumbled to himself. "This was a mistake. This is why humans and Shifters don't fucking mix!" His cat was on edge, and he was confused and angry. Pogue settled her on her feet, picked up her sweater and jeans from the floor, and handed them to her.

He would explain once they'd both calmed down.

But Pogue hadn't counted on the look in Grace's eyes. He also hadn't counted on her pulling on the sweater and jeans and kneeing him hard enough that he saw stars. She fled the room a second later.

He would smack himself, but he was too busy trying to retrieve his aching balls from his stomach. *Yeah, I deserved that. So not only did you let her humiliate herself, you called her a fucking mistake to her face.* He threw his fist through the wall by the door just before he shifted to fix his broken eardrums.

Pogue didn't move until Caden had banged the door open in his face. Stepping to the desk, Pogue quickly pulled his boxers and jeans back up and took a step back, to lean against the desk.

"Sorry it took so long, I got...–Woah!" Caden held his arm up in front of his face, coughing and sneezing. He froze and looked at Pogue, a horrified look on his face as he noticed the mess on the floor.

"No! No, you didn't?!" The sexual pheromones would be like a hot poker up his brother's nose.

Caden popped him on the head. Twice. Then he walked briskly to the windows and opened one, giving Pogue a dirty look before he turned around to look at the desk.

"Poooouge," he drawled. Pogue still wasn't moving.

"Pogue!" he eventually shouted in his face, snapping Pogue out of it.

"Tell me you did not *fuck* Grace on the same table we work at daily! You know, the human who was mentally broken when she walked in! Are you really that much of an asshole?"

Pogue turned to look at his brother.

"No," he said quietly.

"No, what?" Caden pressed.

"No, I didn't fuck her on our desk."

Caden scrunched up his nose.

"The whole room smells like sex; you have blood running down your cheeks, and last I checked, you didn't wear female underwear. Shredded female underwear." He pointed to the panties on the ground next to Pogue. "You didn't do *nothing* Pogue."

Pogue was still in a daze as he tried to explain.

"I fucked up, Cades. And I fucked her up against the door," he mumbled almost as an afterthought.

Caden looked at him for a beat before roaring his laughter as he repeatedly clapped Pogue on the back hard enough to hurt. Yeah, Caden was not proud of him right now.

"The most strong-willed man I know! You really have that little self-control around her, huh?" he said sharply. "Micah is gonna kill you. And we're gonna have a long talk about sex in the office. Like how we agreed we didn't do that. Ever. Pogue, what the shit?"

Pogue just nodded, still standing there in shock like a dumbass.

"I thought... Well, it sounds fucking dumb now," Pogue said quietly. "I nipped her ear to try and snap her out of it. I even carried her to the door and told her no. She was crying, Cades." He looked up at his brother. "She was hurting so bad. So I... Well, I thought..."

"You were trying to comfort her like a Shifter? Like a Mate? Anchor her with touch?"

Right now, Pogue loved that his twin was very adult regarding feelings and shit. He would have torn his face off if he'd started joking. He felt like the lowest lifeform right now. Pogue nodded.

It took a full half hour of Caden feeding him cigarettes after having fished them out from the trash can, and coffee before Pogue finally felt back in control. His cat was as content as ever, yawning and curling up inside him. They'd marked her. She was theirs now. He didn't have the heart to try and explain that all they'd done was scar her. He'd have to get Doc to fix that.

"All right, let's get on top of this. Oh wait, you're already on that," Caden snorted and laughed, and Pogue punched his shoulder.

"On the no sex in the office?" Pogue said, trying to dig up some resemblance of a smile.

Caden looked at him.

"Yeah?"

"I walked in on you, Elijah, and Laney last month. On the desk."

Caden blushed. Pogue knew Caden was a little sensitive about the fact that he had an ongoing agreement with two Nomads from up north.

"I wasn't on the desk," Caden muttered.

Pogue snorted.

"No, Cades. You're right. Laney was on the desk. You were on Laney; Elijah was on you. On the desk..." he said dryly.

That's when Caden went to grab another cup of tea

Chapter 29

G race ran, well, waddled to her room, ripping off the sweater the second she entered. She was furious and had never showered so fast in her entire life. And hurt. And humiliated.

All she wanted to do was go home. Home where it was safe - *oh wait, not safe. Well then, home where I have... What do I have aside from Sophie? A job? Nope. Boyfriend? Nope. A gaping hole in my chest? Yup. So same, same as here,* she concluded as she yanked on the yoga pants Nadya had donated and a T-shirt Micah had left there. It smelled like him.

"Whatever! Fuck him! Urgh, I need to go!" Grace yelled at no one as she paced the room. She didn't know where anyone was, but she needed to get the hell out of this room and this Den.

She literally ran into Hannah by the front door. Damn magical doors! Grace had been attempting to open it, and the stupid thing wouldn't budge.

"Hullo. Where's the fire?" Hannah asked, a grin on her face. Grace turned and looked at her. Hannah's eyebrows shot up. "Oh, okay. Uhm, follow me." Grace trailed down a slender side passage after Hannah until they arrived at a crimson door. With a gentle push, Hannah invited Grace to enter. Stepping inside was like stepping into a genie's lair. The walls were adorned with expansive swaths of vibrant fabric and a massive metal lamp dangled from the ceiling. Hannah had no kitchen, but a kettle sat on a small table. Grace watched as Hannah quickly scooped up some clothing from the floor and nonchalantly kicked a couple of boots under her large, fluffy bed. She promptly turned on the kettle and pulled two cups from a small cupboard by the door, pointing to the bed. Grace climbed up -yes, up. Grace had to jump slightly to scramble onto the mattress because the bed was so high. Hannah waited quietly for the water to boil before making two cups of coffee for them. Then she hopped up and sat cross-legged in front of Grace, huffing her breath.

"From the top, please," Hannah smiled and blew on her coffee.

Grace replayed her equally fantastic and humiliating encounter with the idiotic Alpha, exhaling sharply when she was done.

"I fucked up so bad, Hannah. I think I forced Pogue into having sex with me. Or... Well, I had sex. Good sex. No, wait," Grace signed. "Gods, I was so out of it. I think I maybe goaded him into treating me like a Shifter and just fuck away the humiliation of crawling all over him in a fugue."

Hannah frowned. Grace noticed Hannah's fingertips glowing slightly as tiny electrical sparks hopped from one finger to the other. When she looked into her eyes, she saw the same sparks in Hannah's eyes. "Uhm, Hannah? You're... sparking?"

Hannah blinked.

"Sorry. Okay, so just so I understand. You had an episode? Micah told me about them." Grace nodded. "And when you came out of it, you what? Cause I'm not really sure who's the jerk here," she admitted with a wry grin.

Grace let out a long sigh and took a sip of her coffee.

"I came out of it *on* him. Like physically straddling him. I... I don't know, Hannah, I think I was- am just so damn tired of not feeling in control and not feeling safe, and for some ungodly reason he feels... Safe. Pogue feels safe," Grace said, her voice becoming smaller as she spoke. "I remembered Brody telling me about Shifters and intimacy, and I guess some part of my brain- that would be the dumb part- just kinda panicked a little when I found out he wasn't gay, and all this stupid sexual tension and-"

Hannah held up a hand to stop her.

"Woah, a little less levio, a little more no, no. Pogue is an Alpha Grace. If he really didn't want to, he wouldn't have, but the timing sucked. Okay, so you guys had sex," Hannah shrugged. "This isn't the end of the world. Are you hurt?" She asked, and Grace could hear the sincerity in her voice.

Grace shook her head.

"My wrists are probably gonna bruise a little. I'm kinda sore, and this thing hurts, but that's it," Grace answered, motioning to the mark on the crook of her neck. She tugged down the T-shirt slightly to reveal it to Hannah. Hannah's eyes widened, and she nearly dropped the cup, cursing as warm coffee splattered across the bed. "What? Is it bad? I didn't really look at it."

"Grace, he marked you! That's a mating mark!" Hannah sounded excited but shortly after frowned. "Hang on, he fucked you, *marked* you, and *then* told you it was a mistake?!" Grace just shrugged. "The Maternals are gonna kill him. If Micah doesn't do it first," she fumed. "And if I don't get to him first! What the hell was he thinking?!"

Grace felt a heavy weight settle in her stomach.

"I pushed him, Hannah. I think I used his instinct against him, and I know that's unfair."

"Grace, you're in unknown territory here. It's normal to be confused or on edge. But the fact that Pogue didn't turn you away—and believe me he could have—means something. He's not a juvenile. If he let it go that far, it suggests he recognizes your Shifter side."

"Tiny part. You said so."

"Yes, it's minuscule, but it exists." Look, It wouldn't have gone that far if he didn't have some interest. This mark proves it. Trust me, Shifters can have mind-blowing sex without a scratch," she added with a wry smile. "They only mark when their human or animal side seeks a deeper connection. I've known Shifters my entire life and lived in StormEdge for many years. Believe me, I know. You know, True Mates often connect through their animal instincts rather than their human side," she explained casually. Grace scrounged up her nose.

"Okay, that part I still don't get. I thought mating was a choice. Like marriage? Not that I'm thinking about Pogue in a mating way or whatever."

Hannah snorted.

"And it can be. "True matings are fate's handiwork. Maybe he's your True Mate? Either way, he messed up. You belong here. Trust that. I'm older and wiser," she winked.

Grace had no idea how old Hannah was. Her age seemed to be in her late twenties. However, she recalled hearing that Wielders aged roughly the same rate as Shifters, who aged one-third slower than regular humans. "I have never seen or heard of a Community doing what StormEdge is doing for you. Submissives and the Beta vouching for someone, that's a big freaking thing, Grace. They want you here. Plus, you're literally family now. I think the Alpha is just too proud to admit his Mate might be a human."

Grace looked up, shaking her head at Hannah. Of course, she wasn't anyone's Mate.

"Are you their family too?"

Hannah's lips thinned.

"It's complicated. Take Pogue out of the equation." Hannah said, non-too subtly changing the subject back to Grace. "Look, what do you want? What does Grace want?"

Grace was quiet for a long time, thinking about it, before answering.

"I want to win this war. I wanna help make sure everyone is safe, and I wanna burn down the Council."

Hannah smiled softly.

"Sounds an awful lot like what family does for each other."

It did. Pogue or no Pogue, she wanted this. These people.

"It does, doesn't it? I do want this," Grace said, determination settling in her bones. She looked around the place and noticed a pair of boots that looked way too large for Hannah's small feet. She pointed to them. "So, who's leaving size man boots here?"

Hannah blushed and quickly waved a hand, levitating the boots under the bed. So cool.

"No one." Her tone of voice made it clear not to ask further. Grace decided to change the subject. "Hannah? How come no one here seems to know a lot about Wielders? You're these magical beings, coexisting with Shifters, but it seems like no one knows a lot about you guys."

Hannah wiggled a bit to free her legs and shrugged.

"Magical laws are many and complicated. I can tell you we need each other?" Grace found it odd that Hannah phrased it as a question, not a statement.

"Can you tell me a little about Wielders?"

Hannah smiled, nodding.

"Wielders have existed longer than Shifters." She stopped as if testing something, then nodded sharply and continued. "My people keep the Barrier up, both the main and the smaller ones. Our abilities are released when we're around seven. That's when we gain what you might call the basic pack."

"Levitation?" Grace guessed.

"Yup. All Wielders can levitate to some extent. I'm better at it because of my sub designation." She explained. Grace prompted her to elaborate. "The basic pack is levitation and your main designation. I'm a mage, so I can create. I can't make it permanent, though. Nigel can. He's a scholar. That's the other designation."

Grace held up a hand.

"So Nigel has to learn spells, but he can do more variety than you. To you, it comes naturally, but you're more limited in scope?"

Hannah's brows shot up.

"How'd you know?"

Grace beamed.

"Super nerd. And I used to play a little bit of D & D with one of my fosters before they kicked me out."

Hannah frowned.

"Kicked you out? That's a thing?"

Grace nodded.

"Yeah. It's all good, though. I survived."

Hannah looked at her, a sympathetic look in her eyes.

"You did that a lot, didn't you? Survive?" Grace just nodded. "Do you want StormEdge because of that? To survive?"

Grace looked Hannah in the eye, willing her to see the truth in her heart.

"No, Hannah. I want it to *live*."

Hannah levitated their now empty cups onto the table, cleaning up the mess on the bed, and leaned over to hug Grace tightly.

"Let's do that then. What are we gonna do to cement you here? And do you want me to fry Pogue?"

Grace leaned back.

"You can do that?"

"My main element is earth, but my sub-ability is energy. I can fry him, or any offending part of him, to a fucking crisp!"

Grace thought about it. She hadn't even tried talking to Pogue about the whole thing, so accepting Hannah's zappy touch seemed excessive. On the other hand, she desperately needed to reclaim some sense of control, even if it was just a fraction. *Okay, Grace, time to put on your big girl pants.*

"Maybe a combo? I think I'd really like the Alphas and Micah to understand why I react the way I do cause I haven't told Micah all of it. I know it's dumb, but I'm not really comfortable talking about it, even if it's probably the smart thing to do."

Hannah nodded sagely.

"And Pogue?"

Grace felt her smile turn savage.

"If he thinks I'm a mistake, I'm gonna be the worst one he ever fucking made. I can be a pain in the ass when I put my mind to it. Maybe if I match his dumb with my dumb, we'll make a plus from two minuses."

Hannah nodded sharply.

"Okay, not a tall order at all, even if we're operating on the same levels as the juveniles here." Hannah gave Grace the stink eye. "About the grown-up part. If you want, I can help them understand. I have a friend who can extract key memories while you catch some Z's. Just promise to close your eyes if you wake up when we're doing it. It won't hurt. Promise. On a side note, Can I suggest you get in on the Vigilia training schedule? And if you know of anything we can use in the war..." Hannah looked down at her fingers, letting tiny sparks dance between them. "Grace, anything at all. They're important to me. I'll help you find your feet here and the whole Pogue thing. But help me in return. Get stronger and really be a help, okay?"

Grace felt how serious Hannah was. These people were her family, whether she would admit it or not.

"Deal. Can I ask one last thing, even though you don't wanna talk about it?"

Hannah nodded carefully.

"Is 'Size Man Boots' good to you?"

Hannah blushed and nodded.

"Very. Can I ask you something in return?."

Grace got up and nodded.

"What set off the episode?

Cold sweat started at the base of her spine as memories came rushing back in. She had it pushed so far back that she forgot about it. Grace wasn't entirely sure what she answered or how she got back to her room, but it must have been a good answer because Hannah hadn't followed her... For the first time in a long time, Grace almost wished someone had.

Chapter 30

P ogue settled beside Caden on the dais. The dining hall buzzed with activity, its eclectic layout seeming more chaotic to Pogue's eyes due to the sheer number of Shifters. His gaze scanned the room. Pogue grew increasingly irritated. He looked for the Vigilia; one of them should be with her, as instructed. Grayson and Beau occupied a corner table with Oliver and Nadya. Mehendi laughed at something Maude said while serving food at the buffet. Henley spoke on the phone by the doors leading to the foyer. *Where the fuck is she?!* His gaze lingered for a moment longer. Dina was perched on Tari's shoulder as he arrived. Micah was busy looking for hiding places for the cubs, and he and Caden were both present. Despite the orders, no one was with her, including himself.

"Where the fuck is Grace? Someone was supposed to be with her," he muttered quietly.

Caden heard him just fine.

"I'll go get her. Grab me a plate, too, will you?"

Pogue nodded and got up to go grab them food. Henley came jogging up to him not long after as he'd sat back down, a grim look on his face. Pogue put down his fork and sighed, giving his steak a longing look.

"What?"

"Seems IceFjord has missing Packmembers. No word on how or why. I approached my contact in RazorSea," he explained, referring to another larger predatory community in the area. There were six predatory and two non-predatory communities in the Canadian/Alaska region. RazorSea, a Sleuth near Cordova, was a two-day journey from StormEdge. Though IceFjord denied any and all dealings with StormEdge, he knew they did deal with RazorSea on occasion, even though they, too, were a mixed Community, unlike IceFjord.

"My contact said that IceFjord has locked down tight. No one in or out of their territory, and they've got patrols 24/7. He said he'd spotted more than one Wielder around their borders, and I'm going to go out on a limb and say that could be DeCoill visiting. But no proof that won't set off the slander laws."

"IceFjord won't back out, and them missing Packmembers is good for us. Stop focusing on that and work on ammunition against DeCoill," Pogue told him.

Henley shook his head.

"I think the disappearances and DeCoill are connected."

"But that isn't a now problem. The Turf War is." Pogue said. Henley's lips were set in a thin line. He wasn't ready to let it go, so Pogue threw him a bone. "Do you have a way in with the Council? To get more info?"

Henley's voice was tight as he answered.

"Not one I'm willing to use."

"Then focus on things directly related to the war."

Pogue grunted before telling the tracker to go get some food.

Caden burst through the door just as Pogue was about to bite. Grace was close behind him, he noticed. She took a seat at Oliver's table. Of course, she'd gravitate toward Oliver. Their snark and aggression matched. If she would just not corrupt Nadya, too. She was a good cub despite her insistence that she was an adult now. Caden snatched a chair and sat down forcefully. Pogue arched his brow but said nothing as he pushed Caden's plate toward him and waited. Caden would talk when-

"You're an idiot, bro!" he snarled under his breath.

Again, Pogue lowered his fork.

"Come again?"

Caden's eyes shot daggers at him. Generally, Caden didn't get angry, as much as he just got disappointed. He leaned in, hissing in Pogue's ear, making sure nearby Pridemembers didn't overhear.

"You marked her! You marked her, and then you told her she was a mistake?! What is wrong with you?!" he fumed. "I know you're rough around the edges, but that was cold, even for you. Yes, Hannah explained she was the one who came on to you, but you're a fucking Alpha! A mistake, Pogue?! Really?! I'm telling you right now, I am officially team Grace!"

Pogue stared in disbelief as his twin stood up, grabbed his and Pogue's plates, and walked down to Juno, Liam, and Claus, offering Claus Pogue's plate. Pogue started at his fork, with a now cold piece of meat on it.

Team Grace? There are teams? Both he and his cat were baffled. *Ok, fine, I'll go talk to her then.* He stuffed a piece of meat in his mouth and strolled over to Grace's table. He was pretty sure someone, probably Hannah, had told her to hide the mark, but he could practically feel the eyes of the Maternals and Submissives boring into him. As he approached her table, even Grayson, his damn Vigilia, shot him a suspicious look. Beau was busy whispering something in Oliver's ear.

That something seemed to be 'don't attack the Alpha.' Beau had pinned Oliver to him. Oliver was living proof that one's designation had no bearing on one's personality. And Oliver's personality seemed to want to shred Pogue right now. The rumor mill at its finest. Great...Super... Pogue was fairly certain Grace and Hannah would not have launched a smear campaign. But Hannah clearly told Caden, and someone probably overheard. Rumors in the Den traveled with the speed of lightning.

He looked down at Grace.

"Come with me," he said before turning around and walking away. He took a few steps before realizing Grace hadn't moved an inch. He spun around, ready to glare at her. She wasn't even looking at him! Marching back, he placed himself directly in front of her, his hands braced on the table. "Well?"

Grayson growled at him. He shot him a quick look, effectively shutting him up. Still, she ignored him, instead pushing her food around her plate. Her lips were tense, and she seemed to focus hard on her plate.

"Shall we?" Oliver said, completely ignoring the fact that his Alpha was standing right there. Beau mouthed sorry just as Pogue growled at Oliver. Oliver's jaw was tight, and he clearly didn't want to back down, but he angled his head in submission, baring his throat. The entire table appeared to take a small breath except for Grace. Grace forced a smile as she nodded.

"Yeah, cuz," she said, still not looking at him. But he saw the tension in her jaw. Pogue was so stunned he didn't say a word as the whole table got up and started walking away from him and out of the dining hall. Nadya looked back over her shoulder just as they exited.

"Will you please get those Pogue?" she asked nicely, nodding to the table filled with trays and empty plates. She didn't bother waiting for an answer.

I am the fucking Alpha!

"Pogue, really? You eat for five, and then you're just gonna leave it like that?" Juno nodded to him as she passed.

And that's when Pogue flipped the table.

Chapter 31

"Thanks, Oliver," Grace smiled, though her insides felt shredded. She understood that sticking it to your Alpha couldn't have been easy for Oliver, though he looked okay with it. Grace really didn't wanna hurt Pogue, and from what Caden said, Pogue knew he'd fucked up. But so had she; Caden didn't mince words explaining that either. She got it, though. Ultimately, she'd concluded that snarky and angry were more manageable for her, so she'd go with that. *You fucked it up with the Alphas. So win the Pride.*

Winning the Pride started with a simple rule: don't make their shit, make your shit. Grace knew she'd have to confess about DeCoill, but thinking about it made her stomach roll. Plus, she was already a burden. Then there was Pogue. *Yeah, not opening that can of worms right now.* She felt like a coward, but she'd rely on her newfound friends for now. She was trying to transform knives into spoons, but it wasn't going well. *Be useful, win the Pride, then win the Alphas*, Grace reminded herself. Hannah had evidently tattled to Oliver, and he had jumped into the mission of driving Pogue insane with an enthusiasm that scared her a little. Beau had invited Grace to train with them tonight, most likely at Hannah's request, and they'd all agreed to leave right after dinner. Shifters apparently didn't need to wait for food to settle, Grace thought as the group approached the upstairs gym.

Beau had barely entered the gym with them when Tari approached him. Grace couldn't hear what they were saying. Oliver, who had just picked up a speed rope, groaned. Grace shifted her gaze.

"What's up?"

"Looks like Beau is changing shifts again," Oliver frowned.

"That's bad?" Grace was still trying to learn how everything here worked.

Oliver let go of the rope and grabed his water bottle.

"Normally, I don't mind, but Tari has been switching patrols with him a lot lately. Fucks up the home dynamic and my meetings with the Submissives." Grace nodded, understanding. "But he's doing it to keep us safe... And, it's good training for the Pride to be flexible and shit, I guess." Oliver grumbled as he put down the bottle.

"On that - the good for the Pride thing. Can I run something by you? About the Turf War?" Grace didn't want to assume anything, but she wanted to offer any help she could, and it had been on her mind ever since Hannah asked.

"Sure, hang on." He looked around. "Gray, Mehendi, you got a sec?" Grayson dropped the battle rope he was working on, and Mehendi jogged over. Grace was confused about why they needed to hear it. She had wanted to talk to Oliver about it. Frankly, she found the large leopard and Mehendi's cheetah a little unsettling. Oliver motioned for everyone to take a seat.

"You can't talk war with a Submissive. You wanna talk that kind of shop, we need the Dominants. They'll be able to give you decent feedback."

"Makes sense, I guess," Grace said as the two Vigilia sat down, looking at her. "I was kinda wondering," she started carefully. "The IceFjord assholes. It sounds like they're like old school, right?" Grayson didn't even bat an eye, bracing his arms casually on his knees. His focused demeanor was almost overwhelming. Mehendi nodded as Nadya came to sit, leaning up against Grayson. She looked so comfortable around all the Dominants. "So, I was wondering, why are you guys doing the same? Like bringing knives to a knife fight?"

Grayson casually draped an arm over Nadya's shoulders as he cocked his head. "Please elaborate."

Grace nodded.

"What if I could get my hands on some high-tech human stuff? My best friend's dad owns this huge security firm, and I'm pretty sure he's got contacts in the military."

"High tech? I don't understand," Gray said.

"Ranged weapons," Mehendi clarified as Grace nodded.

"We could get some guns, tasers, and other things. Maybe a few of those flash-bang things and my recurve bow. I can be useful. If you'll allow it," she added softly. "I mean, is this okay?" I'm offering this kind of support?"

Grace had noticed Nadya leaning closer to Grayson as she spoke. He didn't seem to notice. It was a thing of beauty to behold, and it spoke directly into Grace's heart. Even on a subconscious level, they would offer comfort...

"Of course, it's acceptable, Grace," Mehendi said sternly.

Grayson took a sip of water before speaking.

"But why? I want to know why you would offer? And you will not be fighting," Grayson told her sternly.

"Because she likes us, silly. And the Submissives have all vouched for her," Nadya chuckled, putting a hand on the leopard's chest. "And you can't class a human as a Submissive. I think," Nadya scrounged up her nose. Grace noticed Grays eyes tilting down to Nadyas hand briefly, before returning to Grace. Grace couldn't help a small smile. Nadya's cheeks blushed as she noticed. She quickly straightened, leaning away.

Grayson, again, didn't seem to notice, or if he did, he chose not to react.

"Your intentions are good. I will pledge to you when the time comes," he nodded, apparently satisfied with the explanation. He swiftly got up and returned to the ropes as Nadya got up and grabbed her bottle before leaving, saying she needed to find Claus.

She looked at Mehendi, though she was confused by Nadya's sudden departure.

"What does 'pledge' mean?"

"Your turn," Mehendi said to Oliver as she got up and went to do her workout. Oliver stood and started his routine with the speed rope. He wasn't a large man but well-proportioned and clearly kept himself fit. Grace decided the best she could do to match was crunches.

"Pledging means he will accept you as his Alpha female if that bite means what we think it does. Guess we'll know when you actually show the Alpha." Oliver nodded to the scarf Grace was wearing to hide the mark. "Just so you know, we're all on our best behavior. Don't for a second think we wouldn't love to dig into that whole situation like a bear paw in a honeypot. We're being nice," Oliver smirked. "And the Nadya leaving thing? Yeah, I saw you pick up on it..." He turned to look at the Vigilia working out. Mehendi had placed herself between Grayson and them and put on some music. It wasn't very loud, but evidently enough.

"Nadya is twenty-one years old. You're considered a juvenile until you transition around that age. Nadya's barely out of hers. Grayson would be...." Oliver thought about it as he increased the speed.

"Around thirty-two, I think."

"Ok, so there's an age gap." Grace wasn't sure if it was culturally inappropriate to date with an age difference like that.

"Yeah, but that's not really a big deal. We live for a long time. Most of the males here, him included, still insists on viewing her as a cub," Oliver shrugged.

"He doesn't know she likes him?"

Oliver shook his head.

"And she's very Submissive. Grayson, sweetheart, he is very much *not*. We're trying to be casual about it, but most people in the Den know she's been crushing on him since he showed up about six years ago. We're giving it time. Caden will step in if she gets touch starved. But the fact that he still sees her as a juvenile...? Yeah, doesn't look good for our girl."

Micah had explained touch starvation, emphasizing its importance for Shifters. Touch, ranging from hugs to more intimate contact, released endorphins and helped stabilize their animal. Touch-starved Shifters would turn feral, basically in a mental breakdown. This condition resulted in extreme aggression, particularly towards those closest to them, who carried their scent the strongest. They worked out in silence after that. About an hour later, Grayson and Mehendi came up to them. Nadya hadn't returned.

"You wanna join?" Grace asked, feeling slightly on edge, without knowing why. Mehendi grinned at her, shaking her head.

"Thank you, Grace, but I'm pretty sure I don't bend like you're supposed to with yoga. Unless you can do yoga as a cat?" she smiled. Grace took an involuntary step back, suddenly feeling the urge to run.

"Mehendi, come on, girl, could you not?" Oliver said from where he was unrolling his yoga mat. Mehendi smiled at him, her features softening. That's when Grace realized the smile Mehendi had given her was more feral than any other Shifters she had interacted with.

"Sorry," she took a step back. "My cheetah can be a bit unnerving for some people. Not really sure why," she shrugged.

"You know, you smell like him," Mehendi said quietly. Grace was too stunned to say anything at all. Of course, she'd smell like him. "He's very protective," she said a small smile on her tanned face. "Or possessive as it may be," Mehendi winked

Grace's cheeks flushed as her irritation flared. *So, he doesn't want me, but he marks me so no one else would?*

"Motherfucking dumbass," she groaned.

They were doing the final stretch exercises an hour later. Oliver had Grace's leg over his shoulder and his knee bent by her butt, leaning over her to get the stretch she wanted. Because there were no belts, Grayson had Mehendi gently push his leg as he lay on his back, leg at a 90-degree angle. Oliver's nose twitched, and she noticed his pupils dilate.

"What?" He gave her a sly grin. He was charming in an 'I might tickle you before I kill you' kind of way. She was actually blushing.

"Button pushing time," Oliver grinned. Grace just stared at him, unsure what he was talking about.

Mehendi pushed away from Grayson, both looking to the door, then back to Grace, before a small smile formed on the cheetah's lips.

"Pogue is here. I can scent him," Oliver grinned.

"Oliver..." Grayson drawled, warning him.

The door slammed open, revealing Pogue and Oliver's mate, Beau. Pogue was in nothing but sweatpants, looking like he'd just finished a workout. Grace appreciated the sight until both men advanced, growling. Surprisingly, Pogue's growls were directed at Oliver, not her. Oliver, holding onto Grace, shot her a wink. "More?" he asked her, biting his lips to keep from grinning. *You little devil.*

"Yes, please." Oliver complied, and she tilted her head back, smiling. About half a second later, Oliver was plucked from her like an errant toddler and thrust into the arms of Beau.

"Grace!" Pogue cursed as he hoisted her up, turning her so she faced away from him, her body suspended above the floor.

Beau grabbed Oliver, giving him a playful swat, encouraging Oliver to wrap his legs around Beau's waist.

"The fuck, babe?" His deep voice was a mix of confusion and surprise.

Grace wiggled to get down, but Pogue wouldn't let her. So, she did the only reasonable thing. She bit him as hard as she could on his forearm. Like a fucking teenager.

"Ow! Motherfucker! Stop bi-." She kicked back her heel, catching him on the knee, making him grunt.

"Damnit, Grace!" He snarled and put her on her feet. She turned to face him and flipped him off, not exactly sure where she'd left her big girl pants.

"How the fuck is mountain man over there, the civilized one?!" she exclaimed, looking at a grinning Oliver.

"Oh, trust me, he'll be a lot less civilized as soon as we get home. I hope," Oliver added with a wink.

"Yeah, that would be a resounding no cock for you, honey! Act like a cub. Treated like one." Beau told his Mate, growling deep in his chest. Oliver's eyes widened as he looked at his lover. He unwound his legs to get down, but Oliver held on to him.

Grace concluded that Oliver wasn't nearly as friendly when pissed off, and evidently, Oliver had a temper like a powder keg. Or maybe Beau switching another shift was getting to him a little more than he'd initially let on. He smiled sweetly at his mate before he proceeded to deliver a savage headbutt to the nose, making his man let go in favor of holding his nose.

"Ow! Oliver!"

Pogue let go of Grace and walked over, glaring at Oliver, before smacking Beau's hands away from his nose.

"Hold still," he said as he grabbed his nose and yanked it, a pop, telling Grace that he'd just put his nose back into place. Both men turned to her and Oliver. Beau looked at Pogue, who handed him a small white fabric with dark smears.

"Why the fuck do you get the reasonable one?!" Beau started, his voice coming out nasally.

Mehendi barked a small laugh.

"I think the term reasonable is a bit abstract here."

Meanwhile, Gray watched the whole thing silently.

"Don't you fucking start unless you wanna crash on Grayson's couch!" Oliver pointed a finger at him, his lip twitching just the slightest. The little sadist was getting a kick out of this, Grace noted with no small amount of glee. Grace couldn't help but smile at the tragic look Pogue was shooting Beau or the perplexed look on Grayson's face. She noted Mehendi had taken several steps back, not reacting at all.

Pogue took a step towards Grace.

"The fuck, Grace?!" Then he turned to Mehendi and Grayson. "And why the fuck were you two just standing there?"

Mehendi shrugged and buffed her nails. "I wouldn't, Pogue. May not an ass know when a cart draws the horse," her singsong voice chirped. Pogue seethed. At this point, Grayson was sitting on a yoga mat, watching the whole display like a fascinating movie. He chuckled at Mehendi's words. Pogue shot him a look. Grayson shrugged but didn't say a thing.

"You wouldn't fucking what?! I don't even know what the fuck you just said!"

But Grace did. She bent to grab her water bottle and squirted him in the ear when his face was turned. His head slowly turned to her, his cat looking out at her. She held up a pointed finger when he stepped towards her.

"You have no fucking right to tell me shit!" she tossed the water bottle at him.

Beau and Pogue stared at each other for a couple of long seconds. Pogue looked like he was trying to forcibly extract some kind of solution from Beau. The large man sighed and stepped towards Oliver, who was smiling like a savage, his arms crossed.

"Apologies for the caveman act. Please accept my apology. I'll cook tonight. Love you," he recited, likely a rehearsed speech, delivered with comical monotony. Oliver glanced at Grace and winked before he lavished his large mate with kisses along his jaw, offering a quiet apology. Pogue looked at Beau like the man had gone stark crazy.

"Need help looking for those lost balls?"

Mehendi rolled her eyes. *Yeah, not the smart thing to say, Pogue,* Grace thought. Grace crooked her finger for him to bend.

"Yes?" He leaned down, his hands clasped behind his back. He thought he knew how to handle her, it seemed.

"Those balls," she pointed a finger to Beau, "will more than likely be having the best game ever, while those," she pointed to his crotch, "will be playing the field all alone forever because the player is all balls and no goal."

Oliver chuckled discreetly as Mehendi clapped Pogue on the shoulder, winking at Grace before turning her back to leave. Pogue looked pissed, and Grace considered apologizing for her juvenile behavior. She knew how Pogue dealt with disrespect in the Pride, so she appreciated the leeway he gave her. Yet, she couldn't help but wonder why. Did he see her only as a fragile human, or was there more to it? Shaking her head, she left without meeting his gaze.

Pogue

"You know, humans might not be able to play the field like we do, but they score just the same," Grayson said as Pogue just stood there staring before looking at Grayson.

"She bit me! Me! The Alpha!"

"Pogue, you have lost. Save what's left of your dignity," Grayson said, putting his water bottle down. "I think there's something you should know'. Pogue sat his defeated ass on a leftover yoga mat, feeling confused and angry. He was the fucking Alpha. He wasn't used to feeling this disorganized. Grayson gracefully slid into a cross-legged seat.

"She is astute, your human."

Pogue snorted.

"She's not *my* human."

The large man tilted his head slightly in feline confusion.

"The human weapons she will teach us to use could make a very big difference. She is proving her loyalty - to us, the Vigilia and the Pride." Pogue paid attention. When a Vigila, the Pride's protectors, spoke, he would. Grayson described Grace's eagerness to contribute to the looming conflict, a spark of admiration in his typically stoic demeanor. However, Pogue knew Grayson would lock her away from the fights if necessary. His leopard saw her as weak and, thus, someone who needed to be protected same as the Submissives. Pogue didn't want Grace fighting. Not even a little bit and the thought of her in battle enraged his cat.

"What? Arsenal? Military? She's planning to fight?!"

Pogue felt his heart stop for a beat. His cat snarled and flexed its claws. *When the fuck did she get the idea that she'd be fighting?* She heard DeCoill. He could and would take her in if she lifted a finger against a Shifter. Grayson didn't answer him. Instead, he got up and started walking out of the gym, stopping by the doors to look at him.

"Alpha?"

"Yeah, Gray?"

"I am team Grace."

Chapter 32

Council

C ouncil in session

The Council gathered around a large glass table in downtown Ontario, Canada. DeCoill poured wine generously.

"Let us start. I've drafted new laws for tonight's vote," Myla DeCoill announced, taking a big sip.

"The Global Council sent something urgent, Primus?" Daffid Summer asked, deftly peeling an orange.

DeCoill shook his head.

"This is purely relevant for our region. No Global Council involvement is needed. We have an abnormally high incidence of Challenges, and I have been informed that we must devise a solution."

Harry Archer clenched his jaw, leaning in and adjusting his blazer. "To clarify, was this information from the Global Council or your own conclusion?"

"The numbers support the statement, Archer," Loland Mayflower said, his voice tense. "We've seen a surge in Challenges in our region."

"But as we, the local Council, are the ones approving or denying, would it not be easiest to just not approve them?" Archer countered.

DeCoill bristled. He was sweating and looked paler than usual.

"Every single Challenge approved has been valid!"

Archer didn't relent.

"Like approving a Turf Challenge? An actual war in a time where Shifters are disappearing, and we are on the brink of extinction? StormEdge has proven three times over they are the dominant Community over IceFjord. "Archer seethed.

DeCoill smiled all too sweetly.

"Harry, we serve the people. The recent changes in the mongrel Community justify IceFjords' petition. It's approved, the timeframe set, and the Regulators contracted. Alexander, confirm?"

The Wielder representative Alexander Hayfield confirmed wordlessly. DeCoill continued. 'Now, proposal one, and this one pertains to Challenges in general. Rewrite the law for this region only. 1. A Community Challenged may not make any transfers until the Challenge is over. 2. All members, regardless of rank and place in the hierarchy, must participate in Turf Challenges. Cubs under the age of ten are excluded, of course. If they do not, the defending Community will lose by default. The Council takes their land, and the Community is disbanded. 3. Only one Alpha may participate in a Challenge, and 4. Any Pet participating in any way, no matter how minor, will be sentenced to death. Regardless of why and how they participate. All in favor?'"

"Now hold up," Archer interrupted. "You can't just expect us to vote on something this extreme without discussion!"

DeCoill's smile turned sly as he looked at the wolf Shifter. He then slid a piece of paper across the table.

"Please read this out loud."

Archer grabbed the piece of paper and read it. It was stamped and signed by Kelly Walters. Member of the Global Council.

"Effective today, Primus Myla DeCoill gains temporary sovereignty to address the imbalance in the Alaskan/Canadian region until year-end. He has the authority to enact necessary law changes without further debate on the specifics of the laws for the region's well-being. Amendments require the usual voting procedure—majority rules. In a tie, the Primus has the decisive vote." Archer's face twisted in disbelief as DeCoill gloated.

"As you see, Archer, I can and will. Now, Number 1. All in favor?" The table took a vote. Only the last suggestion was failed, but DeCoill was quick to offer an alternative.

"Amend number 4 as follows: Ownership of the Pet falls to the Council. Under Shifter law, the former owner may contest this with a recognized lawyer. Punishment of the Pet falls to the Council."

Just like that, It was over. Archer and Summer were consistently opposed, while DeCoill and Mayflower were in favor. Hayfield abstained, remaining committed to his magic-related votes. And so DeCoill pushed through the new laws.

DeCoill swiftly moved on. "This last bit is just for your information, as I have been mandated to inform you regarding the annual tally of Shifters in our region.

I'll conduct that myself, as I'm performing a personal tally of all Communities for my thesis on same-sex matings and mixed-blood Shifters to determine the remaining Purebloods for the Global Council. I'll begin with StormEdge, then move to FireQuill, RazorSea, and BlackMoon. Mayflower, can I rely on you to track the Nomads?"

Mayflower nodded.

The anger that burned through Archer as he left the meeting could have set the world on fire.

Chapter 33

24 hours later

G race had slept in like way in. Checking her phone, she saw that it was closer to dinner time than morning. Shifters didn't seem to be constrained by conventional schedules; their animal instincts dictated their sleep patterns. And they slept less than humans did. Grace, on the other hand, was utterly exhausted. *Must have coffee...* she thought as she rolled out of bed and dragged herself to the shower.

The phone rang as she was pulling on her last pair of underwear. *Gotta find out where to do laundry around here.* The pile of dirty clothing in the corner of her room was getting ridiculous. She picked up, recognizing Sophie's number.

"Morning, Miss Allen."

"Evening, Miss... Well, what do I call you now? Have you chosen your brother's name?" Sophie asked with a yawn.

Grace, truthfully, hadn't given it much thought. She'd been a little preoccupied, she thought as Sophie told her about her day. But being a Whitmore instead of Doe did have a ring to it. Grace sighed and sat down on the bed. This would not be an easy conversation, and she had been specifically advised not to reveal any furry information to Sophie. But Grace knew Sophie would send her dad or, well, his security people if she thought Grace was in any real danger.

"Not sure. Thinking about it. But, uhm, there are a couple of things I need to tell you. Followed by a huge ass favor." Grace had been going over it in her head a thousand times. How to lie to your best friend 101.

"Sure, love. Shoot."

Grace barked a small laugh.

"Hoping to. Okay, so..." Grace invested an hour crafting the most pivotal lie of her life. She fed Sophie a story about the base taking in a multitude of wild animals tracked by poachers. Another chunk of time was spent trying to justify the seeming lack of military presence due to personnel being away, leaving mainly civilians. Sophie didn't fully buy it. Grace knew because Sophie outright told her so. Yet, that's what best friends did. One would request an absurd amount of weapons using a terribly fabricated reason. Then the other would tell her that if she could have someone pick them up, she would risk being arrested, drawn, and quartered by the Australian government, the CIA, the FBI, and the Queen of England for gun smuggling. Grace adored Sophie, but where Grace was open to the possibility of the paranormal, Sophie believed only what she could explain.

"I'll get some things ready, but Grace, I want to know precisely where you are. Micah won't tell me. He says it's a non-disclosed base. Why can't you tell me?"

Grace sighed.

"Sophie, I'm really just trying to play nice until I'm better, and they're being really good to me. I promise you I'm safe. You know, apart from the whole Pogue thing."

"Pogue thing?"

Then came the whole 'we had angry sex, he gave me a hickey, and then told me I was a mistake, blah, blah.' Sophie went silent, signaling to Grace that she was processing it all. It took nearly two full minutes for Sophie to finally speak up.

"To be fair, Grace, you might not be the most eloquent person, and it sounds like Pogue might have the same issue. And I know he messed up, but deliberately provoking him seems a bit... catty?" Grace gasped.

"Yes, yes, I know I'm on your side here, and I am. But perhaps disrespecting one of the bosses in public isn't the best approach. Maybe try talking?"

Sophie was making sense, though it did involve donning the metaphorical 'big girl pants,' swallowing pride and discussing feelings. Grace assured Sophie she'd consider it, then spent ten minutes showering her best friend with gratitude for the grenades. They wrapped up the conversation shortly after so Grace could grab some food.

Entering the dining hall, a burst of cheerful laughter caught her ear. She couldn't contain a high-pitched squeal when she spotted him. The abrupt sound made a few Shifters, including Juno, flinch. Without hesitation, she sprinted towards him. Though he'd only been away for a couple of days, it felt like an eternity.

"Micah!" She called out, closing the gap between them. Micah let go of the two duffel bags he was carrying and moved toward her.

"Darlin'!" His face lit up with joy. The commotion drew the attention of several onlookers as she leaped into his arms, wrapping her legs around his waist.

She grabbed his face with both hands.

"Oh my God, I missed you so much!" I know it's only been a few days, but damn!" She exclaimed, gently turning his strong, square jaw to examine his features. Micah had grown a neat blonde beard and shaggy hair that fell into his eyes. Those cute freckles on his nose reminded her of a cross between Heath Ledger and Kurt Cobain. "He knows!" Brody's voice boomed as he stood in line waiting for food. A few Shifters chuckled.

"I do, though." Micah smiled impishly at her and hugged her tight as his muscular arms supported her butt.

"I have so much to tell you, Micah." She felt her smile falter a little. Suddenly, she felt her eyes well up. Micah just shook his head.

"No, darlin', you don't. Sophie has kept me well informed. Very," he ended on a serious note.

"It's not just that. There's more. Like a lot more." Her voice became a little quieter.

Micah guided them to a cozy table by the towering, floor-to-ceiling windows and settled into a seat, keeping her securely wrapped around him. In hushed tones, Grace confided in him about DeCoill being her stalker, the fabricated story she told Sophie, the weapons, and Pogue. Micah listened attentively, his hand gently caressing her back. When she finished, he gently drew her head in for a tender kiss on her forehead. Then, he stood, expertly adjusting his hold to support her as she clung to him.

"Forward me the pictures, and I'll inform the Alphas. I'll tell them about the weapons, too. You did well, Grace. I know it's hard as hell, but try not to worry. I will keep you safe, okay? I promise. He won't get to you! Now, you just let your big brother do big brother things." He snickered as she bopped him on the nose.

"Cause I have one of those, you know," she smiled.

"Yes, darlin', your very own goofball," he smiled as he spun around, still holding her.

A low growl stopped their reunion. Micah swiftly turned them to face a displeased Pogue, holding a travel mug and a ceramic cup.

"Micah," he greeted him with a nod. "Wanna stop spinning my...." He stopped as he seemingly was trying to find the correct label. "Just put her the fuck down!" he growled. Micah smirked and did. He looked down at Grace.

"Darlin', go grab your coffee. I need a word with my Alpha."

Grace wasn't particularly interested in being present for that conversation. Especially with the ache that being near Pogue was causing right now, even if he seemed to have brought her coffee. He shifted his gaze between the cup and her as if contemplating handing it over but then changing his mind. If it meant avoiding this awkward situation, Grace was more than willing to let Micah handle whatever his brothers did. She simply nodded and walked over to the long line, patiently awaiting her turn.

Chapter 34

Pogue watched his Beta closely. He knew what was coming, and it couldn't happen here. He jerked his head toward the steel doors leading out of the dining hall and started walking. Micah followed close on his heels. Pogue didn't stop until they were outside and had walked ten minutes into the forest surrounding the Den. He leaned up against a large oak tree.

"Look, Micah, this is-"

Micah's fist cut him off, connecting solidly with his jaw. It snapped his head to the side, a metallic taste of blood in his mouth. His cat stirred, ready to pounce on what it saw as a threat. But this wasn't a threat; it was a brother defending his sister's honor. Pogue understood family and honor. He would allow this. Another punch followed, this time catching his chin and jerking his head up, almost cracking his neck.

"Ok. Are you-" *Nope, not done yet.* To his credit, Micah's lion was contained, though Pogue was sure the cat would love to strip his hide right now. Micah's lion was mean as hell, and most days, he was thankful Micah could stay coherent when his cat took over. Most Shifters could, but Micah had honed the skill. Hell, the man could play a good game of checkers when he was in his fur. His Beta rained down three more blows before Pogue had enough and started growling at him, his cat fed up with just standing there. Micah backed off and glared at him.

"You're gonna fix this, Pogue, he said, his tone low and his words clipped. Micah never looked threatening. Pogue was well aware that it was on purpose. Underneath the soft muscles and teenage wardrobe, he was a skilled fighter. He'd just learned to hide his dominance. Pogue wiped his mouth after spitting out the blood on the ground.

"I can't have a human here," he said casually." You know it's not safe, even if sending her back isn't either. At least in the human world, there are people who can protect her," Pogue reasoned, though the world tasted foul in his mouth.

Micah smiled- not in a nice way.

"Really, Alpha? You don't think you're doing this push-pull for a reason? You're not just a little bit scared, huh? Because you might actually want her so much, you're terrified this war will end her? You don't think there's a chance she is your True Mate? Or did you mark Rosita, too?" Micah snarled.

Pogue felt his chest constrict with Micah's words, and his fist shot out fast and hard, connecting with Micah's cheek so hard the Beta ended up on his ass. Deep down, locked under layers and layers of pride, that was the very thing that he did not want to admit. He was fucking terrified.

Pogue snorted.

"Of course, I didn't fucking mark Rosie!" he rebuffed harshly. Micah didn't growl. Just kept smiling.

"So, you didn't have to fight your cat when DeCoill paid a visit? Nothing stirred at all watching her being accepted so much that the Submissives vouched for her? It didn't matter that your own Vigilia are telling you with and without words that they're team Grace?"

Yes, it did.

"No."

Micah nodded and got back up.

"Ok, so you wanted her just enough to fuck her *and* mark her. But not enough to keep her. Is that it?"

Pogue let out a harsh breath.

"It's not like that, Micah. And the mark will go away."

"Then explain to me what it is like!" Micah shouted. *Wow, he was actually raising his voice.* "You hurt her, Pogue! You told her she was a mistake! All because you're chickenshit, scared something better comes along, and she won't cut it for you!"

Pogue felt his cat clawing at him. He was at the end of his tether.

"Stop talking, Micah."

"No, I will not stop talking. Clearly, someone needs to. You might be fine with Grace dying or getting hurt like you hurt her, but I won't let you fucking destroy her! I will find her a good male and-"

Pogue's leash snapped, and he backhanded Micah so hard he flew back several meters, landing on the wet ground again with a thud. He was up in a second flat, gracefully surging to his feet. Micah laughed at him. Actually laughed, even as he spat blood on the ground.

"Right, Pogue. You don't want her, but nobody else can have her. Wow... Too proud to be with a human, Alpha?"

"It has nothing to do with pride!" Pogue marched over to him and grabbed him by his thick-knitted sweater. "It has everything to do with her safety! She is human, yes! She is weak! A cub can accidentally kill her! *I* can accidentally kill her!"

"And that's the whole reason you're telling yourself you don't want her, right? Because you're scared shitless, you'll love her, and she'll get hurt."

"I. Am. Not. Scared!" he roared. "And we are fucking done with this conversation, Micah! Stay out of my damn business and do your fucking job, Beta!" Pogue poured every ounce of dominance into his words. Micah shrunk in his grip. Pogue took a deep breath and let him go. He didn't miss Micah's calm, low voice as he walked away.

"Yeah, you are." Micah held up a fist as he opened the front door to the Den. he held up a fist. "Team Grace!"

"Motherfucker!" Pogue shouted, stomping inside, heading for his lair.

Caden caught him just as he entered the Den.

"Emergency Vigilia meeting. Now!" he snapped.

Chapter 35

Pogue trailed into the office right behind Caden. He explained he'd sent an emergency code in a mass text to the Vigilia, Nigel, and Hannah. Tari was already there; whatever Caden was about to share clearly came from him. The news must have been sudden to Tari too. All he was wearing was a long black skirt, and he smelled like sex. A lot, even.

Shortly after, Hannah Displaced into the room. Her short hair was sticking out in every direction, and she was wearing a long silk bathrobe and her chunky black leather boots.

"This had better be an emergency!" she growled, looking from Pogue to Caden. He nodded. *Must be bad*, Pogue thought as Beau came running in, Mehendi on his heels. Beau had obviously been in the shower, judging from the fact that all he wore was boxers and boots, and his hair was wet. Grayson came running in, his leopard huffing and hissing as Micah almost tripped over him as he barged in the door, Dina on his shoulder.

Usually, they'd shoot the breeze, but Caden didn't mess around today. He looked at Hannah.

"Where's Nigel?"

"Dunno. Might be at the Academy with his mentor. He's trying to decide where he stands," she said, disdain coloring her words. Hannah, it seemed, wasn't Nigel's biggest fan these days. But then again, he hadn't been around a lot. He only came in to do permanency spells and walk the halls for a little while before leaving again. That had been his general thing from the start, not like Hannah. Hannah was StormEdge - or as close as a Wielder could get to being a Pridemember.

Caden nodded sharply.

"Henley is with the Dahlings. I'll brief him later. Tari, go!"

Pogue looked to Tari. His serval cat was in his eyes as he spoke.

"In under two hours, DeCoill, with one or more Regulators will show up to do a special tally." Tari reviewed the law changes, one at a time, and Pogue and Caden kept everyone in line.

"This... He can't fucking do that! And what the fuck is a star system?!" Beau growled. Pogue didn't have a clue, and what Tari read out loud didn't explain either. Micah, though, seemed to know, judging by how his claws extended and retracted rhythmically and his canines elongated. Pogue reached out and embraced him, emitting calming pheromones for his Beta. Their previous disagreement was insignificant. Micah was Pride, and Pogue had his back. If Micah withheld information, it was most likely for a good reason.

"I don't know," Tari said. "But Beau, we need you to keep Oliver in check. He will be taken into custody if he steps as much as a claw out of line."

Beau ran his fingers through his wet hair, grabbing the ends and gently pulling.

"I know! But I have no idea how to get him to agree to this. You know his stance. He is gonna shit a brick," Beau said, clearly frustrated.

"And every member of the Pride has to be here?" Caden asked.

Tari nodded.

"Almost. The Council has asked us to send a runner to the Dahlings to explain that DeCoill will be coming there next."

Henley's head shot up.

"I'm going."

"Maybe Oliver- "Beau started, but Henley cut him off.

"Beau, I have to go."

Pogue indicated to Henley.

"Henley goes. I want our tracker moving freely. Beau Oliver's your Mate, but if you can't contain him, I will." Beau nodded.

"Grace?" Micah asked.

"Is with me," Pogue said automatically before he could shut his big mouth. *And now you can't take it back, dumbass!*

"On Grace, there's something you all need to know too." His tone was even, but there was a hint of rage in his voice.

Pogue listened as Micah told him about DeCoill stalking Grace and showed him the incriminating photos. Pogue felt another sharp pain in his chest. De-Coill was hunting her. His human. Pogue was only vaguely aware of Caden's arms wrapping around him, his attention taken up by the struggle to resist the overwhelming desire to shift and pursue DeCoill.

Caden looked at Pogue after letting him go with a sharp nip on his ear. *Yeah, I hear you. Buck up.*

"So DeCoill is hunting her and not Micah. Because he sees her as weaker? Easier to get to? Before at least." Caden asked. No one had an answer.

Micah cleared his throat.

"Are you sure you want to be the one to keep her safe? You're not looking very safe at the moment, Alpha."

Pogue glared at his twin. When Caden just shrugged, he pinched the bridge of his nose. He knew what this was.

"Show of hands. Team Grace?"

Even Dina voiced her allegiance. Did they not understand how fucking dangerous this was to her?

"Team Pogue?" Caden was the only one to raise a hand, and Pogue was sure that was mainly because he felt he had to. He sure as hell didn't look very fucking team Pogue.

Pogue let out a frustrated groan.

"Really?! Why the fuck do you have to meddle?! Let me deal with this! Grow the fuck up and stop picking stupid teams!"

"Grace is our business," Grayson said quietly. "We claimed her as a Pet, did we not?"

Always the fucking voice of reason...

"She is weak!" Pogue growled. *She makes me weak. Makes me scared,* Pogue quietly admitted to himself as he felt his defenses crumble.

Hannah straightened up and pointed at him.

"You have no idea how strong she is!" let me enlighten you on your supposedly 'weak' human. She let me dive into her memories, and believe me, there's nothing weak in there! She was abandoned as a child; she was rejected so brutally and frequently that it's unimaginable! Locked away for hours, beaten, lived on the streets, narrowly escaped assault, starved, and now she's hunted by a Shifter, and she's still fucking standing!" Hannah exclaimed.

Pogue watched as her eyes started to change, tiny sparks of electricity shooting out from them as they did from her fingertips.

"Her mind was violated so early. As a child, she mostly survived on her own! Did any of you do that? Did you need to run from people who were supposed to take care of you? Were you tied to a chair and yelled at, called worthless, weak, and a waste of sperm?! Don't you dare call her weak! As if all she can be is weak and unwanted by the people she wants to help so much!" Hannah turned to Pogue. "Stop fucking around, put your big boy pants on, and act your damn-"

"She is wanted!" Pogue roared. His hands shook as he fisted them by his sides, and his canines elongated.

The room fell silent, and all eyes were on him. Within him, his inner feline sat on its haunches. *She's wanted. She is mine.*

Pogue could feel his blood pounding in his temples and his breath escaping in ragged bursts. He let out a sharp exhale. Caden tapped his shoulder and looked at Beau.

"Beau, get Oliver in line. We have to line up in the dining hall in an hour. Pogue, go get Grace. We have another matter to discuss about the Turf War, but we'll do that this evening. Meeting right after dinner, here," Caden said and dismissed everyone.

Pogue still hadn't moved. His brain was going in circles. Caden wrapped his arms around him, and Pogue leaned his cheek on his brother's shoulder.

"She makes me dumb, Cades."

"I know bro. But your cat wants her. Put your big boy pants on."

Pogue sighed and stood there a little longer, letting his twin soothe him. Then he started the suddenly very long walk to Grace's room, hoping to find her there.

Chapter 36

Grace had just wrapped up a yoga session, which should've left her feeling pretty limber. But she didn't. She felt like a complete mess, and not a single muscle seemed to have eased up. *A lawman Shifter is gunning for me. I'm lying to my best friend. I'm falling for a jerk, and I still don't have any damn shoes. Yeah, life's a real peach these days.* "Go to Canada, they said. It'll be fun, they said," Grace huffed.

A knock on the door yanked her out of her self-imposed rollercoaster of misery. She didn't even get to say a word before Pogue walked in.

"What the fuck do you want?" she snarled, automatically going into defense mode.

Pogue seemed to puff up but think better of it, letting out a long breath between his teeth.

"May I?" he indicated to a spot beside her on the bed. She shrugged. He crossed the distance in two long strides and sat beside her, bracing his elbows on his knees, not looking at her. He took another deep breath. His too calm demeanor worried her.

"We need to talk, but that'll have to wait. Right now, you're gonna do exactly as I tell you. without making me explain." Of course, now Grace needed an explanation, but when she went to speak, he held up a single clawed finger. "I will explain everything later. Later Grace. Not now."

His voice was eerily calm, a stark contrast to the tension In his shoulders and the way he tightened his hands so tightly together that his knuckles were white. Something was up. Her suspicions were confirmed when he turned and looked her in the eye. "I know DeCoill is hunting you. He will be here in forty-five minutes. When he arrives, you will make believe you have no idea that we know. He's gonna do a tally, and you will stand silently and look down at the ground the whole time. Do you understand, Grace?"

The man who wants to kill me. Here. He's coming here. Grace's pulse quickened, and her breathing shallow. Pogue slid his large arm around her shoulder and drew her up against his side. "*Grace*! Do you understand? Don't fight me on this."

"You're not my fucking keeper," she bristled, though with about a quarter of the zest she usually would. Pogue tensed up and growled.

"Do as you're told."

I'm not a fucking child, she thought, trembling slightly in fear. She'd witnessed Shifter strength, speed, and superior senses. She'd have no chance against DeCoill unless she had a weapon.

"Fuck y-"

"Please," he said as if that single word had knocked the wind out of him.

Grace cocked her chin to meet his gaze.

"Did you say 'please'?" Did I hear that right?" she asked, forcing a small, brittle laugh.

Pogue chuckled lightly.

"Don't start expecting it." To her surprise, Pogue gently squeezed her again and dropped a quick kiss to her temple. "Stay behind us. Stay quiet. Can you do that?"

"Will I be protected?" He didn't answer. Just nodded. "Fine. Pogue?"

"Yeah, Grace?" He looked as wound up as she felt.

"Should I wear a scarf?"

He stiffened, as she expected, intensifying the rejection. He simply nodded, and he was soon moving away from her. He spoke with his hand on the doorknob, his back to her.

"I won't let him have you, Grace. Not now, not ever."

Chapter 37

G race, still shoeless, watched as the Pride gathered in the dining hall about thirty minutes later. She'd skipped socks and was dressed in Micah's sweatpants and an oversized T-shirt. The setup was straightforward. Except for Oliver, a Dominant stood on each side of a Submissive. Beau was beside him, and Micah was on the other side. Tari stood next to Micah, and Dina stood to Beau's left. The Maternals were evenly distributed, with roughly one for every five people in the row. She counted forty-four Shifters. Pogue approached with purposeful strides, gently gripping her shoulder, guiding her toward the center, and partially positioning her behind Micah. Leaning in close, he murmured by her ear.

"Stay quiet. Head down."

She looked up at him and couldn't help the slight twitching of her lips.

"And the magic word is…?" she trailed.

Pogue rolled his eyes.

"Please."

She nodded as he positioned himself in front of her. His sudden shift in demeanor left her thoroughly confused. Still, she couldn't deny the sense of security being sheltered by him and Micah provided. Her brother, Micah. Yeah, that was going to be an adjustment. She was surprised at how quickly she'd relaxed when Pogue entered her room. A part of her wanted to scream in rage because he had so badly hurt her. But she wasn't stupid. This was a serious situation; regardless of her emotions, she understood the importance of keeping calm. Despite the fact that DeCoill terrified her. Despite Pogue being a jerk.

The doors swung open, revealing DeCoill accompanied by the familiar Councilman with long blond hair from before. Two hooded figures, the Regulators, trailed behind. Summer, the affable Councilman, acknowledged Alphas, Micah, and the room with a nod. DeCoill looked worse than the last time she saw him. He was clearly sweating, and he looked... *Is he high?* she thought. Grace carefully tugged at Pogue's shirt. He didn't turn around, but his hand came around and grabbed hers, his thumb rubbing circles in her palm. *Oh, he must think I'm scared,* she realized. But the fact that he didn't turn told her not to speak. And to be fair, she was scared. Not just a little bit, either.

"Well, well. I must say, I find myself surprised you could assemble so quickly. After all, I only gave the notice-" DeCoill looked at an old-looking wristwatch. "Twenty minutes ago."

No, you didn't? Grace thought. Pogue came to her room before that. She looked at Micah. He looked just as confused as she felt, but he quickly plastered on a smirk, hiding it.

"Let's get this started, shall we? I have with me a Regulator specialized in Shifter genetics. You will all inform me of your lineage and your... *beliefs.*" He said the word "belief" like poison on his lips.

"It's not a fu-"

"Oliver!" Pogue hissed. Oliver looked livid but clamped his mouth shut.

DeCoill snapped his head toward Oliver.

"Ah, we will have to talk about how to govern a Community, Alphas. Now, if the Alphas will step forward, they may be our demonstration. Summer, hand me the markings."

Pogue subtly gestured for Grace to step behind Micah as he moved out of line. A Dominant, whose name she couldn't recall, widened his stance to fill the gap, protecting Grace. She placed her hand gently on Micah's lower back, observing as Caden and Pogue stood before DeCoill. Caden's words were clipped as he spoke.

"Caden of StormEdge, Pureblood Jaguar. Unmated."

DeCoill rolled his hand, motioning for him to continue, his smile wide. The other Councilman, Summer, sighed.

"Really, Myla, this- "

"Silence!" he screeched and turned to Caden. "And?"

"Bisexual." DeCoill scowled and signaled for Summer. Grace watched in horror as Archer produced a piece of gray fabric—a star. Summer approached Caden, his head bowed and affixed the star to his shirt.

Grace felt a surge of gratitude that most Shifters seemed unaware of the symbol's meaning. Grace, however, recognized it from history lessons about the Holocaust. She wanted to kill that sorry piece of shit. Caden turned around. Grace had never seen Caden angry before, but he was furious. He knew, she realized. *The motherfucking platypus-billed dung beetle!* She cursed silently, clutching Micah's T-shirt. She could feel his back's muscles becoming hard as steel.

DeCoill waited for Pogue, who recited his lineage and stated that he was unmated and straight. A gold star was fixed on his shirt. The humiliating ordeal continued. DeCoill asked. Shifters answered. A Regulator pricked their finger and held it close to its mouth, seemingly tasting the blood to test for... Truth? Grace wasn't sure. Turned out that if you were pureblood and straight, like Pogue, you got a gold star. DeCoill made a show of it, paraded him around and telling everyone that if he mated with another Pureblood jaguar, he could keep it, but if he degraded his bloodline and bred outside his species, a gray star was the best he could hope for.

Grace had begun quietly and invisibly, walking up and down the line, stroking the most tense Shifters' backs. She paused when Oliver's name was called. He glanced at DeCoill, then turned to Beau, pulling him into a fiery kiss before confidently striding up to DeCoill. Grace thought she saw a faint smile on Summer's face, but she wasn't sure. One thing was clear, though—DeCoill was not pleased. Oliver. As he addressed Oliver, his sneer and clenched fists spoke volumes.

"Oliver of StormEdge. Do you classify as Purebred?" he snarled.

Oliver shrugged.

"Define Pure."

DeCoill hissed at him but quickly replaced the grim line of his mouth with a fake-ass smile and answered.

"In your case, pure bears on both sides, for a minimum of ten generations back."

Oliver nodded.

"I guess I lost the gold star, mister Councilman. I can only claim five! Oh yeah, I'm also mated. To a man. In case you're in doubt, cock is my favorite toy!" he mocked.

"You disrespect me with your mockery!" DeCoill turned to the Regulator. "Test it!" The Regulator floated toward Oliver and pricked his arm quicker than Grace could follow. It then turned to DeCoill.

"His blood is...." It seemed to pause, "pure."

Grace thought it was all done when the last Shifter had been categorized. It was not.

DeCoill looked over this clipboard, a disgusted look on his pale face.

"Considering StormEdge is the world's only known dual Alpha Pride, one should think you'd be more selective. Nineteen Purebloods between all of you. So sad. Now, bring me your Pet."

Pogue's voice echoed loudly, likely to mask Micah's growls and Grayson's unsheathed claws behind his back.

"No."

DeCoill's head whipped toward Pogue.

"I think you're mistaken, Alpha. I hold the power here. Gold star or not, you'll obey me. You're welcome to persist in your insolence, but I will take the Pet into custody now. As the human liaison, I must ensure it's in proper condition."

Grace stood frozen in place behind Beau, who tensed as Summer approached, his hands raised low in a placating gesture, his face pleading. She realized he didn't want DeCoill to notice. DeCoill, the sadistic fuck, could and would punish StormEdge for defending her. Several Pride members emphasized the Council's power over Communities. *Win the Pride.* Grace knew she had to act the part.

I'm Oliver Twist, she chanted silently and placed a hand on Beau's waist.

"Please, sir, may I pass," she whispered, trying to sound as lowly as possible. She caught Pogue's eyes as Beau let her pass. He looked like he was ready to blow something up.

Summer stopped before her and gently cupped her elbow with his hand.

"Please, if you would."

DeCoill looked almost gleeful as they approached him, and she recoiled as the disgusting man put his clammy hand on her, roughly grasping her jaw.

"Open up, Pet," he smiled. His breath was foul. *Oliver Twist, my ass, I am not opening my mouth near that piece of shit.* Grace clenched her jaw tightly. Grace realized her error as DeCoill's backhand sent her sprawling.

Grayson was poised to strike as Micah growled. The Regulators reacted quickly to intercept. Beau quickly, more luck than anything, subdued Micah while Nadya's whimper diverted Grayson's attention. *Smart move cuz.* Grace avoided looking back at Pogue as she spat blood onto the floor.

"You will not be insolent, Pet!" DeCoill spat at her. She didn't look up at him. "Stand up right now!"

She did. And then, that little filter she was supposed to have between her brain and her big fat mouth malfunctioned.

"I am not *your* Pet!" she said through clenched teeth.

"That's where you're mistaken, mutt! You are mine to terminate under Council law if I see fit. You see, I am in charge of all Pet matters. If you will not open up your filthy mouth, you will strip down."

Without waiting for her response, he grabbed the scarf and tightened it around her neck, causing sharp pain. His claws scraped down from the collar of her T-shirt, then across her sweatpants twice. She soon stood naked, the ends of her scarf her only cover. He spun her around. DeCoill would understand how most people felt about public nudity. This was a calculated humiliation, and it was working. Tears streamed down her cheeks as he gripped her neck with enough force to leave a bruise. Grace was relieved that all but one Shifter in the room had averted their gaze. But not Pogue.

Pogue looked her in the eye, his hands fisted, blood dripping from his knuckles, pooling onto the floor. Caden was standing behind him. The blood falling between Pogue's legs seemed to be coming from his back. Caden's claws were most likely dug in. Holding him in place. Pogue remained motionless, his eyes on Grace as DeCoill spewed.

"You should be collared," he remarked, his gaze raking over her. "Your condition almost leads me to believe you are not being utilized as a Pet should be."

DeCoill's lips near her ear made her stomach churn. The familiar signs of a fugue started at the base of her spine. No, not now. She steadied herself as he continued, "You are a Pet. Replaceable, disposable, useless. Tell me, what do you do here, Pet? And don't lie. My Regulator will know. Yes, Grace, *I* have Pets too." Grace caught the slightest movement from one of the Regulators. However, their large robes and hoods betrayed nothing.

"I wash the floors and stack dishes," she whispered through her tears.

"And?"

"I... Please, sir, you're hurting me."

Turns out he wasn't. Not compared to the hurt Grace felt when he harshly pushed her onto the floor, making her head bang against the stone surface.

"What else, Pet?" he shouted, his voice breaking as it rose in octaves.

"Whatever they command!" she whimpered.

DeCoill kicked her back, prompting her to instinctively curl into a protective ball. Surprisingly, for a Shifter, DeCoill's strength seemed lacking, she observed hazily. The kick should have propelled her across the dining hall, but instead, it felt more akin to a human's strike—painful, yet not deadly.

"Enough, Myla!" Summer's voice sliced through the air like. "You came for a tally. We lack the authority to harm their possessions. Let's proceed to the next Community."

DeCoill let out an exasperated sigh.

"For the sake of your delicate stomach, Daffid. Very well, we shall make a stop for wine on the way. Now, let's go," he rambled, turning to lead the way.

As soon as the doors closed, Pogue, Micah, and Doc sprang into action. Pogue swept her up, holding her close, while Doc quickly attended to her wounds as Micah stripped off his shirt, covering her as best he could as Doc worked. Caden promptly cleared the room.

"Apologies Grace," Doc said as his hands worked over her gently.

Micah spoke over him, apologizing and fussing.

"I'm sorry, Grace. I'm so sorry," he whispered harshly.

Pogue remained silent. She could feel the tremors running through him, but he stayed quiet. Micah helped her into the T-shirt after Doc finished, and Pogue carried her back to her room.

Chapter 38

P ogue carried her into the shower stall next to the tub, making sure she had space to wash off the blood. But he couldn't make himself move too far, staying within touching distance. He needed a moment to steady himself. It had taken all his strength, along with his brother's claws, to prevent himself from attacking DeCoill. Grace stayed still, and he caught a hint of rotten flowers. Swiftly, he leaned down and gently nipped her ear.

"Stay with me," he ordered. Then, softening his tone, he asked, "You okay?"

She made a so-so hand gesture. Pogue nodded. It was a damn miracle she wasn't in worse condition. DeCoill must be a weaker lion than he had previously assumed. Pogue's mind was whirling with emotions as he remembered DeCoill's pale, sickly face.

"What the fuck do you think you're doing, Grace? Getting in his face like that." Pogue shook his head at her. He could feel her small hands pushing on his stomach, attempting to move him. She ended up glaring at him. *Defenseless...*

"You don't get to tell... Urgh, this is ridiculous. Lift me up so I can glare at you properly," Grace demanded. Pogue felt his lips twitching as he easily picked her up and pushed her against the sandstone wall, her legs winding around him as he braced her on his forearm.

"Ma'am?" He flashed a dimple at her. He knew he should pull away and give her space, but he needed to feel her.

She still glared.

"You don't get to tell me what I can and cannot do, Pogue! I did what I had to! I showed him what he wanted to see, and I was fucking terrified doing it!"

"The fuck I do, Grace! It's my Pride!" he exclaimed. She slapped him on the shoulder as her thighs tightened their grip on his waist.

"I'm not *in* your Pride, and I'm not fucking like you! I'm way out of my league here, so cut me some fucking slack! It's gonna take me a beat to find my goddamn footing and know how to fit in your world! I am doing the best I can! Dumbass!"

"You don't fucking understand our world! He snarled, frustrated, "We steal people from each other! To keep you safe from our highest authority, we labeled you as our Pet! A fucking Pet Grace! That's how backward we are! And I can't, I won't send you back! You can't defend yourself against DeCoill worth a damn," Pogue told her, his voice rising. "And I don't know how to navigate this shit!" he shouted, frustrated, motioning between them."

"I am *not* your fucking Pet!" she shouted back at him, cutting him off.

His cat's roar tore out of him at the end of her sentence.

"You're mine!" he bellowed, his clawed hand slamming into the wall beside her, sending debris scattering to the floor.

Breathing heavily, he gazed down at her, grappling with the realization that he had just roared at her like a caveman. He studied his delicate human, her form now withdrawn, her eyes misting. Her legs lost their hold, and he had to readjust her as he slid onto the ground, cradling her in his lap.

"Stop shouting, please."

"Then start listening! God dammit, Grace." He sighed harshly. "Fuck." He breathed out.

Grace said nothing. He brushed his lips across the top of her head. "Grace?" *Why isn't she shouting at me?*

His cat was pacing inside him. *shit...* She left again, just like before. But this seemed worse somehow. Like she'd shut down completely. "Grace, can you look at me? You there?" He gently pulled his arm from underneath her legs and tilted her face toward him. "I'm sorry. My cat doesn't understand. It's trying to protect you; it just doesn't know how. You're not like us, but you're walking into *our* war. Our very claw-filled war, Grace. That's why we're lashing out," he tried explaining softly.

254

"Say something. Yell at me, hell, slap the fuck out of me if you need to, but please, baby, please just say or do *something*," he pleaded. She didn't answer him. "I would never hurt you."

His cat lay down, head on its paws. Finally, Grace looked up at him, and a cold feeling spread in his chest. There was no emotion in her eyes. His chest tightened with fear gripping him.

Gently, he lifted her into his arms and left her room, heading next door to his place. In his bedroom, he carefully laid her on his bed, tucking her in as she curled up. Pogue lingered by her side for an hour, racking his brain for a way to bring her back. Nipping her ear and commanding her had proven futile; nothing seemed to work. Eventually, he admitted defeat. He needed outside assistance, even if it meant swallowing his pride. For all his 'I'm a protector' claims, he still managed to fuck up with the one person he had explicitly been told to be gentle with.

Grace said nothing as he walked away, texting Hannah and Micah to meet him at the office. He was banking on Caden to be there.

Caden looked up from where he stood next to Micah behind the desk as Pogue entered. They were strategizing for the Turf War.

"I messed up. I don't--" Pogue began but was cut off by Hannah's entrance.

"S'up, peeps?" Hannah greeted cheerfully, tugging on her black and green sweater.

Pogue exhaled for a long beat before speaking.

"I think I broke Grace."

All three looked at him.

"Broke her how?" Micah asked, his cat looking out at Pogue.

"Are we talking body, mind, spirit, what?" Hannah prodded, smirking.

Pogue pinched the bridge of his nose.

"Don't, Hannah, not today. Just please, today, be normal for me." Hannah shot him a dirty look before answering.

"That was a serious question! And I am normal!" she stomped her shoeless foot on the soft carpet.

Caden coughed to cover his laugh as Micah looked away, suddenly interested in what color the ceiling was today.

"No, Hannah, you're very much not, but that's why we love you," Caden commented diplomatically, which seemed to quell her outrage.

Pogue took a deep breath.

"It's like she's shut down on me. More than before... I lost my shit. I fucking yelled at her. And I might have made a hole in the wall... Beside her head..." He hung his head, ashamed.

Caden was furious. "Why would you do that?!" he asked. Micah shifted forward, a growl rumbling in his throat. Pogue motioned Micah to stop, pouring all of his dominance into the gesture.

"Because she doesn't understand how deep in shit she is! My cat doesn't know what to do or how to react, and clearly, the *man* is a fucking idiot!" he clarified, feeling angry, pouty, and sorry all at the same time.

"Clearly," Micah growled, though he stayed put

All three looked at him, waiting for him to explain.

"Did her eyes lose focus? Like the last time?"

Pogue nodded.

"I can't bring her back. Nothing I did worked," he said dejectedly.

Micah looked at him, his expression solemn.

"You pushed her into an extreme dissociative state. You have no idea what you've done..." Micah growled.

Pogue sighed and sank into a beanbag, deliberately positioning himself lower than his Beta, a silent gesture of appeasement.

"Just tell me how to fix this. You were right." Micah scrutinized him for a moment before letting out a breath.

"I am doing this for her. Not you!"

Pogue nodded.

"Noted."

"You gotta stop using normal traditions and routines if you're actually admitting she's yours. She's human Pogue. Adding to that, she's got trauma. There's a lot more you need to consider when dealing with her. At least until she feels safe again," Micah explained.

Hannah held up a finger as Pogue nodded again. She was his. He'd do whatever it took. Hell, he'd learn how to be human! Hannah hopped up to sit cross-legged on their desk. Caden frowned and lifted her off the map she'd sat on.

"You need to know how she thinks," Hannah told him gently as she swatted at Caden.

Pogue numbly nodded again and motioned for Micah to start talking. He needed to understand and actually listen. He had to learn how to speak to her like a human, and he needed to know how to interpret her behavior as a human and not a Shifter.

"I know I said she was adjusting, but do you realize how big this is for her? "I'm not sure if she recognized she was on the verge of a major breakdown," Micah began. "These fugues, Pogue?" They stem from childhood trauma. They happen when she is overwhelmed or when her system is shocked. You know, like discovering Shifters or being in a plane crash and finding out she has a brother. Or a dumb ass Alpha who has the emotional depth of a potato! They happen when her boundaries are violated, Pogue. I can't fathom how she held it together when DeCoill was here, but my best guess is adrenaline. Then, after you messed up. Again, I might add," Micah emphasized, "right after, when the adrenaline subsided? Her reserves were depleted. She had no fight left in her..."

Pogue couldn't remember ever having felt like such a piece of shit as he did right now... Even Caden had sat down on the floor, looking like he'd been punched.

"How do I fix it?"

Micah shrugged.

"Let her go. Let my sister go. She deserves better. Better than you and this shitstorm she landed in."

Pogue leaped to his feet. Caden's intervention was the only thing that kept him from lunging at Micah. Nobody would ever take his Mate away from him!

Hannah jumped off the table.

"Don't make me bubble you, Alpha," she threatened. She was ready when he whipped his face to her, ready to respond to one threat with another. Her hands crackled with electricity, though her following words were calm. "I know how you fix it."

Immediately, his cat sat down inside him, ears forward. Pogue quickly sat back down. He noticed Micah's approval nod, though his arms remained tense, and Caden stayed between them... "She *loves* the idea of Shifters and magic, and she loves this place. She wants to be here, and despite your less-than-stellar performance, she likes you." Hanna sighed before grinning and continuing. "And she is not lying about being good with a bow. So, you let her practice and feel like she's contributing to preparations for a war we all know she won't be a part of. And I think I know how to boost her happy hormones. But I want your word, both of you," she pointed between Caden and Pogue, "that there will be no ramifications for me. And it doesn't get you out of groveling until she's better."

"Which she will be. You need to let her sleep for as long as she needs to, and she shouldn't wake up alone or with a potato Alpha," Micah added.

Pogue stood, nodding to Micah, acknowledging he heard him, before turning his eyes to Hannah.

Caden, ever the tension reliever, smirked and cut him off before he could speak.

"Hannah, may I ask a favor? personal, not Pride." Caden asked.

Hannah nodded.

"It might cost you, but sure," she shrugged.

"Find out how a human can survive a mating bite," he smiled softly. "not a marking bite. A mating bite, he clarified.

Pogue groaned. *Nope. We're not going there right now.* One thing was accepting her as *a* Mate. But it was a long way from that to conceding she was his *True* Mate. One didn't involve a bite that could kill her. The other one very much did and he didn't want to ass any more to his plate. Changing the subject, Pogue asked.

"Have you guys figured out if you can make some defensive measures for the Challenge?" Pogue knew it was ultimately up to the Wielders, but they would also have to talk to the Academy.

Wielders had to stay on their good side if they wanted to buy what they needed for their spells and shit.

Hannah straightened.

"Nigel left for the Academy. He refused to help," Hannah explained through clenched teeth. While Hannah possessed more powerful abilities than Nigel, having his support would have been beneficial. "I'm waiting for my marching orders from the Academy, but I'm staying," she said.

Pogue just stared at her. He hadn't expected her to actually want to stay. Spells and defense magic, yes, but not staying. Hannah snorted at his expression.

"What?! Someone's gonna have to look out for the human, and I like her. She gets my geek references, she's tough as nails, and... Well, I like having a non-Shifter friend here." She blushed.

Hannah took her leave after discussing a few practical details for the Games Night once they decided on a date.

"Oh, and tell her we're playing Quidditch!" she yelled before the door closed.

Caden smirked at him from his spot on the floor as he removed his socks.

"So, you're gonna go grovel, brother dear?"

"On my knees, till they bleed if I have to," Pogue said decisively as he got up and started towards the door.

Chapter 39

24 hours later

Grace awoke in an unfamiliar bed, confused and disoriented. Panic rose in her as she looked around, desperate for any indication of her location or time. Then she smelled something familiar: Pogue. *I'm in Pogue's bed?* Her mind was racing with questions, and she swung her legs over the edge, trying to piece it all together. Grace stood up on the... *what the hell is this?!* The floor was surprisingly soft underfoot, like a layer of stable memory foam. *Neat...* She then noticed two wooden sliding doors. One led to a walk-in closet and another to a large bathroom with a humongous bathtub.

She wriggled her toes, feeling out the unfamiliar texture, as she looked around the room. *Wow...* Pogue didn't just like control. Pogue was a fucking neat-freak.

From the neatly arranged shirts on hangers to the organized shoe racks, tie holders, and drawers, the room exuded order. The room was finished with a full-length mirror and a small wooden bench. But there were no personal touches or trinkets. Grace quickly rummaged through the drawers, selecting a pair of boxer briefs and an oversized, soft green checkered shirt. It dwarfed her. As she stood there, she took a moment to assess herself. Doc had done well, she concluded. She was feeling surprisingly well, both physically and mentally, given... What time was it, anyway? As she scanned the bedroom for a clock, she noticed how similar the rest of the room was to the bathroom—ordered but devoid of personal knickknacks or clutter. The only ornate item in the room was a rainforest painting hanging above the bed. It was stunning.

Her stomach growled, signaling her hunger. She entered the large square living room, noticing the absence of windows and a TV. A beautiful ornate desk with a matching chair stood in the corner. Instead of a couch, there were large, flat cushions, almost like supersized cat beds. Everything was clean and neat but nearly barren. Nothing showed who he was or what he liked. She had an urge to buy some things to inject some personality into the place. *Getting ahead of ourselves much*, she snorted.

On the far end, next to a small kitchenette, was the door probably leading out to the hallway and another door just to the left of it. Grace padded over, enjoying the feel of the spongy floor, and opened it.

"Woah!" she whispered. *Chaos!* The room was tiny, but it was a beautiful mess. Charcoal and pencil drawings covered the walls, and the stone floor was splattered with paint. Easels of all sizes were scattered around, some holding abstract paintings while others displayed rough outlines, perhaps works in progress. Small buckets filled with paintbrushes and paint and an abundance of drawing paper were strewn about. She even stepped on a few sheets, leaving her feet marked with charcoal or pencil or whatever it was. She walked over to a small, rickety desk with a wooden stool. A bright blue splotch on a piece of paper at her desk drew her attention. A closer look revealed a stunningly beautiful, meticulously detailed eye. Little golden flecks were scattered throughout the blue, almost like angry flicks of a paintbrush. Impressive talent, she mused.

Her stomach growled again, loudly this time, at her. "Yeah-na. Coffee, food, then.." *Then what* Grace thought. She shook her head.

"Find coffee, get head on straight. If he put you in here, he must want you here. Right? Head on straight; talk to Pogue. Tell him he's an asshole but, like, in an adult way, yeah? Yeah," she told herself as she opened every cupboard in the small kitchenette, not bothering to close them again as she came up empty.

After pulling out multiple (identical) mugs and discovering an old coffee machine, she finally saw a bag of beans. On the top shelf, way up there. The bench was taller than she was used to, but then again, Pogue was way tall. She pulled out a drawer and used it as a step to climb onto the bench. Grace stood on her toes, wiggling her fingers to reach the prized coffee beans. She almost had them when the door slammed shut.

Chapter 40

P ogue took a deep breath before unlocking his apartment door. He'd just finished a hard workout and a quick shower at Caden's. Grace had been sleeping for over a day. Pogue had remained in his bedroom with her, only leaving when Micah was with her. This was the first time they'd left her alone. Micah had to leave the Pridelands, and Pogue needed to decompress. Before proceeding, he recited his strategy.

"Grovel until your knees bleed". He yanked the door open with a huff, only to have his heart leap into his throat at the sight of his petite human balanced on the kitchen counter. She strained to reach the coffee beans on the top shelf, one foot precariously perched on his worn-out coffee machine.

"Grace, what the fuck?!" he yelled. She stumbled backward, arms flailing, and let out a loud squeak as her foot slipped on the kitchen counter. He caught her quickly, but the force pushed them both back, landing with a soft thud on the cushioned floor. She heeled him in the nuts during the landing. *Of course, you did*, he thought as he cradled her gently, wheezing.

"What th- fuuohmygod that hurt!"

Grace rolled off him to stand up, hands on her hips.

"Why would you scare me like that?!" she screeched.

Give me a second here. Just have to retrieve my nuts from my stomach. Pogue rolled onto his side, cupping himself. Evidently, she didn't know, or maybe just didn't care that he may have to rethink any plans about cubs, as she prodded his shoulder with her foot.

"Well?!"

Pogue held up a finger.

"One second. Give me one second." Shifters might be tougher than humans, but he dared any man to stand up when their balls had just been dropkicked.

Grace settled on the floor, her back against the kitchen cabinets, waiting patiently. Despite the pain, he couldn't help but appreciate how incredibly cute she looked, sitting cross-legged in a checkered shirt and...

"Is that my shirt?" he asked, frowning as the pain slowly subsided.

She shrugged.

"Yup."

Slowly, he crawled over to sit beside her, breathing heavily. He turned to look at her and saw her lips twitching.

"You're laughing," he deadpanned. She held up her fingers to measure out a little bit. He sighed and grabbed her to pull her onto his lap, thankful she didn't fight him. When she wiggled to get comfortable, he winced.

"Gently, you just gelded me." With a long sigh, he continued. "You scared the shit out of me."

She lifted her head to look at him.

"If you hadn't scared *me*, I wouldn't have slipped. Just sayin'..." She didn't look him in the eye, her body tense under his hands.

"I know. I'm sorry," he whispered. "I'm sorry about everything... Can we talk?"

She sighed and nodded.

"Make me a coffee?"

He kissed her temple and got up, placing her on her feet as he got the coffee machine running. *She didn't fight that either. So far, so good.*

"You're wearing my shirt..." He lifted the hem to reveal a pair of his boxer briefs. "*And* my underwear..?"

"Yup," she said, looking up at him, the picture of innocence and a hint of insecurity. He started the brew and leaned against the counter. He would be honest. Lay all the cards on the table. She was his. She might geld him for real or just not trust his sudden change in attitude. He would gladly spend the rest of his days convincing her.

"My cat likes that. Well, the shirt more than underwear." His cat stretched inside him. It didn't care what she wore as long as it was their clothes. Their scent.

"Why?" she asked, looking down at her toes, clearly confused.

"It covers you in my scent and that-... What's that?" he said, pointing to her big toe. She immediately placed her other foot over the top of the offending toe.

"Nothing," she said, flashing him an innocent smile. He playfully picked her up, eliciting a giggle that he'd do anything to hear. Swiftly, he turned her around so she was hanging upside down, her face away from him, struggling to keep the shirt in place. He peered closer to get a good look.

"You've been in my studio! And what's the drawing on your ankle?" He tried to meet her eyes, but the shirt obscured her face.

"Pogue! Put me down! I will hurt you!" she started grabbing for him behind her back. He simply stretched out his arms to hold her at a suitable distance.

"Have you been snooping?" Grace stilled. Then she started swinging back and forth. Once, twice and then...

"Ow. Motherfucker! You little fiend!" The woman had managed to swing into a backbend close enough to bite him just above the lining of his jeans. He flipped her around and helped her to her feet. He grabbed her and pulled her closer to him as she swayed.

"You're gonna be the death of me." He said as he tucked her hair behind her ears. They needed to talk, but Pogue was somewhat grateful for the opportunity to build up to it. Let her and him both relax around each other instead of the awkwardness.

"You ready to talk?"

Grace shook her head and pointed to his coffee machine.

"Nope. Waiting on that dinosaur of a coffee maker you have. Gives me time to convince you I'm too funny and cute for you to be mad at me, which gives me the upper hand because I'm mad at you," she shrugged.

Pogue snorted out a laugh.

"You're not funny."

"I'm hilarious," she told him seriously. Pogue shook his head, despite his cat loving the banter.

"If you're thirsty, you could drink some water," he suggested. Grace scrunched up her face.

"Or we could talk when your Flintstone machine has made golden happy go joy-joy."

For some inexplicable reason, he found that amusing. Flintstone. Coffee couldn't be brewed in a flintstone pot. It would break. He began to laugh. Then he lost it when she made fishy mouth faces at him. He laughed so hard that tears streamed down his cheeks, and he snorted in a highly undignified manner. To be fair, this whole situation was so much of a clusterfuck he could laugh or cry at this point. He had to compose himself on his knees, clutching his side, and it took him five minutes.

Grace moved in closer, and he leaned his head against her solar plexus. She stroked his hair carefully as if she wasn't sure what was going on but rolling with it.

"Done, Alpha McSnort? Not a drawing, it's a tattoo," she smirked as Pogue traced the lines on her ankle, while the coffee finally brewed for two. Pogue got up and fixed them cups and handed one over. He led her to a lounge bed, and motioned for her to have a seat. Then, he positioned himself on the floor in front of her, legs on either side. They both took a deep breath. *She's as on edge about this as me,* he concluded. *OK, calm now. Talk like an adult, use many words,* he mentally coaxed himself.

"I'm sorry, Grace. On a scale of one to ten, how much trouble am I in?" Pogue asked, sipping his coffee.

"About an eight. Me?"

Pogue just shook his head. He was the one who'd fucked up.

"This is going to take a lot of words," Pogue began. Grace simply smiled and nodded as she sipped her coffee.

He took a deep breath.

"Did you know most Shifters mate for life?"

"Like penguins?" she asked, or stated, he wasn't sure.

"Wouldn't know, but sure. Micah explained how the human world's version of mating works. Everything is very different with us. You've adjusted so well, but this, all this is different. Dangerous." Grace opened her mouth to speak when he raised his hand to stop her. "Don't interrupt me. Just hear me out. Please," he added.

Grace nodded, looking down at her toes as if she'd been chastised.

He lightly pinched one.

"I'm not telling you off. There will be groveling. But there are some things you need to understand, and I need to know that you do and will respect them. Yes?"

She raised a finger. He cocked his brow at her.

"Can I ask clarifying questions though?"

"Yes."

"Mkay then. Shutting up now."

Pogue left his hand resting on her foot as he spoke.

"I chose a long time ago to not engage in any permanent relationship unless it was my Mate," he shrugged. "My dad was the same."

"You've never had a girlfriend or boyfriend? But you've had sex, I know that!"

Even though she had just interrupted him despite telling him she wouldn't, he couldn't help but smirk a little.

"Lots. Stop interrupting now."

She snorted.

"Smartass."

Pogue made a zipping motion in front of his lips. Grace mouthed sorry and took another sip of her coffee as he took another deep breath and started again.

"Taking a Mate is equivalent to human marriage to us. Mating with someone as weak as a human would be like a jaguar mating a mouse." When she looked like she was about to protest, he added, "Not calling you a mouse." At least she was following his analogy. "I wasn't joking when I said I didn't know how to navigate this," he said as he sipped his coffee and motioned between them. "Despite that you seem to forget it, I am an Alpha, the leader of a predatory Community. I'm responsible for keeping them all happy and alive. To do that, I need to be able focus, and you crashing here messed that up. I haven't spent a lot of time around humans, Grace. Usually, a Shifter navigates social and intimate situations with the help of all our senses. You don't give out any scents to tell me when you're pissed or scared. I'm not used to having to go purely off body language, and even that's different with humans. You're... difficult... to me."

"Sorry," she whispered. She put her coffee down and clenched her hands by her sides, looking down at her lap.

Oh, for fuck's sake, Pogue mentally slapped himself. *Not what I fucking meant!* He gently squeezed her foot and placed his other hand under her chin, forcing her to look up.

"That's not what I mean. Well, I guess the jaguar and mouse thing is. Look, first, a plane crashed that shouldn't have. Then, a human was brought into my Pride, and my cat went crazy. My cat might be aggressive, but he's never *that* aggressive, and it confused me. Then I find out my Beta's your half-brother, the highest authority in our region, is trying to kill you, and we are about to be invaded by a very dangerous Pack of wolves hellbent on killing us all. And in the middle of all that is you, Grace. My youngest Pridemember is stronger than you, and he's five. My Wielder can accidentally kill you with a ball of lightning. I could kill you if I forget to control my claws. Do you see where I'm going with this?"

Grace looked him in the eye.

"You want me gone."

"I want you safe." He put down his coffee cup, scooted a little closer and placed his hands on her hips. "I want you safe, and I don't think you are here. But I also know you're less safe if you go back. And I told you, Grace. I won't let DeCoill have you. Not now. Not ever. That's the problem, don't you see that?"

She slowly shook her head.

"No, I don't see. You don't want me here, but you won't let me leave. You clearly think I'm a giant pain in your ass, but you have no problem fucking me. You tell me I'm a mistake, but then you do nice shit like hugging and kissing my head. Pogue, I'm tired. I know your world was turned upside down, and I get that having a human here is like sticking a Kiwi bird in with a bunch of tazzies, but my fucking world blew up too. Some of it literally. Give me a little time to bounce back and get my self-confidence up yeah?"

This time, Pogue held up a finger.

"I don't understand your analogy. Wouldn't the bird just fly away?"

Grace rolled her eyes.

"A Kiwi bird can't fly. It's the most useless bird ever."

"Tazzie?"

"Tasmanian devil. Cute, but all teeth," she explained. Her face seemed to light up when she explained. He could see why working with animals was her passion.

Pogue nodded.

"Right. Sorry, carry on."

Grace took a deep breath and settled deeper into the cushion.

"I don't know if *you* forgot, but I literally crashed out of the sky. I find out there are people who turn into animals. I have a brother, my human stalker has claws, teeth and floating henchmen and I'm trying to navigate a completely unknown society, with cultural values I'm trying to wrap my head around. You sniff people, Pogue! Not cool in any society, but here it's like a handshake. I'm scared too. I'm confused, too, and you're the boss around here. I was just beginning to feel like I might be safe here, which is not a common thing in my life, and then you blow up in my face. Not anyone else...You. And I don't know what you want from me 'cause you won't just tell me," she exclaimed on a tired huff.

Pogue took it all in and let it settle in the following silence. Logically, he knew, of course, this whole shitstorm was a lot to deal with for her. Hell, it was to him, and this was his home. He knew the rules and how to navigate. Plus, he wasn't the one who'd been blown out of the sky. But for some reason, logic and Grace didn't fit in his mind. For a while, they just sat there.

"I want to keep you," he said after a long while. "I want to keep you with me and I'm scared shitless. You're not geared for this world, Grace, and that scares the hell out of me."

It took a while for her to respond, but when she did, she placed a hand over his on her hips.

"I'm not completely useless, Pogue."

"You're not, no. You have valuable information and you're good with a bow, according to Hannah. But you won't use it. I need you safe in the clinic, trusting you'll stay put."

Her smile was captivating. He couldn't help but notice her lips' subtle asymmetry.

"Pogue?"

He blinked, drawing his attention back to the conversation.

"Yeah?"

"Do you really want me to stay? With you or because I'm Micah's sister?" Her voice was careful, like she expected him to blow up in her face. He maneuvered his legs under the cushion Grace sat on, effectively pulling her closer to him, so they were face to face, her legs now spread out on either side of his hips.

Pogue locked eyes with her, palming her cheek.

"Grace, let me make this as clear as I can. I am claiming you as my Mate. It's up to you to accept or deny me, but my cat has chosen, despite how much you piss me off at *every* turn." He cracked a smile. "I know this is a lot to take in. Not pushing here. I'm trying to explain my reasoning." In an ideal world, I could wrap you up and hide you away from everything that could harm you, and the fact that you are human doubles that urge. No matter how scrappy you are, you are weak compared to us. Think all of this over, alright? This isn't a couple of months fucking around the clock, and then you get to leave. You say yes, you stay with me. For good."

The look on her face told him she got it. Her lips were tight, and a small frown marred her forehead. She took him seriously. He pulled her in for a chaste kiss before moving on.

"Until I know what you'll choose," he paused, frowning. "No, probably forever; I'll have the urge to keep you safe from anything I or my cat deem dangerous. I will *try* to give you space and time. In all things us." She blushed harder, but to his immense satisfaction, she stroked her hand down his forearm as she listened.

"My cat is territorial, and there's a limit to what I will allow. What my cat will allow."

"Stop. Allow, Pogue? I feel like that should come with an explanation. A very detailed one where you rephrase the word into something that won't make me wanna headbutt you."

Adding Oliver to the no list, Pogue concluded, as he remembered Beau's broken nose. He traced the outside of her thighs with his fingers as he thought it through. Talking out his ass wasn't an option here.

"Don't wear any other male's scent, like their clothes. I'm barely tolerating Micah as it is. When it comes to your safety, you don't argue. And no more playing 'irk the Alpha' with Oliver."

"Oliver, who is gay and mated," Grace pointed out.

"Oliver is male, Grace. My cat won't be very rational until you give me your final answer."

Grace bit her lip as she mulled it over. It made him want to put his own mark on her lips just so he could lick it better.

"I appreciate you giving me time to suss this out in my head. But outside the war, you don't get to order me around and don't shout at me. If you have to shout in general, turn your face away from mine. I can deal then. Oliver is my friend, and I need those right now. Please try and suck it up a little?" she asked.

Pogue looked at her for a beat.

"You really don't understand the concept of me Alpha, you human, do you?"

Grace took one of his hands, turning it over to trace the lines in his palm, following her finger with her eyes.

"That's the thing, Pogue, isn't it? If we do this, you still won't be my Alpha. You would just be Pogue to me. "I'll learn, and I'll follow the rules and respect the hierarchy." But I'm not going to sit back and never challenge you. To be honest, I think we both need the pushback. After I shout and stomp my feet."

Pogue barked a laugh. Then he thought about it. He liked her fire and how she seemed to forget who and what he was, apart from Pogue. Just Pogue.

He smiled at her.

"Okay." She stretched and shot the coffee machine a longing look. He took the hint. "You want more? Maybe some food? You were out for over twenty-four hours, you know."

Grace's eyes widened a little as she let him help her up.

"Aaand my ass is asleep," she mumbled as she crossed the short distance to the kitchenette. "That long, huh? Guess that explains why I'm feeling all energized."

He quickly made her another cup of coffee and watched as she sat on the kitchen counter using the bottom drawer as a step. He went to the fridge to get the ingredients for a sandwich for her. "We're being very adult right now," she casually observed.

"Mhm. Only took a little over a thousand years," Pogue responded just as casually. Grace spluttered in her coffee. To his horror, she then wiped her chin with the shirt collar. His shirt. His cashmere shirt!

"Excuse me?"

He frowned at her, and quickly grabbed a hand towel. He wet it and clasped the collar, trying to remove the coffee before it made a permanent stain.

"You know we age slower."

She nodded.

"Well, yeah, but one thing is knowing you as a... Breed? Species? Yeah, that. It's one thing knowing you age slower, but it's another thing knowing someone you're thinking about naked could be a mummy. Different level of cradle robbing, you know?"

Pogue felt his jaw going slack, the hand towel in his hand forgotten.

"I have no idea what you just said, but I would never rob a cradle!" he told her. "You think about me naked huh?"

Grace cracked up so bad he had to take her coffee cup and place it out of reach in case she accidentally knocked it over. He let her finish her laughing fit as he finished her food.

When she was done, he placed the plate on her lap and cocked a brow at her. "Wanna explain?"

She shook her head and dug into her sandwich, happily, if off-key, humming as she ate.

When Grace had eaten, Pogue led her back to the large round cushion and let her settle in with the thick, soft blanket he'd grabbed from the bedroom. He sat down in front of her. There was something else they needed to go over. He needed to know she understood. He hadn't even thought about it until Micah mentioned it yesterday.

Grace seemed to sense they weren't done with the adult conversations and sat up a little straighter, tilting her head while looking at him.

"We're still adulting?"

Pogue nodded, taking her delicate hand in his, gently massaging it as he spoke. He didn't want to overwhelm her, but discussing this was important. *Better address it now than surprise her later,* he thought.

"Grace, do you remember what you read about the Barrier? How it maintains Shifters and Wielders in optimal genetic condition?"

It took her a second to focus. She was clearly loving the massage. *Good to know,* he thought and filed away the information.

"Mhm," was her only response.

"I had someone look into human/ Shifter matings. From what I know, there haven't been more than maybe ten humans mated to a Shifter in the last ten thousand years. Granted, we don't share information much." *Micah's right. We should share more,* Pogue realized. He shook his head to clear his wandering thoughts. "But he did confirm that if you accept me, you'll gain the longevity of a Shifter. Even if I die, you'll live as long as you stay within the Barrier."

She thought that bit of information over for a while before nodding slowly, her smile waning.

"Sophie..."

"I'm sorry, Grace."

He bent his head and stayed quiet, waiting for her to digest the fact that she'd watch those she loved grow old and die.

"Pogue?"

"Mhm?"

"How sure are you about this? Us trying this?" she asked, gesturing vaguely between them.

Pogue placed both coffee mugs on the floor and dragged her onto his lap. He looked her in the eyes as he pushed a lock of her chestnut hair out of her face.

"I wish I could tell you I could let you go if you're not sure." His smile was tight. He wouldn't. He would hunt her down and drag her back every single time, no matter her objections. "I know you'll need time to deal. I'll rein in my cat. We'll wait. *I'll* wait."

Grace nodded, leaning her forehead against his chest. She started looking tired despite only being awake for about an hour. Micah had told him Grace spent an enormous amount of mental energy trying to wrap her head around this whole new world. "You need to go lay down?"

She took a breath and curled into him.

"I don't even know what time it is," she mumbled.

"Dinner is in about two hours."

"Can we go lay down just for a little? I don't want to sleep, but I think my brain needs a break."

Pogue nodded and kissed the top of her head.

"Alone?"

When she shook her head, Pogue picked her up and carried her into the bedroom. He tucked the duvet around her before lying down beside her in the unmade bed. She responded with a frown but did not say anything. Pogue shifted his weight, resting on one elbow.

"The look on your face is loud. Pawprint for your thoughts?"

She burrowed down into the duvet and shook her head. If she was a Shifter, she would want reassurance, touch, Pogue knew. "Grace, do you want to be held?"

After what felt like a very long minute, she nodded. Pogue stood and lifted the side of the duvet to crawl under it. He got comfortable and pulled her into the crook of his arm.

"All you had to do was ask."

She didn't respond, and he let her have her silence.

Chapter 41

G race had managed to fall back asleep despite her earlier declarations. Pogue's revelations had only added to the whirlwind of new information that had left her mind reeling. The prospect of staying here with him meant witnessing Sophie's inevitable aging and going away for good. Could she do that? On the other hand, this. Despite everything, Grace had never felt more cherished or safe. *He did that*, she thought.

The feel of skin beneath her hand told her he must have gotten rid of his shirt at some point. She understood why, though. He was like a living toaster. Nestling into the warmth beside her, it took a moment to register that it was Pogue next to her. She obviously recognized him, but it still felt somewhat surreal. Pogue lay on his back, his steady breathing accompanied by a faint snore, indicating that he had conked out, too. She was wrapped around him, her leg draped over his hip, and he held her close, one arm cradling her as his other was tucked beneath his head.

Grace's fingers traced the rugged contours of Pogue's body in the hazy realm between sleep and wakefulness. His body was shaped by the life he led. All hard muscles everywhere. Her fingers caressed his sides, gliding up over his pecs and then down across his chest. Chest hair had never been a thing for Grace, but his was surprisingly soft, a gentle contrast to the strength beneath. It kinda added a sexy appeal. Blinking one eye open, she watched his rhythmic breathing, a constant in his slumber, as his golden chest rose and fell. Her fingers continued their journey down his stomach. She barely realized she'd followed the faint trail of hair down to the waistband of his jeans until his breath caught, and she felt the tension in his abdominal muscles. She held her hand still, waiting for Pogue to react. *He must be more tired than I thought,* she concluded when his only reaction was to move his hand from her hip down to cup her ass. A second later, a light snore told her he hadn't done that intentionally. His hand felt huge on her. But then again, everything on Pogue was... In proportion.

Logically, sex should be the last thing on her mind. Still, it was difficult not to think about it when a hand was on her ass, and she was smashed up against a fucking Adonis who smelled so damn tempting. *How the hell does he smell so good?* His scent went straight to her clit! It was like an aphrodisiac or something! Grace squirmed a little to try and discreetly ease the now throbbing between her legs. No dice. *Wonder if sex is a no-no until I'm ready to answer,* she thought. And she would take the time to think about this. Pogue was right, not that she'd ever admit it. This wasn't just a fling and then bye-bye. She respected him enough to actually weigh up the pros and cons. *But can we weigh them up while riding him like a cowgirl?* Her brain supplied helpfully. Without really thinking, her hand traced his... crap! Grace looked at her offending hand like it had just moved on its own to rest right beside a very impressive erection. *Jesus, that thing is thick! Was it that big last time? Wonder-*

Pogue's hips lifted a fraction, and his grip on her ass tightened as he drew in a sharp breath through his nose.

"Grace..." he groaned. She wasn't completely sure if he was telling her off or praying.

She felt like a fucking teenager, lying there debating whether to move, freeze or jump out of bed screaming, 'Ha, ha, jokes on you.' Pogue's arm tightened around her, his hand gently caressing her backside. She hesitated for a moment, then let a single finger graze dangerously close to his arousal. A low rumble of pleasure emanated from him as he inhaled deeply.

Turning to face her, his other arm encircled her, cradling her jaw as he teasingly nipped her lip, a flick of his tongue soothing the small sting. Grace couldn't help but emit a soft whine, berating herself internally for her nerves. *Why am I so fucking nervous?!?* She didn't have time to think about it as his lips descended again, this time with a firmer, more confident touch, though it still carried the gentleness of half-slumber. His hand moved to cup her cheek, his thumb brushing against her lip. Instinctively, she opened for him. His intake of breath and the intensity of his purr indicated that he was very awake now. The tongue that darted out to explore her mouth with control and thoroughness that set her blood on fire confirmed it.

Pogue kissed like he ran his Pride. Control, dominance, and a surprising sense of playfulness. He'd alternate between completely dominating the kiss and nipping her lips and licking it better. Grace surrendered to the moment. As she drew him closer, her fingers tangled in his hair, loving a chance to muss it up. Meanwhile, his hand on her backside began an intoxicating descent, skimming the curve of her ass until his deft fingers hovered just shy of where she craved them. Grace wrapped her leg around his waist, trying to press herself against the enticing hardness nestled between his thighs and get his damn fingers where she needed them.

"Impatient?" Pogue whispered against her lips

Grace whined. Again. Like a woman in control. Not.

"I'm not the one with enough morning wood to build a log cabin," Grace retorted.

Pogue chuckled and rolled them over so Grace straddled said morning wood-well, evening as it was. He gave her one last kiss and then let her sit up straight. He looked too good right now. His lips were slightly kissed swollen, his hair sticking out at odd angles, and his hands gripping the headboard.

"You complaining?" he raised a brow at her and smirked.

God damnit! Urgh stop, she complained internally. *Brain, function. Please!* she urged herself. For some absurd reason, that and his damn dimples were her Achilles heel.

"I would have been thrilled with a hut. Cabins are overrated."

The laughter went out of Pogue's eyes, and he gave her a flat look.

"And yet, you're grinding yourself all over my *cabin*."

Grace looked down. One point to Pogue.

He put his hands on her hips.

"Maybe this isn't the best idea, Grace."

And just like that, her pussy wept a little while her brain frantically tried to come up with a suitable, witty, and sexy comeback. Five seconds later, she had nothing, and the time limit for a snappy comeback was, as everyone knows, three fucking seconds. And Pogue knew it. Of course, he did the sly fucker. He smirked and just lay there looking way too comfortable for someone who was in the process of creating permanent zipper marks on their dick. To his credit, he didn't move a muscle, though his eyes had changed to those of his cat. *Yeah-na, kitty cat, we're gonna play*, Grace smiled to herself.

Pogue

You have control. You are control. You are an Alpha! Pogue repeated the words in his mind as he held on to said control with the tips of his claws. Waking up to soft fingers skimming over his torso was one thing. Both he and his cat liked to be petted. But when those delicate fingers came within touching distance of his now painfully hard cock, it was a different matter. He refused to push her, but by the stars, this was hard. Grace looked at him, her head cocked. It made her look cute as hell.

"Sure, you *don't* wanna test how bendy I am?"

He damn near choked on his own spit. He shook his head, trying for a serious expression. By the look on her face, it came out more sultry than serious though.

"Not even a little bit."

"And this wouldn't do anything?" Grace asked. Then she winked at him and bent backward to the point of putting her head down between her calves. *If I get any damn harder, I can use my dick to hammer in nails in her fucking log cabin*, he thought as she came back up and grinned impishly at him. He didn't say a word for a minute, trying to collect his thoughts. Grace took that as something else, and her face fell a little. Before she could say anything, he did.

"Tell me what you want right now, Grace."

She blushed.

"I thought it was kinda obvious," she responded, looking down.

Pogue sat up and grasped the back of her neck.

"Not good enough. Tell me what you *want*, Grace." He felt his breathing speed up along with his heart as she wiggled to get comfortable. Then she looked him straight in the eye.

"You."

He smiled at her, all teeth and extended canines. Then he bent and nipped her neck gently before licking a trail with the tip of his tongue up to her ear to whisper.

"Do you want me to *fuck* you, Grace?" He clasped her ass with his other hand and ground her down on his erection. Her breath hitched, and he could almost scent her arousal coating the air as a tremor went through her. *So my Menace likes a little dirty talking. Good to know,* Pogue thought as he gently squeezed her neck. "Use your words, Grace," he smiled into her neck and kissed her there.

"Yes," she said on a breath.

Pogue got up and deposited her on the bed. He started to undress. He did so in slow, measured movements, watching her for signs she was backing out. She made a small sound as he pulled down his jeans.

He froze there, looking her in the eye. Her pupils were dilated and she had a nice blush going on. Satisfied the sound was one of need, not fear, he stepped out of his jeans, sliding the boxer briefs off with them. He rubbed a hand over his erection to soothe the soreness from being constricted, and Grace watched his every movement, even as she divested herself of his boxers.

She sat back, leaning on the headboard, her legs casually bent, the knees resting against each other. She looked sexy as hell, especially wearing his shirt and nothing else. Her hair, the color of fallen autumn leaves, was unbound and flowing out over the fabric. He walked to the side of the bed and sat down on his knees, facing her. Her slender fingers were soon traveling over the planes of his chest. Mapping him, petting him. He'd never felt so unquestionably marked as when her fingers traced his pecs, abs, and sides.

"Grace, wait." He clasped her hands to stop her from touching him, primarily because if she kept it up, he would likely lose his ability to think rationally.

"What?" she sat up on her knees and blew a lock of hair from her eyes.

Pogue reached out and tucked it behind her ear.

"What we did in the office. That was nothing compared to what I want to do with you. You *will* tell me if I'm hurting you," he ordered as he positioned himself to lean against the bed's headboard and let her straddle him, her sex pressing against his fully erect shaft. He had to remind himself to breathe and get through this conversation. She needed to know what she was walking into. Mostly anyway.

"I'm dominant. In all aspects. I like to play rough, and I like control. Can you work with that?"

"Can we compromise in the foreplay department? Otherwise, yes, I can work with that."

Pogue's hands took on a life of their own, unbuttoning the shirt, leaving her bare for him as he pushed it off her shoulders.

"Try me," he said. He flattened his hands on her stomach, trailing up to cup her naked breasts. "No bra? Again?!" he asked, swallowing. He should get fucking sainthood for not taking her then and there.

"Didn't fit," she said as he maneuvered them so Grace was on her back, completely at his mercy. He hadn't lied when he told her he could compromise. She'd just have to play him for it. Grace ran her hands through his hair as he began to kiss his way down her stomach and across her hip bone. He placed a long, wet kiss on her soft, red curls and inner thigh, making her giggle.

Her laughter turned into a breathless moan as he tasted her. He lapped, nipped, and sucked until she dripped and writhed beneath him. She damn near came off the bed when he inserted a single finger in her. She was gonna feel him thoroughly. She was so tight and he wasn't small. Her arousal surrounded him, and it drove him fucking insane. He added a finger and started working them in and out of her at a controlled pace, angling his fingers to hit the magic spot with every thrust as he used his tongue on her clit, licking and sucking it gently.

Grace came hard with a strangled cry, one hand clutching his hair and the other grabbing the duvet that now lay crumpled up beside her.

"Ssstop! Pogue, stop."

He looked up, smirking at her as he nipped her waist.

"You done already?"

The look she gave him told him she was just getting started, her eyes burning with need. His cat liked it. Now, she was playing with them. She pushed him up and motioned for him to get on his back.

Pogue hesitated.

"I've never really done that." It felt like a loss of control. He wasn't sure how he felt about it just yet.

"You're about to," she said, smiling as he let her slender hand push him down onto the mattress, reminding himself that he had told her to try him. She wrapped her hand around him. He watched her position herself over his hardness with masculine satisfaction, his hands gripping the wooden headboard as she guided him to her core and slowly started to lower herself onto him.

"That's a lot," she stated, biting her lip.

"You can take it." he smiled smugly.

Then he watched her, her long hair falling around her face and down her shoulders, as she slowly drew him in. He had to fight the urge to mark her again as he palmed her breasts, rolling a taut nipple between his fingers, her soft moans coloring the air. When she began to move, he felt his eyes roll back.

"Ah, fuck!" he hissed as she quickened the pace. She leaned back and rested her hands on her calves while riding him. When she started circling her clit with her fingers, he thought he was gonna pass out; it was so damn sexy.

"Make me come again," she whispered harshly, raising herself from the back-bend. Pogue gave her a wolfish grin and pinched her clit as he changed the angle and drove deeper, keeping an iron hold on her hips as he kept chanting to himself silently, not to harm. His claws were already making small indents on her soft skin.

"More?" he asked as calmly as she could through his quickening breath, keeping a stranglehold on his self-control. His cat wants to bite, taste, and lick. When she didn't respond, he lightly tapped her ass. "Words, Grace," he prompted.

"Yes! More!"

"Good girl."

So he gave her what she asked for until she came in a silent cry, biting her fist to avoid shattering his eardrums, for which he was eternally thankful.

Breathing hard, he hoisted her off him. She looked suitably dazzled, he noted.
"Holy shit. Ok, yeah, that was..."

She thought they were done. *Cute,* he grinned. He cupped her and petted her back down. She looked at him, confused.

"But.. You came... Right?"

He flashed her his best dimpled smile and nodded as he watched his juices run down her thighs.

"Shifter. Extra endurance." She mouthed something he was pretty sure was 'holy shit' as he eased her to all fours. He trailed his hand over her shoulders, down her back, and to her perfect bottom. His fingers trailed through her still-drenched folds, up to her back entrance. She tensed a little.

"No?" He wouldn't do anything she wasn't comfortable with.

She shook her head.

"Just surprised."

She moaned a little as he knelt behind her. He gently fingered her while pressing lightly against her puckered hole with his thumb.

"You're beautiful, Grace, you know that? So fucking beautiful. I'm just about all out of gentle now. This might get a little weird."

She looked up over her shoulder, her lips parted.

"Huh? Oh, don't stop!" she breathlessly demanded as he pressed a little more, and his finger rubbed against her G-spot.

"When I'm in you this time," He added a finger into her tight core and pumped harder. "I can't pull all the way out, okay?"

Her mouth formed an O. He could tell she was close again.

"You... Knot?" she asked. "Like in the books?"

"I hook. Cat, remember?" He nipped her butt in gentle reprimand as he felt her tighten around his fingers.

Shifter anatomy wasn't much different than human. Still, Pogue was pretty sure no human male could damage himself and the woman he was with the way the hook could if you separated during sex.

"You... Oh fuck... won't hurt me," she panted. *Almost there.*

"No, no barb like a wild cat." He leaned down to nip her neck before whispering, "I'm gonna fuck you like there's no tomorrow Grace. And you're going to take everything I give you."

She shuddered around him, her muscles tightening up around his fingers with her impending orgasm. The second she came, he pushed himself into her with a ferocity that made her cry out. He froze.

"Move!" she demanded.

"Yes, ma'am," he ground out. And then he moved. He drove to the hilt, pulled out as far as he could, then slammed back in, a hand on her hips to keep her steady. As he branded her in the most intimate way, she met him thrust for thrust. His scent would linger on her, telling every other Shifter she belonged to an Alpha. To him.

She arched her back, her mouth already open in a silent gasp. Pogue pulled her up, flush against him, and she wound her arms up around his neck as he held her to him, kneading her breasts as he thrust into her over and over again.

"That's it Grace. Come for me now. One. More. Time!" he ordered, voice strained as his hands gripped her tightly.

She shattered around him, in a wordless shout.

Pogue followed, coming harder than he had in his entire life. In the same second, his cat bent its head and bit her other shoulder, marking her again. He stilled in shock, breathing hard. He let go of her hands, palmed her cheek, and turned her head towards him.

"Hey, Grace, Grace, baby, look at me!" he ordered. *Fuck!* he cursed himself silently, wiping his mouth with the back of his hand. *Again?! You fucking marked her again?!* He felt the smug fucker his cat was, almost smile inside him.

They were still joined as he waited for the hook to release. He carefully lowered them onto the bed on his side to curl himself around her.

"You are some next-level entertainment, Pogue." she smiled, stroking the arm curved around her belly as she caught her breath.

Pogue felt something in him loosen up at her words, his lips twitching with the effort not to smile.

"Are. You. Ok?" he said between breaths. Grace sighed, obviously content, her body loose and sated, though she was panting.

"Perfect." she breathed out. "I'm perfect. Might have to get stitched up, though. Also.. a little bit ow," she frowned back at him. He bent to kiss her neck and shoulder, murmuring apologies until she giggled.

"We'll get Doc to heal it. Shower?"

"I'm not sure I can move." she sighed.

After another minute, Pogue slowly slid out of her, exciting a low moan from both of them. He got up on shaky legs and went to turn on the shower. Once done, he returned and picked her up, carrying her to the shower stall. He washed her body with slow, measured movements, then dried her off and hung the towels neatly on the rack, while mentally slapping himself for each of the bruises his fingers had left on her skin.

They needed to head down for dinner, but his cat would want a short nap, and she seemed to need one too. But he wasn't sure what she wanted, and her scent didn't tell him much except that she smelled nice. Pogue carried her back to bed, forgoing his own towel.

"You hungry? Dinner should still be on," he said as he pulled the duvet over her.

She looked up at him, biting her lips.

"Uhm... sure. I guess." She looked away. He knelt on the floor beside the bed, turning her face to look at him.

"Grace? Would you prefer staying here, and I'll call in for some food?"

She nodded, and he pressed a kiss to her forehead before sliding under the duvet. He pulled her close, then reached for his phone on the bedside table. Juno would leave the food outside and signal when it was ready. Pogue's cat purred, simply happy to have her in his arms.

"Dinner in bed it is. With placemats," he said.

Grace chuckled, snuggling closer.

"Sure, Pogue. With placemats..."

Chapter 42

Council

Archer

Archer slammed his phone down on the table in his office. When he heard the tell-tale crunching sound, he cursed and picked it up, throwing it against the white plaster wall of his office.

The Global Council was as useless as the local Councils. Kelly, the current chairman, stubbornly refused to acknowledge Myla's misconduct. This was despite the avalanche of complaints about DeCoill's rampage and the arbitrary laws he was enforcing. What irritated Archer even more and led to his phone's untimely demise on the floor, was DeCoill's failure to issue a letter outlining one specific part of the new laws. 'All members, regardless of rank and place in the hierarchy, must participate in Turf Challenges. Cubs under the age of ten excluded.'

Archer knew DeCoill was attempting to throw StormEdge off guard to find an excuse for further punishment.

Archer had dedicated the past two weeks to uncovering any evidence, no matter how small, of the atrocities he was convinced DeCoill was perpetrating. Yet, despite the diligence and skill of his people, they had come up empty-handed. DeCoill seemed to outmaneuver them at every turn. The one advantage Archer possessed was his inside man—his Mate. Once again, Archer would enlist him to ensure StormEdge came out on top.

He needed them alive. Alive to fight another day. Another war.

Chapter 43

Six weeks later

They had agreed to keep their relationship low-key. It wasn't that Pogue was averse to sharing the news—Grace knew the Pride could use some positive vibes right now. He had been gracious when she'd told him she needed space to process the past two months. She was pretty confident the Pride had caught on, though. Their interactions were just too easygoing for it to go unnoticed.

It's not like he had nothing else to do besides convincing Grace; she was well aware of that. He had a war to prepare for. The Vigilia trained hard, and Pogue had recruited a mated jaguar couple from the Pride to serve as extra team leaders. The rest of the Pride had been put on a training routine to slowly build them up, and Maternals had been stocking up on food. Turf Wars, she'd been told could be over in an hour. They could also turn into a siege and last a year.

Grace woke up feeling delightfully sore. She rolled over to find the spot beside her empty. Pogue must have woken up early, judging from the sound of the shower running. He had learned three things about Grace during the last month. 1. Team Grace was very much still a thing, much to Graces' delight. 2. He had learned that her morning grump was, in fact, not a one-time thing. Grace was cranky as hell in the morning. 3. Grace did not do tidy. At all, and she was cool with that. She also didn't do shoes. Grace found she liked the feel of the warm stone floor under her feet. Yeah she may or may not have fought him a little when he showed up with six shopping bags with clothes and boots, shoes and socks. *Need coffee*, her brain prodded her. Biting the duvet, as she silently squealed and kicked her legs a little, she reached under the bed for her phone, wanting to text Sophie. Today marked a month without fugues. He made her feel centered. He'd been patient when she'd told him she wanted to train with the Vigilia, and he'd

285

taken onboard her suggestions on human warfare. They all came from Sophie, of course, but still. He had really been trying. Just like he promised he would.

> **CatLady:** You up?

> **Miss Allen:** GRNGH.

A minute later, another reply.

> **Miss Allen:** Time zones. U OK?

Grace thought about it before texting back.

> **CatLady:** 4 weeks!!!!! I think P sexed it out, LOL

> **Miss Allen:** Pics, or it didn't happen.

> **CatLady:** sec.

She tiptoed out of bed and made her way to the bathroom. She cautiously looked around the corner. Pogue stood under the shower, his back to her, water cascading down. It seemed he hadn't been there too long; the steam hadn't filled the stall. Her breath caught. He was a sight to behold. His back was a work of art, with broad shoulders and defined muscles. He had the kind of tan you'd expect from someone who loved the outdoors but without the tan lines. Her favorite part, though? The two dimples above his ass. The perfectly sculpted bounce a brick off ass. She quickly snapped a photo with the new smartphone Micah had given her. Pogue's head snapped around at the sound. Grace beelined it for the bed. A second later, the phone rang, and she picked up just as she was getting back under the duvet.

"Hey, babe," she greeted Sophie, grinning.

"Bloody hell, Grace! That's a lot of man. So, what now? Housewife, battle, and babies?"

Grace snorted and turned onto her stomach, facing the simple wooden head-board.

"Calm your tits, cuz. One day at a time, yeah?." She sighed. "Honestly, right now, I'm just happy I haven't fritzed in so long."

"Worried it's gonna come back?"

"Yes and no...I mean, I didn't expect any of this. To feel safe, you know? It's like I'm waiting for the other shoe to drop."

Sophie was quiet for a while before answering, her voice serious.

"Look, Grace. I'll support you; you know I will... But it just seems a bit fishy, doesn't it? We don't lie to each other, and I don't believe you're telling me the whole truth. I mean, you're not exactly a master of deception, and you're going with a secret military base can't handle a bunch of poachers? Please, Grace, at least try to develop something more believable."

Grace chewed her lip, fully aware that Sophie wouldn't buy it. But revealing the truth wasn't on the table. So, Grace lied more, and Sophie played along. Though her concern was almost palpable.

"I'm just really bad at explaining it. Didn't Micah explain, too?"

"He did, and if it wasn't for you also explaining, I would believe it. But you did, and now I don't." Sophie paused. "Anyway, we, Micah and I, uhm, well, we spend more time discussing... Other matters."

Grace snorted.

"Sure, Soph. I'm sure it's dire stuff."

"Don't change the subject! And I'll have you know sexting can be quite serious," she grinned before her voice turned serious again. "I worry about you, Grace. You're my best friend, and I don't like this distance between us, metaphorically and physically. Please, be careful."

"I will, Soph. But..." Grace wasn't sure how to word everything right. "Soph, it feels like... I can't explain it. And Pogue... Something's clicked. I don't know." Grace trailed off.

"Clicked?"

Suddenly Grace noticed the water had turned off. She looked behind her to see Pogue, a towel wrapped low around his waist, leaning on the dresser opposite the bed. He smirked at her, flashing his damn dimples like the cat that got the cream.

"Uh, Soph, I gotta go...."

"Why?" Sophie whined.

"A wet cat just walked into the room. Big one. It's gonna end up leaving a mess everywhere."

Sophie snorted as she said her goodbyes and hung up.

"What was that?" Pogue asked, his cat looking out at her.

"Hey, kitty cat."

"Grace," he drawled and slowly stalked towards her.

She flashed him an innocent look while biting her lip.

"Sophie wanted a picture."

Pogue stopped and frowned at her phone as he wedged his hands under his armpits. He shook his head and sat on the bed beside her, running his fingers through her hair. Grace sat up Indian style before him, the duvet wrapped around her.

"So, uhm, how long were you standing there for?"

Pogue's lips twitched.

"Somewhere around clicked. And if anyone leaves messes, it's not me." Pogue grabbed the duvet, using it to pull Grace in for a kiss. She lingered by his lips for a bit before leaning back.

"Morning to you, too," she giggled.

"You all rested after game night?"

Games night in StormEdge was a unique experience. They kicked off with a game of charades. Grace loved charades, but watching a bear act out "Enemy at the Border and I can't find my paws" was a whole new level of entertainment.

Another interesting aspect was how all the games seemed to tie in with training and sharpening their senses. Pogue clarified that cross-species communication was crucial for a diverse Pride, and Micah had found a way to incorporate learning through play. They tried to have a game night once a month. Kept the Pride happy. Between that and the impromptu dancing that seemed to take place at game nights, too, it made for some fantastic fun.

Grace introduced Twister, and it swiftly became a crowd favorite, culminating in the revelation that Caden was possibly the least flexible Shifter in the Pride.

Caden, it turned out, was not a gracious loser. As a result, Grace's Twister mat morphed into more of a Twister puzzle piece. From her first game night, Grace gleaned a few lessons. Firstly, there was an abundance of excellent dancers in StormEdge. She was not one of them. Second, Tari and Caden should never be on the same team. They became the Shifter version of the movie "Mean Girls." Lastly, playing hide and seek with avian Shifters? Not worth it. Ever.

"You there?" Pogue prodded, dragging Grace back to reality.

She wiped a couple of droplets from his cheek.

"Mhm. Coffee? Now ish?"

Pogue grinned, lifting her up for a moment before setting her down and gesturing towards the walk-in closet. Despite keeping things discrete, Grace hadn't used her room in about four weeks. When she emerged, clad in leggings and one of Pogue's hoodies, he was leaning against the bedroom doorway, a satisfied smile on his face.

"Caden texted. Tari's got some information about the war. We're turning breakfast into a Pride meeting."

He looked serious. Pogue hadn't asked her to join in on any important meetings before, even the ones for the whole Pride. It made sense. She wasn't part of StormEdge. Not yet, at least. Pogue asking her made her nervous because that meant it was something big. She nodded as she debated putting on socks. Pogue had bought her three pairs of boots, a pair of slippers, and one set of sneakers. She'd just gotten used to walking around barefoot, and the inside of the Den was always at a comfortable temperature.

"Sure. Anything I need to know beforehand?"

Pogue picked up the socks Grace had taken from the drawer and discarded them on a random shelf. He held them up in front of her as he answered.

"These have a home. It's called a sock drawer. And yes. We'll be telling the Pride some news that will upset them. I need you to stay behind me, Micah or Caden. I don't want you out in the open."

Grace frowned.

"They won't hurt me, Pogue."

"A wolf in a trap will bite the hand trying to free it. Accidents happen."

She took the socks from him and deposited them back in the drawer, closing them with an exaggerated air of accomplishment. She walked over, putting her arms around him.

"This is an actual safety thing, then?"

"Yes."

"Mkay." Grace decided it didn't make sense to fight him on this. She shrugged and motioned for them to get going.

Chapter 44

P ogue guided Grace into the bustling dining hall. It was as crowded as he'd expected, but the atmosphere was markedly different from the laughter-filled evening of the day before. There was a palpable weight in the air, a sense of unease. Each passing second brought them closer to the possibility of losing a friend, a lover, or even a cub. This wasn't the future Pogue had envisioned for his Pride. He never wanted a war. He found himself reminiscing about Tari's utopian vision, where the Council held no sway over their lives. Right now, that vision seemed like a distant dream—one Pogue would go to great lengths to realize.

"I'll go grab your coffee. Go." He gently pushed her toward the dais where Beau and Oliver sat and headed over to grab their coffees. Glares from the Shifters, who were keeping up the whole Team Grace scheme, followed him. Maude winked at him when he approached and held out two large cups.

"Don't ya worry, honey. I'll always be Team Pogue," she smiled. "But mind you, if you don't claim her publicly soon, boy, I will start replacing your sugar with salt!"

Pogue winched. *Team Pogue my ass.*

"Yes, ma'am," he replied as she poured.

As he navigated through the crowd towards the table near the dais, he spotted Caden approaching from the right, carrying a plate and a coffee cup. Caden took a seat and motioned for Tari to join them. Tari adjusted the chair slightly to face the room. The dais was positioned by the spacious windows, offering a clear view of the entire area. They often used it as a stage for game nights, providing a good vantage point.

Pogue paused, eyeing them all. They gazed back at him with feigned innocence, well, except for Oliver. Innocence wasn't exactly Oliver's forte, even if his life depended on it.

"Oliver, you wanna?" he motioned from Oliver to Beau. Mates sitting on their other half's lap was commonplace for Shifters. Pogue had no idea why. It was just like that.

Oliver smirked.

"Team Grace."

Pogue looked from one to the other. He firmly put down the mugs on the table and glared at them. Every single one of them silently raised their fists.

Pogue huffed and looked at Grace.

"You're not gonna move, are you?"

She pulled over one of the cups he'd placed and took a sip.

"Nope."

Cursing, he picked her up, smirking at her small squeak as he did so. He then sat down and planted her in his lap. She froze for a second but then quickly molded her legs into a cross-legged position on his thighs and leaned back. She didn't understand, but for Shifters, this was a statement. So were the markings on either side of her neck, right where they connected to her shoulders. The rest of the table seemed appeased by his gesture. As did a fair amount of the Pridemembers scattered around the hall, though no one said anything. Respecting his status enough to not dig into it. Grace picked up on some of their looks.

"Uhm, Pogue?" She turned, looking up at him. He put his hand on her head and gently turned it toward the table again. "Shuddup."

"Ok, then," she whispered and silently started drinking her coffee. He caught Caden's look of satisfaction as he was slowly waking up. Cades was not a morning person. He did not function before coffee. But then, neither did Grace, really. She was just more angry than slow. Pogue felt that his cat was immensely pleased with this public display. So, Pogue found, was the man. He smiled to himself and bent to kiss her on the neck as he wrapped an arm around her waist. Grace tensed in his arms as a wolf whistle echoed from the back of the spacious room. He instinctively growled though he wasn't sure who was responsible. But seeing

Grace's reaction to the looks and whispers, Pogue knew he was right to ensure his Pride understood the need to give her space. He hissed low under his breath at anyone close enough to see. His Pride knew when the Alpha was displeased and generally respected his wishes. He wouldn't allow her to be pressured into giving him an answer, not by him or anyone else in the Pride.

Half an hour later, Caden was coherent enough to stand. Grace had slumped back against Pogue's chest, relaxing.

"Alright. Morning!" Caden said.

Brody snorted from where he was still slumped over the table just before them. "No."

Tari tossed a paper cup at him, grinning.

"If you didn't go humping everything that moved all night, you'd be plenty awake, man."

Brody shot him a sour look.

"At least my cock is active."

"Or very sad and overused," Beau smirked. "Hey, where's Mehendi?" he asked. The meeting was mandatory.

"Her mom's still sick. She'll be home tomorrow, hopefully," Pogue responded. Letting a Vigilia leave during a time like this wasn't the best idea. But Mehendi was very tight with her mom, and she was old. Pogue and Caden had decided to let her go for a little while.

Brody flipped him off just as Caden rose and started the morning meeting. The relaxed demeanor of Brody, and especially Tari, reassured Pogue. While StormEdge was a strong Pride, this situation put them to the test, especially with the heavier focus on training and security. But that same focus was also what helped them keep their equilibrium. Well, that and the faith they had in their Alphas.

"I know you've had a lot to deal with lately. This war isn't something any of us want. It seems the Council isn't done adding things to our plate, so I'll ask you to bear a little more. But hear me, StormEdge. We will get through this!"

Pogue watched as the Pride as a whole tensed up. They knew shit was about to hit the fan when Cades started to reassure them before even telling them what the fucking issue was. He bent to whisper in Grace's ear and gently patted her outer thigh.

"Behind me, Micah or Caden." He gave her a quick peck on the cheek and lifted her off his lap, nodding to Micah as he did so. Micah, seated beside Pogue with Tari on his right and Beau and Oliver opposite him, their backs to the room, moved his chair next to Grace's, almost directly in front of her. Meanwhile, Pogue and Beau made their way down to Grayson, who sat at a small round wooden table just below the dais with Juno, Liam, and Claus. Grayson frowned as they approached.

"I am going to get angry, aren't I?" Pogue and Beau nodded. Gray ran a tanned hand through his muddy brown hair. Pogue had always been just a little jealous of his Middle Eastern complexion.

"*Goh*," Grayson muttered. Pogue knew exactly two words in Farsi. 'Shit' was one of them.

"Shit indeed," Beau answered and got behind Gray to hold his arms as Pogue placed a hand on his chest. Gray let them. Pogue knew he would. He trusted Pogue implicitly.

"Deep breaths, big guy," Beau coaxed. "Kinda wish Mehendi was here right about now," he added. She was Gray's best friend. Grayson nodded sharply. Pogue looked up to Caden. "Now."

Caden nodded.

"The Council's changed the rules for the Turf War, and there's no room for appeal. Tari tried. The info didn't even come from the Council. Seems they 'forgot'." Caden said the last part with enough sarcasm to drown a whale. Caden took a deep breath and nodded to Beau, who widened his stance as Pogue grabbed Grays's wrists. "They've mandated that every member of the Pride, excluding cubs under ten, must be actively involved in the Challenge. That means everyone save Doc and Grace." Doc, as a Healer, was sacred, and Grace counted as a Pet. As such, she could only serve, not defend.

The Pride was quiet, clearly confused. Brody raised a hand. Caden nodded for him to speak.

"You're saying the Submissives have to fight too, aren't you?"

"I am," Caden confirmed.

Grayson exploded, though he didn't make a peep. His thrashing did the talking and roaring for him. Pogue had hoped he could calm him, but he was already mid-shift. Grayson, as a rule, did not have temper tantrums. He was probably the most stable Pridemate there was. But the Submissives were a red button for him. Added to the fact, this was a new low for the Council, who were supposed to protect Shifters. Demanding a Submissive to fight was the equivalent of asking a deer to wield a gun. Submissives violate their animals when they purposely inflict harm on someone. This would scar them for life,

"Beau, knock him down," Pogue ordered.

Beau shifted his weight, causing him and Gray to tumble to the ground. He shifted his weight again midair, allowing Gray to land beneath him. Pogue swiftly grabbed his legs to keep him from kicking. When Pogue had told Grace the leopard was lethal, he wasn't kidding. Beau was on the receiving end of Gray's razor-sharp claws in seconds. He would probably regret it later, but for now, his cat was in charge. Gray's feline side was always more prominent than that of most other Shifters. It was evident in his eyes. They were only ever his cats.

Pogue could have subdued Gray with dominance, but it would be the equivalent of rubbing a dog's nose in its own piss. All it taught the animal was to fear the owner, or in this case, the Alpha. It would not promote respect or trust. He needed to be allowed to come out of it without being forced.

Pogue was so busy focusing on Gray that he hadn't noticed Grace hopping down from the dais and coming up right behind them, stopping when she was directly in front of the leopard. She was about to grab him, but Pogue hauled her up with one arm around her waist and pushed her behind him with a show of teeth. She showed him her own but stayed behind him as she spoke.

"Gray, you're scaring the Submissives. Calm down! They need you calm. Grayson, be calm for them, please!" she urged, then called back over her shoulder. "Nadya! I need you." *Oh, you're smart*, Pogue thought.

Pogue allowed Grace to carry on, though he kept her behind him with a firm hand.

Nadya was like cold water for Grayson, being the second to lowest ranking Shifter in the Pride. Nadya was there in a split second, sliding in to lie next to Grace, her head on the floor.

"Talk him out," Grace commanded. "Ground him. Touch grounds you guys, right?"

"Yes," Pogue answered as Nadya laid her hand on Grayson's head. Pogue's cat was fascinated by the fact that Nadya showed no fear toward Grayson. She should, given her place in the hierarchy. "Come back. Reza, come back," she whispered.

Pogue noted the confusion on Grace's face and clarified.

"His first name is Reza. Grayson is his middle name."

She just nodded. His Persian looks probably made a hell of a lot more sense to her now.

It took another ten minutes for him to finally snap out of it, and when he did, he promptly got up and left the room. After another two shifts, Beau accepted the sweatpants Oliver handed him. Pogue, not bothering to hide his need to have Grace plastered to him after watching her in too close proximity to a very pissed apex predator, grabbed her and wound her around his waist as he walked back up to their table.

He resettled her on his lap and held her chin, forcing her to look at him. She poked one of his canines with a slight smile when he bared them at her, his cat needing to convey its irritation that she put herself in danger when he specifically told her not to.

"Don't ever do that again. And stop laughing at my cat."

Grace had the decency to look mildly chastised.

"My bad. And I'm not laughing at your cat. Even if he is adorable."

Pogue just blinked at her, unable to form an answer. *Adorable? Are you fucking kidding me?* It took him a minute to come up with one.

"Fierce, strong, or handsome, Grace. Those are your options. Not adorable. Ever."

Grace didn't reply, ignoring him in favor of the pancakes Oliver brought over. Pogue left her to eat as he, along with his twin, settled everyone down. It didn't take much, as usual. Submissives would take their cues from Dominants, and the

Maternals quickly calmed the Dominant's adrenaline, so they could deal with the nervous Submissives.

By the doors to the dining hall, Pogue noticed Tari gesturing for him to come over. He was waving a piece of paper. Pogue nodded, signaling he'd seen him.

He pinched the bridge of his nose and waved to Caden, who grabbed Micah on his way. *What the fuck now?* Pogue groused as he stomped after Tari.

Chapter 45

Pogue knew something was wrong when he followed Tari into the office, Beau and Henley quietly following. Someone must have signaled Beau and Henley on the way because Pogue hadn't asked them to tag along, and Gray shouldn't even be here. His head must be all over the place. But then again, Grayson's loyalty to the Pride would always exceed how he felt or what else was going on in his mind.

Tari positioned himself behind the imposing wooden desk, creating a barrier between himself and Pogue. At the same time, Beau moved towards the expansive window, blocking it. Grayson nonchalantly leaned against the light sandstone wall near the door, and Henley occupied the opposite side. When Caden joined them, followed closely by Micah, the Beta swiftly closed and locked the door. They both sidled up on either side of Pogue and firmly locked his shoulders with an arm each as they faced him. He met Caden's gaze.

"Cades?"

A million questions were in that one word. Pogue had never known what it was like to be managed or handled. It was, however, a sensation he was having right now, and he didn't like it one bit. Sure, he had a temper, but it took a significant push for him to lose control. But his co-Alpha and Beta's firm grip on his shoulders left no doubt that they were expecting that push.

"Grace?" he tried, looking from Caden to Micah.

Pogue saw a pissed-off lion as he caught Micah's eyes. Yet, Micah had somehow managed to keep his apparent rage under control. *He already knows,* Pogue thought, but it still didn't give him a clue as to what this was about.

Caden gave his shoulder a gentle squeeze and nodded to Tari. Tari's hands were fisted, his stance wide. How he stood now made him look like one of the actors from "The Matrix" Grace had shown him photos of. He almost smiled, remembering the look of horror on her face when he told her StormEdge had one TV and three VHS tapes.

Tari cracked his neck and took a breath.

"I got a... *special* letter two weeks ago. About Grace," Tari winced as he said it. Like it burned his tongue having to say the word 'special.'

Pogue immediately started growling.

"And I wasn't informed why?"

Next to him, both Caden and Micah tightened their grips on him. Pogue looked to Caden for an answer. Keeping him out of the loop was inexcusable. Caden tensed his jaw.

"I needed to give Tari time to find a way out. I knew how you'd react. I'm sorry, Pogue, I really am, and I know this isn't how we run the Pride. But..." he sighed. "These are unique circumstances. If it was me, I hope you'd have made the same choice."

Pogue switched his gaze to Tari.

"And did you? Find a way out?"

Tari shook his head sharply, and his fingernails slowly morphed into claws as his serval cat's eyes looked out at Pogue. He waved the paper around as he spoke.

"I tried to appeal," Tari started. "I had Hannah order a Portal. She and Caden went with me and to Ontario, to the Council offices. DeCoill wouldn't even see us. Hayfield didn't care enough to listen, Archer wasn't available, and Mayflower's only response was that the Primus decided that if we treat Pets as Pride members, they'll be counted as one, with all that goes with it. And before you ask, no, I don't know where he gets his info, and yes, Juno is looking into the history books for precedence. William's helping me dig through the old law books, too," he sighed and put the piece of paper on the table, tapping it before looking at Pogue again.

Pets were, from what Pogue knew, confined to servants' quarters when they weren't working. They did not, he knew, participate in game night, go to Submissive meetings, or eat with the general Community. They also didn't fuck the Alpha.

Pogue felt his whole body tense up, and his hands trembled as he fisted them, ignoring the feeling of his slowly forming claws digging into his human flesh. A thousand scenarios ran through his head in a split second, none of them good, and all of them leading to Grace bleeding on the ground.

"More words," he growled, holding himself still.

Tari took a deep breath. He looked first at Caden, then Micah. They nodded.

"DeCoill has decreed that Grace now falls under the same laws as the Submissives. Active participation." From here, Tari spoke with lightning speed as Pogue's whole body shook with rage. "I contacted the Global Council and managed to-"

"He's gonna-" Micah interjected. He didn't get the rest out.

Pogue's roar ripped through whatever Micah was about to say as he shifted uncontrollably between his jaguar and human forms. In a coordinated effort, Caden and Micah managed to bring him down. Caden grabbed Pogue's head and roared at him to shift to human form. The second Pogue did, Micah took hold of one arm, and Grayson grabbed the other. Henley and Tari skillfully locked down both his legs.

Meanwhile, Beau shifted and literally sat on him while Pogue raged. Pogue knew then he'd lied to Grace. *I will keep you safe*, he's told her. How was he supposed to keep her safe? She had no claws or teeth. She had no magic. This would kill her.

"Micah!!!" he roared. Micah would take her. He would run away with her, Pogue thought frantically as he tried to buck off his friends.

"Let us explain, bro," Caden coaxed as he held Pogue's neck firmly to the ground.

"NO!" he bellowed, looking at Micah. "You get her out of here! You fucking hide her in fucking Siberia! You take her and fucking run!"

It took a long while for him to calm down enough for them to let him go. When they did, Beau shifted back, and they all gave him plenty of space. Caden even grabbed Pogue's cigarettes for him. He angrily lit one and paced.

"You knew?" Pogue pointed a finger at Micah as he paced and smoked like his life depended on it. Beau carefully pushed the ashtray closer to him, then quickly backed up when Pogue hissed at him. Everyone had taken a couple of steps back except Caden and Micah.

Micah nodded. "She's your sister." Again, Micah nodded. "She's your blood, and you didn't run away with her!" Micah looked like Pogue's words were a blow to his face. And yet, he nodded. Pogue stopped and stared at him. "Why?"

For the first time since Pogue had known Micah, his voice shook as he answered.

"You think I didn't consider it? You think this doesn't tear me up inside?! We stay for StormEdge, *Alpha*. For her."

Pogue was about to call bullshit when Henley cut in.

"DeCoill wants Micah dead too. My inside source confirmed it. He wants to wipe the bloodline out. If Micah runs with Grace, DeCoill will send every force he has at his disposal after them. And he has enough to pick us off one at a time while he does it. And he will," Henley finished in his soft, calm voice.

Pogue's head whipped to him.

"Is this the anonymous inside source you won't tell us about?"

Henley's eyes went hard, though he averted them and bared his neck. "Yes."

Micah frowned.

"Why hasn't he come after me then? It's not like I've been hiding."

Henley took a deep breath and sat down, crossing one leg over the other.

"Tell me, Micah, what would cause you the most pain? You dying, or you watching your sister die before your eyes? I know DeCoill knows nothing about our Alpha's interests in Grace, so his motive must, therefore, be solely on you and Grace. He is trying to maximize pain, would be my guess," Henley stated as a matter of fact. "My informant also tells he DeCoill hunted Grace long before she came here, and as to you? Taking out a Beta is a difficult task, especially one residing in a dual Alpha Pride."

Micah blanched. He then turned to Pogue.

"Pogue? I'm going to kill him. A lot."

Pogue took a couple of deep breaths through the cigarette he lit with the butt of the one he was about to put out. Caden didn't comment for once. The room was quiet as everyone digested the news. After a while, Caden motioned for Tari to talk. *So there's more. Goodie.* Pogue swore under his breath. Tari sat in the office chair and linked his hands in front of him.

"The Global Council gave us a little leeway on a few conditions: we stay on our lands until the Turf War. No Portalling for supplies or contacting other Communities. They're clearly concerned about us causing a stir. Rightfully so," he added with a sneer.

Pogue stopped in his tracks and looked at Caden.

"And you agreed?"

Caden shook his head.

"I gave Tari the authority to broker the best deal he could."

It made sense, but it still chafed at Pogue's pride not being consulted. He motioned for Tari to go on.

"I negotiated that she falls under the Healers' clause due to her veterinary nurse education. But she has to do one rotation of three hours out, too. She can't defend by any other means than running, and she can't aid us in any way. No bow, no handing us bandages, no nothing."

Pogue scoffed.

"How the fuck are they gonna police that? And why is DeCoill being so fucking open about everything? He's basically laying out all the cards for us to see. It's sloppy."

Tari nodded and pinched the bridge of his nose.

"Unless he knows he'll win. Look, I know. I asked the same thing about the tracking bracelet. She'll be fitted with a magically enhanced tracker, controlled by the Regulator DeCoill has appointed to oversee the damn show. She doesn't have to do the whole three hours in one go. The tracker comes with a timer that will start when she is more than fifty meters outside the clinic."

"We hide her in the tunnels," Pogue decided as he continued pacing.

Caden shook his head.

"The second she is out of the clinic, she follows Submissives' rules. She must stay above ground. They'd know if we stashed her."

Pogue stopped in his tracks again, jaw slack as he processed.

"This is insane!" I mean, have you ever heard of anything like this happening in any other Community? DeCoill is treating this like his own personal circus, making up rules as he goes. Is he completely insane? And the Global Council, whom we've never seen, is simply giving him the go-ahead, although they have to know he's making up these special rules just for us!? Is anyone else seeing how ridiculous this is? Why isn't the Global Council doing anything?!!"

Tari nodded sadly.

Henley held up a finger and uncrossed his legs, sitting forward.

"I heard a rumor that one of the Global Council's newest members share the same... views as DeCoill," he said, probably referring to DeCoill's Purebloods Only fantasy. "And we know how little the Global Council actually communicates with the local ones."

"I'd also like to add, and Tari, you can back me up here, he's not well, Pogue. I believe something is either physically or mentally wrong with him. He's being irrational to the point of insanity," Henley finished.

Pogue looked to Tari, who nodded vigorously. *So he's fucked up, and no one is rising against him. Perfect*, Pogue mentally banged his head against a wall.

Caden turned to him.

"Pogue, there's one more thing. Grace knows. She's known for a week. Micah and I wanted to give her time to adjust before telling you."

Pogue's world stopped spinning for a second. *Why didn't she tell me? Oh yeah, because this is yet another thing she has to somehow fit into the shitshow that is her life.*

Chapter 46

Liam handed Grace a bowl of popcorn as Claus set down a pitcher of water and kissed Liam's cheek before he returned to the kitchen. It smelled like chocolate cake. Oliver and Nadya had suggested they hang out with them while Pogue was in another meeting. Liam and Claus lived in the most adorable little burrow. Grace could tell it wasn't big, but it was comfortable. There were pictures of them with Nadya on wooden shelves and hung on the wooden walls. Thick green rugs broke up the wooden walls and floor, and two large old soft couches sat on either side of a low sofa table in the living room.

Her mind had settled in here somewhere in the last month. Despite knowing DeCoill wanted her dead and that he had made an extra effort by forcing her out in the open during the war, she was surprisingly at ease in ways she hadn't felt before. Being embraced by the Pride and Pogue convinced her that she was much stronger than she realized.

Doc let her treat minor injuries, such as setting dislocations in their animal forms. Grace also noticed a few Shifters with minor cuts despite knowing that shifting would heal them. Pogue indicated they appreciated her contributions and wanted her to feel acknowledged in the Pride.

She and Pogue were slowly getting into a routine, too. He'd get up before her, and coffee would be waiting when she dragged herself out of bed. She would give his cat trigger point massages and throw away his smokes daily. When they didn't eat in the dining hall, they snacked on leftovers – neither of them cooked. The man couldn't cook to save his life. But despite this oddball honeymoon phase, Grace knew his cat was getting increasingly agitated. She wasn't sure if it was the war or that she still hadn't given him a concrete answer.

"How are you really?" Nadya asked her. She leaned back, resting against the armrest, her feet in Oliver's lap. As soon as her feet landed, he almost automatically started rubbing her feet. She smiled at him and threw a popcorn at his mouth. It bounced off his chin.

Grace thought about it as she stretched out on the couch opposite them. Liam had, in no uncertain terms, told her to relax. He was currently in the kitchen helping Claus with dinner. Her thoughts skipped right past DeCoill to Pogue. Overprotective caveman Pogue these days. He'd growl at the offending chair if she stubbed her toe. When she slid and fell down the stairs, he'd apparently decided she'd forfeit the privilege of walking up or down them for three days...

"If we look past the Alpha," Oliver smirked, probably knowing where her thoughts were going.

"Uhm... I mean, The whole bull's eye on my back is..." Grace waved a hand in front of her face, trying to convey what she was thinking. She should be terrified, and yet, she just felt... "I guess I'm kinda just resigned on the whole DeCoill master villain thing. I mean, I can't do anything about it, and thinking about it makes me shake inside. I try not to think about it."

"Distracting yourself?" Oliver asked seriously. Grace nodded. Oliver was about to say something when Nadya cut him off.

"That's fine, Grace. I think I understand. There's something... Satisfying in letting yourself surrender to the knowing that there's someone stronger than you who will protect you."

Oliver gave Nadya a loaded look.

"Projecting Nadya?"

Nadya blushed and glared at Oliver.

"Leave it be! Please," she added.

Grace wasn't sure, but she thought Nadya might be referring to a certain yellow-eyed leopard. She let it go and let herself sink back into taking a mental stock of Nadya's original question. *How are you really, Grace?*

She got along well with the Submissives and was adored by the Maternals. Of course, unless you messed up, they loved everyone. But pity the idiot who pissed them off. More than one adult male had been dragged along like a cub, quietly accepting his fate and groveling for dear life. They were nice. Savage but nice. Her problem socially lay with a few dominants, mainly Rosita, who seemed to dislike her purely because Grace had taken away her chances at a higher rank. Grace stayed out of her way. She didn't need the drama.

"I think I'm good," Grace finally said. "I just have this ridiculous need to prove I... Never mind."

"To prove you belong lass," Liam said as he entered the room, Claus by his side. They provided an intriguing contrast as a couple. Claus, tall and distinctly Scandinavian, with blond hair, and Liam, with his dark, short stature. They both seemed relatively fit, though Claus had a slight pot belly. Grace hadn't asked how old they were. But with a touch of gray in his chin-length hair, Liam was clearly the eldest, and they looked to be in their mid-thirties. He crossed the short distance and gently clasped her shoulder.

"It's normal, you know. I know you're human, but I'm pretty sure you have some of the same instincts. Your chosen-"

"Or true," Claus interjected. Liam shot him a mock frown.

"-Mate, if you'd just accept him already," Liam smiled softly, "is an Alpha. And you're now in a world where your strength matches that of a ten-year-old at best." Grace snorted at him, but he squeezed her shoulder a bit harder. "Of *course*, you feel you need to prove you belong."

So they know I'm the one who's slow to accept. She really didn't know why that was. She knew she wanted to be with him. There was just something about the concept of forever, losing Sophie, and yes, her having the strength of a ten-year-old at best. It was a lot to consider. Before she could delve deeper into that thought, another occurred to her. She turned to look at Claus, noting the distinctive blue scars, the perfect shape of teeth, on the middle of the neck.

"Can I ask you something?"

Claus sat down on the low table between the couches and looked at her.

"Of course."

"Two questions, actually."

He grinned.

"I think I'll survive two."

Grace sat up a little and faced him properly. Liam stood beside them and ran his hand through Claus's hair. Grace noticed how, almost subconsciously, Claus leaned into the touch.

"Ok, maybe three, but you said yes, so. What's the difference between a Mate and a True Mate? Like, can you choose what to be, and is that what makes the marks blue?"

Claus smirked.

"I take it that was question one. A True Mate is decided by fate, I believe. Doc would tell you it's optimal genetic compatibility. A chosen Mate is just that. Chosen. Like a human marriage, I suppose." Claus gently poked her knee.

"Right, yeah. Uhm. Did it hurt?"

Liam laughed, and Claus hid his smile with a fist. Oliver chuckled while Nadya seemed to swallow up the whole conversation and the popcorn equally. The girl could eat.

"I was a little distracted then, but yes, it did, as far as I remember. Bare in mind, Grace, it's been twenty years," he replied, shooting Liam a fond look.

Liam looked down, frowning a little at Claus, and gripped his hair gently in his fist.

"A *little*, darling?"

Grace didn't miss the tiny movement of Claus baring his neck. That didn't make sense, though. Liam was the highest-ranking Submissive, but Claus was in the mid-tier of the Maternal hierarchy. Thankfully, Oliver clarified.

"The general hierarchy and the household one aren't necessarily the same, sweetheart," Oliver said and winked.

Claus shot him a dirty look, but Liam just grinned and bent to kiss his Mates cheek, his lips lingering as he said,

"How about we kick the youngsters out and-"

Grace jumped when the front door slammed open, revealing Pogue. *Shit. Cat's out of the bag*, Grace concluded as she slowly got to her feet. Liam and Claus backed up a little as Pogue walked in. He respectfully bowed his head to both of them and nodded to Oliver and Nadya.

"Get up. Now," he ordered softly. Grace could see his fists clenching and unclenching, and his jaw was tight. Pogue's demeanor looked like he was two steps from throwing someone through a wall. Looking him in the eyes, she saw his cat looking back at her. She got up slowly and walked toward him. She had expected him to be angry as hell. He was, but unlike the multiple scenarios she'd run in her mind, there was no shouting. No cursing and no telling her off. He walked over to her and pulled her into his arms, standing there for a long while before speaking.

"I won't lose you, Grace."

She ran her hands up and down his back.

"You won't."

"The Vigilia are meeting in ten. I want you there."

"Ok."

He leaned down and kissed her softly in front of the whole room before straightening up and taking a deep breath. He motioned for her to put on her new boots as he grabbed her jacket. And Grace did as she was told. No questions asked.

Chapter 47

Pogue pulled Grace closer, both seated on the desk. She nestled in the space between his legs. For a moment, he savored her presence and the familiar scent of wildflowers that only he could detect.

Moments later, there was a knock on the door, and the Vigilia, plus the two conscripted members, Jie and Lily, walked in. Pogue lifted Grace to her feet to allow everyone to gather around the desk, allowing Micah to roll out a map of the Den and surrounding areas. Pogue knew the map by heart- he was the one who drew it.

The Den stood at the heart of the inner grounds, while to the south lay the aeries and forest dwellings, accessible via narrow forest paths. Only one aerie was visible from the Den. Pogue had long dreamed of making it his home, but for now, it remained vacant. It was too big for just one. *But maybe...* Pogue shook his head, refocusing on the map. Raised wooden walkways interconnected the aeries, with a central path linking the largest one to the second-story gym in the Den. Nestled behind the Den to the west was the playground, partially visible from the dining hall's windows. On the northern side of the Den was the clinic. Between the Den and the clinic stretched an open expanse, with a gravel road leading eastward—the primary entryway into the Den.

Mehendi scooted closer to the table, bumping Jie's hip to get him to scoot over, making him frown at her.

"We're locking down the Den with the cubs inside?" she asked.

"Makes sense. Hannah is warding it to the max."

Beau ruffled his spiky purple hair and pointed to the aeries.

"You still want my group up there?" Caden nodded. Beau grinned at Pogue. "Your girl got us the best toys to play with. We're gonna fuck them up so hard they're gonna be popping out bullet babies".

Pogue still hadn't seen any of the stuff, but he knew she'd shown the Vigilia pictures of the rifles they'd be using. He looked around the table.

"And we're sure DeCoill doesn't know? If he really is the one who got IceFjord to agree to a war, I don't want him to be able to give them a heads-up. Where are the weapons now?" Caden asked.

Tari and Henley nodded simultaneously, although Henley was the one to answer.

"Odd as it may sound, from what I know, DeCoill is so unhinged these days he can barely focus on admin. And would any of us have thought of using human weapons if it wasn't for Grace?"

Everyone shook their heads.

Hannah smirked as she added,

"I've put everything at Pogues place," she shrugged before high-fiving a smirking Micah. *Why is he smirking like that?* Pogue thought as suspicion crept up his spine.

The meeting moved on after a bit of back and forth about DeCoill. In the end, Pogue shut it down. They couldn't do anything about him right now. One war at a time.

Grace had suggested a team man the walkways leading from the Den to the aeries and between them. They'd start in human form and then shift once the first volley of shots had been fired.

Pogue pointed to the clinic.

"Micah, your group will glue your asses to the clinic. I need you to-"

"Keep them from blocking the entrance, I know," Micah said quietly. "I know, Pogue. I know."

Pogue nodded sharply.

"We're going to assume they'll stick to the laws and not breach, but if someone's hurt, there's nothing to stop them from picking injured off as they try to get to the clinic."

"And then we'll pick *them* off," Henley murmured.

"You'd better keep them off my man's ass," Beau warned, knowing that Oliver, along with the other Submissives, would be hiding in the trees near the clinic. They'd opted to keep all Submissives in human form, strategically positioning themselves around the entire inner circle, armed with handguns.

A Submissive would, as a rule of thumb, not attack a Dominant. They were too far removed from each other in the hierarchy. The few times Pogue had seen a Submissive physically attack a Dominant, their animals had shut down afterward. Under normal circumstances, a Dominant wouldn't lay a hand on a Submissive for the same reason. But this wasn't normal, and the wolves at the door would lay more than a hand on any Submissive they found. This way, they were still meeting DeCoill's demand for active participation.

Caden nodded solemnly.

"Alright. Micah, you have the clinic. Mehendi and Jie, initial road defense. Stay behind the minefield until all forty-five have detonated. Grace, you're familiar with handling the mines, right?"

Grace nodded. Pogue watched her closely for any signs of distress. She didn't look scared, but she did look pissed.

"Sophie talked me through it, and I've been watching some videos she sent, too. Once I see what she sent, I'll figure out what goes where."

Pogue stroked his hands up and down her arms as he spoke.

"Henley, runners, Beau, aeries."

Grace described the runners, led by Henley, as 'ninja assassins.' Pogue hadn't seen it that way, but the description was apt. They worked in the shadows, divided between delivering messages and eliminating isolated enemies.

"That leaves forest dwellings, sky, and the playground," Caden added. He continued, "Dina, I know it's a lot. Are you sure you can cover the whole battlefield? I know they won't have avian Packmembers, but we don't know what they *will* have."

"Plus, you'll have to navigate around Regulators and DeCoill," Micah said as he opened a water bottle. Having avian Pridemembers was an advantage. Eyes in the sky.

311

Dina shot him a wolfish grin.

"If my bird accidentally scratches out DeCoill's eye, I'm not gonna cry about it."

Pogue rolled his eyes but smiled at the hawk Shifter.

"I bet you won't," he snickered. "Grayson, that means you have the playground and the Submissives." He nodded towards the large leopard Shifter, who smiled tightly as he twirled a coin around his fingers.

"And I get the forest dwellings," Lily said, her voice somber as she leaned into Jie, who hugged her and kissed her forehead.

"We'll be fine," he reassured her. She nodded and caressed his sharp cheekbones.

Caden tapped the map.

"My cat will take down whomever it deems most dominant, so I'll be all over the place."

"I'll be in human skin to do the overall coordination. And one of us will kill Stellan," Pogue stated, referring to the IceFjord Alpha. He then turned Grace around.

"Now, you..."

He felt a surge of pride when she tilted her chin, looking him dead in the eye.

"I can't hide when I'm out of the clinic, Pogue. We've been over this."

He nodded. They had. Multiple times. And she wasn't wrong in that moving around was safer because even though Grace gave off no scent, the Shifter guarding her did. So, a sitting duck was a dead one. He took a deep breath to center himself. Discussing this made his cat crazy.

"You have to do three hours out of the clinic. We're dividing that into three separate slots. You'll start at the clinic, the first hour. I need to see how fast things progress. I'll come for you, and you'll be with me for an hour. Then I'll hand you off to Micah and Tari, with Beau as backup. We repeat every other hour until your tracker beeps. That'll let us know you did the time."

"No."

Pogue's jaw nearly dropped, and he pinned her with a stunned stare.

"The fuck do you mean, no?!" he shouted before he caught himself. He turned and took a deep breath before returning his attention to Grace.

"Sorry."

Grace rose to her toes and kissed his jaw.

"Thank you for turning away. I have a better idea." She seemed to steel her nerves, stepping away from them all. "You're all too big, and you're too known. Oliver says IceFjord knows who the Vigilia are and even some of the others too. I'm good at hiding and staying small, so I've talked to Oliver and-"

A deep, and to most people probably terrifying rumble sounded from Beau. Grace seemed to have forgotten that, despite his bravado, Oliver was a Submissive with a very protective Mate who wouldn't, not for anything, put Oliver in more danger than he already was.

A small part of Pogue agreed with Grace about Oliver's size. And he wasn't big on going out, so no one knew him outside the Pride. However, there wasn't a scenario where he'd entrust her safety to even the most aggressive Submissive.

Pogue understood her motive, despite him knowing DeCoill had been gunning for StormEdge for years. Long before Grace. But, right now, yes—anyone seen with Grace would become a target. She was trying to divert attention from Micah and himself.

But it came at the expense of Beau's Mate. Even if Oliver was willing—and Pogue discovered he actively encouraged it—it wasn't an option. For hours, they went in circles. Grace even called Oliver in to help her persuade them. All that did was make Grayson throw the office chair through the window, and Oliver break Beau's nose. Twice.

They were exhausted by the time Grace finally caved, and Pogue took her back to their place.

Chapter 48

G race let Pogue lead them to his- now their apartment. As he opened the door, he stopped so abruptly that Grace slammed into his back. He was so damn wide she had to look around him to see why he had stopped.

The living room was a maze of big black boxes, duffel bags, and some Styrofoam containers that had taken over the kitchen. With a little laugh, Grace nudged Pogue inside and stood before him, her hands up and palms out.

"Okay, I know this seems like a lot,"- she looked around the small living room- "and to be fair, it is. But.. Erhm..."

"Grace...?" Pogue's voice was deceptively sweet. "Grace, what the fuck is all this crap, hmm?"

Grace offered Pogue a weak smile, knowing it would upset his neat-freak nature. She approached one of the black boxes was about to open it, when she glanced at Pogue, who had gone to open another box. When she saw what was in his hand, her heart stopped.

"Put *down* the grenade!" she said, feeling her heart in her throat.

Pogue lifted a brow as he shook the grenade.

"What? This tiny thing?"

Grace held up both hands to stop him as she swiftly crossed the distance to fold her hands around his as best she could.

"Honey, baby, sugar bear, I am begging you! Put the grenade down."

Pogue must have seen the panicked look on her face. He carefully lowered both their hands down and placed them gently in the foam holder next to the other ten.

"I think I need to call Soph."

Pogue just nodded and said,

"I think you also need to not *ever* call me Sugar Bear again."

Grace blinked.

"Right, yeah. Okay, this is a little more advanced than what I thought she would send. I mean, how? Martin owns a security firm, not the damn military! There's enough stuff here for a small army!"

Pogue glared at her.

"Call Sophie. Now."

Grace did. Well, she tried, but Soph didn't pick up, so Grace left a message. As she put down the phone, she looked at Pogue, who seemed to be arranging and rearranging boxes everywhere.

Grace rolled her eyes at him and went to take a shower before dinner. When she came out, Pogue was on the bed, shifted into his jaguar. He was lazily lounging on his back. He yawned and stretched as she approached, his prominent teeth standing out against his dark fur. *He really is magnificent*, Grace thought, looking at him. A low rumble told her Pogue's cat loved her appraisal.

She walked over and grabbed his large paws, massaging between the toes. A slow purr started as he blinked at her - the cat version of a smile.

"Hey, kitty," she smiled down at him. "You ok?" He rolled over and sat, his head tilted to the side. A second later, a claw ripped her T-shirt in the middle.

"You're a dick. Shift so I can tell you off." He shifted in a flash of light and grabbed her to stand between his legs as he sat on the bed. He pushed aside her shirt and palmed a breast. She felt the sharp sting of his teeth as they closed around her nipple. Then he flicked his tongue over the sensitive flesh, and she felt like the air had been sucked out of her.

"Pogue?" She tried breathing slowly. She really did. But when he took her other nipple in his mouth to deliver a scorching kiss, she felt her knees buckle a little.

"No more weapons talk," he whispered between his kisses as he ran his hands down her thighs and back up. "It's driving me insane you're so happy jumping into situations that could kill you." His hands tightened a little on her bottom.

She gripped his hair tightly. His hands were making it difficult to have a rational conversation.

"I know," she whispered.

He nodded.

"I know. Just... Just let me pet you a little and try to calm myself down." He pushed her onto the soft mattress, onto her back. The weight of his body, his skin against hers, felt amazing. He opened his eyes to look at her, his pale green human eyes sad.

"Hey, I'm right here, ok? We'll be fine, Pogue; I know we will."

He nodded slightly.

"Just let me."

She did. Pogue pushed himself into her and hitched her leg higher on his waist, slowly loving her. She had never felt so cherished in her life as he slid in and out of her, almost lazily, kissing her lips, neck, and shoulder. Grace kissed him back and ran her hands over his bristled jaw until his dimples appeared and the frown faded. For a man who claimed he didn't do gentle he was a quick study, she mused as he kissed her almost reverently. Grace forgot about wars, and Councils as Pogue thoroughly replaced her thoughts with ecstasy, loving her until she felt practically branded by him. He took care of her more than once before letting himself climax. When he did, he rolled them over so she lay on top of him as they waited for the hook to release.

It felt like an eternity later when he finally let go of her and got off the bed. He returned with a washcloth, having slipped into a pair of loose sweatpants. He cleaned her up, smirking when she hissed and bucked her hips as he cupped her intimately.

"No round three?" he teased.

"Not funny, mister. Come lie down with me a little. Just until I can walk again," she grimaced.

Pogue frowned at her.

"You okay?" he asked. She smiled at him, motioning for him to lie down. He flopped down and popped up on one elbow, gently running the palm of his hand

316

over her breasts and down to her belly, a distinctively smug look on his rugged features.

"I waddled for half a day last time, Pogue. You're not a small man. And the bruises will fade," she said, smiling wryly when he frowned and touched a finger to one forming on her hip.

"Sorry," he said, trying his best to look serious.

"Yeah-na, not even a little," she grinned.

"The bruises, hell yeah. The rest? Not even a little bit," he agreed. "But you're gonna be sore for training tomorrow."

Grace got it. Pogue let her train to satisfy her need to be part of the Pride. She understood she wouldn't be allowed to fight, and that was okay. But with her bow, she could show him she was pretty good.

"Crap on a stick," she groaned. " I was looking forward to training.

Pogue was shaking with silent laughter. She smacked his arm.

"Oh yeah, har har. I'll tell Micah your cock broke me!" she teased.

It only made Pogue laugh harder until he rolled out of bed and curled up in a ball on the floor. Grace tossed a pillow in his direction and decided to ignore him for a moment. Eventually, she saw his head poking out over the edge of the bed. As she ran her hand through his hair, he closed his eyes and leaned into the touch like the cat he was. He looked like he was almost asleep.

"Pogue?"

"Mhm?"

"Your kitty gets lazy as hell after sex, doesn't it?" she commented, making him rumble.

"Why, you want me to carry you to the tub?" he mumbled.

"Might help my muscles, so I don't have to ask Santa for a new pussy."

Pogue snorted and opened his eyes. He yawned, and Grace was delighted to see his canines were slightly elongated. She gently lifted the corner of his upper lip. Pogue just looked at her, a brow raised.

"That's probably the sexiest thing I've ever seen," she confessed, earning her a lazy smile before he got up, slid his arms under her, and walked them to the bathroom.

"Come on, kitty whisperer, let's go fix your pussy."

Chapter 49

24 hours later

"G raaace!" Pogue's frustrated voice rang out from the walk-in closet. "Grahgh"

Minutes later, the bed dipped, and a warm hand reached under the duvet to squeeze her ass cheek. She growled at the offending hand, exciting a chuckle from the owner of said hand. She cursed him in her mind. *Just five more minutes.*

"Remember the talk we had about drawers? When you open something, you close it. When you flick a light on, you flick it off. You know, basic rules one would abide by in a household?" The annoyed voice of Pogue slowly yanked her out of her sleepy daze.

She flipped him off. He nipped at her finger.

"Suck a duck, cuz!" she grumbled. Seconds later, the duvet was yanked off her. She reached for Pogues pillow to cover herself with as she burrowed her head under her own. He yanked the pillow off her head.

"Time to get up, princess! Breakfast and training. You know the training you wanted to do even though you won't be using it? Up!"

She shot him a sour look.

"Go fuck a duck, cuz!"

Pogue sat down and brushed the hair away from her face to whisper in her ear. She lazily debated trying to bite his nose.

"One word, Grace." His voice did beautiful things to her at any other time of the day. Right now, however, she wanted to throw things at him, but he'd removed every object within reach. He lazily kissed his way from her shoulder to her jaw, then her ear. "Coffee."

Coffee? Coffee!!!!!

Grace bolted out of bed, stumbling over her legs in the process, making him laugh aloud as he tried to help her stand like a normal person. She began walking in circles around herself, trying to remember where she had put her clothes, until Pogue finally picked her up, laughing, and carried her to the walk-in closet.

As he set her on her feet, Grace noticed Pogue had made more room in the closet for her. He had neatly folded her small pile of clothing and put it on shelves. Maybe that meant they were going shopping soon. She shuddered at the thought. The shoes and clothes he'd already bought were plenty. More than enough to see her through a week.

She proceeded to yank everything out, tossing it around, trying to find her workout clothes. Finding them in a pile by the corner, she turned around to Pogue, huffing out a breath to clear the hair from her eyes.

He looked at her with a tragic expression on his handsome face, holding out her sports bra. She watched as his expression turned from horror to plain shock.

"What?" she asked, suddenly feeling insecure. *Do I have something stuck between my teeth?* She wondered.

"They're blue, Grace," Pogue said wide-eyed as he reached out to touch the now scars on each side of her neck, where it met her shoulders.

"Yeah, I meant to ask you about that. Noticed it when I got up for water last night," she shrugged. *Can we just go get coffee already?* Her brain prodded. She wholeheartedly agreed. The color of scars just didn't rate over golden liquid.

"No, Grace, they're blue!" he said urgently. She tried to look at them again. It wasn't like she'd spent hours studying them in the middle of the night. Glancing down at them, yeah, they kinda looked dark blue. Almost like a tattoo.

"So they're blue. Super. Now coffee," she grumbled. Pogue didn't move. His eyes were dark green, pupils blown, and she noticed his canines had extended.

"But they're blue," he said, his voice almost a whisper.

Annoyed, she frowned at him. She needed coffee to deal with half sentences.

"Yes, we've established that!"

"They're blue." Pogue barked out a startled laugh. Ok, now he was just being annoying. She glared at him, hoping he'd catch on. It took almost a minute of her glaring at him before he seemed to snap out of it.

"Yes, I'll go make you coffee. Geesh, woman!" he huffed and walked out. She could hear him mumbling about blue marks as he crossed the living room to the kitchenette, only to turn on his heel and walk straight back to her. He stopped in front of her.

"No coffee?"

If the look on his face wasn't a little comical, she'd be worried. He looked flustered, and his pupils really were the size of saucers.

"No! I mean, yes to coffee, but no, that's not why I'm annoyed! You say the scars are blue like the reason is obvious!"

He whipped himself around so fast she heard his whole back crack.

"Shit! Yeah, of course. Sorry." he said and picked her up, slung her onto his back, and headed for the kitchenette again. She couldn't help giggling at him.

"You like carrying me around, don't ya?" He measured out a little bit with his fingers and kissed her shoulder.

"Good. I kinda like using you as a jungle gym. Now, why are the scars blue, Pogue?"

He sat her down on the kitchen counter as he started the coffee machine. He ran a hand over her bare thighs (clothes were just overrated at home).

"It's a True marking," he said, shaking his head, smiling wide. "I can't believe it," he mumbled as he grabbed mugs from the smooth wooden cabinet above the sink. *Yeah, that didn't really clear up much.* She prodded him with her foot. He tickled it before adding.

"You know how we're not sure you'd survive a mating bite, even if you accept?" he asked pointedly. They'd had the Shifter birds and bees talk about a chosen Mate and a True Mate a couple of weeks ago. However, Pogue kinda glanced over all things True Mate related, telling her a human/Shifter True mating was unheard of.

Grace nodded. She was perfectly aware of what Pogue wanted, but she still wasn't sure if... If he wouldn't get tired of her or bored if she wasn't his True

Mate. Or even if she was. Pogue yanked her out of her thoughts by placing a cup of coffee in her hands.

"You still here?" he smiled.

"Yeah, sorry, go on," she said, sipping her coffee.

"Before a Mating, there's a claiming to see if your animals are truly compatible. True Mates. That's where that little jewel comes in," he pointed to her shoulders. "I marked you. Them turning blue means I've claimed you. Blue means positive. It means you're my True Mate. Holy shit, Grace, this means... All you have to do is accept, and we can, Mate. Be mated. You'd be my Mate. A True Mate. Holy shit! This hasn't happened before, I think." he frowned before continuing, "I'm looking for answers on the whole mating bite thing. But all you have to do is accept..."

Pogue was ranting now, and Grace was having trouble wrapping her head around all of it. For some reason, of all things, this was what she couldn't grasp. Claus and Liam were True Mates. That was a forever kind of thing. They were both Shifters. What if Pogue regretted it? Could one take back a True Mate bite thing? Like, was Shifter Divorce a thing?

"How bad is this True Mate bite thing? As in the actual bite," she clarified, trying to stick to facts. Facts calmed her.

Pogue winced.

"Liam's mating bite nearly severed his spine because Claus was a little off-center. He has two rather large scars." Pogue measured them out with his fingers.

"Pogue, that's like ten centimeters!" she exclaimed.

"Yeah"" He paused for a bit before shrugging. Pogue was not a 'shrugger.' At all. But he did and smiled at her. We'll figure it out," he promised as he bent to kiss her. "Let's get dressed and head down for training," Grace told him, feeling a little detached. She put down her coffee cup and headed for the walk-in closet.

Five minutes later, Grace came back out. Her mind was a little scrambled. Why, of all things, is this so fucking hard to deal with? She wondered as she felt the familiar feeling of mentally detaching from the situation. She turned away from him to grab some pieces of leather and a small patch with holes and a metal rod on it. He dropped the bow he'd dug out yesterday from a large hardcase to the floor.

"Nope! Not happening!"

She looked at him, confused, as she picked up the armguards.

"What?"

He gestured to all of her. She stared at him, clearly confused.

"What? I'm dressed for training! What did you think I was gonna look like?!"

Pogue shook his head at her.

"Don't you have some baggy sweatpants and a long T-shirt? Or just wear mine!"

Grace started laughing until she snorted.

"Deal with it, Your Highness! I can't shoot in your clothes; the sleeves will get tangled and shit."

She started to walk past him. He stood up straight, the familiar scowl firmly in place.

"Do not walk out that door, Grace!"

She opened the door.

"Listen to your Mate!" he ordered.

Grace kept walking. *Wear my T-shirt, my ass,* she scoffed as Pogue stood in the doorway staring at her.

"But they're blue!"

"So's the sky cuz. That doesn't get to tell me what to wear either."

Chapter 50

The entire Pride was training today. Thanks to Hannah's dome, the area around the Den was shielded from the biting cold and snow, allowing them to focus on their preparations. With IceFjord looming at the borders, on December twenty-first, in just three days, StormEdge was about to step into what Grace referred to as the "Hunger Games of Shifters." There would be no dome during the war, but there was no point in depleting energy now.

Pogue took on the obstacle course after sparring with the Maternals. Across the inner grounds, the Pride members were divided into training groups and engaged in offensive and defensive scenarios led by Caden. Overall, the Pride was well-prepared, especially given the short time to adjust to the situation. It was worth noting, however, that StormEdge, as a Pride, prioritized combat training for Dominants and the few Maternals who expressed interest.

So far, he had managed to keep his cat mostly in check. Knowing she was theirs pushed him into what Grace would describe as "caveman mode." He was driven to keep all unmated males away from her. Fortunately, his Pride was gracious about his grumbling and hissing, probably thinking he was tense about the looming war.

Pogue knew Micah was worried about her, too, but for a different reason. He kept his group near Grace and kept looking for her. The mood was solemn. Everyone was preparing for a fight they didn't want. One where they would almost certainly lose family members.

Hannah came running up to him.

"I need to talk to you *now*!" She grabbed his hand and pulled him around the back of the clinic, by the aeries opposite the Den. Hannah, in her, for once, all-black ensemble, looked furious. He took a swig from his water bottle before looking down at her.

"What's up?"

Hanna balled up her fists and took a deep breath.

"Know that by telling you this, I am violating a sacred bond between a Wielder and his or her partner. This cannot lead back to me. I need your word," she said, a severe look on her ordinarily jovial or sarcastic face.

Pogue nodded.

"You have my word."

"It's about Grace."

Instantly, he felt his jaw clench.

"What about Grace?"

Hanna lifted her sneakers to a bench to tie her laces.

"I'm sorry, Pogue. One of my old training buddies wondered why Nigel, not me as the Council rep, was meeting with DeCoill. I told him I didn't know what he was talking about." She put her foot back down and kicked the ground absentmindedly with her toe. "I figured out the reason he hasn't been around. He's working for DeCoill!" Hannah kicked the bench lightly. "It's some side project he wouldn't tell me about, but I'm pretty sure some of the information we didn't know how DeCoill got his hands on came from him. The few times he's been in the Den, he could have seen stuff," she finished.

Pogue sucked in a breath, shaking his hands lightly to get his claws to retract.

"Thank you for telling me. I won't say anything, and we'll deal with it." He gently squeezed her shoulder and motioned for them to return to the training area. Pogue seethed, realizing Nigel was a mole. And worse, Pogue knew he couldn't do anything but file a termination notice. If he killed Nigel as his cat demanded, the Pride would lose the right to employ a Wielder forever, and they'd lose Hannah.

Pogue restrained his anger, focusing on the impending war. He asked Hannah to fetch Tari, who arrived shirtless and glistening with sweat from the obstacle course.

He watched as Tari's serval cat pushed its way to the surface with brute force.

"I'll word it right. Hannah isn't going anywhere. I'll let you know when the Academy responds!" he snarled and stalked off, not waiting to be dismissed. Pogue knew Tari was more Dominant and powerful than most realized. It was rare for a Shifter to downplay their strength. But Pogue didn't pry as long as he respected the hierarchy. Tari was essential to the Pride, and Pogue valued their friendship.

As Pogue returned to the training area, he noticed a small crowd gathered around Grace as she unpacked her bow. It looked different from the bows he knew, smaller and with more strings. And a weird plastic thing. *What the hell is that tiny thing gonna do? He* mused as he approached alongside Hannah, who'd jogged up to walk beside him.

Micah was returning from having set up six markers at different distances.

Grace was wearing an arm guard, and the strange leather patch he'd noticed earlier was wrapped around her wrist. She had a longer metal stick with a hook-like end, too. She looked fierce as she picked up the bow, accentuated by her long hair catching the light breeze. She flicked it back with an annoyed look on her face. His cat reminded him that loose hair was a disadvantage in a fight.

"Hannah, you got a hair tie in that magic pocket of yours?" Hannah held up a small black hair tie for him, smirking. He grabbed it and approached the small group as Grace shouted at Micah.

"How many meters is that?"

Micah yelled back.

"Twenty-five meters!"

"Hi," he said, walking up behind her and kissing her neck. He was in no way in doubt that the whole of team Grace, also known as his fucking Pride, either seen his very public display of affection and her blue markings. He couldn't care less anymore.

She smiled up at him.

"Hi back."

Pogue turned his Mate's head and started gathering her thick hair into a ponytail, securing it tightly *My Mate. My True Mate*, he smiled to himself. He leaned in, whispering,

"Don't wanna get the pretty locks tangled in your toy."

She turned around and grinned at him.

"Toy, huh?!" She placed a quiver in front of her and arranged the arrows. With practiced precision, she notched and released each arrow, embedding them securely in the target trees. While they weren't perfectly grouped, they all hit their mark. His cat grinned with satisfaction, noticing many Shifters turning their gaze between her and the targets, clearly impressed. Caden was one of them.

"A little off-center, but not bad," Pogue noted.

Grace just smirked up at him as she yelled to Micah, who was looking at her, a stunned expression on his face.

"Micah, how were they?"

Micah went through all the targets, one by one, then grinned as he gave a thumbs up. Pogue scowled before yelling to his Beta.

"Fuck off, Micah. Don't tell her they're good when I can see they're off!"

Micah crooked his finger at Pogue. He rolled his eyes and jogged down; Caden had been watching on the sideline and followed. He looked at the targets as they trotted down the track. The trees weren't the actual target. The target, to his surprise, was a small red circle about half the size of his hand. An arrow was stuck in the dead center of each.

"If you're not gonna mate that woman, I fucking will," Caden whispered in awe.

Pogue stared at the targets again, then at his brother and Micah, both wearing shit-eating grins.

"That's my girl. That's my True Mate right there!" he exclaimed, a wide grin on his face. Then, without missing a beat, he turned and sprinted back up the track, leaving Micah and Caden in stunned surprise. Pouncing on Grace, he lifted her into the air, easily catching her. Her laughter filled the air as he peppered her face with kisses. The small group cracked up at their Alpha. Their serious, never laughing, always brooding Alpha, who was currently swinging his tiny human around laughing,

"That's my Menace!" he hollered. He kissed her and set her back on her feet. "Gods above, I love you! You're not gonna be using that bow, but I love that you can," he added on a breath.

Grace's body stiffened in his embrace. Pogue sensed his cat's confusion. She looked startled. He cocked his head, studying her. Then he slowly looked around the crowd. All eyes were on her. They seemed to be anticipating her public acceptance. She said nothing. He couldn't deny that stung. He understood her hesitation before her marks turned. Now? No, not really...

Hannah broke the awkward silence by taking Grace's hand and asking if she wanted to try moving targets, swiftly leading her away from the crowd. Pogue just stood there blinking until Caden approached him, a sheen in his eyes.

"Bro..." He said before giving him a hard, fast hug. Pogue finally snapped out of it and frowned at his brother.

He loved her. Not just the chase or the idea of mating her or even the fact that he now knew she was his True Mate. He loved *her*. And she had said nothing.

Caden didn't ask, and Pogue didn't talk. This wasn't the time. They would have time. After.

Chapter 51

The rest of the afternoon was more training, patrolling and defense strategy. They'd do three more run-throughs and then switch to offense for tomorrow's practice. Finally, they needed to stock hiding spots with supplies, check the clinic, and handle other practical matters.

Just before dinner, the entire Pride gathered outside by the playground. Hannah had created a beautiful arrangement of fairy lights that cast a soft glow over the area. Everyone was served a generous spread of sandwiches and drinks. Pogue noticed Grace on the ground, laughing with Hannah and Nadya about something.

"We won't lose the Pride, Pogue." Caden bumped his shoulder, pulling Pogue out of his own head. "And we won't lose her either. We're tough. *She's* tough."

Pogue looked at his brother. He had needed to hear that. He ran a hand through his auburn hair, pulling slightly at the ends. He needed a haircut. It was getting almost to the point where he had to push it out of his eyes.

"We won't lose," he said, locking his fear and rage down.

Caden looked pointedly at him.

"Don't. Don't shut down. I like this new you. Keep it in check, but don't shut down, please."

"The fuck do you mean the new me?!" Pogue groused.

Caden looked at him thoughtfully.

"The whole Pride sees, you know. You talk more and frown less. You're laughing out loud around them. I like seeing my brother happy. Hell, if I'm lucky, I might even get a nephew or niece. But leave it to you to find your True Mate right before we go to war, Pogue. You never do anything half-assed," he chuckled.

Pogue sighed and smirked at Caden.

"If you start bawling, I feel it's my brotherly duty to punch you in the nuts."

Caden glared at him. Right before, he did exactly that. Pogue wheezed and took an involuntary knee as Micah walked by, laughing. Seconds later, Micah was in the same position, one step ahead of him, courtesy of Pogue. It made him feel a little better.

Pogue grabbed some food, walked over to the girls, and sat down behind Grace, pulling her into the vee of his thighs as he raised his knees to lean his arms on.

"Hey, kitty cat," she smiled as she turned to kiss his arm, blushing fiercely.

He handed her a banana and a sandwich, which she immediately tore into. He opted for protein bars.

Caden jumped up on a seesaw, balancing easily like the cat he was.

"Good work today. We're as prepared as we can be. Rest up from here. Just a reminder. All Vigilia, remember to get your collars and earpieces. Micah is gonna set up a radio in the clinic. We'll try to keep you updated."

Grace's friend Sophie had sent over a lot of what she called tactical gear. It included earpieces, some kind of collar with a microphone, and body protection.

Along with Micah, Pogue had gone over who would be shifted and who would stay in their human form. Pogue was surprised that the collars Sophie sent were large enough to fit around even a shifted bear's neck. They could also be adjusted.

The loss of the Wielder, who could make spells permanent, was a setback, but they would deal. Hannah couldn't cast Permanency spells, but she could manipulate existing elements. Grace and Hannah had combined Grace's sci-fi ideas with Sophie's tactical gear, resulting in protective gear for all Submissives and semi-protective gear for the rest. The majority of the neck and stomach were covered.

The only downside was that there wasn't enough gear overall. They'd decided to focus on Submissives and unit leaders. Caden would be shifted and would wear nothing, while Pogue would be semi covered.

Pogue looked around his Pride. They were as ready as they would be with this little time to prepare.

He gave Grace another squeeze and kissed her. Caden turned to Pogue, an expectant look on his face. Pogue lifted a brow at his twin. Caden rolled his eyes.

"And Pogue has good news for you all," Caden said pointedly. Grace looked up at him, a questioning look in her eyes. He leaned down to whisper in her ear.

"Sorry to put you on the spot." Pogue sighed and got up, pulling Grace up with him. The Pride knew he would claim her by now, and some may have noticed the faint blue markings. But Regardless of whether she had fully accepted him, they needed to hear it officially. An Alpha mating was significant because it represented hope for the future and demonstrated unity to the outside world. They needed that right now. Hope and unity.

Pogue knew he was sneaking this up on her, and yes, it was putting her on the spot, but in the end, Grace would understand. She had no idea what presenting his Pride with the Alphas True Mate would do. How much it would inspire and motivate them.

Taking a leaf out of her team's book, he raised a fist high above his head. She frowned at him when he pulled down the collar of her top with the other hand, careful not to reveal anything below her collarbones. He heard the collective gasps of the Pride as they saw the twin blue markings on her skin.

"Team Grace," he said, a grin spreading.

The Pride whooped and hollered as they rushed them. Grace was back to looking startled, though the impressive kick to his shin told him how she felt.

Yeah, she would have his hide later for it. She hated being the center of attention, and she wouldn't understand why he took away her choice to reveal them if and when she wanted. He bent down and turned her head to kiss her, ignoring his Pride as they approached them with hugs and kisses, as he murmured apologies between kisses. He only stopped when Micah came up and physically pulled Grace from him. He didn't even try and stop the growl. Micah stood before him, a severe look on his face.

"With all the respect I can muster. If you hurt my sister, I will fuck you up. Alpha," he added with a quick thump to his chest.

Pogue nodded sharply.

"Noted. Now give me back my Mate."

Micah smiled wide and rumpled his sister's red hair before releasing her to Juno, who released her to Tari, who.... He got his Mate back just before dinner, and by then, it was past midnight.

And she did have his hide. And not in low decibels, either. Thankfully, Pogue had what Grace liked to call 'very specific skills.' They came in handy that night when he explained his reasons for pushing when he had promised not to. She wasn't pleased, but she understood.

Pogue had hoped for an answer. For Grace to accept him.

All she'd said was, 'I'll get there Pogue.'

Chapter 52

"**S**o this is it," Micah said solemnly, slowly rolling his teacup in his hands.

The previous evening had devolved into an impromptu casual party. Odd as it might be, having a party two nights before a war, was what StormEdge did. They needed one last taste of life before it changed forever. The Den was quiet and solemn now, in the cool afternoon. Most Pride members chose to be with their loved ones or to gather with friends in their homes. Pogue had made his apartment available to anyone who desired or needed proximity to the Alphas.

Caden took a swig from his beer and nodded.

"The Council sent word that ten Regulators will be there for the show. Rumor has it, Creed is one of them." He frowned. According to rumors, Creed was so distant—almost inhuman—that he hardly ever attended events that weren't directly related to the Regulators. Creed, the apparent leader of the Regulators, never showed up for a Challenge, even if it was a Turf War.

"It's ridiculous, man..." Micah grumbled.

"Probably wanna watch the show the fucking sadists," Oliver muttered.

Beau chuckled and drew him in closer. They'd settled on the floor, Beau cradling Oliver in the space between his thighs. He playfully nipped at his Mate's ear.

"Coming from you, that's a little much, babe."

Oliver gave him the finger and tossed a nut at a laughing Mehendi, who was leaning against Grayson with Nadya in front of him. Nadya was uneasy, and Pogue had asked Gray to keep her nearby. It seemed to calm her.

Nadya sat with her legs pulled up, her chin resting on her knees. Grayson sat beside her, rhythmically stroking her back. Henley stood quietly by the door, a solemn presence in the room. People coped in their own ways during times like this. The people in the room right now, were Pogue's closest friends. The thought of losing them settled in his gut like knives.

He watched as Beau sighed and looked at Oliver.

"Will you promise *now*? I'm not asking for much here, Oliver." Beau had been trying to convince Oliver not to support Grace's earlier plans to let her team up with him. Oliver rarely gave his word, but when he did, the word was golden.

"I am not promising you shit, Beau. We're gonna be fine, and having a backup plan isn't a bad idea!" Oliver snapped and grabbed Beau's hand, kissing his palm before tucking it into his chest. "We're gonna be fine, sweetheart," he said in a gentler tone.

Pogue waited to see if Beau would fight it. Pogue sure as hell had. He just didn't trust Grace fully on this. She was too stubborn.

"Pogue, Caden," Beau pleaded. He was a proud man, but the thought of his Mate out there, not hiding, was ripping him apart.

Pogue looked at Oliver.

"It's not your decision, Oliver. All he's asking is for you to calm his bear and be fucking safe," Pogue's tone held more force than intended. Caden gave him a subtle tap, signaling him to ease up. Pogue shot his brother a knowing glance.

"Yes, Alpha!" Oliver responded, a little too sarcastic. Pogue growled softly at him. Oliver threw his hands up in defeat. "I'm not trying to get myself killed, but Grace has a point, and you know it!"

Pogue was about to argue when Grace emerged from the bedroom wearing only one of his oversized shirts. She'd been sleeping more lately, often taking midday or post-dinner naps. He got to his feet as soon as he saw her. She raised her finger at him.

"Don't fuck with me right now! You guys woke me up." She grunted a few choice words under her breath.

Oliver chuckled before getting up and starting the coffee maker. She was grumpy, but Pogue ignored her and picked her up to sit on his lap.

Micah got up and grabbed her a blanket.

"Hey, darlin.' Sorry we woke you," he said, kissing her forehead.

"Fucktards," she muttered, playfully pushing away Micah and adjusting herself on Pogue's lap, leaning into him. He liked the feel of her smooth skin beneath the blanket, his fingers tracing leisurely circles on the outside of her thigh. Caden approached Pogue and knelt in front of her.

"Avoid killing my brother for five minutes, and Oliver will have your coffee ready, alright?." Caden leaned down to kiss the top of her head.

Pogue felt his arms tighten around her. He leaned down to breathe her in. He was baffled when she wiped a tear from his cheek with her thumb. She had a puzzled expression on her face. *What the hell?*

He shifted his gaze to Caden. His brother had gone to the cabinet to get some coffee cups. Pogue could see Caden's shoulders shaking slightly as he stood at the kitchen bench with his back to him. Pogue kissed her on the cheek before handing her over to Micah, who wrapped around her like a python and began massaging her scalp. He didn't like it, and it irritated his cat even though he knew Micah was her brother. His stupid hormones were in overdrive, heightened by the pre-fight adrenaline he was starting to feel, making his skin crawl, and he wanted to rip any unmated male near her to shreds. The rest of his friends began to talk amongst themselves.

"You ok?" He put a hand on his brother's shoulder.

Caden had been stirring the coffee cup for a minute now.

"Did you know I feel it?" he said wryly.

"Feel what, Cades?"

"That fear you have clawing at your beast whenever she's not in your line of vision. The rage when a male looks at her. Jesus, Pogue, the rage. I never knew you were this angry all the time," he whispered roughly.

Pogue instantly felt like shit. He knew they had a strong bond, but he never stopped to think about what that might mean if either of them ever mated, and he didn't know how long Cades had kept this quiet.

"I'm not. I think my cat is reaching its limit, though. I need to Mate her." He let out a harsh breath.

He glanced over to find that Micah had connected Grace's phone to earbuds. Micah gave Pogue a thumbs up and resumed massaging Grace's scalp while she lay there with her eyes closed, completely relaxed.

"Cades... I'm so sorry." Pogue squeezed his shoulder.

Caden held up a hand, stopping him.

"The thing is, as much as I loathe being forced to experience that level of fear from someone who doesn't get scared, and even though I hate this emotional battering ram... The way you love her? Gods, Pogue. You have no idea how fucking jealous I am."

Caden laughed as Pogue felt his cat rumble.

"Bro! I don't want *your* Mate. I want my own. I mean, I love her, but in the most platonic way I possibly can," he added quickly.

Caden was usually the one for mushy moments. This time, Pogue pulled his younger brother (by a whole minute) into a tight embrace. They both turned towards the others, seeing Micah capturing the moment with his phone. They simultaneously flipped him off while wiping away their tears and went to sit down again. There was a knock on the door before Hannah and Tari strode in.

Grace climbed from Micah over Caden onto Pogue's lap to curl against him and reached for the coffee.

Hannah started towards her when Pogue pointed to her feet.

"Shoes, Hannah!" She practically growled at him before she pulled off her chunky black boots. Her eyes were puffy, and she looked tired. More tired than Pogue had ever seen her.

"Girls, cavemen," Tari greeted everyone as he made his way to the coffee machine.

Boots off, Hannah walked to Grace and took her face in her hands to squish her cheeks together.

Grace looked at Pogue, annoyed.

"She's touching me!" before turning to look at Hannah. "You're touching me. Before coffee."

Hannah threw up her hands and huffed out a shaking breath.

"Yeah, yeah, super scary. Alphas I have news."

The tension in the room became palpable. Tari returned to Hannah's side, holding a cup of coffee. He squeezed her shoulder before placing his hand on her lower back. Pogue couldn't help but notice that, aside from Beau and Oliver, the people in this room lacked romantic or other close bonds. They formed a small family within the larger one.

"Go on," Tari told her, his voice soft.

Hannah took a deep breath. She started speaking, but a sob caught in her throat. She looked at Tari, a pleading look on her face.

Tari nodded.

"I'm sorry, but we're gonna need the room.

Pogue nodded and looked at Grayson.

"Take Mehendi and Nadya to Liam and Claus if they're up for visitors. Beau and Oliver head home. Henley, I'm sorry. Come back in a bit," he concluded.

In a swift response, everyone rose, offering comforting touches to Hannah's shoulders as they passed. Micah, Caden, and Grace remained. Once the room was cleared, Tari signaled for Hannah to join them. Grace slid off Pogue's lap, draping a blanket around them both.

Tari sucked in a breath through his teeth.

"Hannah tried to help us, and it's backfired."

"How?" Pogue and Caden asked in unison.

Hannah's eyes welled up with tears. Tari quickly handed Grace his cup and hugged Hannah tightly, whispering soothing words as Pogue rubbed her shoulder.

"I'm sorry," she shook her head at Tari. "I just can't."

He nodded and wiped her cheeks before facing Pogue.

"Hannah asked the Academy to fight alongside us in the War, even if IceFjord doesn't bring a Wielder. They refused, so she took it higher, to something like our Council. They not only rejected her request but are now sanctioning her. It seems the Academy doesn't like Wielders forming attachments to the communities they work with.

"They didn't know you were staying, Hannah?" Caden asked her. "I don't understand. Explain the sanctioning part. Why aren't they just telling you no and leaving it at that? Can you-"

Hannah was now sobbing hard. Tari growled at Caden, who looked stunned but quickly calmed himself.

"Respectfully, stop! " Tari ordered. "You deal with me right now. The short version is that Hannah gets to stay so long as IceFjord doesn't bring a Wielder. If they do, she can fight with us. If they don't, she's out, and no matter what happens, she'll be punished."

Pogue frowned, confused.

"Dumb it down, Tari."

Tari nodded.

"For starters, the Academy gave DeCoill sixty seconds of offensive measures against Hannah, using any Wielder he can buy. The only bright side is that he can't physically touch her."

"Stand with them. Feel their claws," Hannah whispered.

"But theoretically, DeCoill can have a Wielder siphon her power and she thinks he will. It'll hurt, and if he weakens her before the battle-"

"She's as easy prey as my Mate," Pogue finished.

"We haven't been informed what the rest of punishment is. All we know is that Hannah should expect more."

Well fuck. Just when I thought it couldn't get any fucking worse, Pogue thought... This was getting worse by the minute.

Chapter 53

December 25th

G race didn't hear him enter the clinic; her human senses were too dull to pick up his silent footsteps, even when wearing shoes. She whipped around when he spoke to her, his voice low and harsh.

"Put down the bandages, Grace," he said as he stalked towards her, unzipping his padded brown vest and leaving it where it fell. His hands quickly unbuttoned his black cargo pants and started to pull down the zipper. Her eyes widened as she started to back up one small step at a time.

"Pogue...? What are you doing?" She slowly backed toward the room's end wall. *What is wrong with him?* He seemed... scared. She'd never seen him afraid, but she was pretty sure this was it. He pulled his skin-tight, long-sleeve T-shirt off as he started corralling her towards a corner.

"Kitty cat..." She drew out the words.

"Take it off. Now." He popped his jaw, his hands fisted at his sides.

It finally dawned on her what he was after.

"What?! Pogue, no! We're about to go to war, for fuck's sake!" She stared at him, her eyes wide.

He'd backed her into the corner of the room.

"I know. I don't care," he responded, his voice low and husky. Grace had all the reasonable responses on the tip of her tongue. *Shitty timing, Pogue. You're acting irrationally, Pogue.* And then she looked at him. This could be the last chance to hold him. To be held by him. She'd divested herself of her Kevlar vest and unbuttoned her jeans before he reached her and lifted her up against the wall, pinning her.

"I want to tell you it's a jaguar thing or even a Shifter thing, but I don't know. Don't make me beg, 'cause I will, and it'll be undignified, not to mention ugly."

Grace took a moment to really look at him when she heard the strain in his voice despite the jovial words. *He's trying to ground himself,* she realized. She wiggled to get down. He let her, and she quickly stripped down, sensing his urgency. She had barely gotten her pants off before his claws cut the panties from her and pushed her back against the wall before roughly pushing his pants down to his thighs.

"Tell me you're ready," he whispered as he stroked her, his fingers shaking. She was. For him, she was ready. He lifted her up and slid into her in one hard thrust, murmuring apologies about not wanting to hurt her as her breath hitched at the sudden intrusion.

"S'ok, Pogue," she whispered as she kissed his eyelids, jaw, and cheeks while running her hands through his hair. It somehow felt so final. It was almost time. She could lose him.

"I'm sorry, I'm so sorry, baby, I can't-" He slammed into her. Over and over again, he slammed every ounce of fear, love, and rage into her. She kept whispering soft reassurances to him and clung to his every touch, despite the borderline pain that came with it.

"Mine!" he hissed.

"It's ok, it's ok," she whispered as she took all of him until his strangled cry tore out of him as he came.

He held her there for the longest time while she murmured soft words of comfort in his ear, and he stroked her hair.

Pogue

Doc's agitated voice from outside yanked them out of their reverie. Pogue looked around for something to clean them and eventually stumbled over to the sink to grab a hand towel. He first wiped himself, then pulled up his pants and turned around. *Shit!* Grace's hip was covered in claw marks, her lips appeared bruised, and her legs trembled. Grace flushed furiously as she quickly cleaned herself up. He grabbed what was left of her panties, tossed them in the trash, and helped her pull up her pants, hands still shaking as he apologized again and again.

"I'm so sorry, Grace, I-"

"Enough, Pogue!" she snapped at him. "Pick me up already so I can glare at you!"

He complied immediately. "I get it. I understand, and it's ok. I needed this, too. You know I'm physically more fragile than you, and I will get an owie from time to time, but we will deal, yeah?" She kissed his forehead. "I'm scared too. But we'll get through this." She thumped his forehead when he didn't answer. He'd never admit it, but he loved how she didn't look at him and see an Alpha. All she saw was the man.

"Ok?!" she repeated, dragging him back to the here and now.

"Yes, ma'am," he smiled, flashing her a dimple. "You stay in here until I come to get you." He pointed a finger at her. She bit him. "Ow! Motherfucker! You little fiend, stop biting me; this is serious!" She giggled. Of course, she giggled... He looked at her seriously, "Grace, I can't lose you." He put her down and kissed her gently, lingering for a moment before he turned and walked towards the door. As he opened it, he turned around, his cat looking out at his True Mate.

"I love you." And then he left.

Grace

Grace watched Pogue leave, telling her he loved her. She wanted to say it back, but the words wouldn't form. *Why can't I just say it?!* She wanted to kick herself when she noticed his smile disappear, and he turned his back, walking away. Her strong Alpha... Doc jolted her out of her thoughts as he walked in the door and swiftly ran back out again, sneezing. She ran out after him.

"What? What's happening?!

The good doctor glared at her as he rubbed his nose.

"Did you know that the amount of pheromones an Alpha releases during intercourse is equivalent to sticking a hot fire poker up another Pridemates nose?"

Blushing, she shook her head.

"I didn't know it was that bad."

"Well, you do now! Never again in my clinic, Grace!"

"Yes, sir."

341

Grace then watched the full moon as the Vigilia organized groups by the Den's entrance, across from the clinic, adjusting gear and earpieces. These connected to Doc's radio and, with the right button, to the Alphas'. Micah and Pogue had spent days learning the system. Unbeknownst to others, Grace and Oliver had secured a set for them, too, with their own channel. Pogue, Micah, and Caden were huddled nearby, engrossed in conversation. Grace was about to walk over when Doc held her back with a hand on her shoulder.

"They will more than likely come by before they leave. Please. Let us make sure we have everything. Ah, here's Lucy now." He motioned to the approaching Juvenile. Lucy wore her long golden hair in a bun, her wolf almost palpable beneath the surface. Claws protruded from her mittens, and her eyes glowed with the golden hue of her beast. She approached Grace and Doc, handing her a green travel mug—Pogue's.

"Coffee. Maude sent it." Lucy's voice was strained, and her eyes wide. She was scared. They all were.

Grace took the cup, nodding to Lucy.

"We're gonna be fine, cuz."

"We know," Lucy and Doc replied, their voices somber.

Micah jogged over. He'd stripped down to his boxer briefs, like the majority of the Shifters who would be in animal form. *Really, Micah?!* she thought, a flash of humor in even the darkest of hours, as she noticed his Iron Man briefs.

Except for Pogue, Henley stood out as the only one still fully clothed. Henley didn't do public shifting, Grace remembered.

Micah hugged Grace in a bear hug. Lucy reached for her cup just as Grace was about to drop it. She wrapped her legs around her brother's muscular waist and locked her gaze on him.

"You'd better come back, bro," she smiled. He locked eyes with her. Micah didn't look like his usual laid-back self tonight. There was a sharpness to him she hadn't seen before. His eyes gleamed, telling her he was ready to fight. To kill.

"You saw I hung your bow by the door?" she nodded. "Not that you'll need it, okay? You know where you'll be?"

"Here until Pogue gets me. Depending on what he says, I go with him for three hours, or you guys play 'pass the parcel,'" she answered, not bothering to hide her annoyance.

Micah booped her nose.

"With Pogue or the team assigned to you. Not Oliver!" She nodded. *If all goes according to plan. Otherwise, sorry, not sorry.* "Good girl. I'll keep the fuckers off your doorstep. You three keep us alive if we need it, yeah?" Micah looked at Doc and Lucy before returning his eyes to Grace. Grace nodded again, feeling her eyes well up. Micah sharply wiped her tears with his thumbs and grabbed her face, holding it tightly.

"No! Not tonight. We are strong tonight! You are strong! You hear me?"

She heard his voice cracking the tiniest bit. Her own cracked just the same when she responded.

"Strong. Gotcha. Go kick some ass. But you come back!"

"You bet I will. Love you, sis," he said solemnly as he put her down and left.

Not a minute later, Caden came over, also sans clothes. Grace blinked a couple of times. Caden and Pogue were twins. Like really twins. Everywhere, it seemed. She shook her head and averted her eyes from his blue boxers. *Awkward much?* She shuddered. He wrapped his arms around her and kissed her hair, his warm body almost enveloping her smaller one. He let out a small laugh and leaned down, whispering.

"Stop staring, Grace. Be good. Stay with the team." *Aaand I'm mortified. Super.* Grace wanted to bury herself. To be fair, she might not need to by the end of this... She took a deep breath and looked Caden in the eye.

"Keep him safe, Caden. Keep *you* safe." She poked him in his rock-hard abs. He smiled down at her.

"We are our brother's keeper. And we don't lose."

The next twenty minutes were spent in the clinic, double-checking that everything was in place. The entire inner area between the clinic and the Den had cleared out, save for Pogue, who stood alone in the center. Doc pointed to the red-capped figures floating in, like the Dementors from Harry Potter. The Regulators. A Portal appeared near a large picnic table not far from Pogue. It looked like a large purple wooden door. DeCoill and Nigel emerged from it. As Pogue closed the gap between them, his rage was palpable. It mirrored her own. Doc and Lucy's rumbles and growls said she wasn't alone in her feelings. Grace couldn't hear what DeCoill said, but her two companions snarled as their animals rose in response. Seconds later, Pogue slammed his palm on the picnic table and roared in DeCoill's face. Both upper and lower canines were fully extended, as were his claws. Nigel quickly erected a shield. He then turned his head toward the clinic.

"Hannah Carmichael! I summon you here by Academy order!" His voice broke on the final words. Despite not having the heightened senses of a Shifter, Grace could tell the Wielder was terrified. His slender frame shook, and sweat appeared on his pale brow. Pogue growled softly as he paced back and forth, the human embodiment of his other half.

Hannah appeared to have been on the clinic's roof. She calmly levitated to the ground. Nigel produced a paper scroll from his long brown cape, widening DeCoill's smile. Clearing his throat, he addressed Hannah, who approached him at a deliberate, unhurried pace. Sparks of electricity danced from her fingertips, leaving a mesmerizing trail of sinuous lightning in her wake.

"Hannah Carmichael. It has been decreed that your sanction for acting beyond your designated role as nothing but a contracted Wielder will be to serve as a collector for those you aimed to safeguard. And everyone else," he added with a sly smile. "With IceFjord lacking a Wielder, your involvement in this Challenge will be strictly limited to this capacity. Any deviation from this decree will lead to a permanent binding of your powers. *What the fuck is a binding? What's she gonna collect?!* Grace thought, utterly confused.

Grace couldn't see Hannah's face, but it must have been something because both Nigel and DeCoill backed up a step. Pogue stepped closer to Hannah. He smiled wide as she spoke.

"My *considerable* powers, Nigel. Especially compared to yours, wouldn't you agree?" Hear me, you slithering sleaze." Her voice rose a little. "I will abide by the Academy's decree, even if it is delivered by a Scholar Mage so weak he's an insult to our race." Hannah spat on the ground in front of Nigel. The second her spit hit the ground, it turned into a ball of electricity. Nigel yelped as he stumbled back several steps before DeCoill managed to clasp the back of his neck and hiss something in his ear that made Nigel straighten up again. His look of horror turned into a sneer as he spoke again.

"I, per the decree set forth by your superiors, the Academy and their Elders, command you bound!"

Nigel presented an old-fashioned pocket watch to Hannah, who instinctively stepped back, finding support in Pogue's hand on her back. Nigel smiled tightly. "Your magic will be limited to collecting the essence of the deceased."

Grace, engrossed, hadn't noticed Tari's approach until he stood a bit to her left by the corner of the clinic. She beckoned him over with a whistle. Tari, having worked closely with Hannah before, was the best bet for someone knowledgeable about this.

"What does that mean?" Even the Portal Wielder, who stood quietly in the background, looked horrified.

Tari cursed.

"Siphoning. The Academy has told Nigel to bind most of her powers. As an added punishment, she has to collect Shifter's essence from the dead. It fuels the Barrier that keeps us hidden and... well, young, I guess," he told her, focusing solely on Hannah.

Nigel began his incantation. Hannah motioned for Pogue to step back, and he complied as she ascended into the air, seemingly not by her own volition.

Tari muttered a curse as her limbs spread and electricity encircled her. After a prolonged minute, the electricity transformed into a mist, emanating from her fingertips and into Nigel's outstretched watch. Hannah continued to rise, her gentle cries of pain piercing the otherwise silent night.

She was so far up a fall would seriously hurt her.

"If he takes her magic, she can't levitate herself, can she? Is Nigel allowed to do that?" Grace asked, though she knew the answer.

Tari shook his head, his platinum blond hair blowing in the breeze. He didn't look at Doc when he addressed him.

"Doc?"

"Yes?"

"You can jumpstart a Shifter's heart, right?"

Tari looked scarier than Grace had ever seen him. His eyes were almost shining yellow, his lower and upper canines extended, and his small claws looked like they could cut through stone. He was pissed.

"I can," Doc told him. He immediately headed inside. Grace saw the defibrillator being unpacked.

Grace felt her insides freeze when Hannah's scream tore out of her as her magic now flowed faster and faster like she was being sucked dry. Tari was about to run when Grace stopped him. The mist seemed to turn darker. Grace had no idea how she knew; maybe it was that little bit of Wielder she had in her. Maybe it was the amount of fantasy books she'd read. But she knew, just fucking knew, Tari couldn't touch her until the mist was black.

"Wait. Wait until it's black," Grace told him. Thankfully, Tari didn't question her but waited until she nodded a minute later when the mist had turned entirely black.

Tari took off toward Pogue and whistled through his teeth. Pogue turned and cocked his head at Tari, who pointed up. Pogue nodded and knelt, creating a stirrup. Tari jumped into Pogue's interlocked hands, and Pogue stood, throwing Tari, as high as he could, right into Hannah.

Tari shielded Hannah as they crashed to the ground, taking the brunt of it. Pogue rushed to Tari's side, while Micah swiftly reached Hannah. Grace stepped away from the door just in time for Micah and Pogue to deliver them. Grace waited for Nigel's reaction, but when she looked back to him, all she saw was a Regulator clasping his shoulder and DeCoill's maniacal expression as he shouted,

"We have begun!"

Chapter 54

Silence hung heavy for forty-five minutes. Doc stood near the open door, while Lucy and Grace looked out the windows. They knew they'd only get serious injuries that wouldn't be fixed by shifting. Henley's fox darted past the window occasionally, and Dina called out from above. The tree next to the clinic where Oliver was hiding rustled occasionally. But for a long time, there was nothing but silence.

Then shooting began from the aeries, and Beau's voice echoed through the radio.

"Four, Ice, black!" Grace pumped her fist in silent celebration. They had a simple system: Ice or Storm. Black for dead, red for injured.

The minefield down the gravel road detonated, resembling a fireworks display. Shortly after, more favorable numbers came in over the radio, and Henley sprinted past, emitting a single yip, despite the blood on his muzzle saying it all. When the words "One Storm, red" rang out twice right after each other, Grace felt her heart stop. They gloved up and waited for wounded Pridemates to rush through the door.

Pogue emerged from the woods, Tari's wounded serval slung over his shoulder. He didn't pause when he hurled it through the clinic door at Doc. Beau crawled through the door in human form just as Doc placed the cat on a stretcher. Lucy immediately began to panic, sobbing as she attempted to help Beau onto a bed. Grace was frozen for a split second. She was trained to treat animals, not humans. She knew she'd have to help them in both capacities, but reality was a slap in the face. Beau's groan jolted her out of it, and she assisted Lucy in hoisting Beau up.

"Gods dammit, Beau! Oliver is gonna rip my nuts off!" Grace snapped, unfairly annoyed the big man was hurt.

Beau grinned weakly, clutching his side as he coughed up blood.

"That man loves balls too much to rip them off anyone," he wheezed. "Please have drugs, Doc. Pretty please." He smiled through tight lips. Lucy stood frozen, nodding at nothing.

Grace grabbed her shoulders and shook her.

"Stop! Right now! You will get your claws out and cut Beau's shirt off, so Doc can see what he's dealing with! Do you hear me?!"

Lucy nodded and did as she was told. Beau had three deep claw gashes from his shoulder across his chest and stomach and down to his thighs. Grace noted, to her horror, that he'd been holding in his intestines with a bloodied hand. Grace nearly screamed, before collecting herself. She turned to Doc.

"If the cat still has its insides actually inside, we should switch, Doc!"

Doc immediately turned around, took one look at Beau and nodded.

"Tari will need both hindlegs set, and you'll have to find out how bad the gash on his side is," Doc instructed curtly as they switched places. Grace noticed from the corner of her eye that Doc was using his healing abilities. He had mentioned he would only do so in life-or-death situations. It consumed a significant amount of energy, and he wanted to conserve it as much as he could. They couldn't predict how many more would come before this was all over.

Grace carefully reset Tari's hind legs, attempting to minimize his discomfort. She then retrieved a wireless trimmer and shaved the hair on his left side to better assess the injury. As the hair fell away, a long, deep gash appeared, stretching from his hip to his shoulder.

"Cuz, what the fuck did this?" Grace muttered to herself. She grabbed the saline solution and began to clean the area. "This is bad..."

"Make him shift," Doc told her as he worked on Beau.

"How the fuck am I supposed to do that, Doc? We didn't cover how to do that!" Grace shouted, adrenaline fueling her.

"You're the Alpha's female. Order it!" Doc told her calmly.

Ok I can do it, I can. I have to, she steeled herself. She clasped his shoulder.

"Tari, shift," she ordered sternly. The serval became a man from one second to the other, in a flash of blinding light. Grace had to blink a couple of times to focus. When she did, her right hand was on Tari's cheek and the left... Well, it wasn't on his hip where it had been when he was a cat. He cursed a blue streak. The gash looked so much worse on a human for some reason. She slapped his hands away when he tried prodding it.

"Yeah, he's gonna need surgery Doc." The blood seeping out from the bottom of the wound was darker than the rest. "I think whatever made this hit his liver."

Doc nodded.

"Grab the staple gun and patch him up temporarily. I'll get to him. Lucy, set up an IV. Grace, get him to shift back."

Grace had barely gotten Tari to shift, when Maude was thrown through the door. Grace ran up to her, almost mowing down Lucy in the process. Maude wasn't moving.

"Doc!" she screamed. Doc dropped the sterile cover he was about to drape over Beau's stomach and ran to kneel in front of the woman. A second later, he shook his head sadly and turned her over, revealing what looked like a spinal cord protruding from her neck. Doc gently picked her up and carried her to a small room in the back.

Grace watched as Doc resumed surgery, and Tari had drifted into slumber. She comforted Lucy and quietly arranged for a replacement. This was too overwhelming for the Juvenile. Too much blood and death. She hadn't consulted Doc, and he hadn't remarked on her decision.

Time blurred, and as Pogue dashed in, she realized it had been three hours. Their agreement was for him to retrieve her after one hour.

Covered in blood, Pogue tossed her jacket her way. It didn't matter to Grace. She rushed into his embrace. He responded with a tight squeeze and a kiss on her neck.

"Your ride, ma'am. Sorry I'm late." He then turned his gaze to Lucy. "Luce, you're gonna run for the front door. Mehendi will meet you there. Straight line! Go!" he ordered. "Doc, Brody is coming."

Doc nodded sharply, not looking up as he was hands deep in Beau's intestines.

Lucy was shaking all over but nodded. Grace grabbed the taser she'd placed on a table just inside the door. She pressed Lucy's hand around it, her index finger on the trigger.

"Point, shoot, run." She told her. Lucy nodded and, ran like hell. Grace didn't have a chance to see if she made it as Pogue swung her onto his back and ran too.

Pogue

Pogue's heart was in his throat as he took them deep into the woods to the burrows. He would have preferred to keep her close to the clinic, but the smell of wolves closing in on it made him change his mind. A sound made him freeze in place. He tapped her thigh, signaling her to let go and jump down. He could scent someone unknown in the vicinity. Pogue slowly backed Grace up to a massive fir, keeping her close to his back. He then motioned for her to stand on his shoulders and climb up into the tree. Grace moved as quietly as a human could, but she let out a small yelp when a branch she was grabbing turned out to be rotten and cracked.

"Dammit!" she hissed. Pogue looked up. She was about five meters up. It would have to do. He left the tree, concealing his path until he reached a small clearing where he faced the tree and Grace. His claws extended as he crouched, surveying the surrounding forest. Although he yearned to be near the tree, lingering there would signal he was guarding something.

Grace would have ascended high enough to have a good vantage point by now. She had, and she was proving very useful, he concluded as her voice came through his earpiece.

"Seven circling you."

"Where?" he whispered.

"Uhm... The four shifted are at..." The line went quiet. "If the broken log on your left is noon, then you have four wolves at twelve, two and six. I think number two is a Submissive. There's a dude right next to it, scuffing it and it's shaking. You have two men coming up behind you. They're passing the wolf on your six now."

"Thanks, babe. Now shut up. Please," he added with a smirk.

The two large, naked males with long blond hair, about Pogue's height, made their move. While one was bloodied, the other didn't look like he'd thrown so much as a punch yet. They attacked without a word. *Idiots.* Pogue grunted and threw the first off balance, slamming him head first into a nearby tree. He received a set of claws to his upper arm from the other in the process, but the sacrifice was well worth it. They were clearly not high-ranking Dominants. It took less than a minute to dispatch them, leaving one with his throat slashed and the other with a broken neck against the tree he'd been thrown at. They showed no signs of proper battle training. They slowly crept closer, claws elongating from their fingers.

"Don't do it. You will die," Pogue warned them, as a grey wolf slowly crept closer to him.

A flash of blinding light signaled that one of the wolves had shifted. He stood tall, though he looked tired. His chest was matted with blood, some of it still seeping from the long gash across his pecs.

"Maybe. But so will you. You never should have stolen from us!"

Stolen what? We didn't take anything! he thought, confused.

Two other wolves came up on his rear. Pogue swiftly turned and managed to grab one of the wolves around the muzzle with his hand, breaking it with a vicious crunch, before using it as a handle, like some cartoon, and throwing it at the human. It knocked him to the ground but gave a second wolf the opening it needed. It latched onto his shoulder and tore. Pogue roared as he grabbed its jaws and pried them apart.

"Incoming. Can't tell what," Grace whispered over the radio. Pogue grinned. They never saw him coming. Grayson raced through the small clearing, slicing open the human Shifter's side and back, while Pogue handled the disoriented wolf. Pogue quickly finished off his prey, and the remaining two were pinned to the ground before they knew what hit them.

"I'm coming down!" Grace yelled.

"NO!" Both Pogue and Gray yelled back. Grace, of course, ignored them, and they, in turn, concluded that someone should probably catch her ass when she made her way down the damn tree. Good thing, too.

"Sorry," Pogue saw her give Grayson a sheepish grin as he caught her just before she hit the ground. The last remaining wolf Pogue could see or smell in the vicinity was cowering on the ground, tail between her legs. She was whimpering. A tall, slim man crouched over her in human form. He looked young, maybe just past transition and Pogue could scent the fear wafting off him, though to his credit, he kept his stance and his eyes darted between Pogue and Gray.

"Pogue..." Grace started.

He pointed a finger at her.

"Wait!"

Pogue then grabbed the male's neck, allowing his dominance alone to subdue the man. When he snarled at Pogue, he pressed harder on the male's neck, allowing Grayson to take over the female wolf. "You move on the human you die. Slowly. You can't protect your own so don't try for mine, pup. These are the consequences of your Alpha's choices. It's too late. You will die here," Pogue told him.

The male shook his head.

"You took our Alphas only son and our eldest five Maternals. How would you have responded?"

Pogue loosened his grip slightly.

"We didn't. We wouldn't. We don't steal cubs and we have no use for your Maternals."

The male fell silent, glancing at the female wolf, Gray, and Grace. Sensing his tension, Pogue applied more pressure.

"Why the fuck should I believe that, huh?" the man snarled softly.

Pogue leaned close to his face and snarled,

"Because I am the Alpha, and I didn't order that."

Pogue could sense the moment the realization hit the young male—that he stood before the StormEdge Alpha, and this would be his final moment. Though his fear permeated the air, the male's voice remained surprisingly calm, almost resigned, when he spoke.

"Let my Mate live."

Pogue shook his head.

"You don't have any leverage here, pup."

Grayson squeezed the wolf's neck gently with his hand.

"Shift, female."

Pogue saw Grace slapping Grays's arm after the female did as Grayson had ordered.

"Let her up. Let her up. She's pregnant!"

Grayson not only immediately let her up but supported her gently as she got up, shivering. Harming a pregnant Shifter was on the shortlist of things you did not do. Ever.

Pogue sighed.

"Fuck..."

The male looked up at Pogue, his eyes pleading, though his words were firm.

"I concede defeat, but let my Mate leave. Please. Let her hide until this is over. She'll stay hidden and she won't try to hurt any of yours."

Grace touched Pogue's lower back. He turned his face to her.

"Pogue? Look at her neck."

She motioned to the woman's neck, where a set of blue markings rested. *Like Grace's*, Pogue thought. *Blue. Like my Mate's.* Pogue cursed and yanked the male up. The thought of losing Grace or her losing him burned like acid in his gut.

"Is she yours?" The male nodded. Examining him closely, Pogue could see the same primal drive to be with her, to protect her, that he felt for Grace every moment. It was a visceral urge. He gripped the male's neck and forced him to meet his gaze.

"You're going to run directly west. You'll get to the river. There's a cave nearby. Stay until they announce our victory. Then run as far as you can away from here. Understand? "

The male nodded slowly.

"Will we truly be safe?" said the female in a trembling, weak voice.

Pogue turned the man's head and used a claw to carve two overlapping circles with a line slashed through, on his cheek.

"Now you will. StormEdge won't touch you. Your Mate is the only reason you're alive," said Pogue, locking the male with his gaze. "Remember that when you think about the people your Pack slaughtered here tonight." The female looked up at Pogue. She was a slender blond woman, naked and clearly close to term. Protecting pregnant females was ingrained in Shifters. Life was precious, and Pogue wanted to make sure she didn't get injured by accident. He stripped off his Kevlar vest and slid it onto her, zipping it up as far as it would go with her belly. The male stifled a growl, but both Gray and Pogue raised a brow at him, though Pogue swiftly grabbed Graces arm and hauled her behind him.

The young Shifter held up his hands.

"Most of us didn't want to, you know. You've won before," she whispered so low Pogue almost didn't catch it.

"And yet you did," Grayson said. As the words left his lips, Gray lifted his head and sniffed.

"Magnus and Nadya," he said, frowning. He shifted and bolted south a second after that, snarling as he went.

The female bowed her head once, then looked to Grace, still held firmly behind Pogue. She peeked out, her hands on his waist. Pogue noted how the women seemed to study each other, but it wasn't his Mate who spoke first.

"You're a Pet and yet you touch the Alpha without deference." It was probably meant as a question, but it came out as a statement, almost an accusation. Pogue felt Grace tense up. When she stepped around him, her back was straight and her jaw tight. The male in front of them wisely took a few steps back as Pogue growled at him, letting Grace walk past him to face the wolves.

"You're seriously gonna bite the hand that set you free? I am his Mate, and you have no right to speak. Be fucking thankful he didn't kill *your* Mate and get the fuck off our land," Grace spat.

The female looked like she was about to respond, but her Mate must have seen something in Grace's face. Pogue gently touched his hand to his Mate's shoulder.

The male bowed his head to first Pogue and then, to Pogue's surprise, to Grace. He picked up his Mate and bolted a second later.

Pogue's eyes swept the area before he allowed himself to do two shifts to heal his wounds. When he shifted back the last time, Grace was standing before him, a soft smile on her face. He leaned down and kissed her softly.

"You sounded like an Alpha's Mate. I'm proud of you," he told her.

Grace blushed.

"I didn't think I guess. Just sounded right."

He had hoped for more, maybe for her to actually say the words he needed to hear. But it was a good step. The fact that the male wolf acknowledged Grace without question was no small thing. Pogue shook his head and kissed her head.

"Speaking of things in water. Let's not make you a sitting duck."

He slung her unto his back, and then they ran.

Chapter 55

Pogue dropped Grace off at the clinic three hours later. Pogue had insisted on staying out of fights to keep Grace safe, so the time had passed with little action, lots of waiting around in bushes, and meetings with team leaders. She knew it was because she was a liability. The few fights she witnessed at a distance confirmed her inability to compete with Shifters in combat. They were too quick, too powerful, and too well-trained. Her domain was the clinic.

He kissed her passionately and told her he loved her again before leaving. And once again, the words she wanted to say wouldn't leave her stupid mouth.

She sighed and forced herself to focus on the situation at hand. Doc was sitting on a chair, his face resting in his hands, looking haggard. Tari was on the floor, looking pale but alive, and Beau was fast asleep. Frigg, a Dominant leopard, and Juno were on a bed each, clearly out, though they seemed to have been patched up.

"Doc!" Grace barked to get a response.

Doc whipped his head around. His white poofy hair was standing on end, and he was pale. Grace went to the back room to grab some food for him but stopped cold when she saw the mass of bodies in there. Too many. She promptly threw up in the nearest trashcan.

"Shit!" she cried and kicked the trashcan a couple of times for good measure. *Get it together, Grace! We are strong!* Breathing deeply, she reached inside the back room for the protein bars on the shelf. Grabbing a handful, she briskly walked over to Doc, opening three on the way. He didn't balk when she gently handed them to him, along with a bottle of water.

Micah's voice over the radio made her jump.

"Dina's down. We can't find her," he said. "I heard her hawk scream." Grace wiped her hands over her face. Dina and their other avian Shifter Mac were tasked with aerial supervision.

"Last contact?" Pogue's voice came through.

"She checked in an hour ago, Told me she hasn't been able to find Stellan or his Beta. Probably hi... Fuck! Get the fuck off me, you fucki-...." The line went dead.

"Micah?" Pogue's voice came through the receiver. No answer. Graces throat locked up.

The forest around the clinic was silent, the sounds of snarls and growls almost non-existent. The only noises were occasional check-ins from the Vigilia and Pogue.

Through one of the windows in the back, Grace spotted Hannah. She was being closely followed by a Regulator. Although she looked unharmed, she appeared pale and shaken. The Regulator seemed to do nothing except walk with her. Grace wondered if it was protecting her or making sure Hannah didn't stop.

Grace turned to Doc.

"Does it hurt what Hannah has to do?"

Tari was the one to answer, from his position by the floor.

"She feels their pain as they die..."

Grace was so stunned she didn't even know what to think.

"Do you think they'll let me give her some water or something?" It seemed so trivial considering what Hannah must have felt, but Grace needed to do something. Anything. Tari shrugged.

"Tap the window. The Regulator will tell you no if it's outside what you're allowed to do for her."

Grace ran over and tapped on the window, holding up a protein bar and a water bottle. Hannah and the hooded figure looked at her. To her surprise, the Regulator motioned for Hannah to go to the window. Grace opened it.

"Can I give this to her?" she asked the Regulator, holding up the water and protein bar. The Regulator nodded, and Grace held out the water and protein bar. Hannah looked dead on her feet.

"Hannah, can I do anything? Anything at all?" She looked to the Regulator. "Can't she have just a little break?" Grace felt something tugging at her leg. Looking down, she saw Tari trying to use her to get on his feet. She helped him. Hannah didn't seem to recognize him, her stare blank. He winced but stood straight, looking at the Regulator.

"Are you here to protect her?" Tari questioned, and the Regulator nodded. Tari's lips formed a grim line. "Good. If she's unconscious, she can't complete her punishment, right? You'd have to wait until she woke up?" The Regulator appeared to consider it before nodding. Tari offered a small smile. "Thank you for looking out for her."

Tari winced as he leaned out of the window to grasp the back of Hannah's neck and whisper something in her ear. He kissed her cheek. And then he punched it. Hard. Hannah went down like a sack of potatoes, her body probably grateful for an excuse to give out.

Tari braced himself on the windowsill and hissed in pain, the wound on his side still healing. "She is injured to the point of being unable to defend herself. Grace, help me." Tari tried to climb out the window, tearing up his stitches. Blood started pouring slowly from his wounds.

"Hang on," Grace said as she crawled out the window. She gave the Regulator an annoyed look. "You could give me a fucking hand, you know. That's my friend. You overgrown, lazy, passive-aggressive Slytherin wannabe wizard!" she muttered as she landed on the ground. The Regulator chuckled. Actually chuckled. And then, while Grace stared in disbelief, it levitated Hannah through the window, where Tari caught her and collapsed on the floor with her in his arms.

The Regulator nodded its oversized hood at Grace and left her to crawl back inside.

Doc laid Hannah down by Frigg on a hospital bed. Grace tentatively assumed command, escorting Tari to a stretcher after tending to Hannah's cheek wound. Doc needed sleep, and she'd see to it that he got it.

For the next many hours, she earned her diploma as a vet nurse again - and probably half a human one too, resetting numerous bones and administering IVs. She learned a terrifying lesson when she discovered that Shifters could indeed heal an empty eye socket, but apart from that it was comforting doing something she knew she was skilled at. But, in the end, exhaustion weighed heavily and her brain was mush.

It was midday the next day when Brody raced through the door, an unconscious Sulis over his one shoulder,

"Doc. Please," Brody pleaded, tears running down his face. Grace ran to them, and quickly helped Brody lay Sulis down on a stretcher. He didn't seem to have any injuries. She turned to Doc.

"I don't understand? There's nothing wrong with him except he's unconscious."

Brody grabbed her hand, his words rushing out.

"He was hiding by the Den. Cubs. The cubs are in the Den! Grace, they're in the Den!" Grace was so confused. That didn't lessen when Brody's eyes rolled back and he too lost consciousness. She looked to Doc as he looked Sulis and Brody over. A moment later he sighed.

"Their animals shut them down. They must have fought Dominants. Why would they-"

And then it dawned on Grace. The cubs were in the Den. Someone got into the Den.

"Doc...?"

"Yes, Grace," he responded, as he covered Brody with a soft warm blanket.

"I think someone got into the Den."

Grace had never heard Doc roar. He was usually so composed. But now he did. Then he took a deep breath. He had barely exhaled when Mehendi dragged herself through the door.

"Second wind. They're coming at us hard, Doc," Mehendi panted before she went slack on the floor. That snapped him back into action and he immediately went to work.

Shit... Grace thought as she weighed up her options. She had just reminded herself that she belonged in the clinic. Right? *But the cubs are in the Den. Probably with IceFjord.* And then she stepped out of the clinic, pushed the button on her mic on the throat collar and adjusted the channel on the small box clipped to her pants. Pogue was going to be so pissed.

"Oliver?"

"Yes." The response was immediate.

"Where are you?"

"Tree by the Den. Straight line to me from the Aerie next to the clinic," he explained.

"IceFjord got inside. Oliver, the cubs...." Her voice broke, but she cleared her throat. "We gotta go get them, Oliver."

"Can you make it to me?"

"I think so. I'll run straight for the front door?"

Oliver chuckled darkly.

"Yes. I got your back."

Grace took one look behind her. Doc was fully occupied. *Sorry, Doc. You have Brody to help you when he wakes up.* And then she ran.

Chapter 56

P ogue leaned against a rock by the lake, his gaze fixed on the ripples in the water. He'd checked in with Cades three hours before and Micah just before taking a break following a fight with three wolves. He was recovering, however, and would return soon. StormEdge had the upper hand after a wave of fights. But their losses weighed heavily on Pogue. Dina was still nowhere to be found, and Mac had been killed the second he landed on the ground to have a small break. The fuckers had been watching him.

He'd checked in with Grace every hour. Sophie's gadgets came in handy. So far, so good. A low beeping sound from his headset alerted him someone was trying to reach him.

He pressed his thumb to the button only to hear a growl he recognized as Grayson.

"Shift, Gray."

A couple of seconds passed.

"Grace is missing *Goh!*" Gray swore a blue streak in his native Persian before switching to English again. "Doc thinks she snuck out while he was working on Mehendi."

Pogue couldn't breathe. He heard Gray calling in Micah over the com, though, relaying the information to him as well. "Anyone have eyes on Oliver?" Micah growled through the headset a second later.

A series of no's echoed from the other Vigilia on the line. And a roar. An earsplitting roar.

"Beau's back?" someone, maybe Jie, asked. Pogue fiddled with the earpiece to stop the crackling.

A series of groans answered that question.

"Doc, if you can hear me, knock Beau out," Pogue finally managed to say. Beau's voice traveled via Doc's mic to Pogue's ears.

"Don't you fucking dare, Doc, that is my Mate ou-"

The line went dead for a minute.

"He's out. I will attempt to restitch his intestines. Again." Doc said, probably using Beau's mic.

"More info," Pogue ordered.

Doc came through shortly after.

"Brody, speak to your Alpha. Now let me do my job!" he snarled. Doc never snarled. But then again, he had also never been to war.

A moment later, Brody's voice came through the receiver.

"Sulis was hiding in the tree by the front door. IceFjord and Nigel were there. The cubs Alpha. I think they're after the cubs. Grace heard."

Pogue didn't need to hear anything else. The unit leaders had spent the last hours drawing IceFjord all the way to the south border of the Pridelands. It would take them time to get back to the Den. He rushed out orders as he started running.

"Micah, take Beau's unit and run to the Den. Grayson, take Tari's and herd IceFjord down toward the river by the east. Keep them moving. I don't want them near the Den. I will find Grace and Oliver. Keep an eye out. Cades, growl if you're hearing this."

He recognized the deep rumble as his brother told him that A. Cades heard him and B. He was pissed. *Yeah, well, welcome to the fucking club, bro! Goddammit Grace! You had one fucking job! Stay at the fucking clinic!*

He'd yell at her later. When he had her in his arms. Alive.

Chapter 57

They entered through the front door, which creaked open slowly, almost silently. Grace had a thing for that magical door. Oliver took the lead, his claws out in front of him, passing a small backpack with grenades and other essential items to her. She caught the eerie night glow of his bear's eyes in the darkness when he turned to motion for her to follow. Oliver lifted his head, sniffing the air. He pointed to the dining hall and held up two fingers, then motioned a hand low to the floor. Cubs. Grace nodded and let him lead the way. She could hear sound coming from upstairs, maybe the gym; she wasn't sure. Oliver heard it, too, and moved faster. Oliver led them straight to the kitchen, passing through the large doors connecting the dining hall to the foyer and then across the large space. Nothing seemed out of place.

He stopped once inside and sniffed the air again.

"Fridge," he whispered. Grace quickly crossed the distance to the cold storage room in the back of the large industrial kitchen. She carefully opened the door. The second she did, she was hit over the kneecap with a turkey.

"Ow!" she hissed as she looked down. "Daniel!"

Daniel dropped the turkey and grabbed onto her leg. He was about four but annoyingly strong. He was terrified and cold as fuck.

"The bad men came in. Claus put me here," Daniel said, referring to Liam's Mate. He was a Maternal and had been tasked with keeping the cubs safe.

Grace bent and picked him up while Oliver kept a lookout.

"I know, little dude, I know. Where did Claus go? Do you know?" Daniel shook his head. "It's ok. We're gonna get you...." She looked at Oliver. She hadn't even considered that the predators out there had noses and hearing just like everyone else. Where the hell were they gonna hide Daniel?

Oliver seemed to think about it. Then he asked Grace,

"Where would you hide? A logical place to you might not be to anyone else."

Grace hefted Daniel up higher on her hip.

"I'd want somewhere where you guys couldn't pick out my scent, and the sounds of my hyperventilation would be muffled."

"Pogue's room?" Oliver asked.

Grace shook her head.

"I wouldn't hide where I thought Dominants would go. I'd probably go for Hannah's or the Submissives' hangouts."

"Let's see if we can get into Hannah's place. I know that's soundproof."

Grace cocked her head.

"How the fuck would you know that?"

Oliver shrugged.

"I'm a bear. We're curious creatures. And I heard her yelling at Nigel one night while walking down the hall, but it stopped the second she closed the door. Hannah doesn't just stop yelling. She kinda tapers it out," he grinned. Grace rolled her eyes and looked at Daniel.

"Daniel, where are the others?"

Daniel wiped his nose on Grace's vest.

"Dayna in there," he pointed to the pantry.

Oliver swiftly walked over to the massive pantry and opened the door. Seconds later, he came out with a whimpering bear cub. He slung her onto his back, grabbing her paws by his shoulders.

"Lucy and Githa?" Oliver asked Daniel. The boy shook his head. He didn't know.

Oliver cursed.

"Shit! Ok, we'll sniff them out."

"No, you won't. You'll be dead." The voice came from just outside the kitchen. The door was swung open, revealing two tall blond men. If they hadn't been evil motherfuckers, they would have been kinda attractive, Grace thought.

They looked Scandinavian like you saw in the Viking movies. All tall, broad, with blond braided hair. Oliver carefully backed up. He didn't look at her as he spoke.

"Grace, take Dayna." He said, not taking his eyes off the Shifters.

"Don't bother," the one on the right said.

"Are you really gonna fucking kill cubs?! Really? You're that kind of man?!" Grace spat. *Brain, filter!*

Oliver didn't take his eyes off the two men.

"Grace, take Dayna now! Go into the fridge. Block the door. Go now," Oliver ordered his voice like steel.

"And once we're done with this Submissive pipsqueak, we'll be right in, honey," the other Viking wannabe grinned.

Oliver's tone brooked no argument. Grace retreated into the chilly room and firmly shut the door. With all the energy she could muster, she dragged a sizable shelving unit in front of the door. It wasn't a fortress, but it was better than nothing. Finally, she turned her attention to Daniel and the bear cub, Dayna.

"Is there another way out of here?"

He shook his head and drew Dayna in closer.

The moment Oliver shifted to his black bear, Grace knew. Oliver may be the worst Submissive on the planet, but his surprise attack must have worked. They wouldn't expect a Submissive to attack. And judging by their yelps and roars, he had. *Yup, you totally underestimated how fucking aggressive StormEdge Submissives are, you lower-class Lassies!*

Grace pulled out her taser and grabbed two grenades from the backpack. She couldn't use them here, but she figured she'd better keep them handy. Then she waited. The roars, yelps, and screams stopped shortly after, and the door was yanked open.

"Let's go already!" Oliver said, grinning. She had never seen him this frightening, drenched in blood as if he'd taken a bath in it. It transformed his smile into something menacing. But his pretty eyes had reverted to the steel gray of his human form, a look that seemed to say, 'I could kiss you or kill you.' She took an unintentional step back.

"You're staring, Grace." His smile faltered.

"I don't know if I think you're the scariest thing I've ever seen or a little bit sexy right now."

Oliver snorted and slung Dayna onto his back once more. When Dayna licked his ear to clean him up, he let out a low giggle. Grace had no idea how he could be so fucking calm right now.

"Ok, kids, we're gonna play the quiet game now. Not a sound, no matter what, ok?" Grace said as they left the kitchen and started crossing the dining hall. Daniel and Dayna nodded.

Oliver froze when they reached the door and quickly motioned Grace to the side. Grace flattened herself against the wall next to the door, as Oliver did the same on the other side.

"I smell them. And blood. In here," a gruff voice said and slowly pushed the doors open. Grace motioned for Daniel to close his eyes and cover his ears. She noticed Oliver covering Dayna's hands while leaving his own exposed. Daniel obeyed her orders without hesitation. Grace held her breath, confused as to why the attackers couldn't smell them.

Then it hit her: Oliver was covered in blood. *That must be overriding the scent of the cubs.*

The Shifters were about ten meters into the dining hall when they noticed Grace, Oliver, and the cubs. Grace quickly unpinned and hurled both grenades, then pivoted just in time for the explosives to detonate with a massive boom, rattling the entire dining hall and obliterating a significant section of tables, benches, and chairs. Oliver's face was pinched in pain as his eardrums burst. Dayna whimpered, and Daniel let out a choked scream.

Grace quickly covered his mouth as Oliver sank to his knees, clasping his ears. If no one knew they were here before, they sure as hell did now. Grace pulled out her earpiece when it emitted a high-pitched sound.

She then steadied herself with a deep breath, pushing aside the cold sweat threatening to overwhelm her. It was too much, but for the first time in a long while, her mind obeyed. They could unravel later. Not now. After shifting to heal, Oliver picked up Dayna. He led them out of the dining hall toward the narrow corridor leading to Hannah's place. The walk was short and uneventful, and everything looked fine until Oliver touched Hannah's doorknob. An electric shock sent him flying back against the wall. Dayna screamed in her bear form before going limp. Grace set Daniel down and bent over to examine Dayna. She'd be fine. She then turned to face Oliver. He groaned as he tried to get his legs under him.

"She's knocked out but seems fine. Can you stand?"

Oliver tried again, but his legs didn't seem to wanna work.

"Fuck! Ok, we might have a slight problem here," he panted.

"What? Something broken?"

He shook his head, a grim look on his face.

"No. I can't feel my legs. Shit! Shit, shit, shit!"

"Shift. Try that!" Grace ordered, feeling her panic rising. Oliver shifted three times. After the last one, he shook his head and slammed his fist into the floor.

"Fuck! Ok, help me up against the wall and take the cubs." Oliver ripped his earpiece out and removed the mic on the collar strapped around his throat. " Fried. Great. Grace Go. Tell Beau where I am and that I love him."

Grace bent down and looked him square in the eye.

"Oliver, I am not leaving you. You are my friend! You're my family. Tell him yourself." Her voice broke. "I don't know if I can do this alone, Oliver. And my earpiece is toast, too. What do we do?"

Oliver hoisted himself further against the wall and pushed Dayna toward Grace, grasping Grace's nape. He pulled her down enough to brush his lips across hers. No Shifter had ever done that to her before. She'd seen them do it to each other all the time. It was a greeting, a reassurance, comfort. It was also a goodbye. Oliver gritted his teeth, pain lacing his features.

"You can and you will. You are my Alphas female, and you are gonna live." Oliver nodded to Grace's transmitter. " The shock must have fried yours too. OK, tell people later. Go now. Now Grace! Take the fucking cubs and go!" Grace relented after a tense minute. She unzipped the backpack and took out two tasers, the remaining three grenades, and a handgun. She hurried to the end of the corridor after quickly arranging everything next to Oliver. She grabbed two dump boxes and dragged them over to Oliver, dumping out the clothes to cover him with. She palmed Oliver's cheek.

"Stay alive, Oliver."

Oliver put his hand over hers, then moved it to kiss the palm of her hand.

"I will. Now go!"

Grace nodded and turned to Daniel.

"Daniel, climb onto my back," As soon as he had done so, she picked up Dayna. "Motherfucker! Are all bears this fucking heavy?!" she grunted as she hefted a limp Dayna into her arms.

Oliver chuckled behind her as she ran. She had a pretty good idea where Lucy would go, but Githa? No clue. Lucy would head straight for the place that smelled the most like safety. Grace sprinted, well, jogged toward her and Pogue's home and was halfway down the corridor when it dawned on her that Lucy would assume Pogue would protect Grace over Lucy because she was his Mate and Lucy was close to transitioning into adulthood. That thought stopped her cold. *What's the next best thing? Another Alpha, duuh,* Grace shook her head. Of course! Grace changed direction and turned back toward Caden's apartment, conveniently located in the same hallway as Pogue's but closer to the front entrance. She reached it quickly and, without hesitating, opened the door. As she closed it behind her, she stood still, enveloped in almost darkness.

"Lucy is here," Daniel whispered in her ear.

"Lucy?" Grace called, keeping her voice low.

"Grace?" A quiet voice somewhere on her left.

"Yeah. I have Dayna and Daniel, too. I need your help. And some lights."

She squeaked when a pair of night glow eyes were almost right in front of her. "Sheldon's balls, don't do that!" Grace hissed as she felt her heart in her throat.

"Sorry!" Lucy hissed back. Can we get Githa, too?"

Grace took a couple of calming breaths.

"If you know where she is, yes." *And then we're gonna run like hell to the clinic, and I'll tell Pogue about Oliver and...*

A pair of slender hands took Dayna from Grace.

"Githa is-"

Grace had to put her hand over Daniel's mouth to stop the sound of a scream as a gun went off. It came from down the hallway. Far enough away that it could have been from the corridor Oliver was bunkered down by. A second of quiet and then another bang, and another, and another.

"Oliver," Grace whispered. Dread crept up her spine. *I am not fucking equipped for this shit!* she screamed internally as she prompted Lucy to tell her where Githa was.

"Dump box by the front door!"

Grace was stumped for a second before nodding, knowing Lucy would see.

"Ok, yeah, smart girl. We're gonna have to go back to Pogue's room first. You'll need a gun or five." No response. "Lucy, are you with me here?"

"I'm nodding!" she growled.

"Well, that's super, except I can't fucking see in the dark!" Grace growled back, though much less impressive, what with her being human and all.

"Well then... Then... Ok, then!" Lucy muttered.

Grace rolled her eyes. As soon as Lucy said she couldn't hear anything, Grace led them to Pogue's room and her arsenal, wondering the whole way why the Den wasn't crawling with wolves. They really needed a weapons room or something, she noted as she pushed boxes out of the way. She equipped Lucy with three loaded guns. Then she strapped a knife to her leg and handed her a taser, too. Grace also handed Daniel a Taser and told him to click the yellow button if a bad man came close. Daniel nodded solemnly. *And we're handing out weapons to four-year-olds now,* she shuddered as she packed weapons for Githa and grabbed a first aid kit. She was not leaving without Oliver. Not this time.

Lucy stopped them when they reached the end of the corridor. She raised her finger, indicating that someone, possibly not from StormEdge, was above them, possibly in the gym. Grace considered her options. Stick with what works, she reasoned. As she crept up the stairs, she motioned for Lucy and Githa to stay. She pulled out the pins on two more grenades as she approached the first landing, tossing them when Lucy gave her a thumbs up, confirming they weren't StormEdge. Githa's scream rang out over the sound of debris, screams, and soft, squishy things landing on the floor.

I am not made for this shit! Grace thought as she held Lucy's hair while she puked. Grace's insides shook as she ran to the dump box and knocked it over, revealing a screaming Githa. Grace knelt and grabbed her shoulders. The teenager's clawed hands shot out, raking Grace's shoulders, arms, and neck despite Grace trying to back out of reach.

"Stop, Githa, stop, they're gone. Shhh," she tried coaxing as she sniffled through her own tears. She didn't know how long it took, but Githa finally calmed down long enough for Grace to hand over Dayna, Daniel, weapons, and a point-and-click instruction. The sound of a gun being fired tore through the Den.

"Oliver!" Grace hissed and ran down the hallway to Hannah's place, yelling over her shoulder for Lucy to get them all safe

The dump boxes had been knocked over, and Oliver lay motionless on top of the clothes, a dead wolf halfway on top of him. Grace slid onto her knees before him and touched his neck.

His head snapped up as his hand shot out, clawing at Grace's side. She had never loved Kevlar more than she did right then.

"Shit! Sorry. You ok?" he asked, panicked.

"Yup. Freaking out, probably gonna go into shock really soon, but I'm totally good." She nodded a little too fast. "Come on, we're gonna go now!"

"Grace, I can't." He rolled over. There was a *lot* of blood seeping from his side and under his armpit. He cupped her jaw, his hand trembling, and breathed through his nose.

"Grace, sweetheart, I need you to go now."

Grace shook her head.

"Shift."

"I did. I don't have any more shifts in me."

That fucking does it. Grace slapped Oliver, which, in hindsight, was really unnecessary. Then she grabbed a pair of leggings that had fallen out of the box, made knots, and wound them tightly around him until he cried out in pain. She then stuffed a stray rolled-up pair of socks into his armpit and ignored his grunts of pain as she called out for Lucy, as loudly as she dared, not knowing who else was in the building. Unfortunately, bear Shifters, even small ones like Oliver, had a substantial weight behind them in human form, too. Lucy came running, Githa in tow. Each had a cub on their hip, though Dayna was still shifted.

"Lucy, you and me are gonna carry this stubborn asshole. Githa, can you carry both cubs?" Githa nodded and shifted Daniel onto her back to carry Dayna under her right arm, as the left held a gun. "Oliver?" When he didn't respond, she slapped him again. Her voice trembled when she tried again. "Oliver? Please... Wake up." She choked on the words.

"Sweetheart, if you don't stop with the slapping, I'll eat your face."

Grace snorted and wiped her cheeks.

"Then stay the fuck awake. I need you to hold a gun or two."

"Load me up," he smirked. Grace placed one in each hand. She knew he was putting on a brave face. He was pale, and his breathing labored, sweat trickling down his temples, making trails in the blood that covered the rest of him.

"Ok, here we go."

If this was a movie, it would look either awesome or terrifyingly dumb, Grace thought as she and Lucy dragged Oliver out. He had his head up, and the guns pointed forward over their shoulders. Githa was right in front of them, staying alert, Daniel pointing his taser in every direction but at them, and Dayna hung there like a limp teddy bear.

Chapter 58

I *am going to murder my Mate!* Pogue thought as Micah alerted him. *How the fuck did they...* And then he remembered being told Nigel was there. They had categorically deemed the Den safe because they banked on the front door, not opening for anyone. Anyone but a Wielder who helped create it.

Micah ran up beside him, flanked by Beau and his team. He could have told Beau to stay put, but the bear wouldn't have listened. He knew Oliver would stick to Grace like glue.

Except it turned out to be the other way around. As they neared the Den's front door, five IceFjord Dominants came rushing toward the Den, following a blast behind them, cutting right in front of Pogue. Everyone stopped cold, as a war party consisting of a 4-year-old with a taser, a teenager with a teddy bear, and two tiny females dragging a bloodsicle with guns. Said bloodsicle had surprisingly good aim. The two wolves in front of them fell, leaving three, who were still so stunned they never even got a chance to fight back before Pogue was on them. He finished them off quickly and made a beeline for his Mate. Beau was right behind him, along with Micah.

"Oliver!" Beau roared. Pogue saw Oliver's head snap up before he dropped the guns and went completely limp. Lucy stumbled, and the three of them went down in a heap.

"Get the cubs," Pogue shouted at Beau's team of five Dominants and a Maternal.

He knelt down before Grace and lifted her head.

372

"Grace! Hey, Grace, baby, look at me! You ok?" He stood her on her feet and looked her over. His cat quickly deduced she was okay. Scratched up, banged up, and bloody, but alive. And well enough to smile at him.

"Hi, kitty cat."

He forgot everything around him for a second as he held her tight for a second before remembering DeCoill could be watching. He quickly released her. He hadn't been worried when they were in the forest, but out here, they were visible. Sitting ducks. *Shit...*

He barely moved in time as a wolf came flying at him from the left. He managed to rip its throat out before it could do any harm. It was more luck than anything else.

"Go, go, go!" he yelled, looking around him. Beau's team was running full speed with the cubs toward the clinic after Beau, who carried a now completely limp Oliver. That left him and Micah. And Grace.

It seemed the IceFjord Beta had finally emerged from whatever sad hole she'd been hiding in. Unfortunately, she had her top dogs with her, and all ten converged on Micah and Pogue. Henley's team came running from behind the clinic and ran straight for him. He held Grace close, trying to get his bearings. When he looked over his shoulder, Micah was fighting for his life as Mehendi and Grayson, with their teams, shot out of the forest and came to his aid. And in the middle of the fray, huddled in his arms? His fucking Mate. The person he wanted here the least right now.

"Run!" he shouted at her, shouting for Mehendi to cover her. Thankfully, she did, and Mehendi was right on her ass.

The following minutes were a blur of teeth, fur, and claws as Micah and he fought with everything they had to get the fuckers down.

Chapter 59

G race slid into the clinic, a wolf hot on her heels. It stopped only because Brody shot it in the face. He kicked the thing until it tumbled out over the low porch in front of the clinic. Mehendi had been held up a few meters before taking out another wolf.

"Doc, where do you want me?" Grace asked as she tried to catch her breath.

"I need the blood bags from the back room, the green liquid, and an IV in both Oliver's arms right now, please."

Beau ran for the blood as Brody deftly inserted the IV like he'd done it a million times before. As Grace tackled Oliver's other arm, Beau slipped in a pool of blood as he came out from the back room and sort of pushed the blood bags the rest of the way. He snarled at Grace as she picked them up.

"Beau, you will remain calm or leave. I cannot save him if you keep growling at my assistant!" Doc snapped.

Beau ignored both Grace and Doc. He stumbled to Oliver's side and stood there motionless. Grace ran over, grabbed a chair, and got him to sit. At least this way, he was out of the way.

"He will make it, Beau. I know he will. He killed those wolves like they were made of paper mâché. He's strong as fuck, cuz," she said as she deftly started cleaning the wounds and placing sterile sheets over Oliver's shoulder and his right arm. Beau nodded numbly as DeCoill suddenly appeared, standing in the doorway, Nigel by his side. The whole room seemed to stop what they were doing. Grace felt her insides freeze. He grinned as he looked at them.

"If you are not fatally injured, you are violating the rules," he giggled.

"Grace has been conscripted along with Brody. Everyone else here is mortally injured. Please leave," Doc finally said calmly while continuing his examination of Oliver.

DeCoill laughed outright, and Grace had to fight not to grab the gun strapped to Beau's thigh and shoot the Councilman.

Beau looked up at DeCoill. His voice was so deep and gravely Grace almost couldn't make out what he was saying.

"I hope to every god there is, that you will never find a Mate."

And then he did grab the gun strapped to his thigh. And shot himself in the stomach. Grace screamed as Beau fell to the floor, muttering.

"Mortally wounded enough, or do I need to bang my head against the floor too?"

DeCoill actually looked stunned as Nigel recited some kind of incantation, levitating DeCoill up into what looked like a giant soap bubble, and floated his beady-eyed ass away.

"Beau, for fuck's sake!" Grace screamed at him as she bent to staunch the blood. Doc didn't even look at him when he spoke.

"Beau, shift. You *stupid* bear."

Beau shifted twice. Just enough to pull him out of danger.

An hour later, Oliver was stabile, Beau next to him on a stretcher, was bandaged, and had been adequately shouted at, courtesy of Doc. Grace had cleaned up the worst blood so no one else would slip.

She stood and looked out the door. How long had it been since it started? Forty-eight hours, maybe? Longer? She wasn't sure how long she stood there.

Her eyes caught a lion ambling towards the clinic. It seemed sluggish. *Micah!* She knew him even from afar.

"Brody!" Grace called and waved him over.

"Shit! Run, Micah!" Brody shouted, grabbing the doorframe to keep himself from running out to him. He was strapped up to a blood transfusion machine, donating the blood Oliver needed. The lion faltered in his steps and went down. Grace felt her heart stop. *No!*

"Micah, get the fuck up! Get up now, Micah! Don't make me come get you!" she screamed. A roar told her Pogue had heard her words from wherever he was in the fray.

Micah seemed to hear her threat. He sluggishly got to his feet, semi-walked, and crawled towards her, his eyes never leaving her. Out of the corner of her eye, she saw who she thought was Pogue.

From there, it all seemed to happen in slow motion. Micah was under 20 meters from her when a large, brown, dirty wolf ran up on him from the right. Grace felt her hands reach for her bow, hanging on a hook beside the doorway, and shoot an arrow at the wolf, who went down and rolled a couple of times, but not before it got a swing in on her brother, knocking him onto his stomach.

She heard Brody and Doc yelling her name. She felt icy patches under her boots as she rushed out the door. She weaved between Shifters on the ground to get to Micah, grabbing the lion's mane and attempting to drag him with her. She looked up as she heard Pogue yell her name. Taruk's powerful arms yanked Micah away from her and hurled him towards the clinic. Beau dashed out to grab him and assist him the rest of the way in, reopening his gunshot wound in the process. Micah would live. He had to.

Grace turned to see if Pogue was coming.

She didn't see the other wolf coming up from behind him until it was too late... All she saw was him. He tackled her, and something hit him from behind and then from the sides. As they hit the ground, she didn't feel his weight. Her brain stopped working. Everything was blurry and felt surreal. *Why wasn't he helping? Why is he doing a plank pose? Isn't this a weird time to do a workout, Pogue?* she thought. Then his weight came down on her, and she could feel him move as something hit him again. Everything came rushing back as she managed to roll Pogue off her after three attempts, straddling him in the process.

"Pogue?!" He lifted his pale green eyes to her, his eyes unfocused. When she looked down, all she saw was blood. There was so much blood. She pressed her small hands into the gaping wound in his stomach and sides, forgetting all her vet nurse training and everything she'd learned since. Grace panicked and screamed for help. *Is blood supposed to pump out from there? It looks like a fountain, she mused.* A part of her knew she was losing her grip on reality. But for some reason, she couldn't seem to snap out of it. Pogue wasn't supposed to get hurt. *He's the Alpha.* She barely noticed the brawl going on around her. Pogue was all she saw.

"No! No! Pogue please, no, no, no!" She screamed at him. He lifted his bloodied hand to cup her cheek, tears spilling from the corners of his eyes.

"S'ok. Gonna be ok. So beautiful. My Mate. True..." He coughed, and blood was coming out of his mouth. He laughed a little, wheezing as bubbles of blood formed around his lips. "Guess. No goodbye kiss, huh?" Grace couldn't see through the tears.

"No! No! We don't say goodbye!" She watched him close his eyes and gently slapped his cheeks. "No... Goodbye means going away. Please, please, Pogue, don't go away! I accept! I'm your Mate! Pogue, please! I accept, OK?! Just stay! I love you so much, please!"

Pogue's hand fell from her face, and she heard him whisper.

"Took you long enough." He flashed a dimple at her and then nothing. She felt herself being levitated into the air and watched as Caden clawed his way through so many wolves. She watched him as he, his brother's keeper, lifted Pogue into his arms and carried him into the clinic, uncaring about the mass brawl around him. Her last thought before she felt herself slip away was that there wouldn't be enough room in the back. He was too tall.

Chapter 60

Afterword

Not much else to say is there?

Gotcha! There's so much more to say, but I will leave it with promising you that book two is right around the corner and book three is right behind.

I hope you enjoyed Pride, and I hope you'll do all authors out there a solid and review.

Wanna catch up and get the latest scoops, teasers, and publishing info?

Follow me on social media!

You can find me on Facebook (www.Facebook.com/Vanda Tawhai) & Instagram (www. Instagram.com/@Vandatawhai)

To say this book was all just me, myself and I would be a lie. I cannot thank the people helping and supporting me through this, enough.

Satine, I love you as much as I curse you. For every 'rewrite' and 'but why?' I am reminded of your scary intellect and insightfulness. Thank you will never be enough. Like ever.

Grayson, I am so sorry for the ten times I made you read Pride draft 1-? . I am so damn lucky to have you to place random food in front of me, making sure I remember to stretch and generally just human while writing. Thank you for your unwavering support and endless patience

Bjørn, your calm is astounding! How you can just go "no worries, it will be fine" at 01.20 when I'm panicking about the book cover, is beyond me. Thank you for taking on this task, and for the amazing result. You truly are an artist.

Milton Keynes UK
Ingram Content Group UK Ltd.
UKHW010858081223
434021UK00001B/93